Glimmer in the DARKNESS

A Novel

Nicole Hampton

Printed and bound in the United States of America

ISBN: 978-0-9965397-0-8 (Paperback)
ISBN: 978-0-9965397-1-5 (eBook)

Library of Congress Control Number 2015944867

Published by
Didactic Elements Publishing
PO Box 1233
Morrisville, North Carolina 27560

For inquiries, contact the publisher.

ACKNOWLEDGMENTS

In loving memory of my Aunt Mildred Taylor. You are greatly missed, but your passion for reading will forever fuel my fire for writing.

To say I am elated with having completed my first novel would be an understatement. I feel a mixture of emotions ranging from disbelief to relief. However, I know that I would not have gotten to this point if it were not for the loving grace of God and for that, I am thankful. Without Him, I would not have had the strength or the courage to press forward and dare to dream. I am thankful to God for all of the people He has placed on my path, that have helped me along, sometimes gently guiding, other times boldly holding my hand. He has always manifested in my life in a way that has shown me how much He loves, protects, and provides for me daily.

Thank you to my magnificent husband, Corey Smith. From the moment I met you at the front desk of the residence hall in college, you have always taken care of me. In fifteen years of marriage, you have stood by my side and supported me in everything I have done. I am grateful for your unconditional love and will forever love you with all of my heart and soul. I am blessed to have you as the head of our household and father of our six beautiful children: Amari, Corey, Jaylen, Justin, Jyorden, and Charlize. Although, the way we came to be a family is different, with God in the forefront, we will conquer all of life's obstacles. I love all of you to pieces.

To my mom, thank you for your love and sacrifice over the years. I hope that I will one day be able to make your journey easier. To all of my siblings, both by blood and otherwise, I truly appreciate your love and support. I am blessed to be a part of a wonderful family. I am grateful for my nieces and nephews, aunts, uncles, and cousins. I wish I could address you all individually, but that would take another novel. Just know that I love you and am thankful for you.

To my dad, thank you for the impression you made upon me over the years. I can honestly say that it has helped to mold some of the most crucial decisions I have had to make as an adult and all has been well.

To my friends that I have grown close to over the years, you know who you are. Each of you holds a special place within my heart. You have gotten into a place in my life designated for a special few. Now that you are in, you stay in. I would like to extend a special thanks to Erica, Yolanda, Cyndell and Juneve for reading the novel first and giving me your honest feedback.

Thank you to my dynamic editor, Jessica Tilles of TWA Solutions. You are a fascinating person. I am truly grateful for all of your help, and your beautiful personality. I would be remiss not to say a special thank you to fellow author, Trice Hickman, for taking me under your wing, showing me the way, and guiding me in the right direction. I would also like to thank fellow author, Rysa Walker, for your years of encouragement, and willingness to share your journey with me.

Finally, thank you to those who support me by reading Glimmer in the Darkness and my many novels to come. I have a lot going on in my mind and I am excited to share it with you.

God bless,

Nicole Hampton

Prologue

In her two-door luxury car, Vaneetra James sat across the street from the lavish home where she would soon ring the doorbell, contemplating exactly how she would execute her next move. She studied the expanse of the blonde brick and lush green landscape, as if she needed to memorize every detail. For a moment, she admired the abundant plant beds, adorned with budding flowers and shrubbery about which she knew nothing. Gardening was not her thing and she doubted it was Daniel's, but more a pathetic, unsuspecting stay-at-home wife. She imagined herself pulling into the circular driveway, parking her car, ringing the doorbell and turning his wife's pitiful little fantasy life into a nightmare. One in which Vaneetra was the star.

When Vaneetra met Daniel, he appeared frustrated, more like angry and fed up with his home life. As they had become familiar with each other, Daniel would complain about how his wife, whose name Vaneetra vaguely remembered as being Shannon, complained all the time about him being at work, or about how he never spent enough time with her and the kids. He confided that it pissed him off that she refused or could not understand that he worked hard for their family. He spent long hours building his now successful law practice so that she could stay at home with their kids and be a happy housewife, except according to Daniel, she acted far from happy.

Daniel had also confided that his wife seemed downright unappreciative of all of his hard work and sacrifice, and he frankly, was tired of constantly trying to please her. He expressed to Vaneetra that he was at his wits end.

Vaneetra, of course, would sit and listen to Daniel for hours, allowing her heart to reach out to him. He was every woman's dream—tall, good looking, educated, hardworking, paid—and based on his swagger…endowed. She could not fathom why a woman would be unhappy with a man like Daniel.

For a married man and single woman, they grew too close. After a few months of listening to Daniel's frustrations with his wife, and calculating how to become more than just his friend, Vaneetra made her move. It was much easier than she thought it would be. She told Daniel some pathetic lie about losing her keys, convincing him to take her home for the spare key and the rest was easy. By his uptight demeanor, she could tell he had not been getting any at home, so when she offered herself up to him, he quickly accepted.

For a few months, they were hot and heavy. Daniel spent so much time with Vaneetra; she felt it should have been easy for him to leave his wife and kids to be with her. When she demanded he make an honest woman of her, Daniel withdrew his affection and time, eventually telling her that giving up his family was something he simply would not do. He went even further by ending their relationship, leaving her hurt and embarrassed at how she had freely given so much of herself to a married man, something she had never done before.

Daniel ended the affair. He stopped taking Vaneetra's phone calls, emails or text messages, which was another reason she found it necessary to pay his wife a visit. Had Daniel bothered to respond to her messages, telling him that she had something important to discuss, his wife would not be the first amongst the two of them to find out the good news. Vaneetra dreamt of this day when she decided she wanted Daniel for herself.

A UPS truck zoomed past Vaneetra, startling her from her deep-seated thoughts. She started her car, yanked the gear into drive, making a sharp left turn across the two-way street into Daniel's driveway, stopping abruptly at the front door. Getting out the car, she strutted up the front steps with purpose. Daniel had slid into her life, making her feel like she was the only one he loved, only to quickly snatch his love away. Now, she would ruin him forever, and make him regret the day he first sat down and shared his life with her.

Shannon Johnson added the finishing touches to the lemon and herb seasoned chicken she was preparing to roast for dinner. It was the rare occasion where both boys were gone for the afternoon—Jeran playing at a friend's house in the neighborhood and Zach with Ms. Whitmore, a kind elderly woman from their church. Glad for time alone to think, Shannon spent most of it cooking—something she loved to do—praying and trying to figure out how to relieve the tension between her and Daniel.

For months, Shannon had been racking her brain, trying to figure out how and why she and Daniel's relationship had gotten off track. They hardly ever talked. When they did, it turned into an argument. Admittedly, after they moved to North Carolina, a mild depression had settled over her for several months. During that time, she became distant, not wanting to make love, and feeling like he did not spend enough time at home. He just could not seem to understand how she felt.

After the kids were born, she and Daniel's lovemaking diminished from daily to once a week, eventually to once a month, but now their sex life had dwindled down to once or twice every other month, at the most.

Her depression had gotten better once they joined a church. Attending church helped Shannon realize that part of her depression stemmed from being far away from family and lonely.

Shannon grew to love their church family. They helped her and the kids to feel at home. She attended Bible study on Wednesday nights and service every Sunday.

Shannon did not attend church growing up, and only sporadically during her time at college and as a young adult. Once they moved to North Carolina, Shannon happened upon her current church and knew from her first visit that she and her family belonged. It was at this church where she began to truly learn and understand about Christ and how to identify him in her life.

Another lesson she was beginning to learn, more slowly, was how to be a submissive wife, according to the Bible. She had to admit, it was a bit hard for her. Raised to be strong, independent and never to completely give in to a man, her examples of fathers and husbands growing up left a lot to be desired. However, Daniel was different, which is why she was willing to work toward making her marriage better.

After a few months, Shannon felt close enough to one of the female ministers to share concerns about her marriage. The minister, who had been married for over twenty-five years, listened intently and afterward began to help Shannon learn how to pray over her marriage and her husband. Several months had passed, and although Shannon felt better, she and Daniel still argued about the time he spent away from home, how they spent their money, and his unwillingness to communicate with her in general.

Daniel had not taken to their church in the same manner Shannon had. To her, his attendance seemed more obligatory than out of desire. She did not believe he prayed any more than to bless dinner on the nights he managed to get home in time to eat with them.

Within the past few months, Daniel had grown even more distant, and traveled much more frequently to different conferences. However, Shannon decided not to dwell on those things, and actually do something to break the ice between them. Knowing he would be late, she decided to put the boys to bed early, light some candles, take a bubble bath and make love to her husband. She hoped her plan would be successful enough to ease the tension between them. She longed to turn their relationship around.

The minister she had been meeting and praying with had suggested instead of trying to convince Daniel to talk about their problems, to give them to God. She recommended that Shannon spend time alone praying and fasting, and spend her time with Daniel getting reacquainted, citing that now that they had kids, their time together was limited, making it even more precious.

Shannon had gotten up to get a drink of water when the doorbell rang. She walked to the front door, thinking that maybe it was the FedEx man delivering the contract for her new writing assignment. Without bothering to look through the peephole, she opened the door, ready to retrieve her package. She was surprised to see an unfamiliar woman standing on her steps with one hand on her hip, the other poised in front of the doorbell.

"May I help you?" Shannon's eyes grazed over the beautiful woman standing in front of her. She took note of the annoyed look on her face, and her defensive posture.

"I am sure you can't, but I am here anyway." Vaneetra looked Shannon up and down, smirking at how clueless she was about the fact that her life was about to change. She gave Shannon the once over, noticing her lean legs covered by black leggings, and how her waist did not indicate she had given birth to children. Nevertheless, Vaneetra knew this pathetic version of a housewife could not hold a candle to her, not even under the current circumstances.

Vaneetra's condescending attitude rubbed Shannon the wrong way. "Excuse me? Do I know you?"

Vaneetra turned as if looking around, and set her focus back on Shannon. "You have a nice house. Daniel has good taste…in homes, that is."

"Do you work for my husband? Are you a new assistant at his firm?" An uneasiness about this woman rose from the pit of Shannon's stomach. She sensed she was trouble and would suggest that Daniel fire her.

Vaneetra laughed. "I guess you can call me an assistant. For the past several months, I have been assisting Daniel with some pretty important issues—helping him to stay *hard* and on his game is a better way to put it." She took step closer to Shannon.

Fed up with the woman standing at her door, Shannon snapped, "Look, I don't have time to play word or guessing games with you. You need to get off my property. While you are at it, collect your belongings from my husband's firm, you won't be working there anymore." Shannon turned to close the door, but Vaneetra's next words stopped her dead in her tracks.

"I don't work for your husband. I have been fucking him." She stood stark still, a full grin spread across her face.

Shannon turned around and stepped back onto the porch, stopping centimeters from Vaneetra's face. "Excuse me? What did you just say?"

"Honey, you have not displayed any indication of being hearing impaired so I know you heard me, but I will repeat myself. The look on your face was priceless. *I* have been *fucking your husband.*"

"I don't believe you. My husband takes out the trash. He does not sleep with it. Now, get off my property before I have

Raleigh Police escort you off." Shannon's body tensed in an effort to maintain her composure and not tear this strange woman to pieces. Her mind was spinning, trying to comprehend what she had just heard. She needed to get this woman off her property so she could call Daniel.

Vaneetra held her position for a few moments, satisfied with the completion of part of her mission. This bitch wasn't fooling her. "I know you believe me. You don't have to admit it. Besides, it doesn't matter what you believe. I will deliver proof in six months." She turned, proceeding down the steps, but stopped to look back at Shannon. "By the way, Daniel doesn't know yet. Do me a favor and tell him he is going to be a daddy... *again*." Vaneetra watched Shannon's expression, as she began to comprehend what she had heard, winked, smiled, walked down the steps to her car, got in, and drove away, never looking back.

Shannon closed her front door and raced down the hallway to her phone. First, she dialed Daniel's office number, then his cell. Not surprised that he did not answer either one, she called and left a message with his secretary, only telling her that it was an emergency. For the next hour, Shannon paced the entire first floor of her home, trying to make sense of what the woman at the door had told her. She would not allow herself to believe any word of it. They were having problems, but she just knew Daniel wouldn't cheat on her.

Shannon needed to prove to herself that the woman was lying. She went to Daniel's home office, logged onto his personal laptop, using the password he had given her years prior to their moving to North Carolina. Daniel must have forgotten that he had given it to her, because over the next two hours Shannon combed through Daniel's credit card statements, finding charges that did not make sense. On many nights he had claimed to work late, there were charges to various restaurants. That alone did not prove anything, but the uneasiness she felt when she first laid eyes on the person she was beginning to believe was the other woman, began to increase. Shannon pulled up old phone statements and found what she was looking for—the same number listed countless times for both phone calls and text messages. The number was unfamiliar. She did not bother to call it; she already knew who would answer.

Shannon, closed the laptop, tried to calm her ever mounting anxiety with prayer, but to no avail. She walked to the kitchen in search of a bottle of wine, glass, and a corkscrew. Having found what she needed, she opened the bottle, filled the glass to the brim with the gold-colored liquid. She brought it to her lips, taking a long swallow before cupping it against her chest. Shannon closed her eyes and focused on the warm sensation the wine created from her esophagus down to the pit of her stomach. She took another swallow, this time draining the glass. *How could he betray my trust and sleep with another woman? I love him. Sure, we have been having our problems, but I've remained faithful. I take my marriage and covenant with Christ seriously. How could he just toss it to the side for a fling with some random tramp?*

Salty tears seeped through the opening of Shannon's lips. Not being able to stop them from falling, she cried as the magnitude of what the other woman had said sank in. Daniel had an affair and now his mistress was pregnant. The wine glass shattering against the stainless steel refrigerator door startled Shannon. Engrossed in her thoughts, she had not realized she had thrown it. Shannon grabbed another glass, the opened bottle of wine, and a corkscrew. Stepping over the shards of glass, she walked to the living room, pulled herself together well enough to call Ms. Whitmore and lie about wanting to spend some quality time with Daniel, and asked her to pick up Jeran. Ms. Whitmore agreed, offering to bring both boys home just before their bedtime. Shannon thanked her, hung up the phone and waited.

As soon as Daniel pulled into the garage, he could smell something burning. Seeing Shannon's SUV, he hurried into the house to make sure she and the boys were okay. He felt his way through the dark, smoke-filled mudroom, family room and into the kitchen. Daniel grew more concerned when he felt and heard the crunch of what he suspected to be glass under his shoes. He called out for Shannon and the boys. No one answered. On the stove was the source of all the smoke. What looked like the burnt carcass of a chicken lay inside of a shallow roasting pan. Racked with worry, Daniel turned and started to look for his family, but a forceful blow struck him on the side of the head, behind his right ear. He was ready to strike, but stopped, recognizing Shannon's silhouette through the stream of light from the kitchen window and the smoke. Her chest was heaving, ragged sobs leaving her body with every rise of it.

"Shannon, what the hell is going on? Why are you crying? Why is there burned food on the stove? Where are the boys? Why did you hit me?" Confused, Daniel wanted answers, especially to his last question.

"How could you? How could you sleep with another woman?" Shannon's words came out slurred, but Daniel understood them clearly.

How did she find out?

"Shannon, you're drunk and delusional. You have no idea what you are talking about." He brushed past her, walking to the living room. He had to figure out a way to get away and call Vaneetra. He needed to know how Shannon had found out he had cheated on her.

"I am not delusional, Daniel. I know what I am talking about." She followed him to the living room.

He knew she was lucid, but pretended that he didn't. "Shannon, I don't know what you are talking about. You have been drinking too much. Tell me where the kids are, and go to bed. I'll go get them. We can talk about all of this in the morning." He hurried past her again, needing to get away. She grabbed at his arm, but he yanked it, hard, out of her grasp. He had just reached the entryway to the kitchen when something flew past the left side of his head, just barely grazing his ear, before shattering against the jam of the sliding doors in the kitchen and falling onto the floor, bits and pieces scattering everywhere.

"I am not delusional, nor am I drunk." Her breaths came out in gasps. "What I am is pissed off." Her screams pierced the air. "Some tramp came to our door, to our home, Daniel, and told me that the two of you having been sleeping together and now she is pregnant with your child! Tell me it's not true, Daniel! Tell me this crazed tramp is lying!" Shannon stood her position in the middle of the foyer, fists clinched, breathing hard, staring at him, as her eyes pled for him to say something…anything. Instead, Daniel dropped his head and walked out, not uttering another word.

Daniel sat in church next to Shannon, thinking about the past few weeks. Days passed before he confessed to having an affair. He finally told Shannon that Vaneetra James, the woman who had come to their door, was someone he had met several months ago. They had a brief relationship, but it was over. He told her that he did not believe she was pregnant and was just saying that for added impact, possibly to hurt Shannon more deeply.

However, about a couple of weeks after Shannon confronted him, Daniel received a package at his office. When he opened it, he found ultrasound pictures, with a note attached: *We're having a girl, motherfucker! Don't bother showing your sorry ass face around my house, job, or any place else. When it is time to run me my money for child support, I will let you know. In the meantime, kiss my ass. P.S. How is your bitch? Has she left you yet?*

Daniel never told Shannon about the ultrasound pictures. She had not had much to say to him since she found out about his indiscretion. She avoided him as much as possible, but he knew by the bags that accumulated beneath her eyes that she cried often. He wanted to reach out, to say he was sorry for causing her any pain. He wanted to assure her that his relationship with Vaneetra was over, but he couldn't. He knew she would not welcome any comfort from him. He also knew his relationship with Vaneetra was not over. He vowed never to sleep with her again, but he believed the child she carried was his. He would have to step up and take care of his daughter. He made a mistake and now had to be a man and face up to what he had done. He had to be a father to his child after she was born.

The sermon ended. The pastor invited those who wanted prayer to come to the altar. Up to this point, Daniel had not really taken church serious. However, he now hoped that prayer would help him out of his current situation. He took hold of Shannon's hand and stood. She tried to pull away, but he would not let go, leaving her no choice but to follow him. They had gotten halfway to the altar when Shannon slapped the back of Daniel's forearm, causing him to let go of her hand. He turned just in time to see something fall to the floor, as she ran out of the sanctuary, slamming the doors against the walls, as she crossed the threshold. It seemed every pair of eyes in the sanctuary glared at him. Embarrassed, Daniel walked toward the doors. An usher bent down, picked up the object that had fallen from Shannon's hand, and gave it to Daniel as he passed. He grabbed it without looking, or expressing thanks.

When Daniel made it outside, he caught a glimpse of Shannon burning rubber out of the parking lot. She did not have enough time to get their sons. They had to be in the children's wing still.

Finally, he looked down at his hand. The usher had given him Shannon's wedding rings. He knew they had not just fallen off. She took them off and dropped them. Frustrated at the implication of what Shannon intentionally dropping her wedding rings meant, Daniel walked back into the church, hoping to find a deacon that was willing to take him, Jeran and Zach home, but first he returned to the altar. He ignored everyone looking at him. He knew his problems were much bigger than speculation by on-lookers. For the first time in his life, he hoped prayer worked, because he was going to need a miracle to save his marriage.

Chapter One

Shannon — The Secret Revealed

The traffic on Interstate 90/94 seemed to move much slower than I had remembered. Snails could have moved faster. After what should have been a forty-five-minute drive from O'Hare Airport, but took two hours, Daniel pulled up to the curb in front of his parents' brown, brick bungalow on Chicago's Southside. A blizzard blanketed the city like none seen in Chicago since March 1998 when one foot of snow fell overnight. We picked the wrong day to travel for the Christmas holiday from our home in Raleigh, North Carolina to Chicago, Illinois. I now wished, more than ever, that we had stayed home, but our sons, Jeran and Zachery, would have plotted to have us executed if we had not brought them to visit their grandparents. There seemed to be no end in sight for the enormous headache that plagued me. This trip would prove to be interesting, to say the least. Daniel and I would reveal a secret that we managed to keep while over seven hundred miles away, and everyone would be sure to have an opinion.

Jeran jumped out the rented SUV as soon as Daniel put it in park, and bolted up the steps, two at a time, of his grandparents' house. I looked at him, amused at his excitement and innocence. He was the spitting image of Daniel. He was charming, handsome and exceptionally tall for a five-year-old, all of which he used to his advantage. He knew people found his warm, dimple-framed smile hard to resist.

Zachery sprinted up the steps right on his big brother's heels. I knew he was hoping to ring the doorbell, but before he could make it to the top step, Jeran extended his longer arms and pressed it.

"J, you stink!" Zach said, frowning at his older brother. At three years old, Zachery was extremely articulate. Like his brother, he was tall for his age with the same captivating smile and dimples.

I dreaded getting out of the car. Neither Daniel nor I have told our families about Madison. Madison was Daniel's three-month-old daughter he fathered with another woman. I had been too angry and hurt to tell anyone in the family about Madison. It was embarrassing to have my husband of seven years father another woman's child, resulting from an ongoing affair that began fifteen months ago and supposedly ended before Madison was born. When he found out this woman was pregnant, he thought standing up and sticking by her side was the right thing to do. His choice caused many intense arguments in our home, not because I did not want him to take care of his responsibility, but because he had the responsibility in the first place. We compromised, he would provide for the baby *if* it turned out to be his. If he wanted to do anything prior to that, he would have to do it living outside of our home and on his way to divorce court.

After Madison was born, it did not take long for DNA to reveal she was Daniel's daughter. While noble of him to stand up and accept his responsibility, it made my life pure hell. Why I was still with Daniel, I wasn't sure, other than our two sons. If we were to divorce, they would be without a father in the home. I didn't want that to happen. He was a lousy husband, but an excellent father.

Daniel probably had no idea what to say to his parents, and neither did I. I was more concerned about how his mother would feel about the situation than anyone else. I didn't expect his father to say much. He had never gotten deeply involved in the personal affairs of his adult children. He was the strong silent type, spending most of his time observing and letting his wife be their mouthpiece.

However, as much as Daniel may have dreaded telling his mother about Madison, he probably dreaded telling his sister, Jolene, even more. Jolene was the older of the two. She and Daniel were close. He cherished her opinions and she liked me. Over the years, we grew to be like sisters. I was sure she would be upset about my not telling her what was going on, but how could I? We may have been close, but Daniel was her brother. It would have been wrong to bring her into the middle of our shattered marriage.

"You may as well get out and go in. You can't hide her forever."

Without responding to me, Daniel got out of the car. I had been getting a lot of that for the past couple years. I watched him open the rear passenger door of the SUV and take out the car seat that held Madison as she quietly napped. He slammed the door behind him and headed for the house.

"Can you grab her diaper bag?" he called out, not making eye contact with me.

"Sure, why the hell not?" I rolled my eyes. "This is going to be a very long ten days."

I grabbed the bag out of the rear of the SUV and trudged through the snow toward the front steps. I didn't think either of us noticed his mother standing on the porch, staring with what appeared to be a perplexed look.

"Hi, Mom!" I attempted to sound excited, but don't think I pulled it off.

"Hi, how are you?" Mrs. Johnson asked.

"Hi, Grandma," Jeran and Zach said in unison. The boys wrapped themselves around their grandmother, almost knocking her over. This was probably the tenth time they had said "Hi" to her since she opened the door, but they were so excited to see her, they could not help themselves.

"Where's Auntie Jolene?" Without waiting for an answer, the boys bolted inside the house, shouting for Jolene, who was not far from the front door. Jolene lived at home with their parents. She moved back in several years ago after going through a rather nasty divorce so that she could help them out, since they were getting older. She never had any children of her own. I once asked why, but she did not want to talk about it.

I didn't quite know if Daniel really appreciated Jolene for how helpful she was to their parents, but I did. I used to wonder if she would ever remarry. However, short of a miracle, I didn't believe another man would stand a chance in hell getting her to open up her heart again. From where I stood, I didn't much blame her.

Daniel climbed to the top of the porch steps and was now standing in front of his mother, grinning nervously. "Hey, Momma! How's my suga woo?" He hugged her with his free arm.

"Oh, I'm doing good. Boy this is a big surprise." She laughed and gripped her son tightly. "I didn't think y'all were coming, because of the weather being so bad. When did you get in?"

If our being here is a shocker, this next surprise will knock her off her damn feet, I thought.

She looked at Madison. "And who is this?" She must have been reading my mind.

"Mom, let's go in the house. It's cold out here." Daniel held open the door, ushering his mother inside. He attempted to do the same for me, but I grabbed hold of it and motioned for him to go instead.

"You should get her out of the cold."

Once inside, Jolene greeted us with big hugs and kisses, as she eyed Madison with curiosity, but had not yet said anything.

"Hey, Shannon, how are you?"

"Hey, Jolene, I'm fine. Glad to be in out of that blizzard. Girl, it is horrible out there. I didn't think we were ever going to get off the Dan Ryan. The roads are really bad." I stomped the snow off my boots.

"I know they are! I heard on the news that the salt trucks didn't get out until after the storm had started. By the time any got to the South side, there was already a foot of snow on the ground."

"I believe it!" Daniel interrupted our conversation. "What good is salt on top of a foot of snow?" He hugged Jolene tightly. "Hey, sis!"

"Hey, Dan." She returned his embrace. "Who is that you got in that car seat?" Although she posed the question to Daniel, her eyes moved between the both of us. I didn't bother to answer. I sat down and placed my purse on the floor beside me, but kept on my coat. I wasn't sure if I would be leaving soon.

I guess Daniel finally realized he could not avoid the question and I was not going to answer, because he took a deep breath and slouched down on the love seat, placing the baby carrier on the floor. He was silent for a moment, absentmindedly wringing his hands that now seemed foreign to me. I looked at his broad shoulders weighted down with responsibility he should not have. They no longer commanded attention to his long, muscular frame that once dominated any room he entered.

I remembered the first time I laid eyes on Daniel. I immediately fell in love with his light brown, perfectly tanned skin, almost perfect teeth, and those hands…well just the sight of them alone sent my imagination on a wild ride. Now, it all seemed so foreign to me. I did not recognize the man that sat only a few feet away—the man I called my husband.

Not sure what they were about to hear, Mrs. Johnson and Jolene slid onto the sofa opposite him. The look on their faces indicated that they knew it was not going to be good news.

Daniel avoided eye contact with everyone. I sat in the chair alongside the sofa, staring at the wall. I did not want anyone to see the pain on my face; I had been desperately trying to hide for months. For a fleeting moment, I felt a little pity for him, but pleasure in his discomfort won out. *This is what his sorry ass gets*, I thought. However, after a few minutes, I looked down at the plush, tan wall-to-wall carpet, wishing I could sink right into it and disappear. Whom was I fooling? This wasn't easy for me either.

Jeran and Zach had long since disappeared into the back of the house, chatting with their grandfather, Mr. Johnson, who had recently had knee surgery and had not ventured to the front of the house.

After what seemed like forever, Daniel looked up at his mother. "Mom, I'd like you to meet my daughter, Madison."

Mrs. Johnson looked confused. "What did you say?"

"Madison is my daughter."

"What do you mean your daughter?" Astonishment covered her face.

"Madison is my daughter," Daniel repeated, but with more strength in his voice.

"Wait!" Mrs. Johnson's voice raised a few octaves. "Did the two of you have another baby and didn't think to tell your family?"

I could feel her and Jolene staring at me for answers, even though they posed their questions to Daniel. I took a moment from gazing at the carpet and glanced up at them, before returning my gaze to the same spot on the carpet. They looked as if the world was ending and neither had made it into heaven after working a lifetime to get there.

"No, Mother Johnson, I have not had any more children." I looked at Daniel as those last few words crossed my lips. I wanted to get the point across that when Daniel said "My daughter" he did not mean *our* daughter. He meant *his* daughter.

"Mom, Madison is my daughter from a relationship with another woman." Daniel's words lingered in the room like stale fried fish.

"What?" Mrs. Johnson gasped. "What do you mean a relationship with another woman?" One hand was propped on her hip. She looked like she was ready to jump over the cocktail table separating her from her son, and slap his head right off his shoulders. She was in her seventies, but spry.

"Are y'all still married?" Jolene crossed her legs and arms, glaring at Daniel.

"Yes," we replied in unison.

Jolene had been quiet, but it did not surprise me that she wanted to know if we were still married. She was probably thinking I was stupid as hell to be with him. Men did not get a second chance with Jolene.

"Hmm…" Jolene got up and walked out the living room.

The rest of us sat silent. Thick, heavy tension hung in the air. Nausea overtook me, forcing me to rest my head on my forearms. No one seemed to notice. All eyes were on Daniel and Madison. The anger and hurt I had been feeling since this other woman came into my life and turned my world upside down, came rushing in all at once. What was I doing sitting here? I felt like a complete fool. I had not filed for divorce, nor had Daniel moved out the house. I felt stuck and confused. I spent most of my time steeping in my own anger. I didn't know if I even still loved Daniel. If I did, it would not be enough to get me through this.

Madison's low, lusty moans of discontent startled us out of our thoughts. She had been asleep since we arrived, but squirmed uncomfortably in her car seat. Daniel reached down, unfastened the harness of the baby carrier and picked her up. I looked at the plump baby he held in his arms and, as much as my heart ached for it not to be true, for the DNA test to be wrong, there was no denying their kinship. Madison had a very strong resemblance to Jeran and Zach. They shared the same smooth creamy skin, like a cup of warm milk with just a hint of black coffee. Her lips were full and pouty, with a natural soft brown lip line. Dark brown curls covered her head like Zach's, when he was her age, and were very soft to the touch. All three inherited most of their features from the lineages of Daniel's parents. None of their grandchildren favored the other parent. They were the only family I knew, whose children were interchangeable from one sibling to the next.

I remembered when Daniel first brought Madison home. I had been a nervous wreck, because I did not want to see her. Unfortunately, he had already told the boys of her existence and they wanted to meet her. I felt like I had no choice but to let this child, Daniel had forced into my world, into our home. I most certainly was not going to let them go over to that other woman's house. I have to admit, part of me needed to see Madison. I needed to determine, with my own eyes, if this child was my husband's seed. The man charged with loving, honoring and cherishing me.

I desperately wanted it not to be true. Before ever laying eyes on her, I prepared an argument to conduct another DNA test.

However, the minute I looked into her eyes, I knew the truth. She had Jolene's eyes—delicate and light brown, with the look of pure innocence. The first time she looked at me, it felt like she was looking into my soul and I then knew my life would never be the same. I was stuck in a conundrum. I could not hate this innocent child, but having her around constantly reminded me of Daniel's indiscretion. I simply could not handle that. After that day, whenever he brought her over, I would leave and stay gone until she went home. If I happened to stay, I offered minimal assistance to him—enough to keep up appearances in front of Jeran and Zach.

Deep in thought, Madison's cries, which had grown louder and stronger, startled me. Daniel held her in his arms, attempting to soothe her, to no avail. The more he rocked and cooed at her the louder she cried.

"Is she hungry?" Mrs. Johnson expressed with concern. "When was the last time she ate?"

"I fed her a couple of hours ago at the airport. She is probably ready to eat again." Daniel reached for her diaper bag.

I jumped at the opportunity to escape the tension and stress dominating the air space in the living room. "I'll warm up a bottle for you." I grabbed the diaper bag and fast-walked out of the room. I didn't wait for him to say thank you. On my way to the kitchen, I took off my coat and hung it on the back of the dining room chair. I figured I would stay awhile and see how this all played out.

Jeran, Zach, and Jolene sat at the kitchen table, watching a rerun of *Matlock*. They would only watch it with her. Any other time they wouldn't even consider it. I prepared the bottle, put it in a cup and let hot water from the faucet run over it. Madison was whaling, giving Daniel the blues. A smile tickled the corner of my mouth. He had not been deeply involved with the care of our children when they were infants. He lacked that special touch and timing it took to keep a baby happy. I did not even know if I wanted to stay with Daniel. Each day it got harder. I was beginning to feel like I needed to let him go.

I returned to the living room with Madison's bottle. Daniel took it, not even bothering to check to see if the formula was too hot before placing it in her mouth. She hungrily latched on to the nipple, quieting down immediately. Mrs. Johnson sat on the other side of the room, seemingly trying to take it all in. I silently wished her luck.

Not wanting to be around Daniel, I made a beeline for the den where Mr. Johnson was watching television. He looked curious, but remained silent.

"Hey, Pops, how are you?" I bent over the old man and kissed him on the cheek.

"Better than most, and better than many." He kissed me back. I never really quite understood what he meant by that phrase, but he had been saying it for years. "How are you?"

"I'm doing okay."

"How was the flight?"

"Good. We were delayed in Raleigh for a few hours, because of the storm. When we landed, we heard all other flights out of Raleigh to Chicago were cancelled, because it had gotten worse. Our flight was the last flight to be let in to Chicago. We were lucky." I did not really believe the last part of that statement.

"You don't say? How was the traffic from the airport?" He used his cane to shift himself in the chair.

"Terrible. People act like it is not snowing outside. It really gets under my skin that some people think they are invincible and drive like complete fools."

"Shoot, these Negroes don't care! They'll tear your car up." His voice rose a bit. "That's why I don't go out on days like this."

I smiled, because I knew he tried his best not to go out on dry, sunny days either.

"I'm sure glad you all made it. Your mother didn't think you were coming. Is that a baby I heard a while ago?"

"Yes it was." I eyed him.

"Who else is in there?" He spoke with caution.

"No one."

"Well, whose baby is up front?" He looked confused.

"The baby you heard is Daniel's child with another woman." I leaned back on the sofa and let the news resonate with my father-in-law. He was slow to respond, but after a few moments, he placed his hand on his cane, hoisted himself up out of his chair and moved toward the living room. I was not expecting him to say much when he got there, so I didn't follow. Instead, I returned to the kitchen.

I prepared myself a plate of spaghetti with Alfredo sauce and sat down next to Zach. My stomach growled when the aroma of food wafted up my nostrils. Jolene got up from the table and made herself a plate. She looked at me, but did not say anything. I knew she wanted to say something about this whole ordeal with Daniel.

"Hey, Zach, come on and let's go and play with Maddie." With full stomachs and empty plates, the boys were ready to get into something else.

"Okay, she likes when I make funny faces at her." Zach jumped down out of his chair and ran up the hallway with Jeran right behind him.

They were not gone thirty seconds before Jolene started the interrogation.

"So, Shannon, what in the hell is going on? When did all of this happen? I thought you two were happy."

I took a deep breath and began explaining the situation to Jolene by telling her that last April my doorbell rang and a woman, whom I had never laid eyes on before, introduced herself as Vaneetra James and told me that she had been having an affair with Daniel, was pregnant and thought I should know. Not bothering to give her the details of the conversation, I went on to tell her that I confronted Daniel about it that evening. He admitted to the affair and to possibly being the father of the woman's unborn child.

"So what are you going to do now that you know the baby is his?" The stern look in Jolene's eyes demanded an answer.

"I don't know. We don't talk and when he brings her over, I leave. I am considering filing for divorce."

"What about the boys?"

"I don't know that they really understand, because their lives are primarily the same. They really enjoy having a little sister. Jeran came to me and asked if it was okay for him to love her even though I wasn't her mother. His question surprised me. I realized then that I have to do something, because I don't want them to feel like they have to take sides or not love their sister."

"Well, how do you think they will feel if you and Daniel split up?" Even though Jolene had not accused me of anything, she sounded a little accusatory.

"They would be devastated and it would probably be difficult for them at first, but they will eventually adjust." I ate a couple forkfuls of pasta.

"Right, they would be devastated. This is why you and Daniel have to do whatever it takes to work this out and come to a resolution for this situation." I don't think she even heard the "they will eventually adjust" part of my statement.

"What do you mean me and Daniel?" It shocked me to hear those words come out of her mouth, of all people. "I don't have to do any—" Before I could finish my sentence, Jolene cut me off and laid into me, as if this whole situation was my fault.

"You have to start acting like a woman and stop running from the problem. It doesn't seem to me that anyone has really given a whole lot of thought to how my nephews feel about this, or how they will take it if they lose their father." She pushed her plate aside. "You're sitting around acting like you are not involved in this situation, lurking around the outside of everything, while Daniel seems to be running around here playing happy pappy and my nephews are just taking it all in. I love you and my brother, but I love Jeran and Zach more, which is why I am telling you to get yourself together before the three people innocent in this whole mess get hurt the most. You obviously don't want to leave, or you would be gone, so you need to stop doing nothing and do something to make your marriage work." Having said all that, Jolene walked out of the kitchen, leaving me sitting at the kitchen table with my mouth wide open, with no words to say, staring at two plates of unfinished spaghetti.

It felt like a bag of ice water slapped me in the face, bursting wide open. Jolene has never suggested that a woman stay with a man who has done her wrong, yet here she had stood, virtually demanding that I do that very thing. My shock morphed into rising anger. I pushed my plate away a little too hard. Spaghetti spilled over the edge. Just because Daniel was Jolene's only brother did not mean he got a pass to be a liar and a cheater.

I knew it was time for me to stop running from the truth and to face it full force. However, I was not sold on making my marriage work. I didn't want my boys to be hurt, and even though Madison was not mine, she does not need to grow up in a situation that could be harmful to her either. I would have to make a decision soon. However, whatever I decided would have to wait. There was commotion coming from the living room, and from the sound of it, an intense argument was ensuing.

Chapter Two

Daniel

Look, Mom, before you say anything, I know I was wrong for cheating on Shannon and I messed up. I never meant for it to happen, but it did and now I have a daughter. It's something that we will just have to deal with."

"Yes, you were wrong, but you didn't just mess up. Messing up happens by mistake. You intentionally had an affair. You did not consider the consequences of your actions, how they would affect not only your life, but also the lives of everyone involved. You may have ruined your marriage and damaged the relationship with the children you already have." She moved from her seat and sat beside me with a look of concern and frustration on her face. Seeing her like this made me feel like less than a man, like a little boy who had let her down. "This is not like walking out on an argument or forgetting to pick up milk at the grocery store. You were unfaithful and you now have a child as a result of it and from the looks of it, you expect everyone else, especially Shannon, to be okay with this."

I felt like I had to make her see things my way. "Mom, Shannon and I were having a lot of problems and had grown apart. Vaneetra helped me work through my frustration and things went too far. I know this would have been easier to handle if Madison had not been created in the process, but I can't change the past and I won't turn my back on her. I am her father."

"Boy, no one is asking you to turn your back on anyone, but you do have to be a man and men don't run around on their wives. That is what boys do." Dad spoke up for the first time since coming to sit in a nearby dining room chair. "Son, to hear you talk, it sounds like you think what you did was okay. It was not, and if it is still going on you need to end it. I raised you to be a man and to take care of your family, not to run out when things get tough and pick up with someone new. Shannon has done nothing but love you and you repay her by laying in the street with some other woman. You're lucky she hasn't left you."

I grasped for the right thing to say. "Dad, I know what I did was not okay, but it just happened. Vaneetra made me feel like a man, like I was important to her. I wasn't feeling that way with Shannon. She never included me in anything that had to do with the house, or the children. Not to mention she walked around with an attitude all the time. Every conversation turned into an argument. The smallest things set her off."

"Boy, are you hard of hearing?" I obviously had not found the right things to say. "You keep offering up excuses for what you did. There is no excuse. A man does not cheat on his wife, that's what boys do. Men work out their problems, so that they can keep their families together. And you have not answered the most important question. Is this affair still going on?" Dad spoke firmly, but the anger and disbelief had subsided from his voice and what remained felt like genuine concern.

"No, Dad, I ended it, but we do have to have some kind of relationship because of Madison."

"How'd she do that?" At first, Mom's question made no sense, but soon became clear. "How can a woman make a man feel like a man? I don't understand that one." She threw her hands in the air and rolled her eyes.

"I can't believe you would do something like this. Why is it that men never stop for a moment to think that the stupid stuff they do will have consequences that will hurt other people more than it could ever hurt them?" Jolene stood in front of me, ranting and raving about how I was destroying my family and setting a bad example for my sons. I don't know what happened between her and Shannon, but she came back into the living room shouting and flailing her arms at me. I figured she would not want to hear me out; she was on a man strike.

Mom noticed Jeran and Zach sitting nearby, wide-eyed, open-mouthed and taking it all in. "Boys, why don't you guys go in the den and watch television while the grown-ups talk?"

"We don't want to go," the boys said in unison. They looked somewhat scared, but mostly captivated. They had never seen my parents or their aunt express such frustration.

"I know you don't, but it will only be for a little while. We are almost done. "

"But, Daddy and Mommy send us out of the room when they talk, and we can still hear, so let us stay, Grandma." Jeran presented his argument to his grandmother. Too bad he didn't know that no one won against his grandmother.

"Listen to your grandmother, and go in the den," Shannon spoke up. "If it is okay with your father, Madison can go with you." She leaned against the wall connecting the kitchen to the dining room, rubbing her forehead. I stared at her for a moment, taking a good look at her for the first time in months. She looked exhausted and like she had lost weight. Her eyes lacked the life she had when we were first starting out together.

Shannon was a strikingly beautiful woman, with flawless brown skin. I loved looking at her tall frame, endowed with plump breast that stood at attention, curvy hips, and just enough butt to make any man want to get to know her better. She usually kept her natural hair styled with a lot of neat two strand twists that she would take down for the weekend when we would go out, but lately she kept it pulled back into one puff that sat at the back of her head, a sign that she had not been taking time to care for herself.

This entire situation had definitely taking its toll on her, but she would never admit it. Shannon used to be the voice of our marriage. Now she barely talked to me at all. Most nights I had to ask her how the boys were doing. I realized a long time ago that I messed things up, but I thought once she got over being mad we would be able to move on. After all, she found out about my affair nine months ago and we were still together. I planned to keep it that way. I could only hope that I could fix the damage I caused.

Realizing that everyone was waiting for my answer, I picked up Madison's carrier to head for the den. When I reached where Shannon stood, she pressed her body against the wall so I would not touch her. I wanted to reach out and stroke her hair, kiss her cheek and whisper in her ear that I was sorry, but I walked past without saying or doing anything. I just took Madison into the den and the boys followed. "You two can talk and play with her, but don't take her out of her carrier." I placed it on one end of the L-shaped sectional sofa.

"Okay, Daddy," they spoke at once.

Jeran grabbed the television remote and flipped through the channels until he found his favorite cartoon. Then he joined Zach, who had sat next to Maddie's carrier. I have some good-looking children. All three looked a lot alike. No one from the outside would ever guess Madison had a different mother, but I knew it and now my family did, too. I headed back into the living room, dreading the continuation of the current conversation.

Shannon was now sitting in the chair. I am sure she did that so I could not sit next to her. All the years she had been coming to my parents' house, whenever she sat in the living room, she sat on the love seat, or on the floor so I could sit next to her, but not today. I took a deep breath, ready to pick up my defense.

Jolene picked up right where she left off. Her tone mellowed from angry to concern. "Look, Daniel, obviously you and Shannon have some issues going on right now, but the two of you need to work them out. My nephews are in the middle of this and I don't want them hurt."

"Jolene, no one is trying to hurt the boys. I don't even think they understand what is going on. All they know is that they have a new sister and they love her. I am not going to do anything that is going to bring harm to my children."

"What you have done so far has brought harm to them. Anything that damages your family hurts your sons. Can you tell me that you and Shannon are getting along just fine? Are the two of you still doing stuff together with the boys as a family?" I could barely keep track of her questions. "Do you still even discuss their well-being? Boy, you have a real mess on your hands. While you are around here playing at being super dad and living up to your extra marital responsibilities, you need to make sure you still meet the needs of your family." Jolene sat down and crossed her arms and legs, leaving dead space in the air. Everyone, but Shannon, stared at me with a mixture of pain and sadness on their faces. I could not find the words to make this better. Desperate, I racked my brain trying to conjure up something to make everyone understand my point. Having Shannon in the room made it even more impossible to find the right thing to say.

"Jolene, I love my kids…all of them! I know what I have done has added a hardship to my family, but I feel that it is more so between Shannon and I than the boys. Obviously, things are not perfect between the two of us, but we work hard to make sure the boys are happy." I stopped short of letting on just how bad things had gotten between us. Prior to my having an affair, she had become distant. The only emotion I seemed to elicit from her, if any at all, was anger. I started staying at work late, getting home in just enough time to spend time with the boys before they went to bed. After that, I would go in my home office and pretend to work until well after she had gone to bed.

"All I am saying is that you two need to stop putting yourselves before your children. That is how kids grow up to be all messed up." Jolene continued her rant. "Their parents get too involved with their own issues and never take time to think about how the kids feel. By the time they notice anything is wrong, the kids are doing bad in school, are fighting and getting into all kinds of trouble." She leaned back against the sofa, looking as if I had caused her some serious pain. I guess in a way I had.

I didn't have a response for Jolene's last comments. What she said really put something on my mind and I needed time to think. Shannon had sat quietly the entire time, tears dancing on the rim of her eyelids, her hands bawled into tight fists, as if trying to squeeze out the hurt I had caused her. I could tell she agreed with my sister. Despite what anyone else might think, I had been thinking about how my actions affected Jeran and Zach. Even with all the tension in the house, they seemed fine.

I didn't know what was going to happen between Shannon and me. I couldn't help but feel like she was only around because of the boys and not wanting them to hurt. She barely allowed me to touch her. Her face registered pure disgust when I would try. It seemed like she would never find it in her heart to forgive me.

She didn't seem to understand that I made a mistake. One I will never make again.

"Well, we might as well eat." Mom broke the silence in the room. "Nothing will get solved on an empty stomach. Come on in the kitchen and I'll fix you a plate of spaghetti and fish." She spoke to no one in particular.

Chapter Three

Shannon

At the end of the heated discussion at the Johnson's, I left with the boys and headed to the South Suburbs to Mom's house. It had stopped snowing and the roads were a little better. Even though I dreaded fighting the snow, I needed to be with Mom, if for nothing else but to be in her presence. Not knowing how she would respond to the news, I thought it best to break it to her alone. Daniel did not seem pleased with my decision to leave, but I didn't care.

I was not too concerned about telling my father, as he and Mom were never married and my relationship with him was strained. We talked a couple of times a month, but nothing more. I doubted if I would even see him during this visit. He had his life and family, and I had mine. He lived the good life when I was a child, taking care of another man's children while I suffered. I used to wish for him to rescue me, to save me from the pain and turmoil of my childhood, but he never did. I have no use for him now.

Mom has five children: Terrance, Craig, Raven, Lisa and me. I am the oldest. Terrance and I are two years apart. His father died in a hiking accident while on leave from the Marines right before Terrance was born. She married Craig, Raven and Lisa's father, when I was five years old, giving birth to Craig and Raven early in the marriage. Lisa came along much later, at the end of it. Craig, Sr., drank all the time, using that as an excuse to slap Mom around and display disdain for Terrence and me regularly.

Mom struggled, working minimum wage jobs, and getting help from government programs to make ends meet until she got up the nerve to go to nursing school and leave her abuser. My childhood years felt so cold and lonely. Mom was very protective and endured a lot just to keep us safe. During the week, all was quiet, but on the weekend, the fighting began, lasting the entire weekend. On Sundays, Craig, Sr., would lay holed up in their bedroom, miserably hung over and waiting to make up. I vowed never to be the type of woman that would allow a man to mistreat me.

When I met Daniel, I found solace. I knew he would be different. What initially attracted me to him, after I got past his good looks, was that he filled the void left by not having any type of real relationship with my father. A girl should feel loved and protected by the men in her life. Instead, I felt tossed aside and meaningless. Daniel made me feel like I was the most important person in his life; he was always attentive to my every need, listened to my every word, made love to me—physically and emotionally. Being with him intoxicated me.

In the beginning, I thought he was nothing like my father or Craig, Sr. I did not believe he would ever cheat on me, or turn his back on his children. I found out that he would not turn his back on his children, any of them. I don't know what hurt more, the fact he was unfaithful, or the realization that he was just like all the other men that had been a part of my life—those charged with the responsibility of protecting me from harm, but had caused it instead.

After an hour, I pulled into Mom's driveway and turned off the engine. Jeran and Zach had fallen asleep during the ride. We had been up since four o'clock that morning. The toll of the long hours had taken its effect on my babies. I hated waking them, because they looked like angels, sleeping so peacefully. Neither was happy about being awakened. I had to carry Zach while Jeran clung tightly to my right leg, afraid to fall on a sheet of ice accumulating on the walkway leading to Mom's front door. I used my key to let us inside, anxious to put down my forty-five-pound bundle of joy. "Hello, Mother! Your loving daughter has returned home." I helped Zach and Jeran out of their coats and boots while waiting to hear a response.

"I'm in my bedroom," she yelled from the back of the house. "I just got out of the tub. I worked today."

"Where is Lisa?" I walked to her bedroom.

"She is spending the night with her friend, Kaitlynn. I had planned to work a double and didn't want her here alone."

"What made you change your mind? I didn't tell you that I was coming for sure."

"Did you see all that snow outside?" Her voice elevated. "I didn't want to try to drive home at eleven o'clock at night on that mess. So at three, I punched out and began my snail crawl home. You know I hate driving in the snow."

"You hate driving period. The only reason you have a license is because I moved out." I sat on her bed while she finished getting dressed.

"For your information, I like driving! It gives me independence." She came over and kissed me on the cheek. "I know I waited until I was damn near forty years old to learn, but since I have, I love it! I don't have to wait on anybody to take me here or there and I don't have to put up with their nasty attitudes."

"Well, I never treated you like that! So you could have kept that last part to yourself." I rolled my eyes.

"Oh, you used to get a 'tude, sister girl, especially if taking me kept you from Daniel. The only ones you didn't have a problem doing anything for were Lisa and Craig. You spoiled them, you know."

"Yeah, I did spoil them." My tone dripped with arrogance. "And for your information, I did not have a *'tude*, because you kept me away from Daniel. I had an attitude, because instead of learning how to drive, you preferred to run all of the energy out of me. And by the way, I did not complain about taking any of you anywhere either." If I had stayed away from Daniel, I wouldn't be in this predicament. But I would not have my beautiful angels, who were miraculously still asleep on the couch.

"I did not!" Mom became defensive.

"Oh no? I guess you don't remember that Sunday you got mad at me for waiting until an hour before you got off work to take Terrance back to Northern, which, by the way, is a ninety-minute drive. You refused to get another way home and waited until I got back just so I could pick you up, even though you had said that morning you would ask one of your co-workers to bring you home."

"I don't remember that." Mom cut her eyes at me in a way that let me know she remembered. "Look, I was scared to learn how to drive and I needed you. I didn't realize until I got my own car just how much you did for us. Now I have to run your sisters all of the time. You would think that Raven would find her own way around or at least take the bus, since I keep her kids during the week." Raven was twenty-six years old, with three kids and no husband. She chose not to go to college and worked two jobs to get by.

"Don't complain. You know you like the boys around. They give you something to talk about and someone to fuss at.

Besides, she needs the help. She is trying to better herself." Mom rolled her eyes, squeezed lotion into the palm of her hands and moisturized. "You'll be off the hook soon. Craig is buying a new car and plans to give Raven his current one." I did not tell her that Craig and Terrance had actually bought Raven a car for Christmas. She had a tendency to talk too much at times.

"I can't wait until he does." She turned and walked out her bedroom.

I followed her out. "Some people like to save so they can better afford the things they like instead of settling."

"Well, what does that have to do with me? I should not have to suffer." She walked into the living room, leaned down, kissed the boys on the forehead, and sat down in a chair near the fireplace.

"Well, you have to pay it forward, Camille, and you owe a lot." I rolled my eyes this time. "So how are you, Mother dear?" I blatantly changed the subject. "I have missed you so much, and just travelled through the frosty equivalent of hell to come and see you, so perk up and act like you are happy to see me, woman!"

"I am happy to see you, darling, just ecstatic!" Her response seemed genuine.

"Good! Let's stop wasting time rehashing yester year."

"Where is Daniel? He didn't want to see his mother-in-law?"

"He stayed at his mom's. He's coming here tomorrow."

"Why didn't you just wait until tomorrow? It is really bad out there tonight."

"I wanted to spend my first night here with you." I looked at my babies, so I could avoid eye contact with her. Although this statement was partially true, the entire truth was that I needed to be away from Daniel and hoped to find peace at her place. However, thinking about it now, once I break the news to her, peace may never come. I knew I needed to tell her before the boys spilled the beans.

"I am hungry. I haven't eaten all day." Mom stood up. "Let's go in the kitchen, so you can finish cooking."

"So I can finish cooking?" She had a lot of nerve. "I did not travel eight hundred miles in a snow storm just so I can cook. It smells like dinner is done." The aroma of pot roast cooking in the kitchen invaded my nostrils when I arrived, but our conversation sidetracked me from the delicious smell. I did not eat my spaghetti at the Johnson's and could have passed out from hunger.

"Come on and make my gravy for me and whip up some mashed potatoes. I have some string beans in the refrigerator that I cooked last week and froze for later. I took them out this morning before I left for work. All you have to do is heat them up." Mom's voice dripped with sweetness, like sap from a maple tree. I almost got a toothache just listening to her.

I succumbed to her wishes and completed dinner. "You are lucky I am beyond starving, or you would be out of luck, Mother dear." I used the time to figure out how I would bare my soul to her over pot roast. "So, I have something important to tell you and I may as well do it now before the boys wake up and tell you." I looked away, hoping she would not notice the tears forming.

"Are you and Daniel getting a divorce?" Mom asked jokingly. "Maybe."

Mom looked at me, baffled.

Not knowing how to put it nicely, I sat down at the kitchen table and blurted out, "Mom, Daniel had an affair and fathered a child with another woman." I exhaled. There, I said it.

For a moment, Mom was silent, but then she started to laugh rather strangely. "You have got to be kidding me! You need to work on your jokes, because this one is not funny!"

I did not respond, because I knew she knew it was not a joke.

"When did this happen? Is the baby born yet?" She asked in disbelief.

"Well, the baby is three months old, so you can do the math on the rest," I replied in a dry tone.

"Are you two still together?"

"We live in the same house together, but that is about all. Our marriage is in shambles; we don't talk, or do anything else. We are present in the home, but not accounted for, as least not as husband and wife. We do all right as baby momma and baby daddy."

"Well, what are you going to do?" She stepped closer to me.

I waved my hands in the air and slapped them down on the kitchen table. "Why does everyone want to know what I am going to do? I don't know and really don't understand why I have to do anything. He cheated, he broke the covenant of our marriage, yet everyone wants to know what I am going to do!"

Mom rolled her eyes and hissed at my overly dramatic response. "I want to know what you are going to do, because it is obvious that he is waiting to find out what you are going to do."

"Camille, how could you possibly know what Daniel is waiting on?" I called her by her first name, hoping to sidetrack her. I knew she hated it. She thought of it as a sign of disrespect. It didn't work though. She was so immersed in our discussion that I don't believe she even noticed.

"I know, because he has not left yet." She raised her voice a few octaves. Before I could respond, she continued with her verbal rampage. "Girl, that man still wants you. If he didn't, he would have moved out."

I reminded her that we have two kids and I only work part time as a freelance writer. "It is cheaper to keep me. I can't afford to maintain our home on my salary."

Resting her palms on the table, Mom leaned in so close to me, her breath engulfed my entire face. In a very low tone, she said, "Sweetie, when a man is through with a woman, he walks away. A good man will continue to take care of his kids and make sure they have a roof over their heads, but he leaves the woman. Women are the ones that hold on to lifeless relationships that are beyond repair."

I stood up, walked to the stove, and whisked the gravy. I pierced the potatoes with a fork, pretending to focus on cooking, because I did not want Mom to see my tears that I was trying to suppress quickly rolling down my face. I did not think Daniel wanted to salvage our marriage. I assumed he stayed for the kids and was waiting for me to file for divorce. We had not really talked much in the past few months. Our marriage lacked communication. We never discussed anything more than the needs of the kids. He did not help around the house, with managing the finances, or anything else for that matter. He went to work and brought a check home. He did not deal with any of our problems and ignored my attempts to address them. He had hurt me horribly, yet I had not let go.

I finished preparing dinner. Mom and I ate in silence. The boys slept so deeply that I wondered whether they were unconscious. Finally, I broke the silence. "Mom, I really don't know what to do! I am so hurt and embarrassed. How could he do this to me? I didn't deserve it. I followed him to North Carolina, putting my career on hold for his and for the well-being of our family, and he says *thank you* by cheating on me." Warmth crept over my face. "He just throws all those years we put into each other out the window for some other woman. How could he do that? I wouldn't and didn't do it to him. He should have just left. That would have hurt a whole lot less than this. I could adapt to living without him, but this…this is too much!" By this time, my voice was barely audible and tears were pouring down my face.

Mom was gravely silent. She handed me napkins and I wiped my face. Then she grabbed my hands and squeezed them tightly. "Shannon, I know what you are going through. I was in a similar situation with Craig Sr. You know all the shit I took off him and for how long I took it. Take it from me this is not the worst it can get. You had been telling me for a while that you and Daniel were having problems before all of this happened and he has turned to another woman instead of trying to work them out. Now, you don't have to stay, but I can tell you from experience that there are men out there that are a lot worse than Daniel."

"Mom, what am I supposed to do? If I leave, my boys will be without their father. If I stay, I have to be bothered with Vaneetra James and all of her crap. I just don't think I can put up with the baby mamma drama." I finished the rest of my dinner.

Mom sighed and continued to eat her food. "I can't tell you what to do, but whatever you choose, you have to make sure you and your sons can live with it. Why don't you and the boys go to bed? They can sleep in Sebastian, Andrew and Mekhail's room, and you can sleep in Lisa's room. I will clean up the kitchen."

Although it was still early in the evening, I didn't argue. I felt like I was weighted down with chains and cement blocks. I managed to get the boys into their pajamas and bed before turning in myself. Sitting on the edge of Lisa's bed, I was consumed with hurt, pain and confusion. I pulled off my pants and shirt, and lay my head down on Lisa's down pillows.

My mind and body were not in sync. I lay in Lisa's bed for a while, trying not to think. I felt weighted down with exhaustion, but my brain would not rest. I kept thinking back to when life was better between Daniel and me, trying to figure out what went wrong. I wanted to pinpoint when he fell out of love with me, what part I had played in turning him away. There was a time in our lives when we were happy and in love. It seemed as if we thought of nothing other than making each other happy. I was so in tuned with Daniel; I knew what he was thinking before he ever spoke a word. He knew when I need to be held, and when I needed to be left alone. As quickly as they came, those times were gone, leaving despair where love once resided, replacing calm with anguish. He stopped caring about what I needed. Sleep finally came, but peace of mind did not.

Chapter Four

Daniel

After Shannon and the boys left, I borrowed Jolene's car and went over to Parker's house. Parker was more like a brother than a cousin. His mother, Aunt Mildred, was like my second mom. She died a couple of years ago. His father, a well-known pastor, committed suicide when Parker and his sister, Sylvia, were young, leaving Aunt Mildred broke and struggling. My parents stepped in and helped her out. Parker and Sylvia practically lived at our house. My father acted as the man of both households back then.

Things had calmed down at my parents' place. Mom and Jolene didn't let my infidelity stop them from immediately bonding with Madison. Before I left, Jolene was holding her while Mom started preparations to give her a bath. She pulled out the same foot-and-a-half-by-one-foot-wide plastic, white pail she used to bathe Jeran and Zach when they were infants. She filled it with warm water and Madison's baby bath, placed it on the kitchen table surrounded by oversized, soft, white cotton towels. Jolene turned up the thermostat, so the already warm house could get warmer. She went through the luggage and found Madison's bag, pulling out a fresh pair of lilac, footed pajamas, a pink, cotton T-shirt and a gigantic bib that had a picture of a cocoa brown baby sporting a teeny-weeny afro that read: Daddy's Sweet Little Angel in large curvy letters.

Ice sheeted the streets leading to Parker's house. Mounds of snow piled high on the curbs, as high as four feet. A very familiar scene forever embedded in my mind, because I lived it as a kid. Milk crates and old, vinyl covered chairs with back pads lined the curbs as a way for people to reserve their parking spaces. Back in the day, moving a chair and taking a spot were grounds for getting your tires slashed.

As I drove, the wind blew a rusty, old folding chair out of one of those precious parking spaces and into the middle of the street. The poor soul who put it out was going to be pissed when he returned home to find his spot gone. Being able to park on the street was such a big deal. In the city, houses did not have driveways. Most houses had detached garages situated in the rear and were only accessible through an alley. Unfortunately, during a snowfall, an alley was virtually impossible to pass through.

I parked a block from Parker's place and trudged through the snow and bitter wind to his front step. This would not have been so hard if everyone on the block had bothered to shovel the sidewalk. Standing in what had to be the equivalent of the Arctic, waiting for Parker to answer the door, nearly drove me to make the journey back to Jolene's truck. Just as I turned to go, he answered the door with a grin that covered the lower third of his face.

"Hey, man, how long have you been standing out there? Come on in!" He gave me a big bear hug, practically dragging me over the threshold. Parker was a big man, tall with broad shoulders. We were about the same in stature, but that did not stop him from showing off his strength.

"Hey, dude, what's with you leaving me outside to freeze? If your wife won't let you have company, you should have said something before I came over here."

"Man, she don't run nothin' 'round here. I say what can and can't happen. Now hurry up and let's go downstairs before she sees you." He laughed, as he closed the door behind us.

Parker led the way down to the basement he turned into a miniature theater and game room.

"So, what's been up, man? Your mom said that y'all weren't coming. Boy, I know she was excited to see y'all."

"Oh yeah, you know she was. She didn't even want me to come over here. You know how she gets. She wanted you and your family to come to the house. I had to sneak out!" I laughed, somewhat exaggerating the truth.

"Ah, man, we would have come over. You know I got that big Suburban in the garage and can just roll down the street like the snow isn't even out there."

"I know you can, but I wanted to talk to you first. Where are Laura and the kids?"

"They are at her parents' house. She goes over there a few times a week to help out a bit, since they are getting up in age. I was going with them today, but when you called I told her she should go ahead without me."

"How are Mom and Pop Perkins?" I was stalling.

"They're good. So, what do you want to talk about? Jolene sent me a text message saying you really messed something up and that I needed to talk to you." Parker was serious, with a concerned look on his face.

"I should have known Jolene couldn't keep her mouth shut!"

"Keep her mouth shut about what?"

"Oh, you mean she didn't tell you?"

"No, she didn't! She just said you messed up. Why don't you tell me what she is talkin about?"

"I had an affair and Shannon found out." I blurted the words out without thinking about how he would react.

"Aww, man! How did she find out?"

"The woman I was cheating with showed up to our house and told her."

"Whoa!" Parker took a step back and placed his hand on my shoulder. "How did she know where you live? What did Shannon say?"

"She could have gotten my address off my license when we were together. You can imagine what Shannon said. The affair is not the jacked up part. I mean it is bad, but the story goes on."

"Then you go on and tell it!"

"I have a three-month-old daughter by this woman."

"What the hell! Boy, how did you let that happen? Man, If you gon' step out on your woman, you are supposed to strap it up. You don't bring anything back!" Parker was pacing the room, but then turned back to me. "Are you and Shannon still together?"

"Yes, we are still together."

"Have you thought about how this whole ordeal will affect your relationship with your sons? You and Shannon may be together now, but what if she decides to leave you?"

Everyone was so concerned about Jeran and Zach! Didn't they know that I would never intentionally hurt my boys and I didn't plan for my relationship with them to change? I would do anything to keep that from happening. "Look, man, I know I screwed up, and I have a lot of fixing to do. I am not sure how I will do it, but no matter what happens I will always be there for my sons."

"Hey, dude, I know you will, but you have two women to deal with and Shannon is a handful by herself. What did she do when the other chick showed up at your door? Did they fight?" Parker's eyes got wide.

"Man, I wasn't there when it happened, but no they did not. When I got home, Shannon had finished a bottle and a half of

Moscato. She had burned dinner and the house was filled with smoke.."

"Dude, you kiddin'?" Parker shook his head in disbelief. "Shannon got wasted? I don't believe it."

"Believe it! She went bizerk. At first, she seemed so relaxed that I thought she was going to pass out on me. All of a sudden, she was rambling on about being a good wife and mother, and sacrificing her career advancement for mine. Then she started talking about people doing dirt and thinking they would never get caught and being stupid. At first, I didn't catch on. Then she honed in on her point, and suddenly she seemed sober as hell. She called Vaneetra a tramp and said she came to our door and said she was carrying my baby. I almost didn't believe her, until she described Vaneetra. I thought she had found out some other way and was trying to trip me up."

Parker slapped me on the back a little too hard. "Playa, how did you handle that?"

"At first, I accused her of making it up, even though I knew she hadn't. I walked into the kitchen and blew her off by telling her to ease up on the bottle. I had planned to call Vaneetra to find out what she had planned to accomplish by coming to my crib. Then the crystal vase your mom gave us for our wedding came whizzing past my head. It hit the door jamb in the kitchen and shattered on the floor."

Parker burst out in to loud, rambunctious laughter. I personally wanted to know what he found so damn funny. Between heaves and gasps of breath, he managed to say, "Boy, I know you were happy Shannon was drunk." I must have given him a perplexed looked because he managed to compose himself long enough to explain. "I remember Shannon being pretty good at throwing a softball. If she had been sober she probably would have knocked your ass the hell out with the vase." Ironically, I could not disagree. He finished entertaining himself at my expense and stopped laughing. "Playa, my mom was tight with her money. That vase probably had more lead than a pipe. You were damned lucky, indeed."

"I'm not so sure. Since that day, it has been hell living in the same house with her. She is always mad about something and we go days without speaking. I wish she would just get over this, so we could move on."

"Yep, and I bet people in hell wish it would freeze over, but that isn't likely to happen anytime soon either. A baby ain't nothing you just get over. That's that type of stuff soap operas and divorces are made of. Man, you got your own soap opera going on, you need a network deal." He burst out laughing, again. He was pissing me off and I turned to leave. Parker composed himself, and blocked my way. "Daniel, wait a minute. Don't leave yet, I'm just joking around. Don't be so serious."

I couldn't believe what I was hearing. "Parker, this isn't a joking matter. My life is not a soap opera." I could barely contain my anger.

"Hey, wait a minute, playboy!" He spoke with a level of hardness in his voice that I had not heard him use in years. "You the one went out and banged another woman without strappin' up and had a packaged delivered to your doorstep. I know it's your life, but so did you. You the one who made the joke out of it, so don't get all bent out of shape when people don't feel sorry for you. I'm laughing because I can't believe you got yourself in this predicament." His next words were like a sucker punch to the gut, but they rung true. "You need to man up, accept responsibility for what you did and decide what to do next."

I sat down, feeling defeated. We sat silent for a long time before either of us spoke.

"Look, man, let's have a beer and watch the game. Maybe if you relaxed a little you may be able to think of a way to turn your situation around." He got up, went to the fridge in the corner and grabbed two beers. I really could not see any way out of this that did not involve my moving out of my house and being away from my kids. I couldn't let that happen.

For the next few hours, Parker and I watched the Bulls game and relived old times. We talked about Madison. We talked about how I met Vaneetra. He did not buy my reasons for cheating on Shannon and gave me his version of the dos and don'ts of marriage. Cheating, or at least getting caught, was his number one don't.

I texted Shannon a few times to make sure she made it to her mother's, but she did not respond. I even tried calling once and it went to voicemail. When I left my cousin's house I felt better, but still had no idea how I would work things out with Shannon. I was not even sure I could.

Chapter Five

Daniel

When I returned to my parents', the temperature display in the car read minus five degrees, but with the wind chill factor, it felt like minus fifteen. I was glad I had shoveled the snow from in front of the garage before I left. I backed Jolene's Lexus SUV into it and sat for a minute. It concerned me that Shannon had not called to let me know she and the boys made it to her mother's, but that was her M.O. lately. She no longer bothered to tell me anything.

I'd enjoyed my time with Parker. We reminisced about our childhood and the fun we used to have. We didn't spend a whole lot of time talking about the affair. Instead, he wanted to know about Vaneetra. He wanted to know how she looked, and what she did for a living. Even though I did not like taking about Vaneetra, I answered his questions. Vaneetra was thirty-five years old, tall and in great shape, with smooth brown skin. She had ample sized breasts, with a butt and hips to match. She wore her long natural hair in different styles from week to week. Her beauty was what initially attracted me to her.

We met at a gym in September of last year. I would see her around a few times and we'd have polite conversation. After a while, we started working out together, running the track and lifting weights. She was easy to talk to, definitely easy to look at and had a nice smile.

In addition to her beauty, Vaneetra had a sassy attitude and competitive nature that turned me on. She challenged me and I liked that. Although Shannon is beautiful, she never seemed happy. We argued all the time about everything from my working late, to my never having anything to say. When I hung out with Vaneetra, my stress disappeared. We enjoyed each other's company, always laughing and having a good time. I loved her independence and drive. She worked as a senior director at a technology firm in Research Triangle Park, North Carolina. I guess what attracted me to her the most was that she didn't need me at the time, she wanted me. I had not felt wanted in quite some time. Most days, Shannon didn't even seem interested in my presence. I would walk in the house from work and the dryness in her voice when she greeted me was like sandpaper. She stopped smiling, and her eyes told the truth.

After what I told him, Parker wanted to know how Vaneetra and I went from hanging out to having sex. I told him the story of the first time we were together. Vaneetra had locked her keys in her car and asked me to drive her home to get the spare. When we got to her house, she invited me in and asked if I would mind waiting for her to take a shower and change into fresh clothes. She made me a drink while I waited. When she came back she had on a pair of tight black jeans, and a low cut silk blouse. She walked over to the sofa and, when I stood up, leaned in and kissed me. That began my life, as I know it today. Four hours later, I dropped her off at her car and headed home, thinking of the right lie to tell Shannon.

Ironically, I didn't feel bad after our first night together. I went out of town the next week and found myself talking to Vaneetra more than Shannon. On another occasion, she flew to New York to spend a few days with me while I attended a conference. Things really escalated from there.

Initially, although time with Vaneetra seemed endless, it was never enough. It felt good being in her presence. Time with her was the way my home was not—peaceful, fun, non-committed. She actually wanted my advice on various situations. Whenever we were together, the hours went by like minutes. I was free to relax and release the stresses of the day.

Then oddly enough, she was beginning to sound a lot like Shannon, making demands that I could not possibly meet. She wanted me to leave my family and that was not going to happen. I couldn't see myself walking out on the boys. I was not the type of man that would be okay with another man raising my sons.

Snapping back to reality, I realized the clock read twelve-fifteen. I turned off the SUV and trudged through the narrow path between the garage and the steps leading to the back door. I entered the house, being careful not to make any noise. I'd made it to the refrigerator when Maddie began to cry. The lull of her soft cry came from the front of the house and permeated the air, like the moans of a lonely puppy.

I pulled off my boots and hustled toward the cries, almost colliding into Jolene, cradling my fussy daughter. I offered to take her, but Jolene suggested that I fix a bottle instead. A couple minutes later, I returned with a warm bottle.

I retrieved Maddie from Jolene, who kissed her on the cheek, patted me on the shoulder and went back to bed. Getting hungrier by the second, Maddie's lull escalated to an all-out wail. I put the bottle in her mouth and she sucked fervently. It dawned on me that she usually ate at 1:00 a.m. In North Carolina, it was a half hour past her time to eat. I situated us in an overstuffed chair on the enclosed back porch. It was a comfortable place to sit with Maddie while she sucked her bottle. The space was heated, and had wall-to-wall plush carpet, with charcoal sketches of my grandparents hanging on the wall.

I felt a ping of guilt for forgetting to tell Jolene about Maddie's feeding schedule. Although she didn't seem bothered, I should have remembered to tell her. This was all new to me. Shannon got up with Jeran and Zach when they were babies. I didn't have to do much. She breast-fed them until they were a year. Even then, I still didn't help that often.

After Vaneetra got pregnant, she always talked about breastfeeding and was adamant that she would do it. She told me that I would only be able to visit our child at her house because of it. Now, sitting in the dark, holding my baby girl, I wondered why she had changed her mind and why she let Maddie come with us in the first place. She wasn't the type to be so accommodating.

At first, I didn't think I could handle caring for Maddie alone for two weeks. Shannon had not been going out of her way to help me, and I refused to ask. I didn't feel like I had the right to do so. She flipped out at the idea of my providing Vaneetra with any help at all before I knew that Maddie was mine. I always knew, but did not argue. As odd as it may seem, Vaneetra was a respectable woman. She really thought I would leave Shannon. Truthfully, I never thought that far ahead.

Maddie finished her bottle. I placed her against my shoulder and softly patted her bottom until she burped. I learned that trick from Shannon. She used to do the same thing to Jeran and Zack. She'd always said that Johnson babies took feeding seriously, and nursed with such urgency, it caused gas to settle deep down inside, making it necessary to disturb and force it up from their bottoms. I used to think she was crazy, until I once spent fifteen minutes trying to burp Maddie by patting her on the back. The next time I patted her bottom she burped right away.

Leaning back in the chair, the weight of the day's events settled in on me like a lead blanket. With Maddie in one arm, a canister of milk and bottle of water in the other, I went through the family room and trudged up the dark, rickety, narrow stairwell. Every step whined under the pressure of my heavy feet. I entered the wide-open space with no energy to spare.

Chapter Six

Shannon

Morning seemed to have come too soon. When I opened my eyes, I felt as if only five or ten minutes had passed. I had just fluffed my pillow and rolled over to fall listlessly back into the world of slumber when Zach burst into the room like a hurricane and pounced on the bed. He was the epitome of bright eyed and bushy tailed.

"Mommy, Mommy, time to wake up! There is lots and lots of snow outside and I want to go out and play. Jeran and I want to build a snowman and Grandma says we can't go out without you. She says she's too old to be rolling around in the snow." Words gushed from his mouth like raging rapids, I could barely wrap my mind around his request, or more so his demand.

Before I could raise a good argument as to why Mommy needed three more hours of sleep, Jeran darted into the room, jumped into the air and landed right across my abdomen, as he so often did, knocking most of the wind right out of me. He always managed to leave me just enough oxygen to submit to whatever their demands were at the time. This snowy December morning was no different. Their warm, brown eyes dancing with excitement, and those captivating smiles, made them hard to resist. I caved in to their wants, as I usually did when I knew it would bring them joy.

"Okay, Okay! Go put your clothes on and let me get myself together." As they ran out the room, I shouted for Jeran to find an oxygen tank and bring it to me to replace the wind he knocked out of me.

He halted at the door, turned and flashed me a million dollar smile with his head cocked to the side. "You a big girl, Mom, you can take it." He then disappeared, leaving me sitting upright in the middle of Lisa's bed, grinning.

"I can take more than you could ever imagine, and still come out on top." Having said it to no one in particular, I thought it relevant to our current situation.

Knowing that taking a shower was the most unintelligent thing to do right before going out in thirty-degree weather, I did the basics to freshen up and headed to the kitchen for a cup of coffee. Thankfully, Mom had brewed a fresh pot.

"Good morning," I mumbled, as I poured myself a cup.

"Good morning," she replied, never looking up from her morning paper.

"How'd you get the paper in this mess?" I asked, while popping bagels into the four-slice toaster sitting next to the stove on the dark granite countertop.

"Paper boy lives across the street. He shoveled the sidewalk and as much of the driveway as he could. When you pull your car into the garage, he will do the rest."

"That's nice of him! You must pay him well."

"Twenty well-spent bucks," she stated between coffee sips.

I walked over to the fridge, searching for cream cheese. Surprisingly, I found cream cheese, vanilla almond milk, apples, oranges, and an abundance of other nutritious goodies. Mom had stocked her refrigerator, which was very rare. I loaded up my arms, walked from the fridge to the counter and plopped everything down near the toaster. Pulling plates from the cabinet above the same countertop, I placed warm bagels on two of them and dropped one more in the toaster. Mom had recently had her kitchen remodeled and now had what was called a gourmet kitchen that included beautiful oak cabinets, stainless steel appliances, and ceramic tile floors that reminded me of gold-colored sand with streaks of red clay.

Spreading cream cheese on the bagels and cutting apples into slices, I told Mom that I would put the car into the garage when I took the boys outside. Miraculously, they appeared in the kitchen just as I had set the plates on the large, round oak kitchen table that seated six. They were dressed in sweatpants and matching sweatshirts. As Zach scurried around to sit in a chair in front of the kitchen window, I noticed he still on had his pajamas. I peeked under Jeran's shirt and discovered he, too, had on his pajamas. I chuckled a bit, wondering if they wanted to be extra warm or extra fast with dressing for the outdoors. They hurriedly ate, all the while chatting about snowmen, snowballs, snow angels and forts. They were excited about the amount of white fluffy stuff that covered every square inch of the outdoors. Raleigh did not get anywhere near the amount of snow that Chicago did. Mom added to their excitement by telling them their cousins would be coming over this morning. We finished breakfast. I cleared the table, bundled up and headed outside. I put the rented SUV in the garage, and let the boys loose in the yard.

Within seconds, loosely packed snowballs were sailing through the air with no particular place to go before smashing to the ground with a repetitive thud. Zach was at a disadvantage in the area of strength, so his snowballs didn't go as far, but the little rascal was quick and made up the difference by ducking behind trees and bushes, forcing Jeran to seek him out, and then blazing him as soon as he got within range. I joined in on the fun by pounding snow into small balls and throwing them in the boys' general direction. They took this as a wage of war and quickly joined forces against me. Before I knew it, snowballs bombarded my body, rendering me helpless, as the boys tackled and dragged me down into the fluffy white abyss. Laughing uncontrollably, I raised my hands in surrender begging for mercy. They only released me when three other overly bundled bodies dove into the snow and joined the tussle. Sebastian, Andrew and Mekhail had arrived. We never even noticed them approaching.

Laughing with excitement, all five boys wrestled around, knocking one another down and freeing me up to get away. Cold and feeling my age, I struggled to my feet and walked toward the garage door. I undressed, hung my wet coat on a hook near the kitchen door, and placed my boots parallel to the step leading into the kitchen. Raven stood at the counter pouring a cup of coffee with one hand, taking a donut from a box with the other.

"Good morning." I greeted my sister.

She looked at me and rolled her eyes. "Whatever, you say."

"What's wrong with you?"

"Nothing I want to share."

Giving up on my failed attempt at a decent conversation, I retrieved my coffee cup from earlier. Opting out of the late afternoon jitters that came with a second cup of coffee, I searched for tea, finding the box of lemon green tea I'd left the last time we'd visited. While heating water, I snagged a double chocolate donut. When the microwave beeped, I grabbed my treats and headed for the window seat at the kitchen table, not because I was dying to look out, which I couldn't since my back would be facing it. I wanted the window seat positioned directly over a heating vent because my feet were numb.

"Where's D?" Raven asked in an upbeat voice.

"At his parents' house," I replied, not at all surprised by her sudden mood change. When engaged in a conversation, she was known to have an attitude, but not when she was the one doing the engaging.

"When's he coming out here?" By now, she was sitting across from me with a Bavarian cream-filled long john.

"Not sure." Being evasive, I popped a piece of donut in my mouth.

"Why didn't he come with you last night? It was bad out there!" She kept prying.

"I have driven in the snow before. I don't need Daniel to help me find my way!" I could feel myself getting annoyed. I sipped my tea and changed the subject. "The boys are having a blast out there in all that snow." At that moment, I turned to see a sixth boy bombarded by a barrage of snowballs sailing across the front yard. Since he had a shovel in his hand, I assumed he was the paperboy who also doubled as the snow removal guy. Not to be outdone by five little boys, he dropped his shovel and joined the fun.

"How long you gon' be out here?" Raven wanted to be engaging again.

"Probably until tomorrow, I just want to relax. Besides, I am sure I won't be able to pull my boys apart from yours." Happy she had changed the subject, I spoke with less edge in my voice. I couldn't help but wonder if Mom had told her about my and Daniel's secret. She may complain about Raven, but they were the world's greatest gossip partners. The two of them fussed all the time, except when they were in deep discussion about someone else's business and then they were bosom buddies. One would think they were discussing world affairs as opposed to who was messing around with whom, and who worked double shifts while her baby daddy lay at home all day doing nothing.

"My boys will be happy. They've been talking about how they wanted to see Jeran and Zack since talking to them on Skype last weekend. Why didn't you tell me y'all were comin?"

"That would have meant that Jeran and Zack would have found out, because your boys would have told them, and I would not have gotten any peace in my household." Not that I was getting any anyway. I made it standard practice not to tell the boys where we were going until we were on the way there. For this explanation, I got an eye roll, but before she could say anything, six snow-covered, wet bodies busted into the kitchen through the garage, laughing, shouting, and shaking snow all over the place.

"Hey, hey! Y'all go back to the garage with all that snow on you! The floor will get wet and you'll slip and fall. I don't want you to hurt yourselves." Hearing Mom speak made me realize she had not said a single solitary word since I had come back into the house. That made me a little more curious. She was never quiet this long.

"Boys, go into the garage and take off your wet clothes and then come back in for some hot cocoa." I walked to the sink with my empty cup. "Raven, can you help me get them out of these wet clothes?"

"My boys know how to take off their own coats and shoes! I don't baby them."

Before I could respond to her snide comment, Mom chimed in. "Get up and help those kids out of that wet stuff!"

"They can do it!" Raven fired off. "I don't baby my kids, unlike some other people I know! I teach them how to be independent!"

Knowing she directed her comment toward me, I chose to ignore it, and headed into the garage to help the boys. I started with Zack, who, at three years old, was the youngest. His face felt like ice and his cheeks were almost crimson. I pulled off his hat and scarf, unzipped his coat, took it off, and hung it up on a hook. After all that, the little rascal wanted to take off his own boots and snow pants. I left him to his happy struggle, and turned to help Raven's twin boys, Mekhail and Andrew. As their mother had so loudly uttered only moments earlier, they were very independent, having already removed all their outer clothing. They only asked me to hang their coats, hats, and scarves up for them. Jeran and Sebastian chased each other around in the small space at the rear of the garage, throwing remnants of snow at each other. The paperboy stood near the garage door, still wearing his coat, hat and scarf, laughing at Jeran and Sebastian.

"Boy, what is your name?" I approached him with my hand on my hip.

"Ian." He seemed shy and timid now that an adult spoke to him.

"Ian, why don't you take your stuff off and join the boys for some hot chocolate?"

"No thank you, ma'am. I need to finish the drive way."

"Well, unless the temperature rises, the snow will still be there in an hour or so. That will give your coat time to dry and you time to warm up."

"Will Ms. Camille mind?" He peeked nervously toward the kitchen door. "She doesn't like when I take too long to finish a job."

"Tell me about it! She was a slave driver when my siblings and I were younger and at home. Made me think she believed she had given birth to super heroes!" That got a genuine laugh out of him and he appeared to relax a bit.

"I would like some hot chocolate, please, and I would very much like to stay and play with the other kids. They're a lot of fun!" He hurriedly took off his outerwear and boots. Then he carefully folded his gloves and scarf, placing them inside of his hat, which he pushed into the sleeve of his coat. Lastly, he neatly lined his boots up against the wall. All this careful consideration of his clothes let me know he had been over here before. Mom was obsessive compulsive about neatness.

"Come on in, I will speak to Ms. Camille about you finishing your job at a later time. It is the holiday season, a time to have fun and enjoy life. Have fun now, work later." It was at this time I realized for the first time in months I was enjoying myself.

I sent the boys inside to warm up while I went to the SUV. I grabbed a small suitcase filled with Jeran and Zach's favorite comfort goodies—a canister of chocolate shavings for hot cocoa, mini marshmallows, homemade chocolate chip and peanut butter cookies, and several bags of Takis, which were Mexican corn chips we discovered after we moved to Raleigh. I lugged the heavy suitcase of goodies into the house, closing and locking the door behind me.

I made hot chocolate for the boys with a hint of cinnamon, dropping piles of mini marshmallows in each cup. Mom set the donuts and a plate of cookies on the table, of which all six boys helped themselves to generous amounts even before receiving their cocoa. Zach's ability to keep up with the bigger boys amazed me. He jumped right in, staking his claim to his fair share with no problem.

By the time the boys finished their treats, I had learned that Ian was ten years old. He was exceptionally tall for his age as are my boys, so I wasn't surprised. He lived with his father, who is a widower. His mother died of a brain aneurism when he was six years old. He appeared to be a joyful and well-rounded child, despite the absence of his mother. He and Sebastian played well together. He immediately took on the big brother role, which was not an issue for him or Sebastian.

Raven had disappeared out the kitchen sometime earlier. When the boys opted to play with the Xbox 360 Sebastian got for his birthday in the spare bedroom, I was alone in the kitchen with Mom and I pounced. "Why did you tell Raven about Madison?" For a moment, she looked utterly surprised, but almost immediately composed herself, turning her surprise into defense.

"I did not tell her anything! Why would you accuse me of doing something like that?"

"Because I know you! That tidbit of information was a lot for you to hold on to, so be honest, did you tell her?"

She looked as if she were caught cheating on her taxes. "I told her that you had something to tell her about Daniel, but I did not tell her what it was!" She crossed her arms over her chest like a defiant child. "It's not like your boys aren't going to tell her boys, so you may as well do it."

I pushed out an over exaggerated sigh. Sometimes she makes me tired. "I know the boys are going to tell them. However, I do not have to tell her, or anyone, else anything. Even though I plan to tell everyone, I would appreciate it if you would let me handle my own business!"

"So, if you are going to tell them, what is the big deal?" Mom remained defensive.

"Remember, they grew up around Daniel and will have some sort of feeling about this situation. It is not gossip and should not be discussed as such!" As soon as the final word left my mouth, I knew I had gone too far. "Mom, I am sorry for yelling at you. I should not have done that." Although I felt justified about what I said, I had to be mindful of to whom I was talking.

"I wasn't gossipin'!" Mom snapped at me. "I was trying to warn Raven against saying anything negative, or something else that would piss you off when you told her!"

For some reason, I felt even worse about raising my voice. "I'm sorry. This whole situation has me on edge—" Before I could finish my sentence, Raven reappeared in the kitchen.

"Uhmmm, Jeran and Zach in the back telling my boys that they got a sister named Maddie. They said she with they daddy at Mother Johnson's house." She leaned against the wall with her hands on her hip, looking at me with distaste.

I felt like slapping that look right off her face. "Yes, they have a three-month-old sister named Madison. Daniel had an affair and the woman he was messing around with got pregnant and kept the baby." Mom snatched the opportunity to get out of the hot seat. She practically ran out of the kitchen, mumbling something about checking on the boys.

"Hmm, I thought he was different." Without saying anything else, she walked out of the kitchen.

"Me, too," I said to myself.

I sat quietly for a few minutes, thinking that had gone better than expected. Raven can be quite dramatic. Then she returned to the kitchen unnoticed by me. I swear this girl must have worked for Houdini in a past life.

"I know Daniel cheated on you and all, and your feelings must be hurt. But you need to think about what you did to cause this to happen. "

I snapped my head up, so I could look her in the eyes. I could not believe she had spoken such foolishness to me.

"What?" was all I could manage to get out.

She pushed out a long, aggravated breath and gave me our infamous family eye roll. "I am not saying it is your fault—"

"That is what it sounds like!" I raised my voice and balled my fist, as if ready for combat.

"Whatever, Shannon!" She smacked her lips. "All I'm saying is that Daniel used to run behind you like a sick puppy. It has always been clear how much he loved you, so what happened? It's not all him, but he shouldna cheated."

"Ya think!" I knew I was being acrimonious, but I couldn't help it, or at least did not want to.

Raven glared at me, her eyes cold and hard. "You don't have to be sarcastic! Daniel is not like some of the guys I've dated. He don't just go out and cheat just to be doing something, or because he don't care anything about you, or his kids. There's a reason; it's not a good enough reason, but there's a reason." With that, she walked out again.

I sat alone in the kitchen, again, mad enough to break bricks with my bare hands. How could she possibly believe Daniel had a reason to cheat and that I somehow had something to do with it? All I ever did was love his sorry butt. I gave up my dreams to help see his come to fruition.

Although I love my children with all of who I am, being a stay-at-home mother was not a part of my plan. I wanted to be a world-renowned journalist, with my finger on the pulse of the world. Sure, I wanted kids, but my plan centered on family helping us raise our children, while I worked to build my career. It, of course, did not work out that way, but I never regretted my decision. Even after that tired tramp rang my doorbell and changed my life, I never regretted giving him all of me, even my dreams.

Banging my fist and pushing back from the table, I got up ready to seek out Raven and explode all over her for taking Daniel's side when my cell phone rang. It startled me. I thought

I'd left it in Lisa's bedroom. I answered it without looking at the caller ID.

"Hello"

"Hey, Shannon." I immediately regretted not taking the time to check the caller ID. "How are you and the boys?"

"We're fine, Daniel." I did not want to talk to him and did not hide it.

"You didn't call to let me know that you made it to your mom's. I texted you and left a voicemail message."

"We made it with no problem." If a person does not respond to your attempts to reach them, the next afternoon is a long time to wait to make sure they were okay, especially if they were only going on a thirty-minute drive. An awkward silence hung between us. I think he realized I did not plan to encourage conversation.

"My mom is wondering when you are going to bring the boys back."

"Not tonight. I don't plan to get on the road again until sometime tomorrow." He remained quiet so long; I thought he had disconnected.

Finally, he broke the silence. "What are the boys doing?"

"Playing Xbox with their cousins. Would you like to speak to them?"

"Yeah, I would." His voice sounded weary and deflated, as if those last words had drained the remainder of energy from his body.

I took the phone to Jeran and Zack, passing Raven in the hallway. She looked me up and down with her lips twisted. I glared at her, silently daring her to say something. She didn't. Jingling keys let me know that Mom let her borrow her car. So much for her complaining about all the stuff she does for Raven.

As I approached my nephews' room, I heard the front door slam. "Good riddance," I said to myself. As much as I loved her, we could not get along. "Boys, your dad wants to talk to you."

"Daddy, Daddy!" they chimed in unison. Zach jumped down from the bottom bunk and sprinted for the phone. Jeran, using his size to his advantage, quickly overtook him, but Zack was not to be defeated. He turned around, planted his hands firmly on Jeran's chest. "I want to talk first." Jeran smirked in amusement and conceded to his little brother's demand. He was so sensitive to Zach's desire to be a big boy that he, at times, backed off. I loved that about him. I stood in the doorway, thinking he was mature for a five-year-old.

While waiting for the boys to finish talking to their father, I took in the environment. I found it amusing to watch Mekhail and Andre interact, while playing a racing video game. They are identical twins, with personalities as different as night and day. Mekhail was mild mannered and thoughtful. Andre was outgoing and rambunctious. However, today Mekhail cheered for himself ecstatically and Andre mumbled something that resembled a growl. I assumed Andre was losing. Mekhail confirmed this when he suddenly jumped up, shaking a clinched fist at his twin. "In your face, Dre!" Not easily swayed, or willing to accept total defeat, Andre quickly challenged Mekahil to a rematch.

That got Zach's attention and he practically threw the phone at Jeran. "It's my turn, it's my turn. I want to play!" He snatched the controller from Andre and ran back to the bed to sit down. I tuned in to Jeran's conversation with his dad long enough to hear him begin to recount their morning outdoor activities. Then I shifted my focus to Sebastian and Ian. They sat on the floor in a corner playing with a Kinex set, laughing and talking freely, as if they had known each other forever.

I stepped into the large room for a closer look. A set of mahogany bunk beds, decorated with indigo down comforters, and, knowing Mom, goose feather pillows, encompassed one side of the room. A matching twin-sized bed outfitted in denim was positioned perpendicular to the bunk beds. A sizable double closet with sliding doors made up the inside wall to the left of the entrance. I peeked behind the doors and discovered built-in, custom-made oak organizers divided into three sections. Each boy had his own section, complete with three shelves and two drawers, stocked with jeans, shirts, underwear, sneakers and dress shoes. The top of the closet held three stacks of sweaters and three stacks of jogging suits. Mom may have complained about my nephews being at her house all the time, but she took good care of them.

She outfitted the rest of the room with a long mahogany six-drawer dresser, a flat screen television, and the Xbox 360 system. The walls, painted a warm, masculine green, coordinated well with the furniture. Matching shelves, sports posters, and a beautiful collage of all three boys adorned the additional wall space.

Jeran tapped me on my hip with the cell phone, disrupting my thoughts. "Daddy wants to talk to you. He said he will be out here later and he's bringing Maddie."

"When are they coming?" Sebastian looked up from the Kinex set. "Is she my cousin, too?"

"Yes, she's your cousin." Jeran did not wait for me to answer. "Daddy said they will be here in a little while."

Before anyone could ask me any questions, I walked out and ducked into Lisa's room, closing the door behind me. I knew that Jeran and Zach would give the boys the kid version of the story.

"Hello."

"Hey, I was thinking that I would borrow Jolene's car and come out there this evening."

"Okay."

"Well, is that going to be a problem?"

I couldn't believe he asked me that question. The entire situation was a problem. "No," was all I said.

"I take it you told your family." I could feel his apprehension. It almost made me smile.

"I told my mom. Jeran and Zach told Raven's kids, and she overheard them talking." The pause in the conversation hung in the air like a wet wool coat. I knew he wanted to know what everyone had to say, but I didn't share that information. I felt a small amount of satisfaction from having the upper hand in this conversation.

"Okay, well I guess I'll see you later."

"I'll be here." I pressed the end button on my cell phone and sat on the edge of Lisa's bed with closed eyes. I Don't remember falling asleep, but I awakened to someone leaning over me, their warm breath spreading over my neck, across the side of my face, and up my nostrils, forcing me to lift my eye lids momentarily, at which time I found myself face to nostril with Lisa. I tried to pull the covers over my head and go back to sleep. I wasn't ready to get up yet. However, she had me pinned and the covers would not budge. "I don't want to get up, move off the covers." I futilely yanked at them.

"Okay." She shifted, freeing the covers.

"Where are my kids? It's awfully quiet." I pulled the covers over my head.

"They are in the kitchen eating Chinese food from Liang's."

"Hmm, sounds good, I love Liang's." They have the best Chinese food in the South Suburbs. "Your mother went out in the snow on her day off?"

"Nope, Randall brought it over."

"Randall?" That caught my attention. "Who's Randall?"

"One of our neighbors. I think he and Mamma go together, but she act like they don't." Lisa had a smug grin on her face. Mom had not mentioned Randall in any capacity.

"They go where together?" I removed the covers from my head.

"Don't be a lame." She laughed. "You know what I mean. I think Randall is Mamma's boyfriend"

"What makes you think that?" I sat up in the bed. Lisa had me curious.

"He's always over here. His son is always over here, and Mamma be on the phone whispering and laughing late at night sometimes." She rolled her eyes, still laughing.

"Oh really? Our mother knows how to whisper and talk on the phone late at night? You're talking about a woman who can usually be found with her head thrown back with drool dripping from her bottom lip, and growling like a bear by seven-thirty on any given night." I could not believe what I was hearing. Mom had not shown interest in any man in over a decade.

"Yep, she's the one and the same."

"Wait, wait, you said his son is always over here. Are you talking about Ian?" I put two and two together.

"Yes, that little creepy crawler is so annoying! He's over here even when Sebastian, Andre, and Mekhail ain't, which is hardly ever."

My mind would not move past Mom having a boyfriend, but I tried to focus. "What's wrong with him? He seems like a sweet boy."

"He's always asking me questions! The boy don't know how to shut up and leave me alone."

"Does he have any brothers or sisters?"

"Nope, the little twerp is the only one, thank goodness!"

"If he's an only child, he may be lonely." I felt sorry for Ian.

"For the most part so am I. I love being alone and doing my own thing. I don't have to share, or be bothered with anyone else, if I don't want to. What part of that screams come and talk to me ten-year-old boy."

"True." I had to agree. Lisa was not sympathetic to the plight of children. She had never had to share, and was extremely selfish. At least she knew it.

"When did all of this happen?" I tried to pry more information out of her. She lay across one of her pillows, getting comfortable.

"Well, they met when he moved in across the street last year." Lisa pursed her lips, and squinted as she always did when thinking. "Yeah, he and Ian have been living over there about a year. At first, they would just talk in passing, and then Mamma found out that he was a carpenter and owned his own business. She told him that she wanted the kitchen redone and he offered to do it for her for just the cost of the material. After that, he came around more often, doing more stuff. He built the shelves on the walls in the bedrooms and the closet organizers. He said he got the wood from scraps left over from various jobs. All Mamma had to do was buy the stain and polyurethane.

"Cool!" Camille had snagged herself a handyman and, judging by what I saw in the boy's room, he took pride in his craftsmanship. "Well, well…Mamma is finally getting back in the game."

"It's about time." Lisa laughed. "I'm going to be leaving for college in a few months and she needs something else to do with her time. She won't have me to drive crazy."

I resorted to the overly dramatic eye roll. We are the eye roll experts in our family. "Yes, I am sure she only lives to annoy you…

whatever will she do when you are gone?" My voice dripped with sarcasm. Clueless to it, Lisa continued to speak quiet seriously about the subject.

"I guess she will still have Sebastian, Andre and Mekhail to keep her busy and her mind off me not being here." Laughing at her self-absorbed attitude, I threw a pillow at her. It smacked her right in the back of the head. Not to be out done, she flipped over, cocked her arm back and delivered a quarterback-style throw that landed the pillow square in my face.

Before I could retaliate, there was a soft knock at the bedroom door. "Come in," we said in unison, between hysterical bursts of laughter. Jeran and Zach tiptoed into the room. Zach carried a bowl of chicken and broccoli. He couldn't contain his smile and giggles as he handed me the bowl. "Here Mamma, I brought you dinner!"

"And, Mamma, I brought you the last Coke Zero. Mr. Randall, Grandma's, uhm…Grandma's, uhm. I don't know what he is to Grandma, but he brought Chinese and some soda, and everyone is eating and drinking up everything." He had such a concerned look on his face.

"Yeah, Mamma, they are eating up everything, so we wanted to bring you something," Zach said in a voice that closely resembled the sound of a cat in distress, but his high pitch only added to his charm. Jeran, my quiet child, had a deep husky voice. However, as different as they sounded, their voices commanded attention.

Jeran's serious demeanor tickled me, but his considerateness warmed my heart. I graciously accepted my aromatic and flavorful dish, beaming from ear to ear. "Thank you, boys, you brought me all of my favorites. I just love Chinese Chicken and Broccoli with a Coke Zero."

"We know," Jeran said seriously, but with a half-cocked smile.

"Hey, where's my food?" Lisa asked.

"We didn't bring you any, but it may still be some left in the kitchen," Jeran said.

Zach stayed out of the conversation, choosing instead to help me eat. I followed suit, munching quite happily on a tender, yet crisp piece of broccoli. It really was my favorite Chinese food made in white sauce, as opposed to brown.

"Why didn't you bring me anything to eat? I am hungry, too!" Lisa tried to make Jeran feel bad.

"We just didn't." Jeran looked at Lisa, his voice void of emotion. Her guilt trip attempt failed horribly.

"Let's all go into the kitchen and eat." I put my bowl aside and got up. "That way we can all eat at one time. If we run out, I will go and get more. This is good. They don't have Chinese food like this where I live."

The boys ran toward the kitchen, laughing and racing. I loved to watch the two of them together having a good time.

"Mommy, when is Daddy coming?" Zach pulled at my shirt. "He said he was coming over to Grandma Camille's today."

Suddenly, I felt dread culminating in the pit of my stomach. For the most part, I had been at peace these last twenty hours, with just my babies and me—no drama, no extra babies, no cheating husband—only peace and a moment of happiness.

"Yeah, Mom, when is Daddy coming? I miss Maddie," Jeran said.

"Me, too, I want to see Maddie!" Zach screamed, jumping up and down.

"Who's—" Lisa started.

"Don't ask. You will find out soon enough." She started to object, but saw the look on my face and decided against it.

Mom sat at the kitchen table accompanied by a tall man, with a milk chocolate complexion and clean-shaven head. He looked to be about six feet two inches and two hundred pounds. She wore a grin wider than the Grand Canyon. I had to blink twice, because I thought I saw her batting her eyes and blushing. I suppressed a chuckle. Mom was smitten with this man.

She composed herself once she noticed us standing in the kitchen doorway. Andre and Mekhail snickered and made googly eyes at each other behind her back. Sebastian and Ian looked more than moderately embarrassed. Clearing her throat and smoothing invisible wrinkles from her silk blouse, she introduced Mr. Randall Walker, construction business owner, as the neighbor across the street and Ian's father. She did not mention anything about him being her boyfriend, or middle-aged crush.

As I began to introduce myself to Mr. Walker, the doorbell rang. *Daniel*, I thought. Now, I would get to introduce Mr. Daniel Johnson, devoted father of three, and a lying, cheating, heart-breaking philanderer. Boy, oh boy, what a joy, lucky me.

Chapter Seven

Shannon

"Daddy! Maddie! Daddy! Maddie!" Jeran and Zach bolted to the door, chanting the entire way. Their excitement paralleled my dread and anxiety. For an entire day, I had been able to put the nightmarish shamble of my marriage in the back of my mind. Now, my midnight ghoul stood on the other side of Mom's front door, ringing the bell with his bouncing bundle of joy in tow. Oh lucky, lucky me.

"Jeran, Zachery! Do not open that door. It may not be your father." I reached the door just in time to prevent Jeran from unlocking it and swinging it open. Sometimes his height worked to my disadvantage. "I will open the door. Step back, anxious little sea urchins." I tried not to grin, but could not help myself. Their happiness and excitement to see Daniel manifested out of love and pure innocence.

I opened the door to Daniel holding Maddie in his arm. He was shivering from the hawk like wind beating him from all sides. For a moment, sadness crept over me. However, if it were not for Maddie, helpless in the cold and the boys standing in the doorway jumping up and down, I may have slammed the door in his face. The urge to do so brought me great joy.

I unlocked the storm door and pushed it open, stepping back in order to allow him room to enter.

"Hi." Daniel wore an expression of apprehension.

"Hi."

"Hey, Daddy." The boys hugged Daniel.

"What's up, fellas? What have you guys been up to?" He asked that question already knowing the answer. However, his joy at hearing them enthusiastically retell the day's events seemed genuine.

Zach spoke first. "Daddy, we've been playing video games all day!"

"Not all day!" Jeran clarified his brother's statement. "We went outside this morning and had a snowball fight."

"We already told Daddy that," Zach replied.

All the commotion brought an audience from the kitchen into the living room. Mom, my nephews, Lisa, Mr. Walker and Ian all clamored around us.

Lisa spoke first. "Hey, favorite brother-in-law, glad you made it. I've missed you." She leaned in and kissed him on the cheek. "So, is this who the boys have been talking about?" She pointed at the baby carrier.

"Lisa, be quiet," Mom spoke sternly.

"Well—" Lisa started to respond, but Daniel cut her off.

"I guess you all know by now—"

"I don't know." Lisa interrupted again. "What should I know?"

"If you would just be quiet, you would find out." Mom's voice had grown high-pitched and laden. The room grew quiet, except for giggles from Jeran and Zach, waiting for an answer.

"Well, everyone…this is my daughter, Madison. As you may already know, Shannon is not her mother. You can pretty much figure out the rest." For the first time ever, I thought I detected a hint of shame.

"Wow!" Shock registered on Lisa's face.

"Let's see her." Mom pulled the blanket from Madison's face. "I finally got me a granddaughter." Daniel and I looked at her a little cockeyed, which didn't go unnoticed.

"She is Jeran and Zach's sister and your daughter, so that makes her my granddaughter. We are all family regardless of what may occur in our lives." I was not surprised at how easily my mom could accept Madison as a member of our family. Even still, I bit my bottom lip and turned my head, masking my annoyance.

For the next few minutes, everyone, except me, ogled over Madison. Mom finally found her manners and introduced Mr. Walker to Daniel. "Daniel, this is Mr. Walker, my neighbor."

Lisa continued to fuss over Madison as Sebastian approached. "Uncle Daniel, why do you look so sad?"

"I'm just tired, S man."

"Oh okay, I was going to tell you that you don't have to be sad because your daughter has a different mom from Jeran and Zach." He said it anyway. "I have a different dad than my brothers. It's no big deal. Everyone still loves us, even our dads. My dad brings my brothers stuff and takes them places with us and their dad does the same thing. Aunt Shannon loves her, don't you Aunt Shannon?"

That damn boy! He really put me on the spot. Truthfully, I did not know how I felt about Madison. I did not feel anger. I felt like her mother and father violated the innocence of her existence. "Yes, I love Madison. She is such a sweet and beautiful baby."

Daniel stared hard, as did I, for a long time. I imagined he wondered if I had lied, I did as well.

"Can I hold her?" Lisa didn't wait for an answer. She plucked Madison right out of Daniel's arms.

"Let me get a good look at her. Bring her over here, Lisa." Mom reached out and motioned Lisa to her side. Before long, the spectacle moved to the sofa. Poor Mr. Walker; they wedged him out his spot. That did not stop him from hanging close to Mom. He leaned over her shoulder, gazing at Madison and grinning.

Daniel sat in an overstuffed accent chair across the room. I glanced up just in time to catch him looking at me. I held his gaze, but neither of us spoke a word. He looked tired, but otherwise seemingly unbothered by the situation. I suppressed the urge to walk over and slap him across the temple so hard he would get a blinding migraine. I desired for him to feel the pain that had seized my heart for a year, even if it was just a small inkling of it.

Mr. Walker broke the silence. "Daniel, would you like to go into the kitchen and grab a bite to eat?"

"Sure. What's cookin'?" Daniel seemed startled.

"I bought Chinese. We have a bunch of different entrees, Chicken and Broccoli, which I hear is Shannon's favorite, Beef and Broccoli, Lo Mein Noodles with Shrimp, and Egg Foo Young. We also have House Fried Rice, which is my personal favorite. It has real lobster, jumbo shrimp, beef and pork in it. I had them add onions and mushrooms. There's a bunch of other stuff in there, too; more than enough to share."

"How can I resist such an offer? I'm not turning down anything, but my collar."

Don't I know it, I thought.

"Lisa and Ma, are you okay with Maddie while I eat?" Neither ever looked up from cooing at her. Mom half waved, half shooed him away.

"Shannon, are you hungry?"

"Yes, as a matter of fact I am." I suppressed my previous thoughts. They would do me no good. "Jeran and Zach brought a bowl of Chicken and Broccoli, with Coke Zero in Lisa's room a while ago, but I have not finished it yet. It is in the kitchen on the counter." I rose from the chair and walked toward the kitchen. Daniel and Mr. Walker stepped aside, so I could enter first. The aroma from the delicious food triggered my hunger as soon as I stepped over the threshold into the kitchen; my stomach growled in response. I plucked a small piece of broccoli from the bowl and popped it into my mouth. I could taste the meld of all the delicious Asian inspired flavors. Grabbing my Coke Zero, forcing myself to act happy, I almost skipped to the table. There was no point in fantasizing about things that would only worsen my present situation.

"Shannon, don't you want to heat your food up?" Mr. Walker asked.

"She likes her food and drinks room temperature." Daniel took the liberty to reply for me.

"That's right. I like my food at room temp. I feel like I can really taste the flavors that way."

"That's pretty interesting." Mr. Walker scooped mounds of House Fried Rice and Beef with Broccoli onto his plate.

The three of us sat at the table, enjoying what had to be the best Chinese food I had eaten since the last time we were in Chicago. I made sure to sit away from Daniel.

"Shannon did your mom tell you where she hid the Christmas presents?" We mailed all the presents to Mom for safekeeping a few weeks ago. It was much cheaper than trying to bring them on the plane. Good thing we were able to get a flight in, or we would have been out shopping for the same stuff all over again.

"I haven't even asked her about it."

"Oh, I took them to my house," Mr. Walker said. "Your mother didn't want your nephews to find them. They like to snoop around."

"That was a good idea," Daniel said. Those boys are master seekers. On cue, all six of them filed into the kitchen.

"We're hungry."

"You guys aren't hungry! You ate already," Mom yelled from the living room.

"We didn't have dessert yet." Jeran sounded indignant. He loved dessert. The rest of the crew sounded off in agreement with him.

While the rest lobbied for dessert, Zach stood beside me with his mouth open and eyes wide. I fed him a forkful of my food. "Thank you, Mommy." He remained by my side, happily smacking his lips and chomping on Chicken and Broccoli until we finished every morsel.

"Who wants ice cream?" I pushed my chair back from the table, preparing to get up. Six echoes of "yes" filled the room. "All right then, who can help me get the bowls, spoons and chocolate syrup?" Three of the six scattered to different parts of the kitchen, gathering the requested items and returned them to the counter. I got up from my seat to help, but Daniel insisted on doing it. I did not argue. Instead, I took a long sip of my pop. I managed to finish it before Mekhail evicted me from my seat.

Raven and I entered the living room at the same time, nearly colliding—she through the front door and me from the kitchen. Several large shopping bags hung from each hand. She nearly lost her balance, but quickly regained it, banging my legs with her packages in the process. We stared at one another, but never greeted or apologized. I continued my path to Mom's old-fashioned log burning fireplace to light a fire. I loved everything about a wood burning fire—the smell, the crackle of the embers and the bright orange glow of the dark logs as they burned and disintegrated.

"Where's my niece? Auntie bought her an early Christmas present." Raven, being her usual dramatic, loud and outspoken self, pulled a pink teddy bear with a white tutu out of one of the shopping bags. She dropped the bear on the sofa and leaned over Madison. "Can I hold her?" Not waiting for a response, she picked her up. Lisa relented, got up from the sofa and walked away. Raven noticed, but did not comment. They had a love-hate relationship. Sometimes they got along wonderfully, other times they acted as if they couldn't stand each other. Today they seemed indifferent.

"I think I will have some dessert." Mom rose from the sofa. "Did you finish what you had to do?"

"Yep, I got everything and took it back to my apartment." Raven handed Mom her keys.

"I thought you were going to let the boys open their presents over here on Christmas?"

"We'll come over at about ten o'clock. I want my boys to have Christmas at home, too."

"That sounds like a good idea. My boys and I will meet you guys here at nine-thirty and I can start breakfast." Mom rolled her eyes at us, but refrained from commenting. Instead, she crossed her arms and walked out of the room, rolling her eyes the entire way, at least she didn't stomp.

"Do you have a problem with how we're actin over this baby?"

"No." I looked at Madison in Raven's arms. She had been quite an agreeable baby, considering all the attention everyone showered upon her.

"Are you sure? I know this must be hard on you." Raven actually sounded concerned.

"It has not been easy, but it is what it is." The truth was that the situation had taken over my life. I had missed some major deadlines for some important contracts almost losing them. I had lost twenty-five pounds without trying. Many days I would not have gotten out of bed had it not been for Jeran and Zach. Saying this situation has not been easy does not even begin to describe the hell I have experience over the past year.

"She's so pretty. She looks just like your boys."

"Yeah, she does and they dote over her every time she comes over."

The pain that had become familiar to my heart began to creep up as reality set in once again. My husband had a child he created with another woman. Ironically, my family welcomed her with open arms. I was certain his family would do the same. Tomorrow was Christmas Eve; the rest of Daniel's family would meet Madison. Then on Christmas Day, my brothers would meet her, thus completing the exposing of our well-kept secret. I felt pressured to do something, but I didn't know what.

Chapter Eight

Daniel

Mr. Walker seemed like a nice man. He and Camille met when he moved in the house across the street. He told me he'd remodeled her kitchen and completed a few other projects in the house. The pride he took in his work showed by the immaculate job he had done on the kitchen. He paid close attention to intricate details and it represented Camille's personality well. I had yet to see the other projects, but based on the kitchen, I believed they would also prove exceptional.

Mr. Walker never came right out and admitted to being Camille's boyfriend, but it was obvious to anyone who saw them together. His had always seemed to touch some part of her body. I observed him touching her shoulder one time, knee another and holding her hand often. Camille's continuous smile reached her eyes and her voice possessed a loftiness I had never heard before. My mother-in-law exuded beauty in looks and spirit, but her hardcore attitude overshadowed her softer side most often. Her no nonsense, to the point, hold-the-humor persona dominated how she represented herself on a daily basis. Today, she displayed a side of herself that reminded me of the Shannon I met, fell in love in love with and to whom I subsequently pledged my life.

Raven came in the kitchen with Maddie in her arms. I offered to take her, but she declined. Everyone's acceptance of

Maddie surprised me. Sebastian, Raven's son, even normalized the situation by relating it to the relationships he and his brothers had with their fathers. I knew he was trying to be helpful, but his statement permeated like a sucker punch to the gut. It took me by surprise, because I prided myself on not being "that guy" who had children by multiple women, that guy that did not live in the same home with his kids. Now, not only was I "that guy" who had kids by multiple women, I was on the verge of not living with either of them. Shannon had not asked me to leave yet, but if she did, I couldn't refuse. Even though she worked from home part time, it would not surprise me if she found a full-time job, took the kids and left.

Taking advantage of everyone being in the kitchen, enjoying each other's company, I joined Shannon in the living room. She had wrapped herself in a blanket and sat on the sofa, staring into the fireplace. If she knew I was in the room, she didn't acknowledge it.

"Do you mind if I join you?"

"No." She never looked my way, as I sat beside her.

"Your family seems to be all right with Maddie being here."

"Did you think that they would reject her?"

"No, but I thought they might reject me." I began to regret striking up a conversation with her. She did not seem to want to be bothered.

"No, they would never reject you." She let out a long sigh. "They love you like your blood runs through their veins. You are family and as far as they are concerned, family forgives family."

"What about you?"

"What about me?" She finally turned and looked me in the eyes.

"You're their blood. Why not take your side?"

"They are on my side." She was not hiding her irritation. For a few moments, dead air space hung between us. Shannon sat rigid, her shoulders tensed and eyebrows furrowed, as if deep in thought. After a while, she turned and faced me. "By not getting involved in our marital problems and treating Madison the same as they do Jeran and Zach is showing support for me and you. It's not about taking sides. It is about not making the situation more complicated."

"I hadn't thought of it that way. I figured your mother would at least give me some attitude about it."

"She has always been good at staying out of my business. She may gossip to Raven, but she would not get in the middle of it. As a matter of fact, she and Raven still think the world of you." I thought I detected a bit of resentment in her voice.

"Oh, really?"

"Yes. Raven went so far as to say it, and that you are nothing like the guys she has dated."

"Well, Sebastian thinks the world of his and his brother's fathers."

"Men can be good fathers and lousy significant others."

"What do you think?" My voice was just above a whisper.

"About?"

"About me." She stared at me so long I didn't think she was going to answer my question.

Finally, she spoke. "My feelings for you are complicated."

"What do you mean 'complicated'?" I know I was pressing the issue, but I had to know.

"At first I felt nothing, but anger. I thought it would be easy to hate you." I am not sure why hearing her say that took me by surprise. She didn't even notice my expression had changed and continued talking. "But, no matter how mad I get, I can't hate you. I hate what you have done, but I don't hate you. I hate the state of our relationship; and I hate the fact that I can't just take my sons and walk away from you." Her voice quivered with the last sentence, but she kept talking. "Every day, I tell myself that life would be easier if I just took our kids and left; if I just walked away from you, and the problems that I feel you created. Then I think about how much our sons love you, how much they need you in their lives and I know leaving will cause more problems. So, now I have to decide which problems I want to deal with." Tears were welling up in her eyes. She turned away as the first one fell.

"Shannon, I am not going to give up on our family." I placed my hand on her shoulder. "We can work this out, we have to."

She faced me, tears streaming down her face, but if she noticed them, she did not acknowledge it. "Daniel, you gave up on our marriage the very first time you had sex with your mistress. So, how can you say that you won't give up on our family?" The hopelessness in her voice permeated the air.

"Shannon, I made a mistake, but I didn't give up on us. We have to work it out somehow. You must still love me. You said you don't hate me."

"There is a long distance between hate and love, Daniel." Finally, she wiped away her tears. I stopped pressing the issue. Her last statement felt like a punch to the face. Through all of this, I never even considered that maybe Shannon no longer loved me.

Zach ran into the living room and jumped in Shannon's lap. Wiggling under the blanket, he snuggled up close to her. She kissed him on the forehead and wrapped him in her arms. Seeing Shannon embrace Zach in her arms brought in to full focus the realization that she would sacrifice anything for our kids. She gave them life, her life. I believed she would spend the rest of it making them happy, even if that meant putting up with Maddie and me.

"Mommy, why aren't the presents under the tree?" Zach asked, pointing at the seven-and-a-half-foot, spectacularly decorated Christmas tree. It dominated its position in front of the big picture window. Camille decorated it with a combination of specialty store bought ornaments, as well as hand painted ones decorated by all of her grandchildren. I wondered if Maddie would ever have an ornament hang on my mother-in-law's tree. Anyone ever loved by my wife and her family has an ornament on that tree—a tradition Shannon started the year Sebastian turned three years old.

"Well, Zachy, I imagine Santa does not want anxious little sea urchins like yourself picking at all of the pretty paper that his little elves worked so hard to wrap all of the presents in." She kissed him on the back of his head.

"Oh, Momma, I wouldn't pick at the wrapping paper!" He giggled.

"Oh yes you will. Your tiny fingers are just right for picking wrapping paper off the corners of presents!" Shannon held Zach's hands close to her face, as if inspecting them carefully.

"I can see the prickly, sticky things growing out of the tips of your fingers. They look perfect for picking wrapping paper off presents."

"No they're not, Mommy!" He flashed Shannon a sheepish smile.

"Oh yes they are!" She kissed his hands.

"Mommy, when will Santa put the presents under the tree?" I admired his persistence.

"Oh…I don't know, maybe tonight or tomorrow night. You'll just have to go to sleep and see when you wake up in the morning."

"I'm going to stay up and wait to see if Santa brings the presents tonight." Determination filled his voice.

"Okay, if you insist," Shannon said, exaggerating her words. "If you are going to stay awake, you need to get comfortable." She pulled him close to her and rested his head upon her chest. Only seconds had passed before he was sound asleep.

"He always falls asleep quickly when he is in your arms," I whispered.

"He is his mamma's baby that is for sure." She caressed the top of his head. "Do you think Santa can help bring the presents over here before he leaves tonight?" Surprisingly, she spoke as if everything was okay between us. I could not detect any of the anger and hurt, I heard just moments ago.

"Yes, he can."

When Jeran was three years old, Shannon told him that Santa brought presents to the most precious boys and girls early, in order to make sure that they received all the best toys. In years past, the title of Santa carried special privileges. Those privileges no longer existed. Santa would not be getting lucky tonight. I had only been able to make love to Shannon once or twice over the past several months.

"I'll bring them over after the other boys go to sleep." I forced the idea of making love to her from my mind.

"Let me know when you go, I will come and help you." She pulled Zach tighter and rested her head against the sofa, closing her eyes.

I returned to the kitchen to find Camille and Mr. Walker alone, busying themselves with the dishes. He talked and she laughed. I felt like an intruder standing behind them.

I cleared my throat. "Where is everyone?"

"They are in the bedrooms," Camille managed to get out between smiling and laughing. "You and Shannon's discussion seemed pretty intense, so I sent them to the back of the house through the laundry room.

I had forgotten that the laundry room led to the master bath and bedroom suite. Camille would never let anyone enter the back of the house that way, because it meant passing through her private domain. That was something simply not tolerated.

"Thanks for that. I know how you hate people in your room."

"No problem. You and Shannon have a lot of sorting out to do. Sounded liked you were off to a good start."

"Did everyone hear us talking?" I tried to sound nonchalant and mask my concern.

"When you elevated your voices, I sent the kids to the back of the house. Raven and Lisa took Madison to my room. Zach snuck into the living room when I wasn't looking, the little rascal."

"It doesn't matter what is going on when he gets sleepy, he wants his mother. He doesn't care what else she may be doing." I laughed at the thought. "Speaking of Zach, he gave us the third degree about their Christmas presents. Mr. Walker, do you mind if I get them tonight after the boys go to bed?"

"Not at all, son, I will help you bring them over." His voice boomed. "Camille and I already wrapped them."

"Yeah, we did that when everything arrived. I told Randall how Shannon despises gift wrapping."

"It certainly is not her favorite thing to do. How did you know what belonged to who?"

"She emailed me a list of what would arrive and conveniently put each person's name beside the gift they should receive." Camille rolled her eyes.

"Seems like she was hoping you'd wrap the presents." I let my sarcasm show. I knew that wasn't the truth.

"Ya think?" Camille displayed just as much sarcasm. "I was certain of it when a gigantic box arrived loaded with gift boxes, bows, wrapping paper, ribbon and tape."

I couldn't help but laugh. "Shannon is thorough if nothing else."

"I'll go check on the other boys and if they are asleep we can go before it's too late."

"I am in no rush. We can go anytime you are ready." Mr. Walker put his arm around Camille. She didn't move.

I passed through the living room and noticed that Shannon had dozed off with Zach still snuggled in her arms. I started to take him back to the boy's room, but decided not to disturb them. When I got to our nephews' room, I peeked inside and found all five boys passed out. Sebastian lay on one of the top bunks knocked out cold, one arm hanging over the side rail. Andre and Mekhail shared the bottom bunk. Mekhail's right foot rested on Andre's head. Ian's bony frame was sprawled amidst quite the set of blankets and pillows in the middle of the floor. Jeran appeared to have boldly taken ownership of the twin bed on the other side of the room. He was spread eagle on his stomach, gripping the sides of the bed with tightly clutched fist.

Standing in the doorway taking it all in, I heard Shannon approach, carrying Zach. I lifted him out of her arms. "You did not have to carry him all the way back here. I could have come and got him."

"It was no problem, I can manage myself." She wouldn't look at me, and stepped into the bedroom. I followed.

"I'll put him in the bed with Jeran."

"Good luck with that." She chuckled as she said it, noticing Jeran's position on the bed. "He looks like he had to fight for that spot."

"Yeah, he does." I laughed a bit. "Can you try to move him over?"

"Jeran. Jeran." She barely whispered his name, while gently prying his fingers loose from the sides of the mattress. "Jeran, baby, can you scoot over a little so that your brother can share the bed with you?"

"Mommy?" He stirred in his sleep.

"Yes, baby?"

"Mommy, I saved Zachy a spot on the bed with me," he said sleepily.

"Thank you, baby, you are such a good big brother." She rubbed the top of his head while whispering in his ear. Jeran quickly fell back to sleep, without moving. Shannon managed to adjust his stocky body just enough for me to squeeze Zach between him and the wall.

She pulled the covers up over their shoulders and kissed them on top of their heads, then methodically covered each boy with a blanket before going back to the door and flipping off the light switch. I closed the door and went back to the living room. Shannon took up post again in the overstuffed chair.

"Did Mr. Walker say when you could get the presents?"

"He said anytime. Your mom wrapped them for us."

"I figured she might, since I sent all of the necessary items. She probably thought that I sent them just so she could wrap the gifts."

"That's exactly what she thought."

"I know she did. In actuality, I simply did not want to pack all of that stuff and try to bring it on the plane with us."

"I'm going to check on Madison before Mr. Walker and I go and get the presents."

"Okay, when you are ready, I will help you bring stuff over, too."

"Don't worry about it, we can handle it."

"Six hands are better and faster than four."

Deciding not to argue, I walked down the hall to Camille's room. I heard Raven and Lisa talking through the cracked door.

"I know Shannon must feel stupid," Raven said.

"Yeah, I bet she does, but she doesn't act like she even cares." Lisa gave her two cents. "I wonder if she is going to put him out."

"Hell naw! Shit, he makes too much money. She don't have to work. She bet not try to put him out."

"She has a job." Lisa defended Shannon.

"That freelance writing shit? How much you think she make doing that? She probably does it just to feel like she contributing. She ain't making any money."

Choosing not to listen to any more of their discussion on my life, I knocked on the door with more force than I intended to use. I must have startled Maddie, because she started whimpering. Seconds later, the door swung open and Lisa flashed me a huge grin.

"Brother," she said with overkill. "Come on in."

"I came to check on Maddie." I stepped into the room.

"She is great, basking in all of the attention she's been getting. She was sleeping until you knocked on the door like you were the police." Raven tried to sound annoyed.

"Sorry about that. I wanted to make sure you heard me over your discussion about my personal life."

"You had to know we were going to talk about it." Lisa ignored my agitation.

"I guess I did." I chose not to argue with them about it.

"But it is y'all's business, so we'll stay out of it." Raven's statement surprised me, but it was short lived. "Shannon and this baby mamma must get along real good."

"*Really* good," Lisa added, over emphasizing the word really.

"I thought you said you were going to stay out of our business?" I became exasperated.

"We are," they said in unison.

"But as a woman, if I slept with another woman's man and had a baby by him, I wouldn't let my baby go over the other woman's house. And I definitely wouldn't let my baby go all the way to Chicago with the daddy and his wife, especially not this young." Raven's voice squeaked as she said the last few words.

"That is odd. How old is Madison, two or three months?" Lisa asked.

"Well, I guess she is different from you," I said, shrugging.

"I don't mean to be rude, bruh-in-law, but thinking she was different is probably what got you into this mess." Raven stared at me.

"My daughter is not a mess." My lips tightened pencil thin with tension.

"I didn't say she was. She is beautiful and happy, but the situation is a mess, unless you are one big happy family. I know my sister better than that," Raven fired back.

"Yeah, big brother, we know that Shannon is not that nice or accepting." Lisa laid her head against my shoulder and wrapped her arms around me. "She's nice enough, but she ain't trying to be friends with your baby mamma."

Shaking my head, I changed the subject. There was no winning an argument with these women, any of them, especially when they are right. Shannon was not trying to be friends with Vaneetra. "Do you ladies mind keeping an eye on Maddie while

I go over to Mr. Walker's and get the kids' presents?" Maddie had drifted back to sleep.

"Sure we will, but I hope we have some presents, too!" Lisa smiled at me.

"You sure do! A year's subscription to *How to Mind My Own Damn Business Digest*."

"Whatever! Don't get me started on the subscriptions you should have." Raven winked at me and turned her attention to Maddie.

"Girl, speaking of Mr. Walker, I think him and Mamma..." I walked out as Lisa started gossiping about Camille and Mr. Walker.

Walking back to the living room, something Raven said resurfaced in my mind and curiosity set in. Why had Vaneetra let Maddie come to Chicago with us? She had been very hesitant to allow her to stay overnight with me at home. We had been in Chicago for over twenty-four hours with not a single call from Vaneetra.

Chapter Nine

Daniel

Shannon had fallen back to sleep, so I spared her from having to help bring the presents over. When Mr. Walker and I finished hauling what seemed like a truckload of presents, I went to retrieve Maddie. Camille had evicted Lisa and Raven from her room, and was now softly singing Nat King Cole's "The Christmas Song" to her. I stood in the doorway, as if in a trance, listening to her sweet melodic voice. Shannon would sing the same song to the boys almost every night during the holiday season. When she finished, she stared intently at Maddie, who actually smiled and cooed at her. "I am not a very religious woman, but in my many years on this earth, life experiences have revealed to me that God is a mighty God and can create something great in the midst of destruction." She addressed me, but never even raised her head.

Rubbing my forehead, I started to tell my mother-in-law that I was in no mood, but she raised her hand, signaling for me to hold my peace. She had yet to raise her head and look at me. She kept her face and eyes on my daughter.

"Now, Lisa and Raven told me about the conversation. So, I already know you don't want our quarter's worth of opinion. I usually make it a point to stay out of Shannon's business, but I am going to say my peace anyway." She sat quietly for a moment, waiting for me to respond. When I didn't she continued. "As

I was saying, God can create something great in the midst of destruction. This little girl is the something great. The destruction is the actions taken to get her here. Here, meaning creation. Also, those actions taken by you and my daughter that led up to her being conceived. As people, when this sort of thing happens we have to figure out how to nurture the greatness we are given. "

"Camille, I love my daughter and I will nurture her. I am going to provide her with everything that I give to Jeran and Zach."

"I have no doubt that you love and will pour as much gentleness into her as you do my grandsons. However, if you don't learn to nurture the environment you are raising them in, they will all suffer."

"I know I have to find a way to fix this." I threw my hands up, letting them drop to my sides. "I don't know how, but I will."

"Boy, you can't fix this!" Camille raised her head to face me. "This is broken into a million unfixable pieces. You have to salvage what you can and start anew. Pick up the most important pieces and use them to build a greater, stronger foundation."

"A million pieces is a lot to sort through." I laughed light heartedly.

"The ones worth saving will be apparent. You won't have to look hard if you know what you are looking for." She did not look amused. "Now, go wake Shannon up and the two of you come and get in this bed, because I know you ain't trying to drive back to Chicago tonight. It's snowing again."

"I have to take Jolene's truck back."

"Where's Jolene going? Nowhere at midnight." Camille tossed a dismissive hand.

"Where are you going to sleep?" Exhaustion kept me from putting up an argument.

"Now ya in grown folks business." She rose off the bed. "Go and wake up your wife before she wears a hole in my chair."

"Where are you going to sleep?" I remained persistent.

"Well, if you must know, I have a hot date tonight."

"With Mr. Walker?"

"Yes, with Mr. *Walker*." She elongated Walker.

"Does Shannon know that you and Mr. Walker are close enough to spend the night with each other?"

"Boy, you are the only person that has to answer to Shannon. Now, grab my overnight bag and take it to the door." She turned and started examining herself in the mirror.

"Do you want me to walk you across the street?"

"No, Randall is going to do that. He is a real gentleman. He wouldn't want me to slip and fall on any ice." She applied lip-gloss.

"How long has this been going on?" Now, I was being nosy.

"If you must know, tonight will be the first night that we will spend together. We just thought to do it at the spur of the moment. Lisa's home tonight, Raven and her boys, you, Shannon, your boys and Madison are all here. I thought why not?" She shrugged with this last statement.

Why not indeed, I thought grabbing her bag, which I had not noticed before, and headed to the front of the house. Camille followed me. When she reached the front door, she quietly cracked it open, whispered *good night* and slipped out.

I sat for a while, watching the last of the logs in the fireplace burn out. I closed the flute and woke up Shannon. I couldn't believe she did not resist coming to bed with me or even ask about Camille. I fed Maddie. Then before I knew it, sleep had fallen over me like a heavy wool blanket.

Before falling asleep, I remembered thinking that tomorrow would be the first Christmas Eve that I wouldn't make love to my wife. Even though I was having an affair last year, I still made love to my wife on Christmas Eve.

Chapter Ten

Vaneetra

How could this be happening? Vaneetra James sat in Dr. Chen's office, fighting back tears, ready to punch a wall or throw a chair. Thoughts of a painful death made her shiver. Dr. Gloria Chen, the top oncologist in Chapel Hill, North Carolina, had just delivered the most devastating news Vaneetra had ever received in her life. The tumor detected last month in her left breast was malignant and she had Stage II cancer.

Vaneetra thought nothing of it when her OB/GYN told her that she had a hard lump in her left breast at her late six-week checkup. Further examination of her breast and under arms did not reveal any additional lumps. She dismissed it, thinking it was nothing more than buildup of milk that may have hardened when she stopped nursing Maddie at six weeks old, because Daniel was pestering her about allowing Maddie to spend the night at his house. She refused at first, because of his wife, but finally relented. They had only known each other for a short while before the onset of their affair. She knew his marital status, but did not care. She always got what she wanted and she wanted him.

The affair did not last long. Although claiming to be unhappy at home, Daniel refused to abandon his wife and sons. Vaneetra gave him an ultimatum after finding out she was pregnant and he chose to stay with his family. More pissed than hurt, Vaneetra watched his house for a few days and paid his wife a visit one day when Daniel was not home. She wanted to hurt him as much as he had hurt her, by ruining his marriage. Little did she know that wretched heifer he called a wife would stick around.

Vaneetra had given her OB/GYN her opinion on the lump, but she insisted that she come and see Dr. Chen. Still not taking it seriously, she scheduled her appointment for three weeks out even though she could have gone in sooner. Dr. Chen immediately ordered X-rays and a biopsy. She must have put a rush on everything because, exactly two days after her initial visit to Dr. Chen, Vaneetra sat in her office, listening to this woman deliver the earth shattering news.

"So what do I do now?" Vaneetra asked through clenched teeth.

"That is what we have to discuss, Ms. James," Dr. Chen replied gently.

"You're the oncologist; you should know what to do next." Vaneetra did not hide her sarcasm.

"Let's discuss exactly what the tests have revealed and go over your options." Dr. Chen remained patient.

"The test revealed that I have breast cancer."

Ignoring Vaneetra's understandably seething tone, Dr. Chen continued. "The test revealed a lump that is about four centimeters in size in your left breast near your armpit." She placed the X-rays on a white board and flipped a switch. Light illuminated the dark film. Using a laser pointer she pulled out of her lab coat pocket, Dr. Chen pointed to a white spot near her left armpit, the size of a quarter. "There were also cancerous cells detected under your left arm, but no other tumors. I would like to do a full body scan to determine whether or not the cancer has spread to any other parts of your body." She waited silently, giving Vaneetra time to absorb the information. After a few moments, Dr. Chen continued, her voice gently pushing through the tension and fear in the air. "There are a number of treatment options that we will discuss. At the end, I will give you my recommendation."

"What do you mean recommendation? You are the oncologist. Aren't you supposed to just tell me what I should do?" The words came out like air from a deflating balloon.

"It is not that simple, Ms. James. As a patient, you have the right to choose from any treatment option available, including no treatment at all. As your doctor, I will tell you what I think is your best chance at beating this. However, I cannot force you to make any particular choice."

"Why would I do anything different?"

"I cannot answer that. If I knew why people made the choices they do, I would probably be in another profession."

Vaneetra laughed at Dr. Chen's attempt at humor. It felt odd to do so in the midst of such a serious situation.

"So what are my options?"

"The current treatments for breast cancer are mastectomy, which is the removal of one or both breasts. Having a lumpectomy, the removal of the tumor itself, is also an option. Along with this, you may also need radiation or chemotherapy treatments for a period of time. There is also a hormone treatment for cancer. It is reactive to the hormone levels in your body. The hormone treatment is not an option for you, because your tumor is not hormone reactive. However, I wanted to give you all options currently being used. Lastly, as I stated moments ago, you can choose to not have treatment at all." Dr. Chen waited silently.

Minutes lapsed as Vaneetra tried to process all that Dr. Chen told her. Finally she spoke. "What is your recommendation?"

"Given your age, health and the fact that there is only a small cell cluster under your left armpit, I suggest a lumpectomy to remove it and chemotherapy to kill the rest of the cancerous cells. There are no guarantees, but I believe your prognosis is good."

Vaneetra could only focus on there not being any guarantees. A million thoughts raced through her head, the primary being what to do with Madison. She was only three months old. Vaneetra needed to think of a way to go through both treatment and caring for her daughter. After all, she was a single mom and the father was a married man. Vaneetra refused to consider Daniel as an option, and she would not ask her family for help. She knew immediately that she would have to hire a nanny. As if reading her mind, Dr. Chen verbalized some of what Vaneetra was thinking.

"I understand that you are a new mom. Your medical records indicate that you have an infant girl who is about three months of age." Vaneetra nodded in confirmation. "While I am not certain how your body will respond to treatment, due to the potential side effects, if you are breast feeding I must recommend that you cease doing so. The drugs that you will be given can pass from you to her in your breast milk. You should also consider acquiring help for your daughter. These drugs can also have terrible side effects for you as well."

"I plan to hire a nanny to help me care for my daughter."

"Good. I will schedule the scan to occur tomorrow. I will put a rush on the results, but since Christmas is the day after tomorrow, the earliest we will get them is the twenty-sixth. My plan is for you to start treatment within a day or two of the scan results coming back."

"That is not enough time to find a nanny." An image of Daniel popped in her head, but she dismissed it. Even though she gave in and let him take Madison to Chicago for Christmas, she would not allow Madison to stay with him while she went through treatment. She also wanted to wait until Madison returned home before starting treatment. She had to fight to maintain her composure. She felt pushed around and not in control of the situation, which was new to her.

"Do you have family that can help? Maybe your daughter's father can be of assistance."

"Excuse me…my daughter's father?"

"I did not mean anything by it. I noticed you checked single on the demographic profile sheet."

"I apologize. I should not have taken offense." Vaneetra inhaled deeply, willing her nerves to calm.

"It is okay. You are just fine. I am not known to deliver good news when I first meet people. Emotions run pretty high in here."

Vaneetra bellowed a much too loud laugh at Dr. Chen's second attempt at humor.

"Well, I guess I better get to work on getting my personal affairs in order. I do have someone else that I am responsible for." Vaneetra stood to leave.

"Ms. James, a positive attitude will go a long way on this journey. I know it will not be easy, but do your best to remain that way." Dr. Chen extended her hand.

"Yes, Doctor, definitely easier said than done." She shook Dr. Chen's hand and exited her office.

Walking through the parking lot to her car, Vaneetra thought of a million things, the number one being Madison, who needed her mother. Tears fell from her face like the rush of a waterfall. Blindly, she stumbled upon her car, barely able to find the handle and opened the door. She slumped into the driver's seat, gripping the steering wheel until she could feel her own nails digging into her palms, the skin across her knuckles stretched taught. This type of thing happened to other people, not to people like her. Successful, driven women with children did not get sick and die. No, that could not happen. It would not happen. She would fight. Only, where to start?

Chapter Eleven

Shannon

I don't really know when I crawled into Mom's bed with Daniel and Madison. All I remembered was telling Daniel I would help him bring over the boys Christmas presents, but before that could happen I curled up in my favorite chair. Mesmerized by the jumping blue and orange flames in the fireplace, I had drifted off to sleep.

In the midst of my thoughts about what the day would bring, Madison reached out and grabbed a lock of my hair at the nape of my neck. The feathery touch of her tiny fingers startled me at first, but then an indescribable wave of emotion washed over me. My face became tingly; an ache massaged my heart. Memories of Jeran and Zachery as infants flooded my frontal lobe. They used to pull gently on my hair in that exact spot when they were ready to be fed. I gingerly pried open her tiny fingers and moved my head. Pushing myself up in bed, I scooped Madison into my arms. Her eyelashes rested together in such a way that her face had an angelic peace to it. Her pursed lips moved in a sucking motion just as her brothers' used to do when they were hungry. I placed her back onto the bed and prepared a bottle. Daniel made a habit of bring water and bottles with formula powder to bed with him when he kept Madison overnight. He seemed to be comatose beside us. I picked her up again and nestled her in my arms to feed her. She latched on to the nipple, sucking out formula with an urgency that seemed almost lifesaving.

As I held Madison in my arms, a second myriad of emotions engulfed my senses. Hurt, anger, and vulnerability attempted to take up space in my mental capacity at the same time as the feelings of wanting to protect my sons and Madison from this disastrous situation. Realization of this situation not being all about me pushed for a position in my already full mind. Sitting and holding a child that was not mine, but who was a permanent fixture in my life, because of the actions of my husband, poured hurt into my soul. I asked myself repeatedly, *What in the hell have I done to him to deserve this?* The answer kept coming up the same. I had not done a damn thing. I did absolutely nothing to deserve this! I am not innocent in our marital problems, but I did not deserve for him to cheat on me and bring home his baggage. The fact that I did not see it coming and that this Vaneetra woman knew about me made me feel extremely vulnerable. Especially since I had no clue of her existence prior to her making it her business to stomp into the middle of my life. I felt that as long as I stayed married to Daniel he could do whatever he wanted to me.

I was numb to my falling tears, only noticing when one landed on Madison's face. It trickled down as if it flowed from her eye, streaming across her cheek, down her neck and back onto me. I watched another and another flow along the same path until a small puddle nestled between the space where her head, neck and shoulders rested against the exposed skin of my breast.

I reached over to the nightstand and grabbed a couple of tissues. I knew Daniel had awakened, because I could sense his eyes staring at me. I also noticed a change in his breathing. It had gone from heavy and raspy to light, almost nonexistent. I wiped my and Madison's faces, silently wishing for Daniel not to say anything. He granted my wish and never uttered a word.

Chapter Twelve

Daniel

I woke Christmas Eve morning to Shannon moving around in the bed. She was feeding Maddie and crying. She cradled my daughter in her arms, as if cradling her own flesh and blood. The moment seemed almost perfect, with the exception of the flow of tears cascading from her face. I wanted to say something, but I couldn't conjure up what I thought were the right words to say. So, I kept quiet and just watched. Although she never acknowledged it, I knew Shannon realized that I was no longer asleep. She shifted her body slightly to hide her face from my view. I wanted to reach out and pull her close to me, to hold her until all of the pain that I caused went away, but I didn't do it, I couldn't. I didn't believe she would let me. She no longer trusted me enough to be vulnerable.

Still, I had not heard anything from Vaneetra. On one hand, I felt relieved not having to engage in a bitter conversation with her. She always tried to dictate the type of relationship I could have with our daughter. On the other hand, something seemed very wrong. On any ordinary visit, if she texted me once, she did it fifty times. I resolved that I would call her in private, once I got back to my parents' house.

A loud, inhumane sound broke the silence in the room. Apparently, my daughter found that moment to be the time to release all the gas in her body, through her rear end. After the gas came grunting, twitching, a sigh, and then silence. Shannon pursed her lips, scrunched her nose and spoke for the first time since I woke up. "I am go to go and check on the boys. You can clean up the shit." She handed Maddie to me, got out of bed and walked out the room, closing the door behind her. So much for perfect, I couldn't even get progress. One minute she nurtured and cared for Maddie, the next, she was spitting daggers at me.

Not long after I cleaned up Maddie, Shannon returned to the room with Zach, who bolted from the door and jumped on the bed, making his sister bounce a couple of inches off the bed. "Can I hold Maddie? I'll be careful!" I smiled at his enthusiasm over wanting to hold his sister. Our families had taken to her well and had fallen in love. However, I could not say the same for Shannon. One moment it appeared she was accepting our present circumstance and my child. The next, any hint of acceptance was gone. I tested the waters to see what type of mood she was in today.

"When Jeran wakes up, I would like to get ready and head over to my parents' house. Is that okay?"

"Yes, that is fine."

"Do you want to come with us?"

"Yes, your mother probably wants me to bake and I want to get it done, so that I can have time to bake cookies with the boys."

"Cookies! Yay!" Zach startled his sister who had been gazing up into his face, smiling. I looked up and found Shannon looking at the two of them. Her face looked softened, her gaze tender. Maybe our situation would work out…maybe.

Back at my parents', Zach and Jeran exploded into the house and ran straight to Aunt Jolene. She then proceeded to spend the next forty-five minutes chasing them around the house and crawling under the dining room table.

Dad sat in his recliner and held Maddie. Shannon and Mom were busy in the kitchen, preparing breakfast and Christmas Eve desserts. Shannon, of course, took charge of all the baking, while Mom prepared, bacon, eggs, rice and toast for everyone. Taking advantage of the moment, I darted upstairs to call Vaneetra. She answered on the third ring.

"Hello, this is Vaneetra James."

"Hi, Vaneetra, it's Daniel."

"Hello, Daniel." She seemed distracted.

"We made it to Chicago yesterday with no problem."

"I looked for you to call yesterday, but I guess late is better than never."

"I wondered myself why you hadn't called me to check on Maddie." Her sarcastic tone irritated me.

"I did not know that I needed to track you down."

"Oh, that's surprising any other time you do. I guess I just assumed you would—"

"Word of advice, Daniel, don't make assumptions. The last time I did it, I ended up a single mother." The phone line went silent. I thought she had hung up on me, but then I heard her breathing. For a moment, I thought I heard her crying.

"Look, I didn't call to argue. I just wanted you to know that Maddie is okay."

"How is your family taking to her?" I imagined her speaking through tight lips, her tone clipped.

"They have welcomed her whole heartedly." A long pause hung on the line.

"And what about your in-laws?"

"What about them?"

"Well, have they seen her and how did they react? After all, she is your illegitimate child." She sounded bitter.

"My daughter is not illegitimate!" I fought to suppress the anger rising inside me. "I would not let anyone mistreat her." This time I clipped each word.

"You did not answer the question, Daniel."

"They love her and welcomed her with open arms."

"I find that hard to believe." She sniffled. I became sure she was crying, but I did not entertain the thought of asking why.

"Look, I don't have time for this, Vaneetra."

"Who cares what you have time for? You are lucky that I even let her go with you at all. If I did not want—"

I cut her off. "If you are going to play games, I will file a motion for joint custody when I get back."

"We are not married, Daniel, remember?"

"Yeah, but I have already established paternity when I started paying child support through the court system, remember?"

"Well, you do what you have to do, because when you get back—"

"Look, as I just said, I did not call you for all of this."

"When are you bringing my daughter back?" Vaneetra's tone became frigid.

"We are scheduled to fly back home on December 28 in the afternoon. I will bring her home early evening."

"Have her back by five. Do not be late," she snapped.

Her attitude exasperated me. "If you were going to act like this, why'd you let her come with me in the first place?"

"I was trying to be nice and civil," she snapped at me, again, and hung up.

I sat on the edge of the bed with the phone to my ear, thinking that Vaneetra James has not been nice or civil since we called it quits. That definitely was not the reason.

Chapter Thirteen

Vaneetra

Vaneetra clutched the edge of the brown leather ottoman so tightly she might have torn through it had it been of poor quality. She had just finished having an argument with Daniel, one she started for no real reason. Truth told, she was so preoccupied with her visit to Dr. Chen she had not even thought about him not calling her. She knew Daniel would not let anything happen to Madison. He had been very active in her life since her birth, too active for Vaneetra's liking. Many days she regretted ever going to his house and confronting that bitch he called his wife. Who knew she would demand a paternity test and then accept her husband being involved in his illegitimate child's life? Vaneetra assumed Daniel's wife probably had something to do with his level of investment in Madison. Most women would have been out the door the minute DNA proved their husband's infidelity, but not this chick. She hung on to her man.

Had Shannon left Daniel, they would probably be together and she would not have to face the greatest ordeal of her life alone. Vaneetra pushed those thoughts out her head. After all, she no longer wanted Daniel. She considered him as a weak man. He chose to stay in a relationship with a woman he did not love. How could he love her? If he did, Madison would not be here.

Well, more power to them both. She had more important and pressing issues to worry about, such as her life, her daughter and the next few months. Vaneetra had not shared her news with anyone. Hell, no one knew that she had allowed Daniel to take Madison to Chicago. She never planned to let her go anywhere with him, but not knowing how her visit to Dr. Chen would turn out helped her to make that decision. She figured she would need time to think if the lump turned out to be something. Being a new mom with no husband left little time to think.

Vaneetra had good taste, if nothing else. She sat alone in the living room of her townhome amidst expensive furniture and artwork. Everything, from hardwood flooring to African art adorning the walls, was of the finest quality. The room looked almost masculine. The dark brown, Italian, leather upholstery, while soft to the touch and quite comfortable to sit on, was oversized and stretched tautly over the frame of the furniture, giving it a firm appearance. Cocktail and end tables were handcrafted mahogany. The only feminine items in the room were the plush area rugs, the largest costing five thousand dollars. It laid in the center of the living room, partially covered by the cocktail table, the remainder of it resting in front of the gas log fireplace.

Rising from the ottoman, Vaneetra sauntered into the kitchen in search of a bottle of wine and a glass. She'd planned to drink half the bottle and sleep the rest of the day, but the house phone rang. Deciding to ignore it, thinking it was either Daniel calling back, or her mother calling to pester her about coming to Christmas Eve dinner, a newfound tradition that she planned to skip. She just could not deal with her family and their questions. When her mother found out she allowed Madison to go to Chicago with Daniel, she would sense that something was up and would hone in on it like an eagle on its prey.

Snatching a bottle of chilled white Moscato from the refrigerated wine rack, a corkscrew, and a glass, she went back to the living room, flipped on the switch to the fireplace and sat on the sofa, wrapping herself in a cranberry throw. She opened the wine, filled the glass to the brim and slowly took her first sip. She replayed the events of the past few days in her head. Since her visit to Dr. Chen's office, Vaneetra had called several nanny service agencies and scheduled visits with three of them. She knew the cost would be astronomical for what she needed, but when given an estimate, she began toying with the idea of demanding Daniel pay half the expense. She quickly disregarded that thought. To make such a demand meant having to share the reason she needed a nanny. She also thought that he might get the crazy idea of having Madison come to stay with him. Both options were out of the question.

Vaneetra had almost finished her first glass of wine when the phone rang, again. She ignored it, but whoever it was would not give up. After the fifth time of not answering, she picked up the phone, annoyed. "Yes."

"Neetra!" She hated when her mother called her Neetra. "Dinner starts at six, but I need you to come early."

"Mother, I am not going to make it tonight." Vaneetra did not offer an explanation.

"Why aren't you coming?" Mrs. James sounded surprised.

"I have a lot on my mind and I do not feel like socializing." Vaneetra did not see the point in trying to make up a lie. The truth worked just as well.

"Well, we would like you to join us, but will you at least drop Madison off? I haven't seen my grandbaby in a week."

Again, knowing that lying would not help, Vaneetra opted for the truth. "Mother, I let Daniel take Madison for the holiday. She is not here."

"You did what?" Mrs. James's voice raised a couple of octaves.

"I let Daniel take Madison for the holiday."

"Vaneetra James, why in the world would you let your baby spend her first Christmas away from you?"

"As you just said, she is *my* baby and that is the decision I made."

Not the least bit deterred, Mrs. James fired back. "Look here, girl! I don't know whom you think you're taking that tone with, but you'd better get it straight. Now, I know when something is going on with you and I was willing to leave it alone, but this is too much. I want you and my granddaughter here at five o'clock sharp. Call this Daniel person, that's got you all messed up in the head, and arrange to pick up my granddaughter. You can take her back after dinner tonight, but I want her here. Oh, and by the way, be ready to talk about whatever it is you got going on." Mrs. James spoke with finality.

"Mother, it is not that simple…"

"Why isn't it? Just go and get her! I don't have time to argue with you, Vaneetra. Summer is here to help me finish cooking for tonight. And bring a couple bottles of wine with you. I know you have enough to spare. Good bye." With those last words, her mother hung up on her.

Knowing there was no point in calling her back and standing her ground, Vaneetra finished off her glass of wine. She knew from whom she inherited her personality. Her mother could be very demanding and cutthroat when she wanted to be. Besides, Vaneetra did not see the point in being the cause of the old woman having a coronary, which would likely happen when she found out that Madison was in Chicago, Illinois.

Chapter Fourteen

Shannon

When we arrived at my in-laws, we found Daniel's mom standing at the stove cooking breakfast. I jumped right in to help, placing orange juice and butter on the table, and popped bread in the toaster. Just as I buttered the last slice of toast, my two hungry jacks ran into the kitchen, smoothly taking their seats like professional eaters. Mrs. Johnson piled large spoonfuls of rice onto their plates, much more than what I would have given them, with at least three full slices of bacon each. When the plates where placed before them, they busied themselves eating delightfully. I studied their eating habits for a few moments, noticing that Jeran hums while he eats. Zach eats very slowly and deliberately. They truly enjoyed every bite.

Against my desires, I walked upstairs to tell Daniel that breakfast was ready, but stopped dead in my tracks when I heard him having a heated telephone conversation. Guessing he was talking to Vaneetra, I quickly turned around and went back down, exasperated. My mind would not comprehend the idea of my husband arguing with some other woman.

Pops stopped me as I passed through the den on my way back to the kitchen. "Daniel has a real problem on his hands."

"Yeah, a real humdinger." Leaving it at that, I walked away.

After breakfast, I busied myself making desserts for the evening festivities. Mrs. Johnson had gone to another part of the house to do who knows what. She liked me to bake and learned a long time ago that I do my best work alone. If she stayed in the kitchen, she would try to help and that usually did not work out very well. We had different ways of doing things. She had everything I needed for apple pie, sweet potato casserole and orange cranberry cake. I pulled out what I needed to make cookies for Santa with the boys later.

Sometime, in the midst of my making the dough for my apple pie, Daniel appeared in the kitchen alone. He made himself a plate and ate not so quietly, absentmindedly slamming things around, appearing very agitated. I ignored him, not caring to know the topic of his argument with Vaneetra. After some time and much to my chagrin, he finally decided to speak.

"I talked to Vaneetra to let her know that we had gotten here safely."

"Okay."

"I thought I heard you on the stairs."

"You did."

"You could have come up. I only went upstairs for the quietness."

"The conversation sounded rather heated and, to be honest, I just did not want that drama in my space today." This situation permeated every aspect of my life. I refused to allow it to dominate my mind on Christmas Eve.

"Oh. You do know that I am not trying to hide anything from you and that my relationship with her is strictly about Madison, don't you?"

"No, I do not know that. I know that is what you tell me." *It's not exactly like you have not lied to me before. Why should I set myself up to be lied to?* I thought.

Jolene appeared just in the nick of time and asked Daniel to take her to the store. She was not one to stay in one place too long and suffered from cabin fever. She just had to get out and peruse the aisles of Marshall's. The boys, of course, wanted to go with her. I attempted to bribe them not to go with making cookies, but it didn't work. Daniel asked his mother to keep an eye on Madison, and she readily said yes.

While they were gone, I worked peacefully in my baking zone, forcing myself not to think about Vaneetra James, Daniel or the fact that he snatched his love from me without warning and gave it to her. Time flowed while I worked my dough and created something close to heaven with flour, eggs, sugar and lots of butter. Several hours passed in complete silence. Daniel, Jolene and the boys returned just as I pulled the apple pie out of the oven, arms overflowing with bags from more than just Marshall's.

Not far off their heels were Parker and his family. Mrs. Johnson and Jolene took over the kitchen. I used the time to steal a few moments to myself and say a little prayer, asking God to keep me in the place of peace I found when spending the afternoon baking. I asked Him to help get me through the rest of this vacation and back home.

I must have fallen into a semi coma, because the ringing of my cell phone startled me. "Hello"

"You okay?" My youngest brother, Craig, spoke in a deep gruff voice.

"You heard?"

"You know those cackling sisters of yours blew my phone up this morning."

"Yeah, I just know they did. I am surprised they waited until this morning. I am all right. It is what it is."

"Oh, you mean they knew yesterday?"

"Yes, they sure did."

"That is surprising, but whatever. Maybe they were trying to give you a chance to tell me."

"Possibly, but unlikely; they were probably too busy discussing it amongst each other last night."

"Yeah, that is most likely the reason. You know I am going to talk to him, don't you?"

"Yes, I know. I just want you to remember that he is still my husband, the father to your nephews and, most importantly," I sighed heavily, "I can handle myself."

"Yeah, I know all of that, but I am going to let him know what he did was foul. I'm hurt, because he taught me how to be a man and I looked up to him. I still love him, but this shit ain't right and we need to have a man-to-man."

"Okay, but don't fall out with him."

"I won't. I'll hit you up later. I'm about to jump in the shower and then hit these streets for a minute."

"Don't be—"

"I know. Don't be drinking and driving. I won't. I'll only do it before and after I drive."

"You are not funny." I laughed anyway. I knew he would not do any of it, but I said a prayer anyway. God knows that outside of my sons, Craig was the only person who always brought a smile to my face.

Christmas Eve dinner went very smoothly. Daniel's family fussed over Madison the entire evening. Some of Mr. and Mrs. Johnson's extended family stopped by, one or two at a time, each expressing surprise over the new addition to the family, but not making a big deal out of it. I am sure they will spread the word to everyone else before the New Year.

Seven o'clock rolled around and Zach suddenly remembered that they needed to bake cookies for Santa. Jolene, Parker's wife, and their kids joined us in the kitchen for the baking festivities. We had a blast watching the kids cut out odd shapes that were supposed to resemble miniature Christmas trees, stockings and candy canes. At the end of the evening, we had five dozen cookies, half of which Parker and his family took home. Jeran and Zack made a dessert plate for Santa, with a glass of milk and thank you notes. By the time the last person left, my body was heavy with exhaustion. Excited to go to bed so that tomorrow could hurry up and get here, Jeran and Zach led me upstairs. I tucked the boys in, put on my nightgown and slipped under the covers of the bed Daniel and I would share. I don't remember anything after that.

Chapter Fifteen

Vaneetra

At three-thirty, Vaneetra slipped into a pair of black jeans, a red sweater and applied a minimal amount of makeup. She dreaded the evening and conversation to come, but knew she could not avoid having it. She would not be able to hide the chemotherapy treatments from her family. Grabbing a bottle each of red and white wine, she put on her half-length black wool coat and walked out the door. The drive to her parents' house took fifteen minutes, but it seemed much shorter. Ringing the doorbell, Vaneetra geared up for battle, but her sister, Summer, opened the door, embracing her tightly and grimacing.

"What is wrong with you?" Vaneetra knew she did not have to ask, but did it anyway.

"Your mother is nuts! She invited a bunch of people over here at the last minute and is driving me crazy trying to get prepared. Then to top it all off, she asked me if I really wanted Courtney to come tonight."

"Did she really?" Vaneetra knew her sister's lesbian lifestyle was a major cause of conflict between her and their mother. Summer came out shortly after graduating from college several years ago. It did not surprise Vaneetra when it happened. Although Summer was very feminine, she never took a serious interest in the opposite sex and was still a virgin when she graduated high school. That little fact made their mother proud. She just knew Summer had chosen to save herself for that special man. The very thought of the truth made Vaneetra laugh aloud.

"What is so damn funny? This old lady is killing me in here." Summer did not hide her annoyance.

"I just thought about how it almost killed her when you professed your love for Courtney and she found out that Courtney was not a boy."

"Well, it's been four years. One would think that she would be over it by now. Dad is cool with it."

"Now you know Daddy and mother are like day and night; Daddy being night, dark and silent. Well, I have some news of my own that should bump you out of the spotlight for a long while."

"If having Madison out of wedlock…hey, where is she? Don't tell me you didn't go and pick her up. Now you know Evelyn is going to blow her top. She's been bitching ever since she hung up on you."

"She may as well get over it, because Madison is in Chicago with Daniel and they will not return for another four days."

"What? Why in the hell did you let that happen?"

"I have my reasons, which I will explain later."

"Not sure what makes you think you'll be able to wait that long. You know how she gets."

"Yes, I do, but she is just going to have to deal with it. Now let's crack open one of these bottles." Vaneetra held up the bottles of wine and walked off toward the kitchen.

Summer trailed behind her sister, anxious to hear her news. She knew a little more about the situation between Daniel and Vaneetra than her parents, like the fact that he was married. So if Vaneetra let her three-month-old go to Chicago with her father, the news she had to share must be major. Suddenly, she felt like Courtney's presence would prove not to be such a big deal.

Vaneetra braced herself for confrontation, as she entered the kitchen. Her mother started in on her right away. "Where is my grandbaby?"

"She is with her father, like I told you over the phone."

"I know what you told me, but I asked you to bring her with you tonight."

"You did not ask me anything. You demanded that I bring her."

"Lord forbid, you do what I tell you to do. Would it make a difference if I asked you now to go and pick her up?" Mrs. James's voice elevated with each word.

"No it would not, because they are in Chicago."

"They're where?" Mrs. James stopped what she was doing and faced Vaneetra.

"Madison is with her father visiting his family for Christmas." Vaneetra held eye contact with her mother.

"Why in the hell would you let that happen? She's only three months old!"

"Look mother, I am not going to discuss this right now." Vaneetra walked away from her mother.

"Vaneetra James don't—"

"Evelyn, leave the girl alone." Marshall James had appeared in the doorway unnoticed. A massive man, standing six-foot-five and weighing two hundred fifty pounds, he filled the space easily. "Now, she said she did not want to talk about it, leave it alone. Vaneetra come and help me set the dining room table. Let your mother and sister finish up in here."

Mrs. James did not argue with her husband, but his command did not stop her from demonstrating her frustration by slamming cabinet doors and bowls on the counter until Vaneetra and her father were out of earshot.

In the Dining room, Mr. James addressed his daughter. "Baby girl, you've been keepin' too many secrets. When do you plan to explain the thangs that are going on in your life?" Mr. James gently embraced Vaneetra by the arms.

"Daddy, I am not keeping secrets. I have had a lot going on this past year, but truthfully I did not think that I had to explain myself."

"You don't, baby girl, but you should. You date and have a baby by a man we have never met. Then you break up with him. Now he has your daughter all the way up in Chicago and she is only a few months old. Don't you think you should at least try to help us understand what is going on? Do you even want the baby?"

"Daddy, yes, I want my baby! Why would you ask me that?"

"Because she is not here with you and she is so young. I am not going to push the issue, but I am a little curious."

"Daddy, I have a perfectly good explanation, but I would like to wait until after the dinner party is over to share it."

Mr. James stared into his daughter's eyes just long enough for her to believe that he could see her soul before finally agreeing. "We'll end this party early, so that you can tell us what is going on with you. Now, let's get this table set."

The gathering at the James's home couldn't be over fast enough for Vaneetra. Yet, at the same time, she dreaded the conversation to come after all the guests left. Mrs. James rolled her eyes and glared at her daughter and husband throughout the entire evening, refusing to speak to either of them, which suited Vaneetra just fine. However, Mrs. James's icy attitude did not seem to affect Mr. James's mood at all. He laughed and joked with their guests without acknowledging his wife's attempts to demonstrate her displeasure with him and Vaneetra.

It became evident after dinner that Mrs. James planned to use her newfound tradition as a way to show off Madison. During dessert, she stood up to toast the arrival of her one and only grandchild into the world. She shared with her guests that included friends and family that her brand new grandbaby was spending her very first Christmas in Chicago, with her daddy, whom no one knows anything about, and his family. She went on to say, that the Lord only knows what type of people they are. Mr. James interrupted her by saying that there will be many other occasions for everyone to meet Madison, ending the conversation about it. He then announced that the evening would end promptly at nine-thirty, so that he and his wife could attend the 8:00 a.m. service at church the next morning.

When the last guest left, Summer and Courtney began cleaning the dining room. Vaneetra, who had been standing in the kitchen, turned to go and help. Before she could place a foot across the threshold of the kitchen, Mrs. James started in on her.

"Vaneetra, I think I have waited long enough to know why you sent my grandbaby away for her very first Christmas."

"After that stunt you pulled at dinner, you are lucky I am still here to tell you anything. Where do you get off embarrassing me in front of all of those people?"

"The way you walk around here, acting like no one else matters, I didn't think you could be embarrassed. That type of feeling is reserved for people who care what others think."

"Let's just go into the living room." Mr. James, who had been standing in the shadows of the hallway, interjected before Vaneetra had a chance to carry the argument with her mother any further. Without waiting for a response, he walked away.

Vaneetra followed, leaving her mother no choice but to do the same if she wanted to get the answer to her question. Having heard bits of the conversation from the dining room, Summer and Courtney followed behind everyone else.

"Courtney, if you don't mind, can you clean the kitchen? We're about to have a family discussion." Mrs. James spoke in a dismissive tone.

"Courtney, you can stay. Mother, it is rude to ask someone to clean your kitchen, while at the same time suggesting they are not family." Vaneetra glared at her mother. While she did not understand her sister's way of life, she loved her and thought of Courtney as family. Mrs. James pursed her lips, but opted not to comment. Anyone who would listen already knew how she felt about the situation.

After moments of awkward silence, Vaneetra, not really knowing where to start, plunged right in. "I let Madison's father take her with him to Chicago, because I had a lot on my mind." Feeling flutters in her stomach, she paused for a moment, thinking she may have another episode like the one in the parking garage of Dr. Chen's office. Mrs. James started to speak, but Mr. James signaled for her not to. Silence hung thick in the air. The only sound came from wind rattling the windows.

"When I went for my six-week checkup, my OB/GYN found a lump in my left breast near my armpit. She referred me to an oncologist in Chapel Hill. I decided to send Madison with her father just in case I needed time to think."

"Oh my, Lord!" Mrs. James clutched her husband's hand, as he remained silent.

"Have you gone to see the oncologist?" Summer sat next to her sister.

"Yes, I initially went a few days ago, she sent me for tests. I went back yesterday for the results."

More silence. The expression on Mrs. James's face changed from aggravation to worry. Finally, Vaneetra took a deep breath and spoke. "The lump is malignant. I have Stage II breast cancer."

"So what happens next? What can we do to help?" Mr. James leaned forward and rested his arms on his knees.

"My oncologist sent me for a full body scan yesterday to make sure the cancer has not spread anywhere else. I go back in a couple of days for the results. If it has not spread, I will have a lumpectomy. That means the tumor will be removed. The oncologist said that I will likely have chemotherapy, before and after the lumpectomy."

"What will happen to Madison?" Mrs. James asked.

"I am going to hire a nanny. I already have interviews set up."

"Why would you hire a nanny?" Mrs. James did not hide her disgust.

Vaneetra ignored her mother's tone. "I don't know how sick I will become."

"You don't need a nanny. We can help. You obviously feel comfortable with her father taking care of her. He should be made to help, too." Mrs. James offered her opinion.

"I don't want to inconvenience anyone and I don't want her father involved."

"You let us worry about what we can and cannot do. Her father needs to be involved. He had something to do with making her," Mrs. James insisted.

"Mother, stop trying to take over everything! I am going to hire a nanny and that is the end of it." Vaneetra spoke with finality.

"Wait a minute, young lady." Mr. James finally spoke up. "Your mother is just trying to be helpful. There is no cause to take that tone with her."

"Vaneetra, Courtney and I will be happy to help. We can come over during the evenings. If you get sick, I can take care of you, and Courtney can tend to Madison." Summer attempted to ease the tension in the room.

"We sure can, Vaneetra. It would not be a problem at all and I would love to care for Madison." Courtney supported Summer's comments.

"Look," Vaneetra sighed heavily, "I know everyone is willing to help, but I do not want any help. I can do this on my own. I will get the treatment and be back on my feet in no time."

"You may not want any help, but you are going to need it. We can and will help and so should Madison's father." Mrs. James continued to press the issue.

"Mother, he does not even know what is going on and I do not plan to tell him."

"Why not, Vaneetra? As a man and a father, I think he has the right to know and the responsibility to be involved." Mr. James tried to reason with his daughter.

"Your father is right. Besides, how do you plan to keep it from him? I do not even want to think of the worst, but what if… Madison will have to go and live with him?"

"Mother, I am not even going to entertain the worst that could happen. I will be fine. If not, she cannot go and live with him anyway. I will get my affairs in order and appoint you and Daddy as her legal guardians."

"Now hold on! I love my grandbaby and want to be a part of her life, but I am done raising kids. I am sixty-four years old and there is no since in either of us believing that your father and I can raise a baby. We can help!"

"Baby girl, what is wrong with the man? You don't want him to help you now and you don't want him to raise his daughter, if he has to. You are sending mixed signals, girl. You trust him enough to take her across the country, but not to be of some real help? That just does not make any sense to me." Mr. James raised his hands in exasperation.

"Daddy, it is complicated. Things did not turn out the way I had planned. I realize that I made a mistake in becoming involved with him."

"What does any of that have to do with him helping you with your child? Like I said, what is wrong with him?" Mr. James's voice elevated just a little bit.

Summer and Courtney knew the answer to that question. They stared at Vaneetra, wondering if she would tell her parents that Madison's father was married.

"Daddy, there is no—"

Mrs. James cut Vaneetra off mid-sentence. "Is this man married, Vaneetra Renee James?"

"Mother, why would you—"

"Don't lie to me, Vaneetra. Now, I am going to ask you again, is he married?"

"Why would you think that he is married?" Now Vaneetra demanded to know.

"Because, you ain't never been one to relieve people of their responsibilities. You are cut throat about that type of thing." Vaneetra knew her mother was right. It was her "stick it to them, hold everybody accountable" attitude that torpedoed her up the professional ladder at work.

"Yes, he is married." Vaneetra responded with a little too much dignity.

"Oh my, Lord! Why did you go off and get involved with a married man? Never mind, I really don't want to know." Mrs. James got up and walked out of the room. Mr. James stood up to follow. Before he left, he addressed Vaneetra.

"Baby girl, we are here for you and will help. Whether you want it or not, you are going to need it, but you need to think long and hard about how much you want Madison's father involved, because you are going to need him, too. I know you think you have it all figured out. Let me tell you, you don't. Life happens and figures a way to mess up the most thought out plans. Now, I am going to go and calm your mother down. There's been too much excitement for her tonight. You know how she gets herself all worked up. You girls set the alarm and lock up when you let yourselves out." With that, he turned and walked out of the room.

"She seemed to have taken the news a lot better than I thought she would." Summer rose from her spot on the sofa.

"Yeah!" Courtney stayed put.

"Good night." Vaneetra got up and walked out the house.

Chapter Sixteen

Daniel

The Christmas Eve gathering at my parents' house went better than expected. No one appeared too upset or disappointed that I had a daughter by another woman. By mid-evening, I had long forgotten about my argument with Vaneetra. However, I noticed that Shannon kept her distance for most of the evening, except when she, Jolene and Parker's wife baked cookies with the kids. She didn't interact with Madison at all and, when everyone left, went up to bed with Jeran and Zach without even saying good night.

I helped Jolene straighten up after Parker and his family left. Then I sat on the stairs for a long time before going up, thinking of what to do next. I knew the first thing on my list was to file a motion for joint custody of Madison. I wasn't playing games with Vaneetra when it came to the time I spent with my daughter. Secondly, I had to make things better between Shannon and me. I listed that as second, because I felt like it would be almost impossible to do. I can't even say if she still loves me.

Christmas Day Jeran and Zach woke up excited. They clamored down the stairs, waking up everyone else in the house—shouting and squealing from the living room when they discovered presents spilling from under the Christmas tree. I brought them up from the basement before going to bed last night.

"I am going to do present control." Shannon got out the bed and plodded downstairs. She looked tired.

Madison remained surprisingly quiet while I cleaned her up. When her brothers thundered down the stairs, they startled her, but she did not cry. When I finished, we went downstairs to join the rest of the family. Shannon and Jolene sat on the floor in the living room, flanking the tree with presents looming above their heads and spilling out into the living room from the space between the two of them. Each took charge of passing them to either Jeran or Zach. Mom hurriedly shoved torn wrapping paper into a trash bag in an effort to keep up with the rate in which Jeran and Zach ripped it off the boxes containing new toys and gadgets, tossing it over their heads in the process.

Maddie had quite a few gifts under the tree. Shannon managed to slip one under there from her without my knowing. Jolene must have bought most of them when I took her shopping. Jeran and Zach stopped playing long enough to say thank you to everyone and helped me open Maddie's gifts. Mom gave up trying to manage the wrapping paper. Shannon handed Jolene and Mom envelopes containing cards and money. She learned a long time ago not to try to figure out the perfect gift for them, cash worked best.

"Shannon, what time do you want to head out to your mother's place?" I asked her, hoping she did not have an attitude.

"Anytime between eight-thirty and nine o'clock will be fine. Given that it is only five-thirty in the morning…that should give sons number one and two plenty of time to play and for me to get another hour of sleep."

"Mommy, you can't go back to sleep. You have to watch me and Jeran play with our new toys." Zach's voice always sounded like a cat in distress.

"Well in that case, I better make a pot of coffee, because I am going to need it." Shannon tried to hold back a yawn as she spoke.

"Shannon, I'll make the coffee. I could use a cup myself." Mom got to her feet. "Do you mind if your father in-law and I go with you all to your mother's house?"

"Not at all. You are always welcome at my mother's house," Shannon said, stammering over her words.

The shock I felt, reflected on her face. Mom never visited anyone during the holidays. She liked everyone to come to her house, which is why Parker and his family always came over. However, she was usually a trooper when things didn't turn out, as she would have liked.

"I'm going, too!" Jolene said. "I'll drive."

"I'd better wake your father up so that he can get dressed and eat something before we leave."

"You do not have to cook, Mother Johnson, unless you want to. We will have a huge breakfast with tons of food at my mom's." Shannon spoke cautiously.

"Not really, not today. I think I want to relax and enjoy the day outside of my own kitchen."

I made the coffee along with a bottle for Maddie. Jolene fed her, while Shannon managed to doze off on the sofa with Jeran and Zach playing with toys all around her.

The festivities were already underway when we arrived at Camille's house. Donnie Hathaway's "This Christmas" played in the background. Mr. Walker and Camille partly cooked, mostly patted and flirted in the kitchen, their affection for one another obvious. A much larger mountain of presents engulfed Camille's tree. Camille and Mr. Walker must have added more presents after we left yesterday. Knowing that Jeran and Zach had their fair share under the tree, I wondered how much it would cost to ship all of it home.

My parents and Camille embraced each other like old friends with tight hugs and kisses. Camille introduced Mr. Walker as her gentleman caller, which was old people talk for boyfriend. Jeran and Zach crawled over and around presents, looking for their names. Zach knew enough of his alphabet to be able to identify his name. Ian, who had been sitting quietly, joined them, successfully helping Zach snag four rather large gifts, before procuring four equally sized ones of his own. My little guy independently labored, hauling them across the room to a corner where he started his own pile. Ian, on the other hand, moved with ease to a location just a short distance from Zach. Jeran claimed the entire front side of the tree as his space.

For a while, all went well. Jolene found her way to Lisa's room for a girl chat. They have that mother-daughter, sister-friend type of relationship going on. Shannon went to the kitchen to pick up where her mother and Mr. Walker left off. Although she loved to cook, I got the feeling she used being in the kitchen to hide away from everyone. As long as she cooked, everyone left her alone. I offered to help, but she quickly turned me down, stating she had everything under control. My insides cringed at hearing her say that. Somehow, I felt like it referred to more than just cooking.

The doorbell rang just as Lisa and Jolene emerged from the back of the house, giggling like two schoolgirls. The problem with that was only one of them was school age. Being as though I was the only one unoccupied, I answered the door. I was nearly trampled by Sebastian, Andre and Mekhail, jetting over to the mountain of presents, stopping just long enough to pass out hugs and kisses to Camille and Mom. Raven and Adam, Sebastian's father, stood just inside of the door. Raven asked if Adam could stay for breakfast. I think everyone found that too strange since they had broken up several years ago. Camille gave the okay, and acted as if it were not an odd request.

Not long after breakfast started, Shannon's brothers, Craig and Terrance, came over. Both were single and usually never brought dates to family functions, unless involved in serious relationships. This time neither had dates.

Terrence, always the life of the party, started in on me as soon as he walked through the door. "Brother-in-law! Let me see this new baby you got." He walked over to Camille, who had Maddie sitting on her lap, and picked her up.

"Oh, boy! Here we go!" Jolene released an over exaggerated sigh. I knew she loved it when Terrance started in on someone.

"Well, well, well, she is a cutie; looks like my main men, Jeran and Zach. Boy, you got some strong genes. How do you have three kids, by two different women and they all look just alike? Speaking of having kids by two different women, you must sleep with one eye open!" That got a burst of laughter from everyone.

"Naw, man, I don't have to do that." My muscles tensed and neck got warm.

"Man…you better start. I remember when we were kids. I broke one of Shannon's favorite records, Bon Jovi's "Slippery When Wet." She had already told me to leave her stuff alone. She didn't say anything right then and there. Quite a while had passed and I had forgotten about it." Terrance hunched and threw up his hands. "Then one night at about two o'clock in the morning, I woke up to her chocking the shit out of me! She had me in a head lock, talkin' about she wanted to listen to her record, but couldn't, because I broke it. Now, that was over a record. Imagine what she might do to you for having a baby by another woman. Man, I told you when y'all got married she was crazy. You obviously didn't believe me." The entire room roared with laughter at the story, including Shannon, who pleaded the fifth.

After the family enjoyed a good laugh at my expense, the rest of the day went without incident. The boys spent hours playing with their new toys and eating. Our families held and spoiled Madison. No one said anything more about my affair. At one point, I caught Adam staring at me from across the room while Raven whispered in his ear, but he never approached me to ask about Maddie.

Shannon appeared to enjoy herself. She even gave me a gift, but when caught under the mistletoe together, she would not kiss me. At the end of the day, Camille announced that she had one more gift to give everyone. She went to her room and came out with a Macy's shopping bag. She then proceeded to give everyone small, square boxes, even Adam. That let me know that he and Raven must be back together. She gave me two boxes. Each box contained a beautifully designed Christmas tree ornament. One of my boxes held a small, brown baby sleeping with her head on her hands, covered only by a pink blanket and a card. The card read: *Welcome to the family, Madison. Love, Grandma Camille.* A smile spread across my face. I looked up from the ornament to find Shannon staring at me, tears welling.

Chapter Seventeen

Shannon

The rest of our time in Chicago turned out to be pleasant and uneventful, and I could not have been happier. We had actually done something we had never done before—our families, with the exception of Parker and his family, spent Christmas Day together at Mom's house, and everyone exchanged gifts. As much as I did not want to, I bought Daniel a gift card to Belk. He bought me a tennis bracelet. It was still in the box. My forgiveness cannot be purchased.

Our last two days there, I stayed at Mom's house. It felt good to be able to relax and not have to spend all my free time thinking about the mess I now called my life. Jeran and Zach spent the remainder of their time between my in-laws' and Raven's place. My brothers bought Raven a car for Christmas, and she gladly transported my boys back and forth. She brought them to Mom's one evening, so they could play with Ian one more time, but for the most part, I hardly saw them.

I had not seen Daniel and Madison until the day we left town. In fact, he went out with my brothers the night after Christmas. After such time, Craig called and told me the three of them had a man-to-man talk. He did not give an opinion as to how he thought I should handle my situation. He only told me that I had to decide if what Daniel did was bad enough for me to take an otherwise good Black man away from his young Black sons, which was something to ponder. Daniel sent me a text message saying he felt like he would have to work hard to earn Craig's respect again, but he thought Terrance either forgave him or chose not to formulate an opinion. I did not respond.

Raven took Jeran and Zach to Daniel the night before our return flight home. I missed my boys, but their enjoyment of our family was evident every time I spoke to them on the phone, so I did not feel bad about having some alone time. I got up early that morning and left when Mom went to work. We hugged and I promised to call when I got home. She promised to tell me all about Mr. Walker one day soon. I picked up Daniel, our sons and his daughter, said my good-byes to my in-laws and went to the airport. Back to life as usual. I cried. Jeran and Zach asked when the rest of their toys would arrive. They each only brought one full suitcase with them on the plane. They would not even let us check them. The rest we sent two-day express mail.

Our plane was delayed, so we did not land in Raleigh until late evening. On the way home, we stopped and grabbed dinner to go from the Carolina Ale House. Vaneetra started calling Daniel the minute we stepped off the plane. I mean, literally, the very minute his feet went over the threshold. I wondered if she had a GPS tracking device implanted in him somewhere. Daniel dropped the boys and me off at home before taking Madison to her mother. Good move on his part. I knew where she lived, but had no desire to go there. We ate, showered and were in bed by ten o'clock. Even though I loved visiting family, it felt good to be home. The fact that Daniel had not returned home from dropping Madison off by the time I went to bed did not even bother me. I was too tired to care.

At ten in the next morning, the doorbell woke me up. I grabbed my robe and stumbled down the stairs to find Daniel hauling in three very large boxes filled with games and toys. I noticed he had not changed clothes from yesterday, but kept quiet about it. A wave a relief came over me at seeing the boxes. That meant that I would not have to spend the day reassuring my sons that nothing happened to their toys and that they would arrive as promised. Surprisingly, I did not see them downstairs at the door. I figured they were still sleeping. Daniel confirmed this, as I tried to help him pull the boxes into the living room. Not really being successful with this, I opted to start breakfast. Jeran made his way to the kitchen table as I pulled the last waffle off the iron, and Zach headed to the living room.

"Hey, big boy. Don't you want to go and check out your toys?" I placed a small carafe of warm maple syrup and a dish of soft butter on the kitchen table.

"No, Mommy. I'm hungry. I will play with my toys after breakfast. Are we having pancakes?"

"Nope, we are having waffles, with Mommy's homemade turkey sausage and some freshly squeezed orange juice."

"All right! I'm going to tell Zach and Daddy to hurry up, because I'm hungry." He scooted off his chair, ran out of the kitchen and down the hall to the living room. I placed a tray piled high with warm waffles and turkey sausage in the center of the table. Jeran returned with his brother and father on his heels just as I sat down a pitcher of orange juice. Daniel offered to get plates, glasses and eating utensils with Jeran's help. Zach said the grace.

"Daddy, did you sleep in your clothes?" Zach asked with a mouth full of sausage.

"Yes, Zach. I slept in my clothes last night."

"Why?" Jeran took over the interrogation. "Mom does not like for us to sleep in our clothes. She says that when we do that, we are getting dirt and germs from outside on our bed sheets."

"Mommy is going to be mad at you for getting dirt and germs on the bed sheets, Daddy." Zach giggled at the thought of my scolding his daddy.

"Zach, Daddy is an adult and can do what he wants. Mommy can't get mad at him." Jeran tried to sound like an expert on the subject.

"Uh-uh, Mommy stays mad at Daddy, don't you Mommy?"

I nearly spat out my orange juice. "Well, baby, Mommy is not always mad at Daddy. We just don't always agree."

"Your mother is right, fellas. Sometimes grown-ups don't agree, but that doesn't mean that we are mad at each other." Daniel looked a bit uncomfortable, his voice hesitant.

"Like when you brought Madison home. Did you and Mommy agree on that, Daddy?" Nothing got past Zach.

"No, Zach, Mommy and Daddy most definitely did not agree on bringing Madison home. That pissed her off!" Jeran's eyes widened with excitement.

"I will agree that bringing Madison home did not make Mommy happy, but I would not say that it 'pissed her off'." Daniel tried lightening the tone of the conversation. I wondered what he would say. Jeran's observation was accurate. I knew I should interject, but I just could not bring myself to do it.

"No, Daddy, I think she was pissed. She used a lot of bad words the day you brought Madison home." Zach supported his brother's opinion. I wanted to say something about them using the word pissed, but I know whom they picked it up from—me. I continued to eat and watched the conversation unfold, like an innocent bystander.

"Fellas, let's not use the word pissed." Daniel took a stand. "You can say angry or upset, but not pissed."

"Why not, Mommy does all of the time?" Jeran always demanded a reason why.

"Mommy should not use the word either, Jeran. I am going to work on not using it, because I don't want you to use it." I sided with Daniel.

"Okay." They shrugged and continued to eat. Then they dropped a bomb that brought the magnitude of this situation to the forefront.

"Daddy?" Zach took a sip of his juice, sat the glass back on the table, picked up his fork and continued to eat his second waffle. He has a huge appetite for three years old.

"Yes, son?"

"When Jeran and I are grown up, can we have a wife and a girlfriend, like you do, Daddy?" I choked on my waffle, no one noticed. Daniel choked on his orange juice.

"Are you okay, Daddy?" Jeran was always the concerned one…they both were. Daniel looked at me. I returned his stare, waiting for a response. All eating at the table ceased, waiting for him to answer Zach's question.

He released a huge sigh. "Okay, boys, I am going to try and explain it the best way I can, so that you can understand. So listen up and tell me if there is something that does not make sense to you." I wondered what he thought he could possible say that made sense to them. It still did not make sense to me, but I listened. "Boys, it is never okay for a man to have a wife and a girlfriend."

"But you do, don't you, Daddy?" Jeran seemed so innocent and sincere. He really wanted to know.

"Yes…I mean, no…I mean, I did, but not anymore." Daniel stammered over his answer. "Daddy did begin a relationship with another woman, but I did a very bad thing. Married men should not do things like that."

"What's a reblationchip and why did you do that if it was bad, Daddy? Mommy always says to never do bad things on purpose. God does not like it." Zach had no idea the wisdom he possessed.

"It's relationship, Zach, and that is when you really like someone and spend a lot of time with them, like friends and stuff." Jeran did his best to explain it to his little brother.

"Oh I get it, so we can have a wife and friend and if our friend is a girl, we can get a baby with her!" I almost felt sorry for Daniel. Poor Zach just could not wrap his mind around the situation, and he should not be able to at three years old. It surprised me that he figured out girls could have babies.

"No, son, it is not okay to have a baby with a friend and you have a wife. Men should only have children with their wives."

"But you did, Daddy. You had a girlfriend and now you have a baby with her and she is our sister. If it is bad why did you do it?" Jeran really needed to understand. I felt that familiar ache grip my chest cavity and tears stream down my face. I quickly wiped them away with a napkin. I hoped my boys never experience this type of drama in their adult lives.

"Look, boys, I am not doing such a good job at explaining this. I can only say that I did a bad thing and now that you have a sister, I have to do the best I can to fix it. I don't want you guys growing up thinking that it is okay to have wives and girlfriends and children with anyone other than your wife. I am sorry that I put our family through this."

"It is okay, Daddy. We are happy that Madison is our sister. I like being a big brother." Zach started to eat again. "How can you fix it? Are you going to give her back?"

"No, son, I am not going to give her back. When I say fix it, I mean make sure we can remain a family and never do anything like this ever again." The boys shrugged. I don't believe they truly understood, but decided not to push it.

"Mommy, will you ever be friends with Madison's mother? Can she come over and have dinner with us?" Jeran put me on the hook for answers.

"Sweetie, I don't think that I will ever be friends with Madison's mom. As for her having dinner with us, I won't say ever, but not any time soon. Your daddy and I have a lot of grown up things that we have to work out and I only want to focus on that."

"Will you guys get a divorce?" Jeran looked worried.

"It is—"

Daniel cut me off. "No, Mommy and Daddy are not getting divorced." I just stared at him. I was not sure how he could make that statement.

"Mommy, please don't divorce Daddy. He is sorry for what he did." Jeran obviously did not find comfort in his father's statement.

"Sweetie, Mommy and Daddy have a lot of things to work out, but we love the two of you and will do what we think is best for everyone. Now finish eating so you can start moving your toys up to your playroom." Seemingly satisfied with my answer, they switched subjects to talk about their new toys. I thought about how divorcing my husband would affect our sons. Craig's question resonated with me. Did I really want to separate a Black man from his young Black sons? Did I still think he had any good left in him? Up to this point, his worth wasn't given any real thought.

Chapter Eighteen

Vaneetra

This shit is frustrating. These people must be out of their damn minds!" Vaneetra voiced her thoughts aloud to no one. After interviewing several nannies from her top three agency choices, she finally narrowed it down to two women she thought might work out, but the cost to have someone ten to twelve hours daily would easily deplete her savings within weeks. She knew she would have to start using Madison's child support money to pay, but even that would not be enough. She thought about cutting it down, but remembered her last meeting with Dr. Chen, where she found out that although the cancer had not spread, the tumor did appear to have grown and there were more cancer cells in her lymph nodes under her left arm. Dr. Chen informed her that she would have to start treatment tomorrow. She did not have a plan for who would look after Madison and did not like the idea of asking her family to come and stay with her for a few days until she could find someone. She refused to ask Daniel to allow Madison to stay with him for a few more days.

He finally brought her home last night after five o'clock. Even though Vaneetra knew the flight arrived late, it did not stop her from chewing him out. He did not even bother to respond. He just handed Madison to her and walked out. She followed him outside in the rain, down the driveway, cursing him out, threatening never to let him see their child again. He never even looked back; he simply drove away. This infuriated her to the point that it took her a moment to realize that the blanket had fallen off the carrier and Madison's face was exposed to steadily increasing rain. She retrieved the blanket and went into the house, slamming the door behind her. She leaned her back against the door and slid to the floor, crying. Madison's soft wails penetrated her ears enough for her to pull herself together and tend to her child. Falling to the floor crying did not befit her personality, but for the first time in her life, she did not have control, and that she could not deal with.

After her crying episode, Vaneetra bathed her daughter, put her in new, footed pajamas and went to bed. Having missed her, she let Madison sleep in her bed. She needed to feel the closeness of her baby. However, sleep did not come easy. She did not know what to do.

Madison squealed, causing Vaneetra to shift her focus from nannies and the prior day's events to her child. She made a mental note not to use profanity in front of Madison. Vaneetra walked over to her swing and watched her baby move her mouth in urgent sucking motions—time to eat. She made Madison a bottle and took her into the living room to feed her, but the doorbell rang. Making a detour to the front door, she cursed, again, under her breath at the sight of her mother and sister. So much for mental notes. Vaneetra did not want to deal with them, but opened the door anyway. "Good afternoon, Mother… Summer."

Mrs. James ignored her daughter's cool, formal tone. "Hi, Vaneetra. May we come in?"

"Hey, sis. We thought we would stop by and see if Madison made it home. I hope that's okay?" Summer spoke in a warm and gentle tone.

"Of course it is okay." Vaneetra lied. "It is time to feed her, maybe you could do the honors." Vaneetra waited until her sister took off her coat and handed her Madison. She glanced at her mother, whose face showed pure annoyance. "Mother, may I take your coat as well? The two of you can go into the living room while I hang them up."

Having hung up their coats, Vaneetra returned to the living room to find her mother feeding Madison. She knew she should not make a big deal of it, but decided to do so anyway. "Mother, I don't remember asking you to feed my daughter. I asked Summer. She is perfectly capable of feeding her niece."

"I know who you asked and that she can do it. I wanted to do it." Mrs. James continued to feed Madison without looking up. "Do you have a problem with my feeding my only grandchild?"

"No, Mother, I have a problem with you coming to my house unannounced and taking over."

"Vaneetra, how do you figure I am taking over? I only asked to feed my grandchild. I should be able to do that. After all, I have not seen her in over two weeks."

"Oh, Mother, please! It has not been that long," Summer spoke up. "You are being dramatic. Vaneetra, let her feed Madison. You know she is going to gripe and complain if you don't."

"I know she is going to gripe and complain regardless." Vaneetra took a cheap shot at her mother.

"Since when is it okay to just speak so disrespectfully about your mother right in front of her?" Mrs. James placed the bottle down and began to burp Madison.

Summer ignored her mother's annoyance. "No one is disrespecting you, Mamma. We are just discussing historical observations of your behavior."

Vaneetra thought it best to change the subject. "So what did I do to deserve a visit from the two of you today?"

"I wanted to see my grandbaby."

"Why else are you here?"

"You are way too suspicious, child. Been like that all your life; always wanted to know why, never trusted anyone." Mrs. James shook her head, giving Madison the rest of her bottle.

"Well, I wanted to see Madison and to talk to you about how the nanny search is going. I also want to know if you have gotten the results of your full body scan." Summer got comfortable on the huge, overstuffed, leather sofa.

"Thank you for your honesty." Vaneetra's words were wrapped in sarcasm.

"Child, please! Naturally, I want to know about all of those things, but I could have called for that. I cannot call and see my grandbaby." She pulled Madison closer to her.

"Vaneetra, do you feel like sharing right now? If not, we can wait." Summer's gentle tone possessed genuine concern.

"I don't mind talking to you about it. I may as well tell you now. My full body scan did not show cancer in other parts of my body, but the tumor has grown and there is an increase in the amount of cells in the lymph nodes under my left arm." Vaneetra worked hard to keep her tone void of emotion.

"So what are they going to do?" Mrs. James's voice elevated with concern.

"My doctor wants to start chemotherapy right away. She hopes to shrink the tumor before surgery."

"When is right away and how long before you have surgery?" Mrs. James asked.

"I am supposed to have my first treatment tomorrow, but I need to put it off for a few more days. The surgery is scheduled for the end of January."

"What do you mean you need to put it off for a few more days? This is not like going to get your hair done." Mrs. James placed the bottle down again. This time a little too hard and it fell on the floor.

"I still need to secure a nanny for Madison and make arrangements with my job to adjust my schedule to accommodate my treatments." Vaneetra bent down to pick up the bottle and placed it back on the table.

"When do you plan to do those things?" Mrs. James's voice rose even higher.

"Mother, I am working on those things now. I have narrowed my selection down to two people. Now that I know what my treatment plan will be, I will make the necessary arrangements with my job."

"I will take some time off from work and come over and help you out. Courtney will help, too. Depending upon how you feel, we can come in shifts and stay with you overnight if that is what you want or need, until you hire someone."

"Why haven't you told your job yet? This is serious. They need to know that you will be off work." Mrs. James pressed forward with her questions.

"I have not told them anything yet, because I did not have anything to tell. I don't plan on sharing everything with my job, just what I feel is necessary for them to know."

"So what exactly do you plan on telling them? You have to tell them more than you are having a procedure done. You could end up being off work for months." Mrs. James handed Madison to Summer.

"I only plan to tell them that I have a minor medical issue that requires attention and give them the dates I will need to be out of the office. I am only taking off for the surgery and maybe a week or so afterward. I will work from home the days I have to go for chemo treatment."

"Girl, to be so smart, you really are naïve. You are not going to be able to work after those treatments. You arc going to get as sick as a dog and all you will be able to do is go to bed."

"Mamma, some people do not have terrible side effects with chemo treatments. Vaneetra may be one of them," Summer said, trying to diffuse the situation.

"I have never heard of anyone having chemotherapy and not having bad side effects." Mrs. James shifted her body in annoyance.

"Look, I will be fine. I am going to put off the treatments for another week or so, hire a nanny and move on with my life."

"If you have it narrowed down to two people, why will it take you a week to hire?" Mrs. James asked.

"If you must know, Mother, the cost to have a nanny for the amount of time that I will likely need is going to eat up my savings and I have to liquidate some assets."

"Why are you going through all of that when this child has a father that can help?" Mrs. James stood with her hand on her hip.

"I am not going to get in to this with you. I have not told Madison's father about my condition and don't plan on it. I will be fine and no one needs to help me."

"You need to tell him, Vaneetra Renee James. Why won't you ask him to help? Are you afraid that his wife will do something to Madison?"

"No, that bitch may be stupid, but she ain't crazy." Vaneetra sneered.

"From where I am standing, she is not crazy or stupid. She didn't sleep with the married man, who, by the way, is still at home taking care of his family."

"How in the hell would you know what he is doing? You don't know him and you don't know a damn thing about his family."

"Vaneetra, don't you take that tone with me and don't curse when talking to me. I am your mother, not one of your girlfriends. I deserve respect. And if he has a wife, he has a family. Family does not necessarily mean kids, but he probably has some of those, too. Regardless of his family status, he has a child over here that needs his help and you need to ask for it."

"Are you finished? If so, then I need to do a few things. You will have to leave. I am done talking to you about my personal life."

"Mamma, let's go and let Vaneetra get some rest." Summer handed Madison to Vaneetra, caressed her mother's elbow and steered her toward the door. After retrieving their coats, she gave her mother the keys to her car and instructed her to go and wait.

"Vaneetra, you should not have spoken to Mamma so harshly. She is scared for you…we all are. You need to call her later and apologize. In regards to starting chemo, you just said the tumor has grown since you found out a couple of weeks ago. I don't suggest you wait. I will plan to be off starting tomorrow to help you out. I can take a week or two. That should give you enough time to hire someone.

"Summer, I will be fine."

"You say that, but you really don't know. I am taking off. I also have some money saved. It is yours if you find that you need it. I won't give an opinion on asking Madison's father for help. I understand why you don't. It is your choice."

"How could you understand what I am feeling? You have never been in my shoes." Vaneetra sneered at Summer.

"I know that if I needed help and my child's father, who just happens to be married, is able to help, the only reason I would not ask would be because I did not want his wife involved."

"Your child would not have a father, you are a lesbian, remember? Your child would have a sperm donor."

"You get my point, so don't try and act like you don't. Just call me and let me know what time to be here tomorrow. Never mind, I will come back tonight to stay over."

With that, she opened the door and walked out, leaving Vaneetra standing alone with Madison in her arms in the foyer. She knew her mother and sister were right. However, she refused to entertain the thought of having to ask Daniel for help. After all, he chose not to be with their child. She walked back into the living room, sat on the sofa and wrapped a throw around her and Madison. She knew she might need help, but refused to ask Daniel. Vaneetra would not even allow herself to think about the possibility of dying, even though the idea lurked on the edge of her mind daily. If she died, Daniel would get custody. How would that bitch wife of his treat Madison? She was determined not to find out, but knew death was something she could not control.

Chapter Nineteen

Shannon

How was the trip to Chicago?" LaVonda asked over the phone.

"Cold!" I knew LaVonda's question had nothing to do with the weather in Chicago.

"Um hmm! How cold?"

"Very… It snowed the day we arrived and the next. After that, the temperature dropped to the twenties and stayed there."

"Girl, you know doggone well I am not talking about the weather! Did you and Daniel get to spend any time working out your differences?"

"We talked, but did not resolve anything. LaVonda, I am not sure there is anything to resolve. How am I supposed to get past him having an outside baby?"

"You take one day at a time and learn to forgive. Now, I am not taking Daniel's side. He was as wrong as two left shoes, but it has been about a year since you found out. You obviously are not going anywhere, so you may as well start working toward healing."

"Easier said than done, my friend. I can barely stand to look at him."

"You're still sleeping with him. How bad could it be?"

"That is all I am doing is sleeping, nothing more."

"What? Shannon how long has it been since you made love to your husband?"

"LaVonda, one has to be in love in order to make love."

"Since you want to be technical, how long has it been since you and Daniel joined together in the biblical sense?"

"It has been a while…a few months. Every time I give him some, I think about him being with someone else and get mad all over again." My answer was indignant.

"Girl, you must want that man to step out again. I can't believe you're holding sex over his head!"

"I am not holding anything over his head, but at what point am I supposed to forget that he has been daddy-long-dicking some low-life chick and just keep giving my body to him?" I put my hand on my hip. "I tried to forget, but I can't!"

"Calm down and get your hand off your hip!" My irritation did not faze my longtime friend.

"I don't have my hand on my hip!" I took my hand off my hip.

"Lying is not your thing, Shannon, so don't try it."

"How did you know I had my hand on my hip?"

"Girl, we have been friends since college. I know your every move and when you will make it. Now back to my question. Do you want him to step out on you, again?"

"LaVonda, I did not want him to step out the first time, but he didn't ask me!"

"No he did not, not many men would, but that is beside the point. Stop dancing around the subject. You will eventually have work toward having a normal sex life with your husband."

"Why?" I walked to the boys' playroom and peeked in on them, then returned to my room.

"Stop being childish; you know why! The Bible says that sex should not be withheld in marriage."

"It also says that the marriage bed should not be defiled. My bed has been defiled."

"Girl, I am not going to argue biblical points with you. If, for no other reason, you need the intimacy! Women also have needs."

"My needs are just fine, thank you." I paced around my bedroom.

"Yeah right, I know you are not doing anything to relieve yourself in that manner. You are way too uptight for your other options."

"You don't know what I am doing. For all you know, I could have someone on the side, too."

"Do you?" LaVonda was being sarcastic.

"No."

"I didn't think so. What toys do you have?"

"None."

"Have you learned the art of manual—"

"Enough already! I am in the midst of a very dry spell! Can we talk about something else? Didn't this whole conversation start with you asking me about my trip to Chicago?"

"Okay, how did things go in Chicago?"

"Everything went okay. Our families know about Madison."

"Any drama?"

"Not at all."

"Not even from your family?"

"Not from anyone. Everyone has accepted her existence. Jolene and Raven went out and bought Madison Christmas presents at the last minute and my mom had Raven buy her an ornament for the tree."

"Wow, Shannon. How did you feel about that?"

"I felt fine. I did not want there to be any drama. There has been enough of that lately."

The doorbell rang. I ignored it, thinking Daniel would get it. A couple of minutes later, it rang again.

"LaVonda, hold on. My doorbell is ringing. Daniel is downstairs; I am not sure why he won't answer it." I stomped down the stairs so he could hear me. I looked through the peephole and saw an older Black woman and a much younger version of her. "Hold on, LaVonda. There are two women at my door and I don't know them, probably Jehovah's witnesses."

"Uh huh! Remember the last time a strange woman came to your door?"

"Girl, hold on." I opened the door. "Hi, may I help you?"

"I most certainly hope that you can, honey. I am looking for a Mr. Daniel Johnson and his wife," the older Black woman stated, as she looked up at me.

"I am Shannon Johnson and Daniel is my husband. Who are you?"

"My name is Evelyn James and this is my daughter, Summer. We need to talk to you and your husband."

It took me a moment to comprehend the identity of the women standing at my door. LaVonda caught on right away.

"Who did she say they were? Did she say James? Is that—"

"Let me call you back." I disconnected the call before she finished asking her questions. "How may I help you, Ms. James?"

"Its missus and I came to speak with you and your husband. May we come in? It is mighty cold out today and my arthritis does not respond well to winter air."

For a moment, I did not budge. I did not want another James in my house, definitely not two of them.

The younger one chose to speak. "Mrs. Johnson, we are not here to start any trouble. My mother wants to talk to you and your husband about a personal matter."

"I am not sure what you could possibly want to talk to me about, but come in. I will get Daniel for you." I moved aside and let the decade's-apart twins into my home. Tension gripped the back of my neck and my shoulders began to ache. This could not be good. "Please, follow me." I led them into the living room. "Have a seat. I will go and get Daniel for you."

"Please return with your husband. What I have to say pertains to both of you. It is important that you are present to hear it."

"As I said before, I don't know what you have to say that would pertain to me. Your daughter and my husband have a child together. That is as far as it goes. I assume you know that or you would not be here."

"Yes, I know and that is part of the reason I am here. I will wait for you to return with your husband." I could not believe this old woman just dismissed me in my own house.

I considered asking her to leave, but Jeran and Zach ran down the stairs. "Mommy, can we have some lunch? We are hungry." Jeran rubbed his belly.

"Yes, sweetie, give Mommy a few minutes and I will make grilled cheese and soup for you and Zach."

"Hi! My name is Zach. Who are you?" I turned to find Zach shaking hands with Mrs. James and her twin, what's her name. Realizing that we had guests, Jeran ran into the living room.

"Hi, I'm Jeran."

"Hi, boys! My name is Summer and this is my mother, Mrs. James."

"Summer is not a name, it is a season," Zach stated, as if the young lady in front of him misspoke.

"Why don't you boys go back upstairs for a little while? I will call you back down when your lunch is ready."

"It's okay. I wouldn't mind getting to know my granddaughter's brothers." Mrs. James patted Zach on the hand.

"You are our sister's grandmother?" Zach never left any question unasked.

"Yes I am, suga."

"Can we call you grandma? Our real grandmothers live in Chicago." Apparently, Jeran does not either.

"You sure can. I would like that very much." Mrs. James clapped her hands together.

I left before I lost my cool. Where in the hell did this old ass woman get the idea that she could come into my house and accept the status of grandmother over my sons. We are not one big happy family. I searched for Daniel. After not finding him in the kitchen, family room or his office, I looked outside. He was walking toward me with a bundle of wood. I motioned for him to hurry.

"You have guests," I told him when he got within a few feet.

"Who is it?"

"Your baby mamma's mother and sister." I think my response left him speechless. He did not react to my quip about Vaneetra.

"Why are they here?" he asked when he found his voice.

"I do not know. She said she needed to talk to us about something, but would not say what."

Daniel walked past me and sat the load of wood down by the door. He proceeded toward the front part of the house and into the living room. I followed.

"Hello, ladies. I am Daniel Johnson. My wife tells me that you are Vaneetra's mother and sister." He shook their hands.

"Yes, I am Evelyn James and this is Vaneetra's younger sister, Summer. I am not one to waste time so I will get right to the point. However, maybe we should speak without the children present."

"Jeran and Zach, let's go into the kitchen and I will make your lunch." I turned to Mrs. James. "Feel free to start this discussion without me."

"We'll wait. This is a great opportunity for me to get to know my granddaughter's father." I looked at the old woman and walked out.

"But we want to stay!" Zach protested.

"You guys can stay until your lunch is ready. After that you have to go and eat." Daniel gave in. He probably did not want to be left alone with Vaneetra's people. I continued into the kitchen without comment.

When I finished making lunch, I returned to the living room and the boys went to the kitchen to eat as promised. Mrs. James did not waste any time.

"Young man, I am here to talk to you and your wife about my daughter and grandbaby."

"Mamma, I really think we should respect Vaneetra's wishes and stay out of this."

"Summer, I asked you for the address and a ride, not your opinion. " Mrs. James's sharp tongue lashed out her daughter.

Summer pressed the issue. "Vaneetra is going to be mad at us for getting involved in her business. We should really leave."

"Do I look the least bit concerned about how Vaneetra might feel? I am here for her benefit and the sake of my grandbaby."

"Maybe the two of you should come back when you have worked out your difference in opinion on this subject, whatever it is." I really did not want to be a witness to their family argument.

"There is nothing to work out. I have a reason for being here and I am going to share it. As I was saying, I am here to talk to the two of you about my daughter and grandbaby."

"Mrs. James, if you are concerned about whether I am taking care of my responsibility, I am. I pay child support and Madison comes over most weekends when Vaneetra will let her."

"If you are concerned about how she is treated, as you can see, our sons love having a sister and I would never mistreat her." I stood with my arms crossed.

"No, I am not here for that. The fact that my daughter let Madison go away with you for Christmas tells me all I need to know about those subjects."

"Then why are you here?" My impatience took over.

Mrs. James stared at me for a long moment before responding. "I am here because Vaneetra is sick and will need more help with Madison than you are currently providing."

"What do you mean sick? She seemed fine when I took Madison home yesterday." Daniel's voice elevated.

"She has—"

"Mamma, please just stop! We should not be doing this." The younger twin made one last plea.

"Summer, you are not doing anything, I am." Mrs. James raised her voice at her daughter. "Now be quiet and stop interrupting me."

I wished they would just leave. Whatever she had to say, I did not care to hear.

"Vaneetra has breast cancer and is to begin treatment tomorrow. She is talking about putting it off until next week when she can hire a nanny, but I don't think she should. Madison needs to come and live here until this ordeal is over. My daughter needs to focus on her health, so that she can be around to raise her child to adulthood. "

"With all due respect, ma'am, but that is a decision that Vaneetra and I will need to make. Of course I will help her any way that I can, but I need to talk to her first." Daniel seemed flabbergasted.

"With all due respect, when it comes to who lives in this house, you talk to me first. Then you go present your options to your mistress."

"Shannon, do we really have to go into this now. Of course I am going to talk things over with you, but I have to find out what it is Vaneetra needs."

"I see why Vaneetra did not want to tell you. Your wife obviously has a problem with my niece." Summer piped in on the defensive.

"I don't have a problem with Madison, whatever your name is, but your mother just dropped two major bombs on me. Surely, you did not think I would just grin and say okay. My husband and I need to discuss this. I am the primary care giver for the children in this home and I most certainly will have something to say about what children I raise. Do you understand the magnitude of my taking care of my husband's child that he had outside of our marriage?"

"What does any of that matter? My sister could be dying." Tears formed around the corners of her eyes.

I wanted to sympathize with her, but I couldn't. "It matters a lot to me! I hate what Daniel and your sister did to me and I should not be saddled with the result of it." The room grew silent with the weight of my words.

Mrs. James spoke first. "Honey, I've been where you are right now, and believe me when I say, I know what it is like. It feels as if your very soul is on the outside of your shoes being crushed, scratched, bumped and bruised against the pavement. And like the heels of them are on the inside of you, kicking you every step of the way. But you are still here." She stood and walked toward me. "I am not proud of what my daughter has done, but I won't let that get in the way of what I need to do right now. The fact is, Vaneetra needs your and Daniel's help. As a matter of fact, she needs you more than him." Mrs. James pointed at Daniel.

Each of Mrs. James's words felt like an iron ball dropping in my lap, weighing me down and making it even harder to run away from this never-ending nightmare. I kept my cool and my stance. "As I stated before, Daniel and I have to discuss all of this, but I really do not see myself being of any help to your daughter. I am truly sorry for what happened to her, but I can't just step in and be a mother to her child with my husband."

"Honey, you are going to have to find the strength and forgiveness to help. My granddaughter needs a mother, not a nanny. These first few months of her life are the most important. She don't need to be raised by no nanny."

"Mrs. James, if that is what Vaneetra wants to do, how can we stop it? She and Shannon are not exactly on speaking terms and we barely get along." Daniel asked a valid question and made good points.

"I hear you are a lawyer. I know you have a way to make it happen, so do it." I couldn't believe the ruthlessness of this woman.

"Are you suggesting that I sue Vaneetra for custody of Madison? You did just say that she is sick. Why would you want me to do that?"

"I know I sound cold and heartless, but I am thinking about the future of my granddaughter. Breast cancer is a dangerous beast. And while I believe my daughter can beat this, there is always the possibility that she won't." For the first time since she arrived, Mrs. James's voice quivered.

"You have to understand that this is a highly unusual request. I would expect for you, as Madison's grandmother, to want to raise her." I voiced my thoughts.

"Honey, I want to be a grandmother. I raised my kids and did a good job, regardless of the decisions they have made." She shifted her eyes, briefly glancing at what's her name. "Besides, my husband and I are getting older. We are well into our sixties and Madison is three months old. We can't keep up with no baby."

"What about her?" I pointed at Summer. Daniel looked at me, but didn't say anything. I knew he disagreed with what I was suggesting, but I didn't care.

"Courtney and I will be happy to raise Madison." What's her face spoke up.

"I don't approve of Summer's lifestyle. Plus, she has no say so in this matter either. God forbid Vaneetra was to die, Madison needs to be here with her father. "

"No one knows if she will die. We need to find out what is going on before we go any further." Daniel seemed at a loss.

I needed a drink. I sighed and all the fight left me, along with my breath. "Mrs. James, would you like a glass of wine?"

"What are you serving, white or red?"

"I have it all."

"How about a glass of sweet red? Red is good for the heart. Lord knows my heart needs something good."

"Would either of the two of you like anything?" I swept a glance at Daniel and Summer.

"Do you have beer?" Summer asked. "I could go for one of those."

"Me, too," Daniel said.

I turned to find Jeran and Zach standing with their mouths wide open. "Go on in and sit with your father, boys." The looks on their faces told me that they heard more than they needed to know. There was no point in sending them away now.

Chapter Twenty

Daniel

Vaneetra never talked about her family. Our relationship did not include hanging out with or discussing them. We spent most of our time in bed. The visit from her mother and sister left Shannon and me uptight. Shannon took the boys and left, without telling me where they were going, or when they would return. Needing to get out of the house and take my mind off what Mrs. James asked me to do, I ended my vacation early and went to the office to get some work done. When I arrived, I found my business partner and longtime friend, Josh, preparing for an upcoming case.

Joshua Belanger has been my sounding board through this entire situation with Vaneetra, being brutally honest and not caring how I felt about it. Although single, he valued family more than anyone I knew. Growing up in an upper middle class, two-parent family in Upstate New York, he only strayed from his roots or family values once.

We were college roommates and remained good friends after we graduated. When I told him about Vaneetra, he told me I was stupid and didn't try to hide his disappointment. After a couple of days trying to convince me to end it, he finally started hearing me out. Josh had a lot to do with my ending my relationship with Vaneetra. He never let up on two things: the first being that even though Vaneetra seemed perfect she had flaws, and second if I left Shannon, Vaneetra may not want me broke, which is what I would more than likely be if I walked out on my wife and two small children.

"Dan, my man, what are you doing here? I didn't expect you back another week."

"What's up, Josh? Man, I needed to get out of the house."

"Things aren't getting any better?"

"Man, I don't know what things are getting. One minute Shannon seems cool and she helps with Madison, the next she turns all cold and callous."

"She's cold and callous toward Madison?"

"No, toward me, but when she is that way with me she keeps her distance from both of us."

"How did things go in Chicago?"

"They were great! Our families were cool with Maddie. It went much better than I thought. Shannon spent a lot of time with her mom and the boys rotated between both families. Shoot, we didn't see much of each other the last few days we were there."

"Sounds like a drama-free time. Why did you end vacation early? Did you need to work off some sexual tension? Is Shannon still holding out on you?"

"Josh, don't even bring that up. I got bigger problems than that now. After yesterday, Shannon is probably going to leave me."

"Dan, it has been almost a year. If Shannon wanted to leave she would have done so already."

"I thought the same thing, but after last night a lot of things will change."

"What happened, did you get caught talking dirty to Vaneetra on the phone or sending freaky text messages?"

"Man, no! I am done with that, even though no one should blame me, since I am not getting any action at home."

"Well, if you want your marriage to work, you better wait until she is ready."

"Aren't you listening? Didn't you just hear me say that my marriage is over?"

"Technically, you did not say that."

"Look, man, do you want to know what happened or not?"

"Okay, I'm listening. What happened?"

"Vaneetra's mother and sister came over last night."

"No way! You are joking, right?"

"No, I am not joking. They actually came to my house."

"What did they want?"

"Her mother came to try and convince me to file for custody of Maddie."

"That's some cold-hearted stuff. What mother would do that to her daughter? Is Vaneetra that bad as a parent?"

"No, she has breast cancer."

"Aww, man, I am sorry to hear that. It's gotta be tough finding that out and being a new mother. That still does not explain why her family wants you to sue for custody."

"It's not the family, just her mother. Believe me, I thought the same thing you are thinking. But after I listened to her reasoning, I understood and actually agreed with her."

"What reason could she have?"

"She's afraid that things may turn out for the worse with Vaneetra and if that happened, as Madison's father, I should be the one to raise her. Mrs. James feels that she and her husband are too old to raise Maddie and I agree with her. Regardless of whether or not Vaneetra's family is able to take care of Madison, I am her father and should do it."

"You make some valid points, but there are just a couple of issues. One, you are still married and your wife would have to agree. Two, it just does not seem right to put a sick person through the ordeal of a custody battle." Josh got up and walked around to the front of his desk.

"Those are both problems that I need to figure a way around. I will talk to Shannon tonight about it. I was planning to file for joint custody for both legal and physical anyway. While we were in Chicago, Vaneetra started threatening not to let me see Madison anymore. Now that I know she is sick, I don't want to put her through that process, but I have to get her to agree to let me keep Madison more often while she is going through treatment. And, after all of that is over, I will deal with the legal end of it."

"You are right to not pursue any legal action right now, but without it you may not get what you want. There is also that little matter of getting your wife to agree to taking care of your former mistress's daughter." Josh stood with his arms folded across his chest, wagging his right index finger in front of him.

"What can she say?"

"She can say no, Dan, she can definitely say no." He looked at me like I had two heads.

"Josh, I honestly don't think she will say no. She has to know that I am going to be in my daughter's life. So if we are going to stay together, she has to accept Maddie."

"What you said makes perfect sense, but will it turn out that way?"

"It has to turn out that way. I just don't know how it will."

"I wish you the best of luck. If it turns out that you have to sue for custody, I will represent you pro bono. Looks like you will be broke anyway, that's the least I can do, seeing how you are fifty percent of this business."

Josh's effort to break the tension worked. I laughed for the first time in a few days. "While you are being so generous, can you convince my wife to agree to what I am about to ask her to do?"

"Only God can help you with that, my friend. Better yet, forget about luck and start praying. You need to pray that the mothers of all of your children will let you be a father to them and not just a financier."

I found it profound that my friend easily identified who had the final say about the type of father I could be to my children—their mothers. I would definitely take his advice and start praying. I had not done that since Shannon walked out of church on me the day I asked her to go to the altar and pray with me. We have not been since that day. I personally felt embarrassed, because of my infidelity and having fathered a child outside of my marriage. I loved my daughter, but I knew what I had done went against everything I had learned in church. Some of the men at church left messages asking if we were okay and stating that we were in their prayers, but I had not responded.

I worked for several hours in my office, answering emails and returning phone calls, before going home at six-thirty. Shannon and the boys were eating dinner. I joined them and did my best to deflect what seemed like a hundred questions about when Maddie would be coming to live with us. Neither Shannon, nor I had addressed what they heard from Mrs. James. Considering I did not know how the situation would turn out, I had nothing to tell them.

At eight-thirty, Shannon and I shared the responsibility of getting the boys to bed. I helped them clean up their playroom. She gave baths and we both read bedtime stories. Once we finished, I snagged the opportunity to discuss the inevitable.

"Shannon, do you mind if we talk about Vaneetra's mother and sister's visit yesterday?"

"Do I have a choice?"

"Shannon, you always have a choice, but I would like you to choose to discuss this issue."

"Since when do you want to discuss anything? Why don't you just sweep this issue under the rug like you do all the other issues in our marriage?" She pushed past me and went into our bedroom. I followed.

"I don't want to argue with you, but this situation affects all of us." I stood in front of her, careful not to touch her, even though my manhood rose just by her being close to me.

"So have all of the other decisions you have made over the past year. What makes this one so special?" She tried to push past me again to go into our bathroom, but I would not move. If she felt my hardness, she didn't let on.

"Shannon, I am trying to do the right thing for everyone. I could go off and just make a decision without you, but you said you wanted to discuss it. No, you said we had to discuss it! Well, I am trying to discuss it!" I took a chance and caressed her shoulders, trying to keep her close.

She pulled away. "Okay, let's discuss it. What is it that you would like to do? What would you like for me to do, Daniel? The way I see it, I am going to end up on the losing end of any decision made in this situation, so you just tell me what you want to see happen."

I forced out an exasperated sigh and moved out of her way. "I want you to do what is comfortable for you, Shannon."

"No you don't. You want me to do what is comfortable for you. Why don't you tell me what it is you want to do?" She walked over to the bed and sat down.

My erection deflated. I walked over and sat next to her. "I think we should have Madison come and live with us until Vaneetra is able to care for her. It may only be a few months."

"You want me to take care of your child that you had with your mistress? Did I hear you correctly?" She moved away from me on the bed.

"Vaneetra is not my mistress. My relationship with her is over, but I still have to do what is right for my daughter. Mrs. James made a good point when she said that if Vaneetra dies, Madison should be with us." I reached out to take hold of her hand, but she pulled away.

"Daniel, keep in mind that Mrs. James's opinion is just that, her opinion. It does not reflect the thoughts or feelings of either of the women actually involved in this situation." She folded her arms across her chest.

"I know how you feel, but tell me what you think we should do. I need your support on this, Shannon. I need to know that you are okay with this." I moved closer to her. She pressed her back against the headboard. Being this close to her on the bed reminded me of how long it had been since we made love. I pushed those thoughts out of my mind.

Her silence was deafening, until she spoke. "Daniel, I don't want to have your daughter come and live with us. I am still adjusting to the fact that you have a daughter. However, you do what you feel is best and I will do the same." With that, she jumped off the bed, ran into the bathroom and slammed the door. I knew that would be as close to a yes as I would ever get.

Now I had to have this same discussion with Vaneetra, but decided to wait until I would pick up Madison on Friday to talk to her. I needed the rest of the week to figure out how I would convince her to let Madison come and live with me, without taking her to court.

Chapter Twenty-One

Shannon

I simply could not believe Vaneetra's mother showed up at my house with her other daughter, demanding Daniel and I let Madison come and live with us. This seemed like a nightmare that would not end. I cannot even begin to conjure up the words for how I felt about Mrs. James's bright idea that I take on the responsibility of being a stepmother to my husband's illegitimate child. I could best relate it to being stabbed in the heart so much that you go numb, but God is not merciful enough to let you die.

Unfortunately, Jeran and Zach overheard most of the conversation about Vaneetra's situation and I spent the following day doing my best to answer all their questions without actually giving a real answer. The idea of their sister coming to live with us excited them. I actually envied them. I wish I could be young enough not to understand this mess.

Daniel made his feelings crystal clear. He wanted his daughter to come and live with us, like we are one happy family. I told him how I felt and left it at that. I did not say no, but I refused to say yes.

That night I slept downstairs on the sofa. The next morning, he tried to talk to me, but I refused to acknowledge him. He did not seem to understand the magnitude of what he wanted me to do and why I just could not say yes.

Once he left for work, I got up, made the boys breakfast, showered and called my mom. I told her what happened and she, of course, said that I should not try to stop Daniel from bringing Madison to live with us. I did not want to hear that. By the end of the day, searing pains shot through my head caused by the stress of contemplating walking out on my marriage or staying for the sake of my sons.

I needed time to think. So, I packed a bag with enough clothes for the boys and me for a few days, and left. I told them we were going on a New Year's Eve getaway. I did not leave a note, nor did I call Daniel to let him know that I would be gone when he got home. I wanted him to hurt, to think that I left for good. It just might have been true.

The first few hours the boys and I went out and had fun. I took them to Marbles Museum, then to Frankie's Fun Park and let them play for a while before eating lunch at the restaurant located on the premises. Eight hours later, we ended up at the front door of Ms. Rosalee Whitmore, a widow and member of the church we attended. We used to go regularly until I found out about Daniel's affair. After that, I walked out at the end of a service and had not been back.

The boys must have really missed her, because when she opened her front door, Zach almost knocked her down, jumping into her arms. Jeran wrapped his arms around her waist in a tight hug. She stood as tall as I am, with a long, but stout frame. Her milk chocolate skin barely held a wrinkle for her seventy-five years of age. Her thick, salt and pepper hair, shining with natural luster, fell softly just below her shoulder. Ms. Whitmore prided herself on walking four miles daily. She lived alone in a four-bedroom house not far from the church.

After fifty-seven years of marriage, her husband, Milford Whitmore, passed three years ago to bone cancer. His death devastated the entire church. Everyone that knew him loved and respected him greatly. He loved his family, life, the Lord, and most definitely his church. He spent tireless hours caring for the church property. They raised five children—all boys—who now lived in various parts of the country, doing well for themselves, but found the time to migrate home a couple times of year to visit. They all have tried to convince Ms. Whitmore to live with them, but to no avail. She said she planned to live out the rest of her days in the place where God blessed her and her husband to live long happy lives.

I admired Ms. Whitmore. Even though her husband was dead, she still managed to live. I once asked her how she continued to smile and live a full life after losing someone she spent most of her years loving. *"God saw fit to call Milford home, not Rosalee,"* she had said. She felt she owed it to God and Milford to continue to live, love and enjoy life, and that she did.

After Ms. Whitmore caught her breath and Zach, she invited us in. She took our coats and shoes, and hustled the boys to the kitchen and gave them milk and cookies, while I sat in the living room. Having gotten them squared away, she joined me with cookies and milk for me, and tea for her.

"Thank you, Ms. Rosalee. You know I love your homemade cookies. I am surprised that you are not traveling. Don't you usually visit your youngest son and his family between Christmas and New Year's?" I devoured a double chocolate cookie.

"Yes, chil, but this year they went over to Europe for the holidays and ain't nobody gettin' me on a plane over a large body of water." Ms. Rosalee sipped on her tea.

"You didn't want to visit any of your other sons? I bet they were heartbroken."

"They'll get over it. This year I wanted to stay in my own house, sleep in my own bed and attend my own church. I just didn't want to go traveling this time of year. I hope they understood, but if they didn't, too bad!" Ms. Whitmore cackled as if she had just heard the funniest joke ever told.

"Well, I guess I heard that!" I took a sip of milk and smiled.

"You sho' did and they did, too! Besides, if I had left, then I wouldn'a been here for you today, would I?"

If I had not known Ms. Whitmore to be a college-educated woman, I would have thought she barely made it out of middle school by the way she chose to speak sometimes.

"Ms. Whitmore, you didn't need to be here for me. I just came by to check on you." I tried to keep my expression jovial.

"Chil', who do you think you foolin'? I could see the trouble on your heart from the driveway. Even though you often drop by just to see how I'm doing, that is not why you here today."

"Nothing gets past you, does it?"

"Nothin, but time chil', nothing but time. So tell me what's troublin' you."

I spent the next half hour telling her everything that had happened in the past couple of weeks, pausing briefly so she could put a movie on in one of the spare bedrooms for the boys to watch. When she returned, she told me that both fell asleep before the opening credits finished.

Ms. Whitmore already knew about Daniel's affair and Madison. I told her about that just as soon as I found out. She prayed and cried with me through the entire ordeal. This time I managed to get halfway through the story before bursting into tears, and sputtering out the rest of it through chest rattling sobs. The entire time Ms. Whitmore sat by my side, rubbing my back and letting me cry on her shoulder.

"There, there, chil', go on and get it all out." She offered me a box of tissue.

"I am not sure why I'm crying. I should have expected more madness to come out of this situation." I gasped and heaved between words.

"Shannon, how could you have possibly expected this to happen? Only God knew that gal would get breast cancer and I doubt He would have shared that information with you. And only God knows what is going to happen to her from here. "

"I know, but it just seems so unfair. Why am I getting stuck with taking care of my husband's illegitimate child?"

"Now hold on one minute. What has that poor, innocent baby ever done to you? Don't talk about her in such a manner."

"She has not done anything to me, her parents did. I call her illegitimate because she was born out of wedlock." I defended myself.

"Well, weren't you born out of wedlock? I distinctly remember you sharing that tidbit of information with me once. How would you feel if someone had spoken about you in such an awful manner?" I did not bother to answer; I just ate another cookie.

"No need to answer, chil'. We both know I'm right. Now back to the problem at hand. Did Madison's mother agree to let her daughter come and live with you and Daniel?"

"No, from what I gathered, she does not even know that her mother came to talk to us."

"So why are you getting all worked up about something that may not even happen? You just have to wait and see and if it is God's will, you will just have to deal with it when the time comes."

"How could it be God's will that I take care of my husband's child by someone else? That hardly seems fair."

"Well first off, how am I supposed to know why God makes the decisions He does? When I get to Heaven I will ask Him, but it will be too late to do you any good. Secondly, you have been alive long enough to know that life is not fair. God did not promise you that it would be. You just have to deal with what He puts before you."

"God did not put this before me, my husband and his mistress did." I ate another cookie. I began to wonder just how many cookies she had given me.

"Now you are mincing words. Daniel and that woman may have entered into an adulterous relationship, but they had nothing to do with that gal getting cancer."

"Are you suggesting that God gave Vaneetra cancer just to teach me a lesson?"

"Of course not, chil', that is foolish! What I am saying is that if He sees fit for you to take care of this baby girl, then you need to seek His guidance and do what you know is right. Maybe I worded it wrong. I am getting old. My mind isn't as sharp as it used to be."

"Hmm, maybe, but how can anyone expect me to take care of this child?"

"Because the child has done nothing to you and if that is what is needed, then that is what you should do."

"Why does everyone seem to think that is what I should do? Vaneetra has family."

"Who is everyone?" Ms. Whitmore sat with her arms crossed over her chest.

"You, my mother, Vaneetra's mother!" I flung my hands in the air.

"Well, I can answer that one. It is because we are all mothers and we know that our job is to take care of children. Now before you think of another argument against why you should do it, let me make something clear. In the event that this here gal should leave this world, you will have to raise her daughter anyway, provided you plan to stay with your husband. He is her father and has a legal right to take custody of her."

"Well if she dies then I will consider it. Until then, I don't want to think about it." I knew I was just being stubborn.

"Now you are being foolish. What choice do you have? If this other woman agrees to let her daughter stay with you and Daniel, what choice do you really have?"

"I can file for divorce." I surprised myself when I said it.

"Would you really do that?"

I thought a moment before I answered. "Yes, I will and I think I am going to do just that. This whole situation is just too much for me and I need a way out. Divorce is that way out." My tears started to run freely down my face again and onto my now empty plate.

"Shannon, it may be a way out of one situation and into another. What about your sons? How do you think divorcing their father will affect them?"

"You know, people have been asking me that question for the past week and a half. I think they will adjust. I will not be taking them away from him. I am more than willing to share custody. I just need to be away from all of this madness." I buried my face in my hands and sobbed.

"Shannon, you are not thinking clearly." She began rubbing my back again. "Why don't you go to the car and get your bags. You can sleep on it and we can talk more in the morning. "

"How did you know I brought bags with me?" I stopped sobbing and looked up at her.

"Like I said before, I could see your trouble from the driveway. God put it on my spirit the minute I saw you that you needed refuge from your storm. Now go and get your bags."

Chapter Twenty-Two

Shannon

I took Ms. Whitmore's advice and slept on my decision of what to do next. When I woke up the next morning, I made up my mind to consult an attorney. Since it was New Year's Day, I knew no one would be available. I checked my cell phone and found twelve voice messages and twenty text messages from Daniel, but nothing past nine-thirty last night.

I showered, dressed and searched the Internet for divorce attorneys in the area. I settled on four that I would call tomorrow. Since I had never done anything like this before, I did not know what else to do. I went downstairs to find the boys eating pancakes and sausage for breakfast.

"Hey, Mommy!" Zach actually got up from the table and gave me a hug.

"Hey, Mom." Jeran stayed in his seat and continued eating.

"Mom, guess who came to see us last night?" Zach climbed back into his chair and resumed eating.

"Who came to see you last night?" I looked over at Ms. Whitmore quizzically.

"Daddy came over and stayed with us." I had to mask my annoyance.

"Yes, Daniel called and asked if I had seen you and the boys. When I told him that you were here, he asked if he could come and see you. I said yes." Ms. Whitmore set a place at the table and gestured with her hand for me to sit down, ignoring my eye roll.

"Did you guys enjoy your visit with your dad last night?" I decided not to make a big issue of it. After all, I could not tell Ms. Whitmore whom to let inside her house.

"Yes, we had a lot of fun! Daddy brought over some of our Christmas toys and played with us until we went to bed."

"Oh really? What time did you guys go to bed?" I poured syrup on my pancakes.

"Oh the boys and their dad brought in the New Year together. They all fell asleep on the floor in the family room at around one." Ms. Whitmore sipped her tea. The woman loved tea.

"He slept here last night?" I held my fork filled with pancakes in midair, feeling a surge of sadness for not bringing in the New Year with my boys.

"Yes, Daddy left early this morning, Mamma. Then we went for a walk with Ms. Whitmore and to the grocery store." Jeran pushed his plate away and placed his napkin on the table.

"You guys walked with Ms. Whitmore? How far did you go?" I nibbled on my pancakes.

"We walked around the block three whole times, I had fun!" Zach held up three fingers.

"We are going to do it again tomorrow, if we don't go home tonight," Jeran said.

"How in the world did I sleep through all of that? I am sorry I did not stay awake long enough to bring in the New Year with you boys."

"I wondered the same thing myself. You must have been really tired." Ms. Whitmore got up to clear Jeran's plate from the table.

"Guess what, Mom?" Jeran got excited for the first time since I came downstairs.

"What, sweetie?"

"Dad said he is going to come and take us to the movies." His grin stretched wide across his face.

"That sounds like fun. Did he say what time he was coming to get you?" I wanted to leave before he arrived, so that I would not have to see him.

"I don't remember. Ms. Whitmore do you remember what time my dad is coming to get me and Zach?"

"I believe he said that he would be here at one-thirty."

"Ms. Whitmore, would you mind keeping an eye on the boys while I run a few errands? I think I want to take advantage of some of the New Year's Day sales." I scrambled for a reason not to be here when Daniel arrived.

"Chil', that won't be a problem at all. You go out and have some time to yourself. Jeran and Zach are already dressed. We will play with their toys until Daniel arrives."

I finished my breakfast, cleaned up the kitchen and the room I slept in. I left the house at twelve-forty five, passing Daniel as I drove down the street. I didn't expect him to be early. He was never early for anything. He honked his horn. I ignored it. He called, I did not answer. I just went about my day, pretending as if he did not exist. I needed to be completely away from him in order to get my head together. He called four more times, then finally sending a text message at six-thirty telling me that he took the boys to a movie, out to dinner, then home and if I did not return home tonight, he would drop them off at Ms. Whitmore's on his way to work in the morning.

I returned to Ms. Whitmore's, who promptly informed me that she had a date with a gentleman caller and for me not to wait up. "When did you start dating? I did not think you would ever be interested in another man."

"Just a couple of weeks ago. I met him when I visited a friend's church. He is an eighty-year-old widower of ten years. It will never be anything serious, just someone to keep me company every now and then." She cackled as she stood in the hallway, looking in a mirror, fixing her hair.

"Well, you go on with your bad self and have a good time. Daniel is keeping Jeran and Zach overnight, so I guess I am all alone tonight."

"Yes, he told me that when he picked them up today. I think that is his way of trying to coax you into comin' home."

"Well, it is not going to work. I still need time to think. Tomorrow, I am going to make an appointment to see a divorce attorney. After that, I will decide what my next move will be."

Ms. Whitmore turned to face me. "Chil', are you sure you want to do that? I think you should reconsider."

"I am just going for a consultation. However, if I have to divorce Daniel in order to get peace of mind, I will."

"Honey please, that man ain't going to let you go. You need to move past your pain and look at your situation clearly. That man made a mistake, but he loves you and he loves his sons. Shoot, he has been over here almost as much as you have in the past two days."

"I can't look past my pain. Besides, he started this and I am going to finish it." I rolled me eyes.

Ms. Whitmore took my hands in hers and stared me in the eyes. "Shannon, let this old woman give you a piece of good advice. Not everything started needs to be finished. Especially if at the end, you will have destroyed everything you worked so hard to build. Now, that man made a mistake. He has never done it before and will likely never do it again. Do you believe that this was the first time he ever cheated on you?" I nodded my head.

"Then you have to find it in your heart to forgive him. You know you still love him. If you didn't you wouldn't hurt so bad, but that pain is something you are just gonna have to face."

Even though I was not sure if I loved Daniel or not, I did not argue with her. "I am not going to make any promises. I am still going to see that divorce lawyer tomorrow."

"Do as you must; I will leave you with one last thing to think about."

"What is that, Ms. Whitmore?" I looked at her skeptically.

"Imagine you were Daniel and you cheated on your wife and had a baby with the other woman. Then you find out that the woman might die and you have to raise your child. You stand to lose your wife and other children because of your sexual improprieties. Would you cheat again?" She stood with her hands on her hip and a smirk dancing on the corners of her mouth. "For one, he is not all that smart. A serial cheater would not be dumb enough to get his other woman pregnant. Two, he should be too scared to do it again. What if the next one gets pregnant and then sick enough to die? Who wants to be bothered with all of that?"

I started laughing and could not stop. As outlandish as all of what she said seemed, she made some valid points. Ms. Whitmore left me in the middle of her hallway pondering her series of questions. However, even if Daniel never cheated on me again, he had already done enough to break up our family.

Chapter Twenty-Three

Vaneetra

Vaneetra's first round of chemo did not go as well as she had expected. Dr. Chen presented her with several options of administering chemo. Vaneetra, with the urging of her father who accompanied her, opted to go into the hospital on an outpatient basis and have the medications administered intravenously.

Halfway through the treatment, nausea overwhelmed her and she became violently ill, vomiting hard enough to stop the chemotherapy until the nausea subsided. Afterward, her father took her home, but the vomiting returned. Dr. Chen told her that nausea and vomiting were common side effects and should subside. She told Mr. James that if it did not, he should call her answering service and have her contacted. She urged Vaneetra to take the nausea medication she prescribed during her last visit. Vaneetra remembered that she never got it filled, but did not tell Dr. Chen. Instead, she told her father when they got in the car and asked him to go and get it filled for her.

When they arrived at Vaneetra's house, Mrs. James, Summer and Courtney were there awaiting their return. As promised, Summer returned the night before to begin taking care of Madison until Vaneetra hired a nanny. Something she intended to do today after chemo, but now thought it better to wait until tomorrow. Vaneetra noticed her sister acted somewhat strangely, almost like she had something to hide. Vaneetra wondered if Summer's job had given her issues about taking time off on such short notice.

Vaneetra walked into her living room with her father's help and sat down on the sofa. "Marshall, don't let her sit in here! Take her to her bedroom and I will help her get in the bed." Mrs. James tried to take over.

"Mother, I do not want to go and lie down right now," Vaneetra snapped. She was in no mood for her today. "I just want to sit in my living room and wait until I regain some of my strength. Then I am going to log on and get some work done."

"Vaneetra Renee James, you need your rest. Why must you be so stubborn?" Mrs. James pressed the issue.

"Apparently, I get it honestly." Vaneetra leaned over to get her throw, but could not reach it. Summer handed it to her. "May I hold my daughter, please?" Courtney, who held Madison in her arms, handed her to Vaneetra.

"Vaneetra, why don't you wait a while before holding Madison? You might drop her." Mrs. James reached for Madison, but Vaneetra turned her body away from her mother, moving her daughter out of reach.

Mr. James put a stop to his wife's demanding attitude. "Evelyn, that's enough. Leave Vaneetra alone. She doesn't need you pestering her. She knows what she wants to do. We are here to help, not boss her around."

"Well if no one is going to listen to me, then I guess I will just go home." Mrs. James crossed her arms and walked to a nearby chair to sit down.

"If that is what you feel like you need to do, then go right ahead. Courtney…Summer, will one of you escort Evelyn home, please?" Mr. James refused to play into Mrs. James's ploy for him to let her have her way.

"I will take you home, Mrs. James." Courtney volunteered.

"That is quite all right, Courtney, Summer will take me."

"No I won't, Mamma. It is almost time for Madison's afternoon feeding and nap. Also, I want to be here just in case Vaneetra needs to go to the bathroom and needs help. Courtney has offered to take you home. If you don't want that then you need to just wait until Daddy leaves." Summer wished she had been so adamant the other night before she took her mother to Daniel's house. She knew Vaneetra would explode once she found out, which is why she does not plan to say anything for another day or two.

"Well, I guess I will just wait. I should have a say so about who takes me home." Mrs. James sat in the chair with her arms and legs crossed.

"Only when you are driving, Mother dear, which by the way you know how to do, but chose not to." Vaneetra stroked Madison's hair, not bothering to make eye contact with her mother.

"Where did I go wrong? I never in my life would have thought that I could raise such disrespectful children."

Giving in, Mr. James walked to the foyer closet, grabbed Mrs. James's coat and returned. "Come on, Evelyn. I am going to take you home. This seems to be a bit much for you. I will bring you back later this evening." Mr. James placed his arm on his wife's shoulder.

"It is not too much, Marshall, I just want to help," Mrs. James whined.

"But you are not helping. You are trying to throw your weight around and that is aggravating Vaneetra." Mr. James held his wife's coat open.

"You guys do realize that I am still in the room and can speak for myself, don't you?" Vaneetra looked at one parent and then the other.

"Baby girl, what would you like for us to do?"

Vaneetra let out an exasperated sigh. "Daddy, do as you please as long as no one is trying to tell me what to do!"

"I think I will go and get lunch started. Vaneetra, would you like anything?"

"No thank you, Courtney. I am not hungry."

"Vaneetra you should try and eat something." Mrs. James could not resist butting in.

"Evelyn, come on and let's go help Courtney with lunch. Baby girl, if you change your mind, just let us know." Mr. James laid the coat down, took his wife's hand and tugged on it.

"But, Marshall, she needs to try and eat something," Mrs. James persisted.

"You know what, Mother? I think I will go to my room. Don't follow me." Vaneetra attempted to get up from the sofa with Madison in her arms and lost her footing, falling back down on the couch.

"You see, Marshall? She almost dropped the baby!" Mrs. James shouted.

"Mother, go home. You just need to go home." Vaneetra shouted, causing Madison to whimper.

"Vaneetra, calm down. Daddy is going to take Mamma home and I am going to just sit here with you and Madison. None of this is helping, so we need to do something else. Mamma, go home. You can come back later after Vaneetra has settled down and feels better." Summer sat next to Vaneetra, placing one hand on her shoulder and the other on Madison.

"Come on, Evelyn, let's go." Mr. James helped his wife into her coat and walked her to the door. "Baby girl, we will be back later today or maybe tomorrow. I will call first. We love you."

Vaneetra refused to respond as they walked out the door.

"Vaneetra, let me have Madison. I will feed her and put her down for a nap. You get some rest. Let me know if you get hungry." Summer gently took Madison out of her sister's arms, turned to leave, but then turned back. "You know, you think you are the only one going through something, but you are not. You may be the one with the breast cancer and the new baby, but you are not the only one going through something."

"Summer, I don't want to hear this lecture you are about to give. You can get your girlfriend and leave, too. I don't care!" Vaneetra shouted.

"I am not leaving, no matter how much of a bitch you are being. You need me and everyone else who wants to put up with you. In case you have not realized big sister, you can't boss cancer around. Believe it or not, you are fighting for your life and everyone that loves you is in your corner trying to support you. You can't do this alone, so stop pushing people away." With that, Summer turned and walked away, leaving Vaneetra fuming. She pushed herself off the couch again, only to experience a wave of nausea and fall to the floor. Unable to move, she lay there expecting her sister to return, after hearing the loud noise of her falling. However, no one came, not Summer or Courtney, so she lay there until she found the strength to pull herself back up onto the sofa.

Vaneetra made up in her mind that she would hire the nanny tomorrow, so that she would not have to put up with the nagging of her family beyond the end of this week. If she felt better, her sister and girlfriend could go home that evening. She drifted off to sleep, still fuming at the events that had just taken place. She would show her family that she could beat cancer without them.

Chapter Twenty-Four

Shannon

I called home to say good night to the children. Daniel asked when I planned to come back. I told him I did not know. Before he would let me speak, he told me that he wanted me to come back home so that we could work out our differences as a family. I told him that I needed time to decide if I wanted to be a family again.

The boys told me all about the fun they had hanging out with their dad. He took them to the movies, back to Frankie's Fun Park, and out to Terrero's Mexican food restaurant. Zach said they bought me a seafood burrito and asked when I would be home to eat it. I asked him to put it in the refrigerator for me and that I would be home tomorrow. He cried when I told him that. My heart could not take it. I called Mrs. Whitmore and left her a voice mail message. I also wrote her a note, letting her know that I went home to be with my children. Then, I gathered our bags and left.

I arrived a little after ten, but did not go in right away. I wondered how I could gain the courage to take my kids away from their father, if I did not have the heart to stay away from them myself. I felt as if Zach sensed something different going on between his dad and me. He did not cry when he stayed away from us in Chicago. Outside of that, he never slept overnight anywhere else. Then I realized, we all were away from home and for as long as he has been alive, I had never stayed away from home without them.

At ten-thirty, I found the boys in the family room in their pajamas, waiting up for me. Daniel sat with them on the sofa. He moved to a chair and I took his place. Zach crawled in my lap while Jeran grabbed the huge, crocheted blanket we always kept on the edge of the sofa and spread it across the three of us. We snuggled together, drifting off to sleep. I woke up a couple hours later with a stiff neck and Zach and Jeran pressed firmly against me. Daniel sat in the same chair asleep. I awakened the boys and took them upstairs. The three of us crawled in my bed. The boys fell back asleep. I lay awake for a while, wondering what would come of my visit to an attorney.

The next morning, Daniel attempted to sneak around our room and not disturb us while getting ready for work. He failed. I awakened and just listened to him moving around, not saying anything. I did not want to talk to him just yet. Before he left, he came over to the bed, kissed the boys on the cheek and me on the lips. I lay very still, pretending not to feel it, but I did.

After Daniel left, I called the attorneys whose names I found yesterday. The fourth one could fit me in at eleven-thirty for consultation. The cost would be two hundred dollars. That kind of money would have to come out of my personal account. Daniel kept very close watch over our household account.

The boys awakened happy to be back in their own home. I cooked breakfast and called my friend, LaVonda. She answered on the first ring.

"Happy New Year, lady!" LaVonda always seemed filled with cheer.

"Happy New Year to you, too! How are you, any resolutions to break?"

"Girl, yes! I decided this would be my year to run a 5K! I am going to start training just as soon as it gets warm." She laughed at herself, knowing full well she had no desire to run a 5K.

"Since you are not going to start today, will you keep the boys for me? I have an appointment at eleven-thirty. It should only take an hour or so." I prayed she did not ask any questions.

"Sure, they can come over. What type of appointment?" She sounded suspicious.

"I would rather not say right now. I will share with you once I come back to pick up the boys."

"Uh huh, okay. But you know I don't like secrets. I will be waiting to hear all about *this* appointment."

"I promise to share and bring lunch. I will drop the boys off by eleven. Thank you, girl, I love you."

"I love you, too. See you in a little while."

When I dropped off the boys, LaVonda did not pry, but I saw the look of concern on her face. LaVonda's son, RJ, short for Richard Junior, had gone back to school after winter break today, but Jeran and Zach were happy to see her anyway. When they were with her, she made it all about them. Unlike some of my other friends' houses, hers was kid friendly and there was always something constructive and interesting for them to do.

I arrived at the nicely decorated law office of Jessica Flipmen with five minutes to spare. When I identified myself, the receptionist handed me a packet of papers to fill out and a clipboard. She instructed me to have a seat on the sturdy wood furniture with fabric upholstery and told me that it would be fifteen minutes before Ms. Flipmen would be ready to see me. I used the time to complete the papers—basic contact information, years of marriage, number of children, assets, employer, what Daniel did for a living and our estimated household income.

My stomach tightened in knots as I provided what I considered extremely personal information. Doing so made the entire situation seem all too real.

In exactly fifteen minutes, the receptionist escorted me back to Ms. Flipmen's office. I found myself looking down at a very petite woman with a girlish face. She did not appear old enough to be out of college. However, her approach offered a completely different view of her.

"Good morning, Mrs. Johnson. My name is Jessica Flipmen. Please have a seat." She pointed at a chair positioned in front of a coffee table. "How are you today?"

"I am doing well. How are you?"

"I am well, but are you really doing well? Most people that come and see me are anything but well. " She spoke in a very direct, matter of fact tone.

"I am just fine, thank you." Her forward attitude and assumptions made me uncomfortable.

"Good, how may I be of assistance to you today?" She did not look convinced.

"My husband and I have been going through a rather serious issue over the past several months and it does not seem to be getting any better. Actually, things have now gotten worse and I think that I want to file for a divorce." I rushed the last few words out of my mouth, as if I were afraid that if I didn't, I would never say them.

"I see. Do you mind expounding on the issue that has you considering divorce?" She picked up a notebook and pen up from the coffee table.

"He cheated on me with another woman and they have a child together." Tears welled. I blinked hard to keep them from falling. She pushed a box of tissue toward me.

"I see. How long ago did he start this affair? Is it still going on?" She wrote something in her notebook.

"From what he has shared their affair started over a year ago. He says that it is over, that it ended after only a few months. As far as I can tell it is, but I really have not made any effort to find out." I pulled a couple tissues from the box.

"How old is the child that he has with the other woman?" She stopped writing and focused her attention on me.

"She is three months, almost four?"

"Hmm." More writing. "Do the two of you have any children together?"

"Yes, two boys. The oldest is five and the youngest three."

"Do your children know about this other sibling?"

"Yes, they know about her. My husband gets her on the weekends."

"Hmm." She wrote some more. "Tell me what exactly occurred that makes you think you want a divorce now as opposed to when this all first happened?"

"It's not that I didn't want a divorce when it first happened. I needed to think things through," I snapped.

"It is not my intention to offend you, Mrs. Johnson, just to gather information." Her tone still matter of fact.

I continued without acknowledging what I considered an apology. "He wants the child to come and live with us."

"Has the mother agreed to this?"

"No, she has not. I do not believe she is aware of it. Her mother and sister came to see us and divulged that she is sick and needs to focus on her health. Given the nature of her illness, they thought it best that the child come and live with us, especially in the event that her mother succumbs to her illness and dies." I did not feel comfortable sharing what type of illness she had. Ms. Flipmen caught on.

"Mrs. Johnson, is this illness something that could have been passed along to your husband?" Her voice actually displayed concern.

"No, it is not, thank God."

"So, it is only the idea of the child possibly coming to live with you that has you considering divorce?"

I hesitated with my answer. "Not just the idea of her possibly coming, but the entire situation. I don't know that I can handle all of this."

"I see." She wrote something else on her notepad then looked up at me. "Have you considered going to counseling?"

"No, I am not sure that counseling will work. I think I just want to be done with this."

"Let me explain how the divorce process can go." She set her pad and pen back onto the coffee table. "In the state of North Carolina, you will have to first file for a legal separation. After one year, a divorce can be granted. Although your husband cheated, you may want to file under irreconcilable differences. Are you employed?"

"I am a freelance writer." I felt tension creep into my neck and shoulders. "I plan to seek full-time employment."

"We don't have to discuss that right now. We can talk more about that down the line. Right now, what is important for me to know is if you plan to seek full custody of your children and what assets you may have that you want to keep. In addition to that, what does your husband do for a living? Would you happen to know his yearly gross income?"

I laughed. She seemed perplexed. I explained why I laughed and provided her with the information she requested. After the meeting, Ms. Flipmen again suggested that I seek counseling with my husband before I made such a huge decision. She also told me that I would need a five thousand dollar retainer. For that, she would start the legal separation process and move forward from there. I left her office even more confused than when I had come in. It would be more complicated than I imagined.

Chapter Twenty-Five

Vaneetra

Vaneetra recovered after two days from her first round of chemo and went back into work. She still did not feel one hundred percent better, but she refused to let this illness keep her from doing what she needed to do. Summer and Courtney left after a rather unpleasant conversation the day after her treatment, but returned each morning to care for Madison. Her parents also returned, but kept their visits short. Mrs. James continued to give her unsolicited opinion whenever she felt necessary, which was all the time. Vaneetra met with and hired the nanny of her choice, Mrs. Lancaster. She appeared to be very professional, efficient and most importantly, not very social. She agreed to start on Tuesday, but would come by Monday afternoon to sign her contract.

Daniel texted Vaneetra on Friday morning, letting her know that he planned to pick Madison up around six-thirty. That evening, as she packed Madison's bag, she decided that she would tell Daniel that he needed to pay for half of the nanny expenses, which included half of the placement fee. She realized that she would need childcare regardless of her health and Daniel should have to pay half.

When he arrived, Daniel seemed tense. Vaneetra chalked it up to the way she behaved when he brought Madison home after returning from Chicago, but she did not care. "I need you to have her back no later than five o'clock on Sunday evening."

"That is no problem, but before I leave, I want to talk to you about something." She noticed he seemed to struggle to keep his tone level.

"Whatever it is, it will have to wait until I say what I have to say." She faced him with her arms crossed over her chest.

"I'm listening."

"Since I have returned to work, I will need someone to care for Madison while I am away. I do not want her at a facility with a bunch of kids that have snotty noses and germs, so I have hired a nanny. She will come in for eight hours a day, five days a week. Her salary will be one thousand dollars weekly, which is a steal. There is also a twelve-hundred-dollar placement fee. She starts Tuesday. My expectation is that you pay half, in addition to the child support you already pay." Vaneetra smirked at him.

"If you wanted me to pay half, you should have discussed that with me prior to now. I have a say in those types of matters." Daniel flexed the muscles in his jaw.

"You don't have a say in anything. We are not married. Without a court order, I don't have to consult you about any decisions I want to make, but you do have to pay."

"I can get a court order. I am a lawyer, or did you forget?"

"Look, Daniel, if you want to play games, you can also get a court order to visit her. Do you really want to play this game with me?" His attitude annoyed her.

"Actually I don't. But, I am glad you brought this up. I wondered how I would address the topic I need to discuss with you. I guess I will get straight to the point."

"Please do, I don't have all evening." She poured herself a glass of wine, took a sip, and almost choked. It tasted strange to her, like metal.

"Should you be drinking that?"

"Why shouldn't I?" She looked at him curiously. "The last I checked, I was a full grown woman and did not need permission from any one to have a drink."

"Look, your mother and sister came to see me Sunday. Your mother told me about your current situation."

"My mother and sister did what? What exactly did they tell you?" Vaneetra could feel her face and chest tighten, but she remained calm.

"They told me that you have breast cancer and had to undergo treatment." Daniel failed miserably at trying to push back the ever-rising tension in his voice.

"Son of a bitch! They had no fucking right to tell you my business. If I wanted you to know, I would have told you my damn self." Vaneetra slammed her wine glass in the sink. It shattered on impact.

"Does it matter who told me? What's important is that I know." Daniel failed at remaining calm.

"It's not important that you know. You are not my husband. You are a non-fucking factor!" She screamed at the top of her lungs.

"Look, I did not come here argue. I came to talk to you and pick up my daughter. I think that Madison should come and live with me and my family until you are done with treatment and can take care of her." He braced himself for what he knew would come next.

"You think she should do what? Did I just here you say you think my daughter should come and live with you, that bitch, and those ratty ass kids of yours? I might have cancer, but you have lost your damn mind. My daughter is not going anywhere with you. Not tonight, not ever. Now get the hell out of my house." Vaneetra hissed out the words and clinched her fists at her sides. Nausea threatened to overtake her. She took a couple deep breaths to hold it at bay. The last thing she needed was for him to see her get physically ill.

"Why don't you calm down so that we can talk about this? If you would listen to what I have to say, you will realize that it is a good idea."

"I don't care what you have to say. Get the hell out of my house."

"I am not leaving until we talk about this like mature adults."

"I said get the hell out of my house!" Vaneetra's scream pierced the air.

"Fine, I will get Madison and go." Daniel inhaled deeply, forcing his own anger down, as he walked toward the door. "Will you go and get her for me? We can finish this discussion later." He clenched his jaw open and shut.

"Did you not hear me? Are you deaf, or just stupid? I said you are not taking her anywhere."She began to push him, the wine bottle still in her hand. Daniel grabbed her arms and held her away from him.

"You better let me go, or I will call the police and have your ass arrested for assault."

"I am just protecting myself. I am not trying to hurt you."He released her arms and opened the front door.

"That won't be what I tell them. Who do you think they are going to believe, a poor woman sick with cancer or your Black ass?" Spit flew out of her mouth, as the words easily rolled off her tongue.

Daniel pulled his hands up to his chest, clinching and shaking his fist, working hard to keep his frustration at bay. He did not put it past Vaneetra to try to have him arrested. "I'll allow you to calm down and come back tomorrow for Madison."

"Allow? You can't allow me to do shit! We aren't married. I do and say as I please and I say that you are not taking her anywhere. Do you think I am stupid? You have already told me what you want. What makes you believe that I am stupid enough to think that you will give her back? You probably have a custody order ready to file." She let her rage explode all over him.

"I don't, but I know there is no point continuing to talk to you now. We will discuss this further at another time, or I will file a court order for permanent custody, sick or not." He stepped backwards out onto her stoop.

"You do what you have to do, motherfucker!" Daniel barely had enough time to duck out of the way of the wine bottle Vaneetra hurled at him and slammed the door in his face. She heard Madison crying from her nursery in the upper level, took a step away from the door and vomited all over herself and the floor. Her knees buckled and she fell. She hoped Daniel had gone and did not hear Madison's wails. She wanted to go to her baby, but her arms and legs died beneath her. She had no idea how long she stayed on the floor before her limbs regained life and she crawled up the stairs to her child. She did know that as soon as humanly possible, she would make sure that her mother and sister regretted the day they decided to butt into her business.

Chapter Twenty-Six

Shannon

After my visit with Jessica Flipmen, I stopped and picked up lunch for LaVonda, the boys, and me. During the drive back to LaVonda's, I kept envisioning having to raise Madison if I stayed and having her as a constant reminder of how I was not good enough for my husband; how I could not satisfy him. Daniel had no right to make such a monumental request of me. Just as I thought I had my mind made up, I would then think about how leaving Daniel would devastate Jeran and Zach. By the time I arrived at LaVonda's, frustration and anguish racked my mind to such a point that I could not speak without crying. Jeran and Zach cried, because they saw me crying. LaVonda took pity on me and did not ask any questions. When I calmed down enough to drive, I told her I would call her in a couple of days and fill her in on everything. I just needed time to process it all first.

As promised, I called LaVonda after a couple of days and filled her in on everything that had occurred.

"Girl, they did what? You can't be serious!" LaVonda shouted into the phone, almost bursting my eardrums.

"You heard me correctly, and no I am not kidding. Vaneetra's mother and sister came to our house."

"Is that who was at the door when you told me that you would call me back and hung up on me?"

"Yes, and I did not hang up on you, at least not intentionally. Their visit took me by complete surprise. I did not even know she had a mother and a sister. Never, in a million years, did I think that they would ask us to let Madison come and live with us."

"Really…you didn't know she had a mother? What did you think that she hatched in a sandpit somewhere?' LaVonda laughed at her own joke.

"Well…don't most snakes hatch in sandpits?" I could not resist the opportunity to be mean. Her hearty laugh bellowed through the phone like waves in an ocean.

"You know you're a fool, don't you? Tell me what else happened." She coughed the words out, trying to catch her breath.

"There is nothing to tell, really. Daniel agreed with them, I did not. The day after they came, we talked about it. He told me that in the event that Vaneetra dies, Madison would have to come and live with us anyway. I did not commit to anything, just told him to do what he had to do and I would do the same."

"What did you mean when you said that?" I heard the seriousness settling in LaVonda's voice.

"LaVonda, I do not know if I can handle having his child come and live with us. Don't you think it is too much to ask me to play Mamma to his mistress's child?"

"Why can't her family take care of the baby?"

"Mrs. James said that she and her husband are too old. She mentioned something about not agreeing with the sister's lifestyle, but I did not inquire."

"She may be a man snatcher, too."

"Maybe, but that should not prevent her from helping her sister with her child or raising her if need be."

"Well, to answer your question, under ordinary circumstances I would say that taking in this baby is ludicrous, but it seems like she needs you."

"I am so tired of hearing that! That child does not need me! My kids need me. What needs to be done is that everyone needs to realize that I am not down for playing stepmammy to Daniel's child."

"So what are you going to do? You said Daniel thinks she should come. Where does that leave you?"

"When you watched the kids for me the other day, I went to meet with a lawyer. I think I am going to file for divorce." I tried to sound matter of fact.

"I figured as much. You were pretty torn up when you got back. Have you thought about how you would take care of yourself? I don't mean to sound harsh, but you don't really have a stable job."

"LaVonda, I can get a job. I am an educated woman and my freelance writing brings in a decent amount of money. I turn down assignments." Now, I was offended.

"Okay, suppose you can get more assignments. That will take away from your being able to take care of the boys. So, their dad will be out of the home and you will have to put them in childcare. Is that really what you want to do?"

"They won't be the only children in the world living in a single parent home and in day care." My tone switched to defensive.

"No, they won't, but that would be three lives altered, yet again, by decisions from others. You may not be concerned about the little girl's life, but you should be concerned about Jeran's and Zach's."

"I am concerned about their lives. I want to protect them from all of this." The tears began to flow, again. They seemed to come more freely lately.

"Shannon, I didn't mean to upset you, but I think you are making a mistake. However, it is your decision to make. I will support you the best way that I can, either way. What did the attorney say?" I shared the details of my meeting with Ms. Flipmen, including her suggestion that Daniel and I go to counseling.

"I agree, except I think you need therapy as opposed to counseling. It couldn't hurt." Her voice perked up.

"You would, considering you are a therapist. What is the difference between therapy and counseling anyway?" I could not resist asking, even though I knew what she would say.

"A counselor talks to you about your problems and tells you how to fix them. A therapist talks you through your problems. First helping you to identify them, get to the core and then helps you to create your own resolutions and coping mechanisms." She spoke with pride for her profession.

"Well, considering we have to wait a year to actually divorce, I will consider it. Maybe it will help prepare us if we split up."

"I am going to ignore the 'help prepare us to split up' part of your comment. I know this is an unbelievable and hurtful situation to be in, but don't resolve to end your marriage over a situation that may not even come to fruition? Come on now, Shannon! You and Daniel can work through this."

"LaVonda, it is not just about this particular situation. I have been considering getting divorce ever since the wench came to my house and told me she had been sleeping with, and was pregnant by, my husband. The idea of Madison coming to live with us is the catalyst that is propelling me into action."

"I get that and understand, but something has kept you there. Figure out what it is and try to build on that. Therapy can help you with that. In the end if you still want a divorce, then at least you can say you gave it your best, because once you sign those papers there is no turning back. I would hate for you to do something that you will regret more than your husband regrets having a child that is not yours."

I hung up from LaVonda, wondering what would happen next. I am sure that Vaneetra will not agree to let Madison come and live with us, but she may not have a choice, which would force me to make one.

Chapter Twenty-Seven

Daniel

I would like to say that Vaneetra's actions surprised me, but they did not. It is not as if we had been on good terms since I broke it off with her. It took a lot for me to maintain my composure, especially when she spoke so badly about Shannon, Jeran and Zach. I wanted to slap the hell out of her when she called Shannon a bitch and my sons ratty, but I could never put my hands on a woman. After I left her house, I drove around for a while trying to calm down before I went home.

After arriving home, I went straight to my home office and stayed there until Jeran and Zach came in demanding that I wrestle with them. We played until we fell out on the floor in exhaustion and gasping for air. Shannon had gone to bed sometime earlier, leaving me to do bedtime duty alone. I was sure she suspected that I had talked to Vaneetra about Madison coming to live with us, but did not ask me anything about it. She had made it clear that she did not want that to happen under any circumstances. However, I had a responsibility to Madison, just like I did to Jeran and Zach, and I was not going to let anyone stand in the way of my being a father.

I felt a little better on Saturday. Realizing I could not make Vaneetra let Madison come and live with me, I decided against filing custody. No matter how much she infuriated me, I would not put her through that ordeal while she was fighting for her life.

The boys and I went out to breakfast, then to the Life Sciences Museum until late afternoon. They loved the interactive exhibits.

Shannon declined to go, claiming she wanted to catch up on housework. While that might have been true, I think she used it as an excuse to avoid being with me. She had not had much to say to me since Mrs. James and Vaneetra's sister came to see us. The way she had chosen to deal with this entire situation had pissed me off. I felt like she wanted me to kiss her ass and forget I had another child, so she could move on. I would not do that.

We returned home to find Shannon folding clothes. I prepared the boys a light lunch and sent them up to their playroom. I checked my email and went back to check on them. They had fallen asleep watching a movie. I figured now would have been a good time to talk to Shannon about my altercation with Vaneetra last night, even though I did not expect her to care.

"Do you have a moment for us to talk?"

"I am not doing anything other than folding these clothes, so I guess I do. What do you want to talk about?" She did not look up at me.

"I went to pick up Madison last night and used the opportunity to talk to Vaneetra about Madison coming to stay with us."

"How did that work out for you?" I knew she was being facetious, but I ignored it.

"Not well, as you may have guessed since I did not have Madison when I came home last night."

"Did you think it would go well?" She stopped folding clothes and looked up at me.

"No, I didn't, but I expected it to go better than it did." I sat on the sofa, leaned forward and placed my elbows on my knees, clasping my hands together. "Needless to say she did not agree with Madison coming to stay with us for any amount of time and threatened to not let me see her again. She stated that she hired a nanny and demanded that I pay half." I left out the parts about Vaneetra throwing a wine bottle at me and threatening to call the police. I am not sure how she would have responded and did not want to know.

"Hmm." She continued folding clothes. I could feel my face warming with frustration.

"You'll be happy to know that I am not going to push the issue, but I am going to present her with an offer to help with child care. Madison is also my responsibility."

She stopped folding the clothes again and faced me. "Look, you sound like you are on the defense. I am not going to fight with you about this. You have already demonstrated that my thoughts and feelings about decisions you make in your life do not really matter. I understand that you have a responsibility to Madison. I also know that you will help her pay for childcare expenses whether you have to or not. It is important to you that you look like a stand-up guy for those on the outside."

"I don't care about how I look to other people. I am only concerned about doing what is right!" My voice elevated almost to a holler. I had grown tired of her cheap shots about my character.

"If you were concerned about doing what is right, then we would not be having this discussion. What would have been right is for you to keep you dick in your pants."

"How long are you going to dwell on that? I am tired of apologizing to you!"

"You don't ever have to apologize again. It won't change anything, the damage has been done and you can't undo it by telling me you're sorry."

"Shannon, what do you want me to do? I am trying to make this work, but nothing I do is to your satisfaction. It seems like you don't want to move on, or you just want me to turn my back on Madison. We can't keep having this argument every time I need to do something for her."

"I do want to move on, Daniel, but you don't get to decide when I do it. We don't have to argue every time you need to do something for your daughter, but don't come at me telling me what Vaneetra demands. As long as we are still together, I am the woman you make decisions with, where as she may have you under her thumb, she does not have me."

"She does not have me under her thumb and you don't either. Don't think you are going to dictate how I take care of my daughter!" My shoulders tightened with tension.

"I am not trying to, Daniel, but what about your sons? When are you going to do what is best for them?" She threw clothes back in the basket and pushed it away.

"Everything I do is for them."

"Not everything. They would have been perfectly fine without a sister."

Thinking that this conversation was going nowhere, I stood up to walk out, but turned back. "When are you going to get over the fact that I had a child outside of our marriage?"

"You said that like you are waiting on me to get over your being late for dinner. I don't know how long it will take. How long would it take you to get over my having another man's baby?" Her voice pierced my eardrums. She shoved the basket of laundry onto the floor.

"I don't know how long it would take, but I would at least try." I managed to calm myself enough to lower my voice.

She walked up to me and stood close enough to kiss me, but that did not happen. "Can you honestly say that you would be able to forgive me for going out and having an affair with another man?"

"Yes, I can honestly say that I would." I placed my hand on her arm. She pulled away.

"Okay, so can you say that you would forgive me for getting pregnant by that man and bringing a baby home to you? You see, because I would have to bring my baby home to you and you would be responsible for it, because you are my husband. Can you really say that you could get past that and just forgive me?" She didn't wait for an answer. She pushed past me and walked out.

I never considered what I would do if Shannon cheated on me. I could not even imagine what I would do if she got pregnant by another man. I never thought that I would soon have an answer to one of my questions. All I knew was that my marriage could not take too much more stress, but I didn't see how to avoid it. I had to take care of my daughter regardless of who does not want me to.

Chapter Twenty-Eight

Vaneetra

Vaneetra woke up Saturday morning still infuriated from her altercation with Daniel the night before. Her mother and Summer had no right getting into her damn business. She found small consolation in the fact that Madison appeared to have slept through the night. She sat up on the sofa, gently stood up for a few moments, then slowly took two steps forward hoping the nausea would not return. When it did not, Vaneetra gathered Madison into her arms, took her into the kitchen to prepare her bottle and feed her. Afterward, she climbed the stairs, ran a bath, placed Madison in her bathtub chair, and bathed them both at the same time.

In order to take her mind off her mother and sister's betrayal, Vaneetra logged onto her computer and got some work done. She balanced working and playing with Madison for a few hours before giving her another bottle, after which they both took a nap. Two hours later, the sound of her doorbell woke her up. Tiptoeing down stairs with Madison in her arms, Vaneetra opened the door to find her mother and father standing on the other side. She nearly lost it.

"You have a lot of damn nerve showing up here after what you and Summer did to me!"

"What in the world are you talking about, Vaneetra? What did Summer and I do to you? Mrs. James seemed genuinely surprised.

"Oh, don't play stupid, Mother. Daniel came over here last night and told me what you did."

"Evelyn, what did you do?" Mr. James spoke gravely to his wife.

"Do we have to discuss this standing in your front door for all of your neighbors to hear?"

"Do you really think that I want you in my house? You went behind my back and did exactly what I told you not to do." Spit flew out of Vaneetra's mouth unnoticed by her. Madison began to whimper, but quieted down when Vaneetra rocked her in her arms.

"Baby girl, let us in so you can get Madison out of this cool air. We can sit down and you can tell me what is going on." Mr. James stepped in front of his wife to shield his daughter and granddaughter from the cold.

Vaneetra stood still for a moment before taking a few steps back to let her parents inside. She turned her back and walked into the living room ahead of them.

"Marshall, please take my coat and hang it up for me." Mrs. James started to take off her coat.

"That won't be necessary. You won't be staying long enough to get comfortable." Vaneetra stood in the middle of her living room, still holding Madison.

"Now hold on, baby girl. What did your mother do that was so bad that she is not welcome in your house?"

"Ask her what she did. Mother, why don't you tell Daddy what you did? He obviously does not know." She rocked from side to side, absentmindedly patting Madison's back.

"May we come and sit down first?" Mr. James asked.

"Sure, come and have a seat. You will want to be seated to hear this anyway." Vaneetra sat on the love seat, as her parents entered the living room and seated themselves on the sofa.

"Now, Evelyn, explain to me what you did that has Vaneetra so upset."

"Marshall, she is making too much of the whole situation. All I did was go and have a discussion with this Daniel person, that's all." Mrs. James clutched her purse and coat tightly.

"First of all, how in the hell did you get his address? You had no damn business going over there!" Vaneetra shouted.

"Now hold on, baby girl. I am going to have to ask you to stop using that foul language around me and your mother. I know she has done something that you don't agree with, but we are still your parents and deserve respect." Mr. James's voice held a gentle, yet firm tone.

"She does not give respect and as far as I am concerned does not deserve any, but I will stop cursing around my baby."

"Thank you." Mr. James turned back to his wife. "Now, Evelyn, go on and tell me the rest of the story. We will get to how you got this young man's address later."

"Marshall, I did what I thought was best. I had Summer take me over to this Daniel person's house and talked to him and his wife about taking care of Madison while Vaneetra is sick." Mrs. James raised her chin in defiance.

"Evelyn, now you know good and well that you had no right to do that. Vaneetra made it as plain as day that she did not want that young man involved. You overstepped your boundaries this time."

"I was only looking out for my grandchild."

"So you thought you would just give her away to her father? How is that looking out for her?" Vaneetra got up and paced the room with Madison.

"I don't think a child this young should be raised by no nanny. You plan to have some stranger taking care of her all day long.

That's just not right, Vaneetra." Mrs. James shifted in place on the sofa.

"Mother, you don't get to make that decision, I do!"

"But why would you do that, Vaneetra? Madison has a father who can care for her." Mrs. James tried to reason with her daughter.

"I don't have to explain my decisions to you. She is not going to stay with him and that is final." Vaneetra resisted the urge to curse.

"You are going to be too sick and will need more help than what you can pay for, Vaneetra. Why won't you listen?" Mrs. James stood to face her daughter.

"You don't know what I will be. I am feeling just fine now," Vaneetra lied. "Besides, how could you possibly believe having my daughter be away from me would be of any help? She is only three months old. How is not seeing her every day supposed to help me? What happened to your offer to help? Not that I want it, but have you changed your mind?"

"No we haven't, but you will need us to take care of *you*. Your father and I are getting up in age and your sister has her own life. Her work schedule gets hectic and you can't depend on her to be here every night."

"Mother, you think you know everything, but you don't. However, like a said before, Madison and I will be just fine."

"Baby girl, we will help you in any way we can. I hope that you don't get too sick, but cancer of any kind is a powerful beast. It will not go down without a fight. Your mother is right about one thing, you will need more help than even your money can pay for. She was wrong for what she did, but you need to think about how this young man can assist you."

"I already have thought about it. He is going to help me pay for a nanny. That's all I will need him to do." Vaneetra finally sat down in a chair with Madison. "I am going to be fine."

"What if you are not? You think you have it all figured out, but you don't! You're not only going to need our help, but his, too." Urgency enveloped Mrs. James's tone.

"What?" Vaneetra could not believe what she had just heard.

"What if you are not okay?" Mrs. James walked over to her daughter. "Women die from this disease every day. Sometimes they fight and fight and fight and they still die," Mrs. James said, slamming her fist at her sides with each word, her chest heaving with ragged breath. "They give it all they have and it just is not enough."

Vaneetra did not expect her mother to become so emotionally distraught. Seeing it deflated her anger a bit. "Mother, my doctor said that my prognosis is good. The tumor is operable. It is very likely that once I go through this treatment it may never come back. "

"But what if it does come back? What if it is in different places already and they just haven't found it yet?" Mrs. James sat down on the ottoman in front of Vaneetra's chair. "You may not believe this, but I love you enough to risk you never speaking to me again. That is why I went to see Madison's father." She placed her hand on Vaneetra's arm. "I can't bare the idea of burying my own child. You are going to need every ounce of energy you have to fight this thing and we will be right by your side, whether you want us here or not. You will still see Madison. She can come and be with you every day, but you need to let this man and his wife help."

Vaneetra could see the desperation and pleading in her mother's eyes, but did not change her mind. "Mother, it is not going to happen. I am not going to let his wife raise my child, not even for a little while."

"Is that what this is all about? You don't want his wife to raise your child? Didn't you know he was married when you got pregnant by him?" Mrs. James stared at Vaneetra in disbelief.

"What does that have to do with this?" Vaneetra could feel her stomach churning. She took a couple of deep breaths to try to settle it.

Mr. James spoke up. "Nothing and a lot all at the same time. What is done is done, but in the event that you take a turn for the worse, I don't think we can keep the young man from his child. However, right now, none of that is important. I am tired of all of this bickering. We are going to sit here right now and work out a schedule of who will be here to assist you on the days you have chemo." Mr. James spoke with finality.

Vaneetra went along with her father's demand, but only listened halfheartedly. Satisfied with the schedule he made up, Mr. James took his wife home, offering to take Madison for the night. An offer Vaneetra accepted even though she was still furious at her mother. Once alone, one thing her mother said stuck in her mind. What if she did not make it? Throughout all that she had processed over these past few weeks, she never once thought that she would not survive. Vaneetra sat in the living room until well past dark, staring out the window at nothing. She could not bear the thought of dying and having Daniel's bitch raise her daughter, but in the back of her mind, she knew all of that was out of her control.

Chapter Twenty-Nine

Vaneetra

On Monday, Vaneetra felt great, well enough to call and curse Summer out for butting in her business. She did not get as much satisfaction from it as she thought. Summer did not even try to defend her actions.

Believing she would feel better after her chemotherapy treatment than she had last week, she called her office and told them to expect her early afternoon. As promised, her parents were right by her side. Mrs. James stayed with Madison and Mr. James drove Vaneetra to the clinic.

At the end of her chemotherapy session, Dr. Chen stopped by to talk to her. "Hello, Ms. James. How are you today?"

"I am doing as well as to be expected given my current situation."

"How did you feel after the first round of chemotherapy last week? My office did not receive a call from you, so can I assume that all went well?"

"I felt fine." Vaneetra lied to her doctor.

"Did you experience any nausea or weakness?"

"No I did not."

"Good. Have you experienced any other symptoms such as hair or weight loss?"

"No I have not. How many more treatments do I have to have before you will perform the lumpectomy?" Vaneetra attempted to rise from her chair, but lost her grip on its arm. Dr. Chen noticed.

"Are you feeling unsteady, Ms. James?" Dr. Chen studied Vaneetra intently.

"No, I think my palms are sweaty. I feel fine. So when can I expect to have the surgery?" Vaneetra changed the subject and ignored Dr. Chen's concerned glance.

"I want you to undergo two more treatments. You are scheduled for surgery in three and a half weeks. That will give us a chance to run tests and determine if the tumor has shrunk or not."

"What happens if the tumor does not shrink?" Vaneetra fought back nausea.

"Since it is smaller than five centimeters, we can still operate, so we will move forward as planned."

"So why am I going through chemo therapy beforehand?" Vaneetra was becoming annoyed.

"We would always prefer to operate on smaller tumors so as to minimize the chance of possible complications. Ms. James, why don't you go ahead and stand up? I want to make sure that you are okay to walk." Dr. Chen took a couple steps back so that Vaneetra would have room to stand up.

"Dr. Chen, I am fine. You don't need to stay and watch me stand up and walk." Truthfully, Vaneetra did not know if she could stand and walk, and she surely did not want Dr. Chen to know this.

"I don't mind and have a few minutes before I have to be back to my office. It is better for me to know now, just in case I need to adjust your medication regimen."

Vaneetra pulled herself to the edge of the seat, not being able to hide the slight struggle in doing so. Then she gripped both ends of the chair and pushed herself up. Wavering, she got to a standing position, but did not trust herself to take a step. "See? I am fine, no problems at all." Vaneetra plastered a phony smile across her face.

"Ms. James, I noticed your struggle with standing. However, I will not change your medication regimen at this time, but please do not hesitate to inform me if your weakness worsens."

Vaneetra sighed and rolled her eyes. "If it gets to the point that I cannot bear it, I will be sure to let you know."

"Please do, because if you don't you could earn yourself a stay in the hospital. I will walk out with you. Do you have anyone to drive you home?"

"Yes, I have someone waiting for me in the lobby." Vaneetra took a cautious step. When her legs did not buckle beneath her, she dared to take another step.

"Your gait is a little unsteady, but I think you are fine to walk." They walked the rest of the way in silence. Mr. James stood when he saw his daughter entering the waiting room. He greeted Dr. Chen and offered his arm for Vaneetra to hold onto, but she declined. They walked out the door, leaving Dr. Chen standing in the middle of the waiting room, watching.

Vaneetra did not make it to work. She vomited as soon as she got to the parking garage, but refused to allow her father to do anything to help her. Mr. James felt helpless. He knew Vaneetra needed more help than she would ever admit and feared her stubbornness would cause her to suffer more than necessary. However, he felt his wife had interfered enough and did not want his daughter to shut them out completely. He resolved to keep quiet and stay close, just in case she got to the point of not being able to turn down his help.

On the way home, Mr. James stopped and bought saltine crackers and ginger ale. He remembered that it helped soothed both his wife's and Vaneetra's upset stomachs when they were pregnant. He figured an upset stomach was an upset stomach no matter the cause.

At home, Vaneetra accepted the ginger ale and crackers and even followed her mother's suggestion to take a nap upstairs. They stayed with Madison until Summer and Courtney arrived later that evening. Vaneetra, still angry with her sister, did not make an effort to be sociable. Summer decided to leave.

"Courtney, will you wait in the car? I will be there shortly"

"Yes, good night, Vaneetra. I made you some homemade chicken soup that you can add rice to. I left the rice in a separate pot, just in case having it in the soup is too much. There are also crackers on the counter. I put a few bottles of water in the fridge, on the counter and upstairs in a small cooler on your nightstand for Madison."

"Thank you, Courtney. I really appreciate your help and your decision to not interfere in my personal life."

Knowing Vaneetra directed the last part of her comment toward Summer, Courtney walked out to the car.

"Vaneetra, you are moving around okay and can't seem to be polite, so I am going to leave you alone this evening. Call me if you need anything. I won't let your bad attitude stop me from being available to you." Summer stood near the front door while Vaneetra sat on the sofa holding Madison.

"How poetic, you could be a romance novelist." Vaneetra's voice dripped with sarcasm.

"And you can be an ungrateful bitch!" Summer slammed the door behind her.

Vaneetra sat on the sofa for a while. She did not want to tell anyone that she really struggled today. She told herself that she did not need them. The nanny would be starting tomorrow and her family would not need to come by again.

Her cell phone rang. Vaneetra looked at the caller ID. It was her father. Opting to stave off an unwanted visit, she answered the phone.

"Hello, Daddy."

"Hi, baby girl. Summer called and told us she left. Are you okay? Do you want me to come to pick up Madison or stay the night?"

"No, Daddy, we are fine. I am going to feed Madison, fix myself a bowl of the soup Courtney made for me and go to bed." Vaneetra put Madison down and started to rise from the sofa, but this time she lost her footing and fell back, dropping the phone. She scrambled to pick it up, hoping her father did not realize what had happened.

"Baby girl! Baby girl, are you alright? What just happened?" Urgency filled Mr. James's voice.

"Yes, Daddy, I am alright. I dropped the phone when I leaned over to lay Madison on the sofa." She lied.

"Okay, I will let you get on with what you have to do. Call me if you need me. I will be up for quite a while tonight, working on some things around the house." Vaneetra could tell she had not convinced her father, but appreciated his willingness not to press the issue.

They disconnected the call and Vaneetra attempted to stand again. This time she did not lose her footing. Chalking up her last slip as poor footing, she walked with a slightly unsteady gate to the kitchen. Courtney remembered to place baby bottles of water on the kitchen counter, but not any formula. Vaneetra reached above her head to get it down out of the cabinet and the entire room began to spin. The formula and Vaneetra both crashed to the floor.

Vaneetra opened her eyes to a stark white light and a piercing beeping sound. The last thing she remembered was being in her kitchen, getting ready to fix Madison a bottle.

"Madison! Oh my, God, where is my baby?" Vaneetra cried out, trying to hoist herself out of whatever had her pinned down, but a sharp pain overwhelmed her senses, causing her to slam her head back against whatever object she was laying on.

"Baby girl, Madison is okay. She is just fine and the doctor said you will be fine, too." Mr. James placed his hand onto his daughter's shoulders, preventing her from rising up again.

"Daddy?"

"Yes, baby girl."

Vaneetra thought she heard her father's voice quiver.

"Daddy, how did you get inside of my house and why is the light so bright? Why can't I get up?" Panic crept in Vaneetra's voice, as she slowly began to realize that she was not on the kitchen floor.

"Honey, you are not at home. You and Madison are both at the hospital." Mr. James rubbed his daughter's shoulders, trying to sooth the fear he could hear rising in her voice.

"The hospital? Why are we here? What happened to us? I have to go see about my baby." Vaneetra opened her eyes again, but immediately closed them to block out the light. Her heart was pounding against her rib cage, as if trying to escape. She tried to get up again, but sharp pains stabbed her behind her eyes and the back of her skull when she moved her head even a little bit.

"Calm down, Vaneetra, and just relax. I didn't like what I heard when I was talking to you earlier on the phone, so I decided to ride over and see about you. When I got to the front door, I could hear Madison screaming her head off. I rang the doorbell and banged on the door, but you never came. So I came into the house through the garage and found the baby on the floor in the living room and you on the floor in the kitchen."

"On the floor? What happened?

"The ER doctor thinks you passed out. You must have hit your head because there was blood all over the floor. I think Madison rolled off the sofa and hit the floor, because her blanket was still on it. I called 911 and the ambulance brought you both here."

"Daddy, I have to get out of here. I have to go and see about my baby." She knew her words were futile. She could not even open her eyes.

"Vaneetra, Madison is fine. However, we had to call her father."

"You did what?" Vaneetra screamed, causing searing pain to overtake her face and all of her senses. The pain was so severe she thought her nose had begun to bleed. She feebly wiped at it, causing her arm to sting where the IV needle penetrated it.

"Vaneetra, we had to call him in order for the doctor to be able to treat Madison. The doctor asked if you were married. When I told him that you were not, he asked if I knew how to get in touch with Madison's father, because he had to sign papers for her to be treated. I did not want to lie, so I called him. Baby girl, I did not want to do it, but I couldn't lie either."

A nurse entered the room, took Vaneetra's vitals and administered something from a syringe into her IV line. Vaneetra began to object, but drifted back into a deep sleep before she could speak a single word. The next time she opened her eyes, Daniel sat at her bedside, his face tight with worry and concern.

"What in the hell are you doing here? I don't want you here." Her voice cracked from dryness.

"I came to see about you."

"Where is my daughter?"

"*Our* daughter is fine. She had a small bruise on the left side of her head, but no broken bones or concussion. The doctor discharged her into my care yesterday."

"They did what? They can't do that. I am going to sue their asses," Vaneetra yelled at Daniel. Pain shot through her skull.

"They can and they did. I brought all of the necessary paperwork to prove that I am her father. Since you have been in and out of consciousness the past two days, I needed to make a decision in regards to her care." Daniel kept his voice calm so as not to upset Vaneetra any more than he knew she would already be, but his jaw tensed so tightly he could feel a headache coming on.

"Take her to my mother's, the nanny is ready to start. We don't need your help."

"I didn't come here to get into another argument with you, but you are done making decisions. Your refusal to allow me, or apparently anyone else, to help you almost cost you your life and hurt our daughter. I have no control over you, but I do have a say when it comes to Madison. She is at my house and will remain there for the time being. You can't take care of her and yourself."

"I hired a nanny, you asshole!" Vaneetra's anger threatened to overtake her judgment.

"Yes, your mother told me that she was due to start yesterday. I asked her to go to your house, wait on this person, and provide her with my contact number. I told the nanny you hired that there had been a change of plans and that her services would not be needed. I agreed to send her two weeks' pay and take care of the placement fees with the agency. No need to thank me. I know you don't appreciate it."

"Go to hell, you bastard. You are going to give me my daughter back." Vaneetra tried to sit up in her hospital bed, but the pain forced her back down. It was not as bad as before, but it still hurt.

"I am not trying to steal her from you, but I am going to keep her safe. When you get better, we will talk. I'm leaving now. I will have my paralegal bring documents to your house in a few days for you to sign. Your mother has asked me if she could keep Madison while I am at work so that she can bring her to see you daily while you go through treatment. I am completely okay with that, but I have to have assurance that you will not try to pull any tricks and not send her back. If you sign the papers, you will see her every day. If you don't, you will only see her on the weekends when I can bring her to you." Daniel rose from his chair to leave.

"How dare you threaten me? Who in the hell do you think you are? I'm not signing a damn thing. You will be hearing from my lawyer."

"I look forward to it. If you want to take this to court, we can. Whom do you think the judge will side with? You could have died, or has that not registered to you yet? From what your family told me, you lost a lot of blood when you were unconscious on your kitchen floor. Like I said before, when you are better, we will negotiate a more suitable custody agreement for the both of us. Until then, Madison stays with me."

"Get the hell out of my room. This shit isn't over." Vaneetra picked up an empty bedpan and used what little strength she had to throw it at Daniel as he walked out. She ran her hand through her hair in frustration, only to cry when she pulled back a hand full of it. The sight of her hair in her hand brought forth a rush of emotion that she could not force back. She turned her heaving body and pressed her face into the flat pillow, sobbing and wailing, barely able to catch her breath. Her nurse entered her room, but quickly ducked out unnoticed. Vaneetra finally grieved. She finally released all of her fears of dying, of not being able to raise her daughter. When her tears subsided, her eyes were swollen and her body exhausted. With having nothing left, she slept.

Chapter Thirty

Daniel—Three Months Later

"Man, I haven't slept in weeks." Daniel yawned, got out of his chair and began pacing in his office.

"Shouldn't Madison be sleeping through the night by now?" Josh leaned against Daniel's office door, watching his friend.

"She sleeps just fine, but I have to do everything for her. As soon as I leave the office, I have to swing by Vaneetra's parents' house and pick her up; where I have to wait thirty minutes to get a complete run down of her day. Then when I get home, I play with the boys, feed Madison, give her a bath and put her to bed. By that time, its ten o'clock and I have to go work on my cases. I can't keep up with the schedule."

"Is Shannon still refusing to help you?" Josh walked further into the room.

"She will do small things, but not much. These days we don't even talk."

"You have to give her more time."

"Give her more time for what? Madison has been with us three months and she has known about her a year. How much more time does she need?"

Josh shrugged. "As long as it takes is all I can tell you. You will have to figure out the rest by talking to Shannon."

"She won't talk to me. On the weekends, she takes the boys and disappears for hours at a time. She will do their laundry and hers, but not ours. Do you know she won't even pick up formula and diapers when she goes grocery shopping? The other night, Madison ran out of formula and I had to take her with me to buy some at midnight."

"Look, man, this whole situation is going to take you a lot longer to fix than it took you to mess up. You might as well buckle in for the long ride. Instead of thinking of all the things that Shannon does not do for Madison, focus on what she will do and go from there."

"The only thing she will do is hold her; and that is only when the boys want to spend time with her and I am busy doing something else."

"Okay, so she is promoting a bond between Madison and her brothers. You have to give her credit for that."

"How is that promoting a bond?" I wasn't following Josh's line of reasoning.

"Look, my sister is a child development professor and loves to talk about this kind of stuff. She has always said that touch is very important in the early stages of child development. If Shannon holds Madison and spends time letting the boys play with her, it is probably going a long way with building a bond between them. I am no expert, but that is what I think. Does she do anything else?"

"I guess you have a point." I leaned back in my chair. "She will give her a bottle and feed her sometimes. Last week she suggested that I start buying baby food. I did and came back with the wrong kind. She did take it back and buy the right stuff."

"The wrong kind? What did you get?"

"She said I got stage two and all fruit and that Madison needed a mix of stage one fruit and vegetables."

"She's doing some things to help you out, but you can't expect too much from her. It may not seem like it to you, but she does not have to do anything."

"I wish she would just get over being so damn bitter…enough already. I can't change the past." I picked up a pen and tossed it across my desk. "Plus I am still the breadwinner in the family."

"Look, man, you got yourself in to this situation, now you have to step up and take care of your child. Like it or not, Shannon is not obligated to help you."

"She has made that clear."

"I have a couple more questions for you then I have to prepare to meet with a client." Josh walked back to my office door.

"Go ahead and ask them."

"Do you think that you are having such a hard time, because this is the first time you have been the primary caregiver of one of your children?"

"That's nonsense. I am the primary caregiver for all of them, Shannon included! I work and pay all of the bills." I looked at him as if he had gone crazy.

"No, hothead…you are the primary provider. Need I remind you that your wife does contract work? However, a primary caregiver is the person that actually physically takes care of a person. Until now, you have spent most of your time working. She runs the house and takes care of the boys."

"Where do you get this stuff?" I looked at him in disbelief.

"My sister, she talks about this stuff all of the time. Some of it makes sense." He shrugged again.

"How hard can it be to cook, clean and entertain our kids all day?"

"It must be extremely difficult, considering the fact that you are complaining about having to do it." Josh laughed and walked to the door.

"What's so funny? I am doing all of that and working sixty hours a week!"

He looked at me for a moment. "You know, maybe you should take some time to consider just how much you value your wife."

"I don't have to think about that. I value her. I appreciate how she takes care of our home and the boys. I just wish she would get over this whole Vaneetra situation already. Her attitude is getting really tiresome."

"Daniel, you just minimized everything Shannon does for your family like it is easy, but you can't seem to do it. Maybe that is one of the reasons you cheated. Maybe you don't value her enough."

Realizing that I was debating with the other best attorney in Raleigh, I conceded to his point. "Okay, I see you point. I don't agree, but I will think about it."

"Look, all I am saying is that while Shannon may not have accepted the fact that you have this child, it is not the real issue. The real issue is what you think of your wife, and why you thought Vaneetra was worth the risk of losing her. Taking care of Madison by yourself and working a full-time job is just your reality right now. Work on fixing your marriage and your reality can change."

I threw up my hands. "Whatever, man! I can't fix this. She has to want to work things out. It doesn't seem to me like she does. What was your second question?"

"You have to give her time, Dan. This is not about you and what you want." He walked over and palmed my shoulder. "The temporary custody order I filed for you will expire soon. What do you want to do about that? That was my second question."

"We are going to need to extend it. I met with Vaneetra over the weekend and she begrudgingly informed me that her doctor ran more tests after her lumpectomy and found more cancerous cells. She will have to continue chemo for at least a couple more months."

"Man, I am really sorry to hear that. I will get a court date and take care of it."

"Thanks, I appreciate it. Vaneetra is not happy, but she is smart enough to realize that she has to focus on getting better."

"Does Shannon know that Madison will be staying longer?"

"Not yet. I plan to talk to her about it this evening."

"Good luck with that!"

My intercom buzzed and Josh walked back to his office.

"Yes, Susan?"

"Mr. Johnson, your two o'clock appointment just called and said that he has to reschedule. He wants to meet this evening at five-thirty. He emphasized that it is important that he meets with you today." This was the last thing I needed. I usually picked up Madison by six. This meeting will take hours. "Okay, go ahead and reschedule for this evening. Please tell him that I have another engagement at eight and will need to end at seven-thirty."

I called Mrs. James and arranged to pick up Madison later. "Eight-thirty is fine, Daniel. Madison is running a slight fever, but I gave her some medicine and she seems to be doing a little better."

"Thanks for doing that. Please continue to check her temperature. If it gets any worse, I will come and pick her up." I hoped that I would not have to pick her up. This was a big client for our firm and putting him off could cost us a lot of money. Money I could not afford to lose.

"Daniel, I have raised two children, I know what I am doing," she snapped at me and returned to normal just as quickly. "I am keeping her away from Vaneetra. Lord knows that she cannot afford to catch a cold or anything else." Mrs. James sounded tired.

"Have there been any other developments since I talked with her this past weekend?"

"She had a very rough day. Her side effects seem to be getting worse." I could hear what I took as worry in Mrs. James's voice.

"Mrs. James, I could ask my wife to come and pick up Madison, if it is too much for you to handle." Not that I thought Shannon would actually do it, but if I had to, I would ask her. "I am sorry to have to ask you to keep her longer than usual."

"Boy, don't be sorry. I enjoy any time I can get with my grandbaby. Vaneetra is asleep right now. She took a couple of pain pills and they knocked her right out. Summer will be here shortly. If Madison does not feel better by the time Vaneetra wakes up, I will have Summer take her to your wife, if you don't mind, or she could just take her home and keep her overnight."

"It is okay for Summer to take her to Shannon, if need be." I lied.

"Are you sure?" I could hear the skepticism in her voice.

"Of course I am sure. Besides, none of you can afford to get sick while helping Vaneetra." I hoped she would go with the change of subject and not press the issue of how Shannon would feel.

"That is very true. I did not think of that. Vaneetra needs all of the help she can get. She fell again yesterday. Marshall was not here, so Summer and Courtney picked her up and put her back in the bed."

"I am sorry to hear that. Let me know if I can help." I said it with sincerity.

Mrs. James chuckled. "Boy, I think you better just focus on being a father to Madison. To try and do anything for Vaneetra might get you hurt by your wife, if Vaneetra does not use all of her strength to do it herself." I knew Mrs. James had a point. I thanked her again before ending the call.

Next, I called Shannon and got straight to the point. She agreed to care for Madison if needed until I got home, which I wasn't expecting. I did not question her sudden change of heart. I simply thanked her and got off the phone, before she had time to realize what she had agreed to. Maybe Joshua was right after all and all Shannon needed was more time…maybe.

Chapter Thirty-One

Shannon

Not sure why I made the suggestion, but I called Daniel and told him to tell Mrs. James to go ahead and send Madison to me. It was not as if I had been taking up a whole lot of time with her. However, I have enough sense to know that she does not need to be around her mother if she is sick. That would only delay the process of her going back home. However, I don't mind helping out with her every now and then. I am not a monster. At least, I do not think that I am.

He never called me back to let me know if someone would be bringing Madison to me or not. The doorbell rang at about six-thirty.

"I will get it!" Zach ran from the kitchen to the front door with Jeran right on his heels.

"No, you will not! I will get it." I ran to catch up with them and opened the door. Summer stood on the other side with Madison in one arm and her car seat in the other.

"Good evening, Summer, come in." I stepped back so that she could get through the doorway.

"Can I carry this for you?" Jeran grabbed hold of the car seat.

"You sure can, little guy." Summer released it and Zach took hold of the other side, walking with Jeran to the living room. Madison squirmed in Summer's free arm, whining and sneezing.

"Why don't you take her to the family room?" I closed the front door and led the way to the back of the house. "She does not seem to be doing any better."

"No she is not. Her fever has gone up to 101. We don't want to trouble you and would keep her, but we cannot afford for Vaneetra to catch whatever she has. We know you have your own kids to worry about." Summer stood in the middle of the family room, rocking Madison.

"It is no problem. The boys will be fine. Why don't you sit down and take her jacket and hat off?"

"I can't imagine that it is not a problem. Why would you want to take care of my niece?" Summer sat down, but never took her eyes off me.

I intentionally strayed away from the underlying question. "I don't mind helping under these circumstances."

"You were not exactly all open arms the last time I was here. What changed?" She removed Madison's jacket, but kept her hat on. I walked over to the fireplace to start a fire, wanting to get rid of the now noticeable chill in the air.

"Summer, I would not have chosen this situation for myself, but it is what it is. I am not a monster and would never mistreat Madison. Daniel told me she was sick and I know having her around her mother is not a good idea." I tossed a match onto the logs and watched them slowly catch fire.

"I can respect that. I can only imagine what you are going through. Anyway, I am going to take tomorrow off, so that I can keep her for my mother. I am almost out of days, but I have to do what I have to do." She stood and handed me Madison. I wondered why she chose to share that last piece of information with me. She did not seem to be trying to manipulate me into volunteering to keep her.

"I know this situation must be as hard on your family as it is on mine. You do not have to take off work. I will speak with Daniel tonight and we will work it out. If need be, she can stay here with me and Zach. He loves having her around. Summer may not have been trying to manipulate me, but it did not stop me from feeling guilty and offering to keep Madison. Damn, Daniel!

Jeran and Zach must have grown impatient with our conversation, because they started clamoring around Summer, trying to get to Madison. I asked them to get one of her blankets from the ottoman so that I could lay her on the floor and they could watch her while I let Summer out. They happily obliged, quickly working together. Summer placed Madison in the middle of the blanket and put her pacifier in her mouth.

"She is not feeling well. We are going to take her upstairs, give her a bath and try to put her to sleep early. Who wants to help me?" They both eagerly volunteered to be my helpers. "Great! I am glad I have my two big boys to help me out tonight. Be careful with her and I will be right back."

"Okay, Mom." Jeran sat beside Madison and held one of her hands. Zach lay on the other side rubbing her head.

Summer said good-bye to the boys and I walked her to the front door. "Are you sure? I could also ask my girlfriend. She would not mind." Something told me that she meant girlfriend as in lover and not just a friend who is a girl, but I did not pry.

"Yes, I am sure. You guys should focus your time and resources on Vaneetra."

"Don't tell me you are concerned about my sister's well-being!" I could sense the sarcasm.

"I can't stand your sister. But, she is fighting for her life and does not need to acquire any type of infections." I decided honesty worked best.

"Point taken, thanks for being honest." Before leaving, Summer offered to take Jeran and Zach on an outing sometime, stating she and her girlfriend would be happy to do it as long as I don't have a problem with lesbians. I decided to stay the honest course and politely told her that I do not have a problem with lesbians, but I am not eager to integrate our families and would rather keep them separate. She expressed understanding of my feelings, but made it clear that as long as Jeran and Zach were her niece's brothers, the offer would always be available and made sure to tell me that whether I liked it or not, we are all family now. She bid me good night and let herself out. For a long time after she left, I thought about how I felt about her last comment. Whether I liked it or not, our families were forever linked.

As promised, the boys helped me bathe Madison and get her dressed for bed. I put the three of them in the bed with me, one boy on each side of a fussing squirming Madison. Jeran and Zach did the best they could to quiet her. My heart wretched, watching them dote over her. I know they will miss her when she goes back home to live with Vaneetra. Although, Daniel and I have not discussed it, I imagine that she will be leaving soon. He told me she had the lumpectomy done and are on the last of her chemo treatments, but that is all he ever said. I would not be surprised if he tried to make this a permanent arrangement.

"Mommy, Maddie is hot!" Zach's statement brought me out of my thoughts.

"She has a slight fever, sweetie. Her body will feel a little warm to the touch." I tried to reassure him.

"No, Mom she is really hot. Come and feel for yourself." Concern etched Jeran's face. I placed my hand on her little body. The boys were right, she felt warm through her pajamas. Her cheeks flamed bright red and sweat plastered her hair to her head.

"Okay, boys, I want you to watch Madison while I go in the bathroom and get the thermometer and some cool towels. When I come back, we are going to take off her pajamas and just keep her in a t-shirt and diaper." I went to the bathroom and returned quickly. For the sake of not making them uncomfortable with this process, I placed the thermometer under Madison's arm. It read one hundred and three degrees.

"Is that bad, Mom?" Jeran asked.

"Is it bad, Mommy?" Zach repeated his brother's question.

"Not too bad, but Mommy needs to get Madison out of these pajama's so she can cool off and give her some more medicine." Realizing that I did not ask Summer what medicine they had given Madison and when, and not having her number, I called Daniel to ask him to find out for me. He did not answer. I sent him a text message, telling him that it was important for him to call home immediately. Five minutes later, the phone rang.

"Shannon, what's going on?" I could not tell if I picked up concern or annoyance.

"Madison has a fever of one hundred and three degrees. May I have her grandmother's number so that I can call and find out when they last gave her medication and what they gave her?"

"Does it matter what they gave her? I'm coming to take her to the Emergency Room." I definitely picked up annoyance that time. I tried to explain to him that if I knew what she had been given, she might not need to go to the emergency room, because I would know what to give her, but he refused to listen. I became annoyed by the complete disregard of my opinion on the matter. He acted as if I did not know what I was talking about. "I would rather just take her to the emergency room. Her temperature seems really high"

Since Madison technically is not my child and I am just a placeholder for her mother, I decided not to argue. "You are right,

Daniel. It is high, but may not warrant a trip to the emergency room. However, do as you please. The boys and I are to keep cool towels on her forehead and back until you get here. You will still need to get that information from her grandmother so that you can tell the doctor at the hospital."

"I think taking her to the emergency room is best, so that is what I am going to do."

"You won't get any argument from me. She is your daughter and you can do as you please." I could not hide my sarcasm.

He picked up on it. "Can we not do this right now?"

"We are not doing anything right now."

"I don't need the sarcasm or you reminding me that she is not your daughter."

I looked over at the kids to find Jeran and Zach staring me in the face and quickly changed the direction of the conversation. I told him to call when he got within five minutes of the house so that I could have her ready to go and made sure to say good-bye, hoping that our sons would not noticed that their father had thoroughly pissed me off.

"Mommy, is Daddy coming to see about Maddie?" Zach crawled across the bed and sat next to me.

"Yes, baby, Daddy is on his way home." Madison's wails permeated every part of the room. I struggled to keep my voice even. Daniel had a lot of damn nerve to question my ability to take care of a sick child. I was the one who took care of our sons when they got sick. I placed the cool towels on Madison's back. She screamed even louder.

"Mommy, where is Dad taking Maddie?" Jeran yelled over Madison's screams.

"He is going to take Madison to the hospital, but before he gets here we are going to get her calmed down and cooled off." I reached across the bed, picked her up and put her pacifier in her mouth. "Come on, boys, we are going to take her downstairs and make her a bottle of juice with ice. That will help." I looked over at the boys only to see them weeping.

"Is Maddie going to be all right, Mommy? I don't want her to go to the hospital." Zach buried his face in the side of my shirt.

"Mommy, I want to go with Maddie to the hospital. I want to make sure she is okay." Jeran wiped the tears from his eyes, trying to be brave.

"Let's just try and get her calm and when Daddy gets home, maybe he will change his mind." I cursed Daniel inside of my head. He could be a real idiot at times. The boys followed me downstairs to the kitchen, sniffling all the way. Madison fussed and squirmed.

"Jeran, can you help me make Madison a bottle of juice?"

"Yes, Mommy." He rushed to the counter and grabbed a bottle, eager to help, making sure to put ice in it.

"Mommy, I will get the juice. I saw Daddy put some in the frigerator yesterday." Zach ran to the refrigerator, pulled it open and grabbed a small bottle of juice from one of the lower shelves on the door. They both ran back to the table, where I sat with their sister. Like a big boy, Jeran made the bottle, but let Zach feed it to Madison, while I held her in my arms. She sucked fervently until she emptied the bottle, only stopping once to catch her breath. I held her close to my left shoulder and gently patted her bottom until she burped. The juice calmed her some, but she started to sneeze and cough, which in turn made her cry again. Ten minutes later, the house phone rang.

"Are you almost here?" I did not bother with niceties.

"No, should I be?" Mrs. James laughed as she spoke.

"Oh, Mrs. James, my apologies, I thought you were Daniel. He is on his way to come and take Madison to the Emergency Room."

"Yeah, he called and told me and to ask what medication I had given her."

"Good, the doctor at the hospital will need that information." I stood up and paced the room with Madison.

"Chil', that baby don't need to go to no hospital. I know you know that." I imagined her waving her hand in the air in a dismissive manner.

"Yes, I do, but that is what Daniel prefers to do." I sighed with exasperation.

"Who cares what he prefers? I gave her some infant Tylenol about an hour before she left. Now you know, too, and can go on and do what you need to do."

"Thank you, but Daniel should be here shortly. I will let him take her to the hospital."

"You will do no such thing! Give that baby whatever you planned to give her and go lay her down somewhere. Grow a backbone. Just because you are not Madison's real mom does not mean you don't know how to be a mother. You already got two kids and they seemed healthy enough to me that time I saw them. Now go and do what you know how to do and be a mother. I will call and check on her in the morning. Good-bye." She hung up the phone. I knew Mrs. James was right, but I did not feel like I needed to argue with Daniel over his girlfriend's child.

I waited a few more minutes, but Madison's body continued to grow warmer to the touch. I asked the boys to make her another bottle of juice and took her upstairs to give her more medication. If Daniel still wanted to take her to the hospital when he got here, he could. Until then, I would do what I knew was best. The boys came up after a few minutes with the bottle. Madison began to drink it, but finally fell asleep after a couple of minutes. Seeing that she had fallen asleep, Jeran and Zach dozed off as well.

About twenty minutes went by when the house phone rang again. Figuring it was Daniel and not wanting to move for fear of waking up Madison, I ignored it. Exactly five minutes after that, I heard the door chimes, signaling his arrival. He ran up the stairs and into our bedroom.

"Why don't you have her ready?" I did not have to imagine his annoyance; I saw it all over his face.

"Mrs. James called to check on Madison. She told me that she had given her Tylenol an hour before Summer brought her here, so I gave her a dose of infant ibuprofen. The two can be given intermittently as long as it is done a few hours apart. She had one bottle and part of another and fell asleep. I did not want to wake her. She has been cranky since she got here." I never bothered to look at him again.

"Well, I think I should still take her to the hospital. That fever has me worried." He started toward the bed, but I stopped him, asking him to get the thermometer off the dresser so that I could take Madison's temperature. He obliged. I sat on the bed, trying not to move and watched him drag his body back across the room. He looked like he could use a weeks' worth of sleep. I felt no sympathy.

"Do as you please, but Jeran wants to go and you will have to sit for hours. An infant with a low grade fever will not be priority." I rolled my eyes at him, while I placed the thermometer under Madison's arms. She squirmed a little, but did not awaken.

"Shannon I don't think one hundred three degrees would be considered a low grade fever. Why are you trying to talk me out of taking her?"

"First off, by the time you get her to the hospital her fever will not be one hundred three. Since I gave her the ibuprofen and her grandmother gave her the acetaminophen, it will likely be lower. Even if it does not go down any more, a couple of hours from now whoever takes care of her at the hospital will more than likely give her another dose of something and you will still have to wait. Secondly, I am not trying to keep you from taking her. I am trying to help. I do a very good job with your other two kids. There is no need to question my abilities now!" I whispered loudly, hoping not to awaken any of the kids. Before he could say anything else, the thermometer beeped. I looked at it and gave it to him.

He read the display. "It's down to one hundred two, but that is still pretty high."

"It has only been thirty minutes. Why don't you go and rest on the sofa for about an hour or so, then come back and check on her? If her fever is not down more by then, take her to the hospital. If it is, just call her pediatrician in the morning and make an appointment for a sick visit." Zach stirred next to me. I absentmindedly rubbed the top of his head to sooth him. Daniel paced back and forth. "Look, make up your mind before you wake the three of them up." My exasperation was apparent in my voice.

He seemed to contemplate my suggestion for a few moments. "Okay, I will wait. Do you want me to take her?" He reached down and touched her hand. I started to give her to him, but before I could, Jeran woke up asking Daniel if he could go to the hospital with him and Madison. When Daniel told him that they did not have to go right away, Jeran asked his father to come and lay next to him. He told Daniel to let me hold Madison for a while. My kids' innocence continued to amaze me daily. They loved so easily and just assumed that everyone else did as well.

"You can stay in here. I think we will all fit." I adjusted myself on my pillows, careful not to wake up Madison. Daniel walked over to the other side of the bed, turning out the light on the way.

Before he settled in, he reached over and placed his hand on top of mine. I could feel an ache take hold of my heart and tears welling. The darkness of the room hid them as they rolled down my cheeks.

"Just so you know, I recognize that you are an excellent mom to our boys and are trying to help. I should not have insinuated that you were trying to keep me from taking Maddie to the hospital."

I did not respond to him. I couldn't.

When everyone settled on the bed, around Zach who never actually woke up, I drifted off to sleep, tears drying on my face, with my husband's baby in my arms, thinking, *I am a stepmother to a child younger than my own, because I married an idiot.*

Chapter Thirty-Two

Daniel

I woke up to find Shannon and the kids were gone. My phone buzzed in my pocket. I pulled it out and answered it. "This is Daniel Johnson."

"Where is my daughter?" Vaneetra did not bother being polite.

"She is with Shannon and our boys." I decided two could play her game.

"Where the hell are they and why isn't she with you?" Her hostility was really getting old.

"We are all at home. They are downstairs and I am upstairs. What do you want, Vaneetra? I don't have time to argue with you today." I sat up and swung my feet to the floor.

"Don't take that tone with me. Bring me my daughter." I could imagine her sneering.

"She is sick. I am going to take her to her doctor this morning and if he says it is okay, I will bring her to you." I walked inside of our closet and pulled a pair of slacks and button down shirt off their hangers.

"I don't give a damn what her doctor says. Bring me my damn baby, you bastard. I don't want that bitch of yours anywhere near her!"

"I have had enough of this. You obviously are not thinking clearly. I will talk to you after I come from the doctor." I disconnected that call. It amazed me that she could still be so hateful, considering how sick she appeared to be. I barely see her when I go over, but last week when I picked up Madison, she was sitting in her living room holding her. She wore a silk scarf on her head, but I could tell that all of her hair had fallen out, even her eyebrows. She also looked to weigh about fifty pounds less. I could tell she was very embarrassed by her appearance, but that did not stop her from being nasty.

I knew I needed to talk to her about the custody. She somehow managed to hire an attorney who contacted our office with threats. Josh responded with a custody agreement that gave me full physical custody until her doctor stated that she was able to resume parenting duties. When she was better, I was willing to share physical custody. Her attorney had yet to respond. I had not spoken to Shannon about it yet. I felt it was still too soon to bring it up with her. Last night was the first time she had any real involvement with Maddie since she came to live with us, and I messed that up big time.

I took a quick shower and got dressed. Vaneetra blew up my phone for the next hour, maxing out my voicemail box with messages that I was sure would make even a sailor's ears burn. I deleted them, without listening to any. I went downstairs to find it empty. Shannon, Madison and the boys were gone. I pulled my cell phone out of my pocket to call her, but stopped when I heard the garage door rise. I went to the door and waited until she got out of the truck.

"Where did you go?" It came out more accusatory than I intended, but I wondered why she would take Madison out knowing she was sick.

"I took Jeran to school like I always do." She walked around the front of the car to the rear, passenger side door.

"Why didn't you wake me up?"

"I did wake you up, but you went back to sleep." She opened the car door, leaned in and unfastened Maddie's car seat from its base.

"Where is Zach?"

"I dropped him off with Ms. Whitmore for a few hours. I have a project to finish." She rolled her eyes at me.

"You know she is sick, you should have woke me up again, instead of taking her out." By now, Shannon stood in front of me with Maddie's car seat separating us. She shoved it at me, but not hard enough to startle Maddie.

"Look, I did not have time to keep trying to wake you up. You are a grown man who knows how to set an alarm. Will you move out of my way so that I can get into the house?"

I stepped out of the door way, but continued the conversation.

"If you really wanted to, you would have woke me up. I just don't understand why you didn't."

She turned back and looked at me. "What are you insinuating?"

"I am not insinuating anything. I am just trying to understand your reasoning. What's the problem in that?"

"Let me ask you a question." She put her hand on her hip.

"Go ahead and ask."

"What do you think I do with Jeran or Zack when they get sick?" I saw the tears forming, but she blinked to keep them from falling. "You don't stay here and help me with them, so exactly what do you think I do with them?"

"Shannon, you are getting off topic, we are talking about Maddie." I tried to avoid acknowledging the point she was clearly making.

"I am not getting off topic. It is the same issue. I take them with me. Not once have you ever volunteered to go in to work late or stay home and help me with them. In case you haven't noticed, we don't have a nanny, I am it!" She failed at hiding her tears. I knew they were tears of anger. "You've been a pappy for fifteen minutes and now you are questioning me about my parenting skills. You have not taken issue with them during the past five years, why now? Do you believe that I don't know what to do with your precious little daughter or that I would intentionally harm her? When one of our sons is sick, I have to take them both out and they always manage to live through the experience. I don't imagine that your daughter is any different!" She turned and walked away. I followed.

"Shannon, I am not questioning your parenting skills. I just asked a question. Can we please just stay on topic?" I knew that she would not harm Madison, but I didn't think she cared enough to think things through before making a decision about Madison's well-being.

We had made it to the base of the stairs when she turned around to face me again. "Daniel I took her with me, because I knew she would survive the trip. Furthermore, this would not even be a topic of discussion if you had stayed off the top, sides and bottom of Vaneetra, so just do me a favor and leave me alone!" She actually stomped halfway up the stairs, before turning back toward me once again. "Oh and for the record, you don't have to worry about us having any more of these types of discussions, because I won't be lending any more helping hands." With that, she stomped the rest of the way upstairs. She slammed our bedroom door with such force, the noise woke up Maddie, who started screaming at the top of her lungs. Then my phone rang again. I ignored it. I could not deal with another angry woman.

After getting Maddie calmed down and back to sleep, I noticed she was still very warm. It reminded me that I needed to make her a doctor's appointment. Then I remembered that I did not even know what doctor Vaneetra took her to see. I never thought about getting that information before now. Vaneetra, of course, did not volunteer the information. I only knew that I carried her on my insurance. I pulled my cell phone out of my pocket to call Vaneetra, but she called me instead. I picked up in no mood for her bull. "Vaneetra, I need the name of Madison's doctor."

"Bring me my baby! I will take her to the doctor. You don't need to know shit." I could not believe her level of hatefulness, but it finally pissed me off.

"I don't have time to argue with you, just give me the name of her doctor so that I can call and make her an appointment." The skin on my hand stretched tight across my knuckles.

"I am not giving you shit, motherfucker! Just bring me my baby."

I had taken all I could take from her. "What the hell type of mother would refuse to give vital information about her daughter's medical care just to get her way?"

"Go to hell, you bastard!" She hung up on me this time. Deciding not to call her back and argue some more, I looked through my estimation of benefits and found the information I needed. I should have looked there in the first place. I made an appointment for Maddie at one-thirty.

I called my assistant who informed me that I had already missed one appointment this morning. She covered for me by telling my client that I had a family emergency and she had not had time between my calling her and him arriving to call and reschedule. I made a mental note to buy a gift card to her favorite department store. She also reminded me that I have ten, eleven and one o'clock appointments that I could not reschedule.

I called Josh and asked if he could cover them for me, but he was in court all day. I needed to find someone to keep Madison, because I could not jeopardize losing my clients.

I called Mrs. James and Summer, but did not get an answer from either of them. I left messages, hoping one of them would call me back right away. In the meantime, I called Ms. Whitmore and asked her to keep Maddie and take her to the doctor for me. She made it clear that even though the idea made her feel uncomfortable she would do it anyway, because she loved me just as much as she loved Shannon and the boys. However, she couldn't take her to the doctor. She had dropped her car off for repairs yesterday and it would not be ready until this evening. I knew now was not the time to ask Shannon for a favor, but I did not see that I had a choice. I had no options left. I only had an hour before my next client.

I went upstairs to our room. The door was locked, forcing me to knock. After a few moments, I heard it click, but it did not open. I let myself in. Shannon stood in front of the dresser, applying makeup.

"I hate to ask you to do anything after what just happened, but—"

"If you hate to ask, then don't." She brushed past me, but I reached out and grabbed her arm. "Let me go. I don't want to be a part of whatever it is you need." She tried to pull away, but I wouldn't release my grip.

"Look, Maddie's doctor can't see her until one-thirty. I have three appointments today that I absolutely can't miss. I need you to keep her for me and take her to her appointment." I thought I would choke on that last sentence.

"Find someone else. I cannot be a part of this." She moved toward the door, but I still did not let go of her arm.

"I called everyone I could think of, including Ms. Whitmore. Vaneetra's mother and sister did not answer and Ms. Whitmore's car is in the shop, so she can't take her." I released her arm. "Shannon, I need you. I am sorry for how I behaved earlier."

She stood still a moment with her eyes closed before turning to face me. "It really does not matter if you are sorry or not. The only thing that matters is that I don't want to be a part of this." She walked out just as my cell phone rang.

"Hello, Daniel Johnson."

"Daniel, this is Mrs. James. I got your message. How is my granddaughter?" I was not in the mood for small talk, but I needed her to keep Madison.

"She still is not feeling well. Did you get my message about keeping Madison for me?"

"Yes I did, but Marshall and I can't come. I wish we could, but Vaneetra is throwing up again. Something has her all upset and when she gets like this, the effects of the chemo gets worse."

I knew what happened, but considering her behavior, I did not really care that she had made herself sick. "Do you think Summer could keep her? I called, but had to leave a message."

"Summer is at work and won't get your message until she gets off. I don't have Courtney's number or I would suggest you call her, even though I would prefer you didn't."

"Well, at this point and time I am willing to take my chances with whatever your concerns about her are. "

"Oh there is nothing wrong with her. I just don't care for her kind."

"Isn't Summer her kind?" I could not resist asking.

"Summer is just confused; she will get past this phase in her life." Mrs. James did not sound convincing.

"Well, I don't mind her kind, so if she happens to call you can you give her my number and ask her to call me? Are you sure you can 't keep Madison and Mr. James care for Vaneetra?"

"Her doctor wants to see her today to go over some test results, which works out, because when we got here we found her in her bathroom throwing up her guts. Marshall wants me to go just in case she gets sick in the car I can help her." I detected concern in her voice.

"I hope it is good news. I have to go and catch Shannon before she leaves. I will call you later." I disconnected the call, and ran downstairs with Madison still in her carrier just in time to stop Shannon before she pulled out of the garage.

"What do you want, Daniel? I told you I am not keeping your daughter for you."

"Shannon, I have three important meetings today. If I don't make these meetings, I stand to lose these people as clients. Shannon, we can't afford for me to lose clients. Look, I apologized for my behavior earlier and I meant it." She finally put the car in park.

"I will keep her and take her to her appointment, but do not throw up in my face what we can't afford." She looked down at her lap. I could tell that she was crying.

"I appreciate your help even if you don't want to do it." I figured that she would respond to my indicating our finances could not take a big hit.

She looked up at me and her tears were gone. "I did not ask for any of this and I feel like things will not get any better. I cannot figure out one good reason why we are still together."

"I can think of two—our sons." I needed to get going, but I knew that leaving now would not be a good idea. Shannon continued talking.

"They were not good enough reasons for you to stay faithful. So, they should not be good enough reasons for me to stay somewhere that I don't want to be." She opened the car door and got out.

"What are you trying to say?" I did not like the shift in this conversation.

"I am saying that I want a divorce. I don't want to be a part of this and the only way I am going to be free of it is to not be married to you."

I didn't know how to respond to her. I knew that she was serious by the look on her face, but instead of dealing with this right away, I chose to dodge the subject. "Look, we can sit down and talk about this when I get home. I will come home early."

"There is nothing to talk about and no need for you to come home early. I have already met with a lawyer and know what I have to do. She recommended that we go to counseling first, but it won't help." She brushed past me to the door. This time I did not reach out to stop her.

"Can we at least talk about it when I get home?" I could not believe that she was ending our marriage in our garage.

"No we can't. I have picked up some extra projects and am going to start looking for a place for me and the boys to live, something I can afford without you." She walked into the house. I stood in the garage in a daze until my cell phone rang again. My secretary informed me that my client would be ten minutes late. I entered the house to an empty downstairs. Shannon had taken Maddie to the second floor. I decided not to press her, grabbed my brief case and left. Not only did I need Josh to represent my custody issues for Maddie, now I needed him to represent me in my divorce. I drove to work with only one thing on my mind. I could not lose my family.

Chapter Thirty-Three

Vaneetra

Vaneetra sat in the waiting room of Dr. Chen's office, feeling like crap. If she honestly believed that, by now she would be back at work and well into the recovery process, she was wrong. Her body and this damn cancer would not cooperate. She finally had to submit a request for short-term disability at her job, because she could no longer keep up with the stress and demands caused by her duties.

Vaneetra did not want to sit in the lobby of her oncologist, waiting to hear whether she would defeat this terrible disease, or if it would overtake her and toss her into an early grave. She had the lumpectomy six weeks ago and does not see an end to her chemo. At first, Dr. Chen delivered good news, stating the surgical team removed the entire lump in her left breast. She stated that Vaneetra would have five to six more chemo treatments and then would return for checkups every two to three months for a year. After the year, she would continue to come in for checkups, but not as frequently. Vaneetra believed the longer the cancer stayed away the better her long-term prognosis. However, Dr. Chen warned her against believing that it may never return. She described breast cancer as a life snatcher that could resurface at any time, with no warning whatsoever.

Arguing with Daniel this morning worsened the nausea she was experiencing. It pissed her off that her mother, once again, made a decision that she had no right to make and sent Madison to Daniel's early yesterday, stating she knew Vaneetra would not allow it and she did not want her to put herself at risk for getting whatever afflicted Madison. This still infuriated Vaneetra. Between the cancer and her mother, she felt as if she had no control over her own life. The idea of Daniel's bitch caring for her baby only added to her rage. She never imagined that her child would be raised by anyone other than herself. Many nights she would lay awake, cursing God for letting her have a child, only to then force her to battle this soul-eating disease. She sometimes thought God saw fit to punish her for being an adulterer. As bold as she found herself to be, she would never share that information with anyone. No one needed to know the thoughts that raced through her head.

"Vaneetra James?" A heavyset African American nurse stood at the entry to the examination area calling her name.

Vaneetra pushed up on the arms of her chair. Her limbs trembled under the pressure. Mr. James rose from his chair next to his daughter and firmly placed his massive arm around her waist to help stabilize her footing. Mrs. James picked up Vaneetra's purse and walked toward the nurse. Mr. James led his daughter in the same direction, greeting the nurse warmly. He gestured for Mrs. James to enter first, so that he could help Vaneetra in. The nurse smiled at the trio, but did not bother to step aside so that Vaneetra and Mr. James could walk through the door together.

Vaneetra stood next to her father on shaky legs; her frame only a remnant of its previous attention-commanding stature. Although her body was now a weakened version of its previous self, her attitude displayed that her mindset remained the same. She snorted in disgust at having to press her way past the nurse's hefty midsection with her father bracing her sides from behind in order to ensure she did not fall. Vaneetra did not care if the nurse heard her, but if she did, she did not let on.

They waited less than ten minutes for Dr. Chen. Vaneetra knew immediately upon seeing her that she did not have good news.

"Hello, Ms. James. Mr. and Mrs. James." Dr. Chen nodded curtly in their direction. "Ms. James, are you comfortable with your parents being in the room while we discuss your latest test results?" Dr. Chen spoke flatly.

Vaneetra turned to ask her parents to leave, but her words got caught on a fresh wave of nausea. Her quivering body fought hard to keep from spilling the bile of her stomach onto the scuffed linoleum floor. Gripping the sides of her chair in a feeble attempt to regain control of her body, she rested her head against the wall, closing her eyes. "They can stay."

"Very well then, your latest test results show new cancer cells in the lymph nodes under your right arm and in both breasts." She paused, waiting for the impact of her news to sink in.

"Oh, sweet Jesus, no!" Mrs. James's hand shot to her mouth just in time to muffle her involuntary sobs.

"Calm down, Evelyn. Let's listen to the doctor and see what else she has to say." Mr. James embraced his wife with one arm. Vaneetra grabbed hold of his free arm, afraid to let go. She thought it impossible, but her body seemed to have gotten weaker. Her head became heavy, her arms hung limp off the sides of the chair.

"So what's next?" Vaneetra pressed her eyes tightly together, fighting back tears.

"Well, since we have not found any more tumors, we will modify your regimen and try another combination of medications. We will extend it for a little while longer and retest in about four weeks. There is not a tremendous amount of new cells and it is possible that they began to grow prior to your initial treatment, but were not detectable."

"Doctor, if that were the case, wouldn't the treatment my daughter is on have helped?" Mr. James's confusion was evident in his voice.

"It is possible that it did help somewhat. I have no way of telling, but without treatment at all, this new cell growth could have been much worse."

Vaneetra now wanted to talk to Dr. Chen privately. What she wanted to ask, she did not want her parents present in the room to hear or to comment. "Dad, will you take mom out to the waiting room? I want to talk to Dr. Chen alone."

"Why can't we stay? I don't want to leave you." Mrs. James objected to her daughter's request.

"Mother, what I have to say is not something that I want to share with you and Dad." Vaneetra turned to face her mother. "Will you please not fight me on this?"

"Whatever you want, baby girl, come on Evelyn. Let's give Vaneetra and the doctor some privacy." Mr. James stood up, holding his wife's hand. "Dr. Chen, please send someone out to get me when Vaneetra is ready so that I can help her to the car." He pulled his wife close as they walked out of the room with her head buried in the side of his chest.

When Vaneetra heard the soft click of the door closing, she immediately shared her thoughts with Dr. Chen. "I have fought hard and I am still losing. I want you to be straight with me and tell me the truth. Am I going to die? Do I need to make long-term arrangements for my daughter?"

"Ms. James, I would not ever give patients false hope, so when I tell you not to throw in the towel just yet, I am being earnest."

"What do you mean, don't throw in the towel? Look at me. I am already dead! I am sick every day. I fall down all of the time. I can't keep anything on my stomach." Vaneetra weakly banged her fist against the arm of her chair. "How long am I supposed to live like this?" Tears streamed down her face, leaving a trail on her ashen dark skin.

"Ms. James, believing that you can beat this is important." Dr. Chen sat on the rolling chair with the circular seat pad.

"How does what I believe matter? I believed that I would have a few treatments and a lumpectomy, a few more treatments and go on with my life as usual. This is nothing like I thought it would be and now you tell me it has gotten worse." Vaneetra inhaled deeply in an attempt to steady her shaky breath.

Dr. Chen studied Vaneetra for a long moment. Her face showed a mixture of pity and disbelief. "Ms. James, I do not believe that I gave you the impression that this process would be easy. Although your prognosis looked good when you first became my patient, I thought I expressed clearly just how difficult it would be."

Vaneetra picked up a hint of defensiveness in Dr. Chen's tone, but did not react to it. Instead, she focused on her words. "Did you say 'looked good'? What do you mean my prognosis 'looked good'? What does it look like now?" Vaneetra used all her strength to lean forward in her chair, careful not to lean too far.

"It is my professional opinion that you still have a chance at recovery. The cancer appears to only be in your breast and lymph nodes. We will continue to monitor it along with treatment." She turned to her computer and began to type.

Vaneetra stared at the doctor and thought if she had enough strength, she would slap the shit out of her. "So, what is next?"

An uncontrollable fear crept up from deep within her gut. She closed her eyes and mentally tried to will it away, but to no avail.

"I am submitting orders for a new chemotherapy regimen. One that I think will attack the cancer a little more aggressively. It will be intravenous and you will need to come in twice a week. However, this medication combination is stronger and the side effects could be more severe."

"How could it be any more severe than what I am already going through?" Sarcasm engulfed her question.

"I said that it may, I have no way of knowing how your body will react until you have actually had a treatment or two." Dr. Chen placed her hand on top of Vaneetra's. "Ms. James, do you have anyone that may be able to move in with you and your daughter for a few weeks?"

"My daughter is staying with her father until this is over. Why do I need a baby sitter?"

"You don't need a baby sitter, but you may need someone around to help you. Cancer drugs can be as bad as the cancer, but the right combination can also be very affective. We just need to find the right combination for you." She stood and walked toward the door. "I have uploaded a new prescription for you into our system. My nurse will call over to the outpatient center and find out if they can fit you in for a round today."

"But I just had a dose on Monday. Don't you think five days is too soon?" Vaneetra knew the doctor was doing what she thought was best, but she sneered anyway.

"Five days is long enough. If they can fit you in today, your new treatment regimen will be on Tuesday and Friday. You will actually be receiving smaller doses, but the medication is stronger. "

Vaneetra rubbed her temples, noticing her hands felt foreign to her own body. "Whatever! When will I know if I can go over today or not?"

"You will know in just a few minutes." Dr. Chen turned toward Vaneetra before leaving the room. "Ms. James, I know this is hard for you and I get the feeling that you are not used to dealing with something that takes away your control. However, as your physician I must advise you that not sharing information like symptoms you are experiencing, and how often they occur, only makes this process more difficult."

"I did not need to tell you anything. I handled it well enough."

"Had you divulged some of the things that you told me today much sooner, I would have made different decisions in regards to your treatment. In the future, remember that as your doctor I can only help you as much as you let me. You may not be able to take another blow to the head from a fall like the one you had at the beginning of treatment. The nurse will be in shortly and I will see you back in a few weeks to evaluate whether the new regimen is effective, unless of course you require a sooner visit." Dr. Chen walked out of the room.

Vaneetra fumed at the doctor's audacity. She knew Dr. Chen was right. She should have shared how bad the side effects were, but thought she would get over them. She thought she was strong enough to beat cancer with minimal help from anyone. As she sat in the cold, sterile exam room, she realized that she had been wrong and now would be separated from her daughter even longer.

Chapter Thirty-Four

Shannon

It had been a week since Daniel and I had our big blow up. Against my better judgment, I kept Madison for the rest of that day, taking her to the doctor in the afternoon. It turned out she had a nasty virus and required plenty of fluids along with Tylenol. Her pediatrician advised to bring her back if her fever had not gone away in a few days.

I knew I blurted out that I wanted a divorce out of hurt and anger, but I meant it. He must not have believed me, because we had not discussed it again after that day and we had not had much to say to each other since. There really was not anything left to say. I was not sure if he took me seriously. He was pretending as if everything were okay.

After he left for his office that day, I called and scheduled another appointment to meet with Jessica Flipmen the next day. I spent another two hundred dollars for her to tell me that I should really try counseling, but if I insisted upon filing now, we would have to do a legal separation first. She told me—after I gave her the five thousand dollar retainer—she would get started on the process.

Since Daniel and I shared checking accounts, I couldn't take that kind of money out without him asking questions. I wouldn't put it past him to move most of what we had to other accounts in order to keep me from spending any on a divorce attorney. I decided to open a separate account and wait until I could save up enough from the money I earned.

I had already started looking for a full-time job, in addition to taking on more assignments on my current freelance contract. I applied for an instructor position in the English department at North Carolina Central University. Dr. Harold Barton, LaVonda's husband Richard's brother, presided as dean of that department. I had seen him at quite a few of LaVonda and Richard's gatherings, but never said anything more than hello. He was tall, very handsome, obviously well-educated and single. LaVonda talked about him often, complaining that he worked too hard and needed to settle down.

When I found out that there was a position open on his staff, I sent in my resume and cover letter. I did not tell LaVonda that I applied for the job, because I did not want her to influence her brother in-law's decision. They don't always see eye to eye. I had heard Richard tell her that Harold would appreciate it if she would stay out of his business.

Since I know LaVonda can be a bit of a busy body, I did not want him to think that I conducted myself in the same manner. Dr. Barton's secretary called me within a few days of my submitting my resume and scheduled an interview for today at one o'clock. The timing was perfect, because Jeran was at school and Zach already had a play date scheduled with a friend.

I dressed in a form fitting, but not tight, black business suit, with a cream silk shirt underneath. I opted for a pearl necklace, bracelet and matching ring to accessorize, finishing off the look with low-heeled, black patent leather pumps. I made sure to apply just enough makeup to be noticeable, but not too heavy, and sprayed just a little of my favorite perfume between my breasts and wrists.

My stomach knotted at the mere idea of entering the work force full time. I enjoyed being a mom with a part-time job that I could do from home. I had become accustomed to the comfortable living Daniel provided, but I could not deal with having to help him raise his child. I truly cared for Madison. She was such a beautiful baby, but she was a constant reminder of Daniel being unfaithful and that was just too much for me to bear.

I arrived at the University twenty minutes early. Dr. Barton's secretary informed him of my arrival and he came right out to get me, not seeming at all surprised to see me. I thought that he would, since we did not really know one another.

"Good afternoon, Shannon. Do you mind if I call you, Shannon?" Dr. Barton escorted me into his office and offered me a seat in front of his massive oak desk. The entire space screamed masculinity and distinction.

"No, not at all, Dr. Barton, Shannon is fine."

He sat in the seat right beside me, positioning his chair so that he could face me.

"Before we get started, may I offer you a beverage? My secretary will be happy to get whatever you would like."

"No, thank you, I am fine." I reached inside my leather work bag and retrieved my resume and tablet. "I hope you do not mind, but I may want to take notes while we talk."

"I don't mind at all. I admire your preparedness." He reached across his desk and picked up a portfolio. "Before we get started, I would like to ask why you chose not to identify yourself as being one of my sister-in-law's friends."

"To be honest, I did not know if doing so would unduly influence your decision to call me in for an interview. So, I opted to earn this interview on my own merit." Perspiration formed at the edges of my hairline from nervousness.

"I admire your desire to make your own way. Let's get started." He sat back in his chair, crossed his legs and opened the portfolio. "I can honestly say that I called you in because of your resume and cover letter. You have a vast amount of experience and attended excellent graduate and undergraduate schools. I see you have also won several awards for writing and journalism. So tell me, what do you think you can offer our university?"

The interview went on for better than an hour. I thought it had gone very well. I explained my love for writing and English, as well as my desire to be in the classroom with adult students. He asked why I wanted to work full time. I explained I was preparing to go through a divorce and needed to become self-sufficient, leaving out specific details. I thought I detected a happier tone in his voice after sharing my plans, but could not be sure.

By the end of the interview, he insisted I called him Harold, and told me that he had a few more interviews to conduct. His secretary would call me if my resume were forwarded to the Human Resources Department with a recommendation to hire. I left feeling optimistic, so much so that I went apartment hunting. I would finally be able to begin my separation from Daniel. I planned to break the news of my and the boys moving out once I was offered the job at the university.

Chapter Thirty-Five

Daniel

I know I should have handled the situation with Shannon better. The pressure of Madison being sick and Vaneetra making my life hell pushed me over the top and I took it out on Shannon. It could not have been worse timing, because for the first time since Madison came to live with us, she set her feelings aside and actually tried to help. I thanked her by indirectly accusing her of not caring for Maddie properly.

Over the past week, our conversation had been polite, but guarded. She stopped sleeping in the bed with me, choosing to sleep downstairs on the sofa. Prior to now, she slept with a pillow between us. We had not made love in months. A couple of days ago she moved some of her things out of the room

After our argument, I told Josh about Shannon's plans to file for divorce and move out. I felt if she were serious and were actually going to go through with it, then I would need him to represent me. When he told me that he wouldn't do it, I couldn't believe it. He said that he cared for Shannon and the boys like they were his family and he was not going to have any part of bringing any more hurt and pain to her.

I understood where he was coming from and why he did not want to get involved, but I felt like he had betrayed me. He was supposed to be my business partner and best friend, but it seemed to me like he was siding with Shannon against me. I knew I created this mess, but I expected his complete support, just the way I had been there for him when his world caved in around him.

Maddie had not been over to Vaneetra's since Summer dropped her off with Shannon last week. Surprisingly, Vaneetra had not called to harass me about it. It felt good not to have my phone buzzing in my pocket every hour with her on the other end being ignorant. She truly made me regret the first day that I ever laid eyes on her.

Mr. and Mrs. James called to check on Madison daily. They did not mention Vaneetra and I did not ask. Summer and Courtney even came by a couple of times when they thought she was no longer contagious. I mentioned that I would take Maddie to her mother in a day or so. They both ignored the statement. I got the impression they did not want to talk about her.

I finally called Vaneetra after a couple days of Madison not having a fever to arrange a time to bring her to visit over the weekend, but she did not answer either of her phones. I began to wonder if something had gone wrong with her treatment. She would not let an entire week go by without threatening me or calling me names. She definitely would not ignore my calls. Since Shannon and the boys had gone out and Madison was napping, I picked up my phone to call Mrs. James to find out if anything had changed with Vaneetra's health when it rang.

"Hello, this is Daniel Johnson."

"Daniel, this is Mrs. James. Do you have a moment to talk?" She sounded like she had been crying.

"Sure, Mrs. James. I had just picked up my phone to call you. I tried to call Vaneetra, but she did not pick up. Is everything all right with her?"

Silence hung in the air like dead space over the phone. Then I heard Mrs. James draw in a shaky breath. "No, Daniel, everything is not okay, but I don't want to talk about it right now. Vaneetra is here with me and her father. She has been since coming from her doctor's visit last Friday. Will you bring Madison over here today so that we can visit with her?"

I got a sinking feeling in the bottom of my stomach. I wanted to ask more questions, but decided against it. "Of course, I will bring her over. What time would you like us to be there?"

"You can come any time you want. I would like for her to spend a few nights with her mother, if you don't mind." Her voice cracked over the phone.

Tension spread across my shoulders. I wondered if Vaneetra was in fact sicker than she had let on. "That is no problem. I will bring enough items to last until next Friday. If you need me to pick her up before then just let me know." She thanked me and hung up.

I put together a small suitcase with all the items I thought Madison would need for a week with her mother and grandparents. As time passed, I grew more concerned about the evasiveness and heaviness in Mrs. James's voice. I decided that I would sit down with them and find out exactly what was going on.

Shannon and the boys came in from spending the morning out while I was in the kitchen packing up Madison's bottles, containers of formula and a couple jugs of water. "Hey, Daddy! What are you doing?" Zach jumped in my arms and gave me a hug.

"Hey, buddy! I am packing up some stuff for Madison. She is going to stay a few days with her mom and grandparents." I put him down and continued placing items in her diaper bag.

"So we will we see her again?" Jeran came and stood next to me. I could tell he was worried.

"Yes, buddy, you will see her again. She is only going to be gone for a few days." I rubbed the top of his head.

"Daddy, is Madison going to live with us forever?" Zach looked up at me from his position at my side.

The question caught me by surprise. "Right now, I don't know. It is possible that she may have to come and live with us forever." Shannon, who was sitting in the family room, looked up and furrowed her eyebrows at me, but did not say anything.

"Well, since we are not going to see her for a few days, can we go with you to drop her off?" Jeran asked. Shannon's furrowed eyebrows grew deeper. I ignored her.

"Sure, buddy, I don't see why not. Let's go upstairs and get Madison ready to go." The boys ran up the stairs. Shannon stared at me as I walked past her, but she did not object. Halfway up the stairs, I heard her slamming cabinet doors in the kitchen.

Mr. James answered his door seconds after I rang the bell. He did not appear surprised or upset that I brought Jeran and Zach along with me, welcoming us as if we were old friends. The boys walked in, staying close to me until they saw Summer. They ran over and hugged her as if she were really their aunt. They turned toward the living room, but stopped dead in their tracks.

"Vaneetra is in the living room resting. I don't imagine your sons have ever seen anyone with cancer before, have they, son?" He patted me on the back.

At that moment, I began to regret bringing them with me. "No, sir, they have not." I swallowed hard. This was the first time Vaneetra had ever seen my sons. I handed Madison to Mr. James and headed toward the living room. Even though I believed she was sicker than she had let on, I did not trust her not to say something inappropriate.

Jeran and Zach stood frozen in place, staring at Vaneetra, who looked up at me with what I thought was nothing less than pure hatred in her eyes. I didn't think she could get any frailer, but she had. She sat on the sofa by the window, wrapped in a blanket with a scarf on her head and gloves on her hands. Her eyes seemed to dominate the top third of her gaunt face.

Without warning, Jeran walked over to her and held out his right hand. "Hi, my name is Jeran and I am Maddie's older brother. Are you her mom?" Vaneetra stared at him so long, I thought that maybe she didn't hear him. Zach walked up and stood beside his big brother.

Slowly, Vaneetra extended her right hand to Jeran. He shook it gently. "Yes, I am Maddie's mother." The room had grown silent. Mrs. James and Courtney had emerged from other parts of the house, but stood by quietly, watching what transpired between Vaneetra and my sons.

"My name is Zach and I am Maddie's big brother, too!" He also extended his hand to Vaneetra, which she shook.

"What's your name?" Jeran asked, moving a little bit closer. Vaneetra looked as if she didn't know how to respond, but finally did.

"My name is Vaneetra."

"I am pleased to meet you, Ms. Vaneetra. Thank you for letting Maddie come and stay with us for a little while. We love her a lot and like being big brothers."

"Yeah, thank you. We love her a whole lot." Zach opened his arms, and without warning, he reached over and hugged Vaneetra, giving her a kiss on the cheek as well. Jeran did the same. When they pulled back, I saw tears brimming in the corner of Vaneetra's eyes.

Summer broke the silence. "Who wants a snack?" Surprisingly, neither Jeran nor Zach jumped at the chance, as they would usually do.

"Ms. Vaneetra, would you like a snack? We can get it for you." Jeran rested his hand on top of hers. Tears started to run down her face.

Zach reached over and wiped her face with his little hand. "Don't cry, Ms. 'Neetra. Maddie is going to stay with you for a little while."

"Yeah, please don't cry, Ms. Vaneetra. It is going to be okay. God is going to take care of you." Jeran stroked her hand gently.

"Thank you, boys, I think I will have a snack, but you eat as much as you want first."

"Come on, fellas, let's go into the kitchen." Courtney walked over and took the boys by the hand, walking them out of the living room. Summer followed her. Mrs. James, in full-blown sob mode, walked over to a chair and sat down. Mr. James walked over to Vaneetra with Maddie in his arms. He gently handed her to Vaneetra and sat close by. I remained standing near the entryway.

Vaneetra hugged Madison and talked to her for a few moments, and then looked up at me. "You son of bitch! Why did you bring those kids over here?" Her voice was barely a whisper and I had to strain to hear what she said.

"It is nice to see you, too. I brought them because they wanted to spend a little extra time with their sister. Thank you for not being as rude to them as you are being to me." I walked a little further into the room, but did not sit down.

"Now that you have dropped my daughter off you can get the hell out." She actually strained to speak this time.

"Look, Vaneetra, I came here to find out what is going on with you. I have called you a few times this week. You have not answered. I am not leaving here until you tell me exactly what is going on." I stood in the middle of the floor as if I owned it.

"Son, have a seat. We are all going to sit down and talk about what is going on. Vaneetra, you may as well tell him. The man needs to know what to expect." Mr. James took Vaneetra's hand in his own. I sat in a chair near Mrs. James.

She rolled her eyes at me and sat quietly for an extremely long time. When she finally spoke, I had to strain to hear her. "Last Friday, when I went in for a checkup, my doctor told me that they found more cancer cells." I didn't know how to respond so I kept quiet. A few more moments went by before she spoke again. "I started a new round of chemo that same day. This time around, I go in twice a week for treatment. I completed my third round yesterday." She started coughing and Mr. James passed her a cup of water that had been sitting on the table. I waited until she finished sipping it before I spoke.

"Vaneetra, I am genuinely sorry that you are having such a hard time, and I will do what I can to help you." In the back of my mind, the idea that she may actually die began to form.

"I don't need anything from you, but to take care of my daughter for a little while longer. I still hate you, but I love my daughter enough to want to make sure that she is taken care of. These past few months, you have shown me that you can at least do that."

"So, what's next?" I turned to Mrs. James this time.

"Well, Marshall and I are going to keep Vaneetra with us until the chemo is over, or as long as she is willing to stay. When Madison goes back to your house, I want you to start bringing her back to me to keep during the day."

"I can do that as long as you are up to handling both her and Vaneetra."

"I am fine, you asshole. I look worse than I feel." Vaneetra spat her venomous words at me. I had grown tired of the name calling, but held my tongue. Mr. James apparently had, too, because he addressed it.

"Baby girl, that is enough name calling. Daniel has not done anything to deserve this type of treatment from you. It is time to let all this anger go."

"Yes, Vaneetra. You are going to have to forgive this man, because you have a child to raise together when you get better." Mrs. James spoke with more hope than certainty.

"Can I please be left alone with my daughter? I don't want to talk about any of this right now." Vaneetra rolled her eyes and held Madison tightly in her arms. She put her face close to Madison's and kept her head down. She actually looked afraid. I wondered if she thought that the cancer would kill her.

"I think we will be going now. I will call and check on Maddie tomorrow. If you need anything, or if I forgot something, let me know and I will bring it to you." I walked into the hallway and called out to Jeran and Zach. They came with a small plate containing half a sandwich and an even smaller glass of milk. Both walked right by me, over to Vaneetra, offering her the treats they brought. She extended them another act of kindness by accepting the snack and saying thank you, which I did not expect. They gave her and Maddie kisses, before going around the room displaying the same affection to everyone else.

I looked back before walking to the door just in time to see Vaneetra put her middle finger up at me. I almost laughed at her level of childishness. At that moment, I began to pity her, because I saw her for who she really was—a lonely and miserable woman fighting for her life, but afraid she will not win.

On the drive home, I thought about how I would break the silence between Shannon and me. That short time with Vaneetra, specifically seeing how Jeran and Zach interacted with her, made me desire to keep my family together. I had to figure out a way to save my marriage, while at the same time raising my daughter, who needed me now more than ever.

Chapter Thirty-Six

Shannon

I hated letting Jeran and Zach go with Daniel to take Madison to her mother and family, but I did not stop them. I simply could not conjure up the energy to argue about it and I most certainly did not want to hurt Jeran and Zach's feelings. They loved their little sister to pieces and they had grown used to her living with us. They wanted her to stay forever and were asking for that in their nightly prayers.

While they were gone, I called my mom and caught her up with everything that had been going on over the past two weeks. We chatted weekly, but I was usually vague about Daniel, Madison and Vaneetra. I lived it, so I certainly did not want to talk about it all the time. I usually spent the time probing for information on her relationship with Mr. Walker. However, today I needed to vent to someone.

"Hey, Mom, how are you?"

"I am doing okay? What's on your mind?" She liked to get straight to the point.

"What isn't on my mind is a better question. There is so much going on. I am just overwhelmed by it all." I tried to fight back the tears, but I could not.

"Shannon, are you crying? Tell me what happened."

"Mama, I…Mama, I—" A rush of emotions overtook me and before I realized it, I blurted out everything that happened between me and Daniel. "Mom, I became so angry that I could not hold in my feelings any longer. I told him I want a divorce." I thought baring my soul to Mom would have helped me to feel better about my decision, but instead I felt as if I were a self-righteous bitch. Apparently, Mom felt the same way.

"Shannon, I know what you are going through is hard. It is more than any one woman should have to put up with, but you have to pull yourself together and think about what is good for your family." I could not believe my ears. My own mother did not even understand. I thought, of all people, she would understand, considering what she went through when she was married to Greg, Sr.

"Are you serious? I am thinking of my family, more so than you thought of yours. Why should I have to put up with all of this garbage?" She really had some nerve. Unlike her, I didn't find it necessary to be a doormat.

"I wondered when you would bring this up. I thought it would be over Christmas, but I guess now is as good a time as any." Her sigh echoed loudly over the phone.

"You act like I am supposed to just sit around and take the garbage that Daniel spews all over our marriage. You may have been a doormat, but I damn sure will not be one." I fought to catch my breath. I was appalled at her attitude. She chose to stay with Greg, Sr. for years, even though he beat the hell out of her and slept around with a bunch of different whores.

"I admit to staying with Greg, Sr., and taking a lot of shit that I should not have. I thought I loved him and that I could make things better if I would only be different. Obviously, I was wrong, but I won't apologize for my decisions. Despite the mistakes I made, you and your siblings turned out pretty well for the most part."

I ignored her statement that my siblings and I turned out pretty well for the most part. "That's why I thought that you would understand my point of view. You lived through it and you could not change Greg, Sr., and I can't change Daniel."

"Shannon, your situation is nothing like mine." Her tone became defensive. "Greg, Sr. was an abusive whore, who did not want anything out of life, nor did he value it."

"Excuse me, but I think having an affair and making a baby while you are married qualifies as being a whore. Abuse does not have to be a part it."

"Having an affair does not make Daniel a whore. It means he made a poor choice. Having a baby with his mistress makes him somewhat stupid and extremely reckless, but not a whore. Daniel is one of the good guys. He made a bad decision and deserves to be forgiven."

"Mom, why are you defending him? You are acting like I do not have the right to feel the way that I do, or make the decision that I have."

"Shannon, you have every right to feel however you want and can make whatever decision you choose, but you are not making decisions only for yourself. You have two children to think about."

"I know that, Mother. They will be fine. I don't think they should grow up in a house where a man teaches them that it is okay to run all over his wife and bring outside babies home." My head began to pound.

"Shannon, is that all Daniel teaches them? Look, I know he hurt you and it will take a very long time for you to forgive him, but don't break up your family. Build it up and make it stronger. Why don't you do as that lawyer suggests and go to counseling? What could it hurt?"

"I don't want to go to counseling. I just want to be done with it all."

"Shannon, divorcing Daniel will not mean that anything will be over. You will just be creating a new set of problems. You will still have to deal with Madison's existence and then you will have to deal with the changes your sons are going to experience by being taken away from their father. Shannon, you cannot run away from this, so you may as well face it head on and deal with it."

I did not want to hear any more. "Mom, I have to go. Daniel will be back soon with the boys and I need to start dinner."

"Where did he take them?"

"He took them with him to drop Madison off with her mother and grandparents." Knowing that she was going to have something to say, I rushed to end the call. "Mom, I really have to go." It did not work.

"No you don't, but I will let you go after I say this one last thing." I did not want to hear it, but listened anyway.

"I made a mistake by staying with Greg, Sr., as long as I did. I thought I was doing the right thing at the time, but now I see that all I did was create an environment that fostered preconceived generalizations of men. It seems to me that what Greg, Sr. did in our marriage hardened you against men more than it did me."

"How can you say that? I loved and married Daniel. It is what he did that has made me this way."

"I think what Daniel has done triggered old feelings that already existed; feelings so painful that you convinced yourself life would have to be horrible to experience them with a man of your own."

"Mom, you are not making any sense."

"Yes, I am. You just don't want to hear what I have to say. Prior to Daniel you never gave any other young man the time of day. He came along and swept you off your feet. You made him the center of your world. He was different from the poor excuse of a man you were raised around, but you never put my past behind you. You never forgave me, or Greg for how we made you live your childhood. I know you swore no man would ever do you the way that he did me."

"Mom, I did want a better life, but I did not judge you." I knew she was right, but felt like I had to defend myself.

"You were right to want a better life and whether you admit it or not, you did judge me, but that is okay. I can't change my mistakes, but as your mother I can try and show you yours before it is too late." I could hear the tears in her voice. "Daniel has broken your heart, but in all of the years you have been married, he made one major mistake. No matter how bad the decision, it should not cost him his family. Find a way to forgive him and work on the issues in your marriage that brought you to this point."

I could not bring myself to argue any longer, so I conceded. "Okay, Mom, I will think about what you are saying."

"You do that. Try talking to someone you trust at the church you guys attend. There has to be someone there that can help you through this." I did not bother to tell her that we stopped going to church several months ago. Maybe it was time to go back.

Chapter Thirty-Seven

Shannon

I received a call from Dr. Barton before ten Monday morning. I found it a bit odd that he called personally, but did not dwell on it. He stated he was prepared to make his hiring recommendation, but wanted to meet with me a second time to tell me more about the responsibilities of the position. I agreed to meet with him on Tuesday afternoon for a late lunch. I asked Ms. Whitmore to keep Zach and pick up Jeran from school, while I went to a job interview. She agreed, but told me while she thought it was nice that I wanted to go back to work, she hoped I was not still considering leaving my husband.

On Tuesday, my nerves were all a flutter with anticipation of my meeting with Dr. Barton. He chose Bone Fish Grill, my favorite place to eat. I wondered if he conducted a second interview with all the candidates, or if this meant that he was going to recommend me for the job. I did not have to wait long for an answer.

"Good afternoon, Shannon. I am pleased that you could meet with me on such short notice." The server offered to seat us at a table in the center of the restaurant, but Dr. Barton requested a booth instead. I thought that maybe he did not want to be in the flow of traffic, once business picked up for lunch.

"It was no problem, Dr. Barton. I am glad you called." I smiled at him, hoping to appear relaxed and confident.

"I am glad you answered. You left me very impressed and intrigued after your interview. We need someone with your passion and level of intellect on our staff." The server took our drink orders. I ordered water with lemon. Dr. Barton ordered a Rusty Nail.

"You are my last appointment for today. I will not be going back to the office, so I am going to relax and enjoy a cocktail." He leaned forward and smiled. "Can I order you a drink?"

"No, thank you. When the interview is over I have to pick up my sons from the sitter." I returned his smile, despite the increasing ball of nerves growing in the pit of my stomach.

"That's right, you do have two small children at home. How old are they?"

"One is three and the other is five. My five-year-old is actually at school, but my sitter will pick him up for me."

"I like a woman, I mean a person who plans ahead. That is a skill that will prove to be very valuable as a staff instructor in my department." He looked into my eyes, but then allowed his gaze to drift and pause a little too long at my breast. I shifted in my seat and cleared my throat, thinking he may notice my suddenly hard nipples pressing against the insides of my dress. He raised eyes up and continued with his conversation. "I wanted to meet with you in order to ask a few more questions before I made my recommendation." Our drinks arrived. I sipped my water.

"I will be happy to answer whatever questions you have." We talked about the position more in depth for thirty minutes, only taking a break to order lunch. I ordered Grilled Salmon. He ordered Bang Bang Shrimp and the Chilean Sea Bass. By the time our food arrived, I had answered all of his questions and felt more relaxed.

"I believe I am ready to make my recommendation. I know I should not do this, but since you are such good friends with my sister-in-law, I will break the rules and tell you that I am going to recommend you for the position. I think you will fit in very well with our current staff."

My heart skipped a beat. "Thank you, Dr. Barton! When can I expect to hear from Human Resources with a start date?" I hoped that I did not sound too eager.

He laughed and took a bite of his fish. "Slow down, the position start date is in June, so there is still some time yet. However, you should expect to hear from HR within the next few days. They will make a salary offer, send you all the necessary paperwork and tell you what you need to do on your end. I will call you in to meet our staff at our May department meeting."

"I am excited to start and look forward to the possibilities and opportunities this position will offer me." I took a bite of my food and savored it. I looked up to find Dr. Barton staring at my breasts, again. A warm sensation rose from the pit of my stomach.

"Shannon, during the first interview, you mentioned that you were getting a divorce. I would first like to say that I am sorry to hear that, but I wonder what happened. I remember seeing your family at quite a few of Richard and LaVonda's parties. You and your husband always seemed quite happy with each other."

I have not been out of the work force long enough to forget that I did not have to answer such questions, but I thought nothing of it since I am familiar with him in my personal life. "Looks can be deceiving, Dr. Barton. Daniel and I have been having problems for a couple of years now." Having relaxed, I went on to tell him my current situation. He listened intently, commenting and giving sympathetic glances at the right moments in my story. When I had shared all I thought that I should, leaving out Vaneetra having cancer and Madison living with us, he reached over and cupped my hand in his.

"I am truly sorry that this type of thing has happened to you. I don't know your husband well, but he has got to be crazy to put you through such an ordeal." His middle finger stroked the palm of my hand. I felt a tingling sensation travel up my arm and shoot down between my thighs. I knew I should pull my hand away, pay my part of the bill and leave, but I just sat there.

"I have to agree with you, but we seem to be the only two who think so."

Dr. Barton pushed his plate aside. I did not touch mine.

"Really, who could possibly think it is okay for a man to cheat on his wife and create a child? The affair is bad enough, leaving evidence is worse." I noticed his choice of wording, but ignored it.

"Everyone that knows about it feels like I should forgive and forget. They feel like I should just move on, business as usual." He gently squeezed my hand, his middle finger now making circular motions on my palm. I involuntarily closed my eyes, enjoying the moisture and warm sensation that now dominated my lower extremities, remembering that months had gone by since the last time I had sex. When I opened my eyes, Dr. Barton was gazing at me with his deep brown eyes, making it difficult to look away.

The server brought the bill to the table along with a dessert menu, which quickly brought me back to my senses. I looked at my watch and shifted abruptly in my seat. "I did not realize the time. I have enjoyed my time with you, but I must go. Please let me pay half on the bill." I took deep breaths to slow my heartbeat and my voice.

"No, I will not allow you to do that. I will pay the bill and walk you to your car." He released my hand to retrieve his wallet. I sat quietly while he paid and the server boxed up our leftovers. He took the liberty of ordering me a piece of chocolate cake to go. I wondered if he knew how much I loved chocolate cake.

At my car, I opened the door and turned toward him. He stood inches from me. I had to tilt my head up to keep from staring at his broad chest. I could tell that he worked out. His cologne permeated my nostrils, intoxicating my senses. "Thank you, Dr. Barton, for lunch, dessert and especially the position recommendation." I took a step back, wedging myself between the car door and the frame.

"Call me Harold and it is my pleasure. You truly are the best candidate for the job. The fact that you are beautiful and about to be divorced are bonuses." Before I could respond, he leaned in and planted his mouth on top of mine. His tongue gently parted my lips, playfully licking the inside rim. I did not pull away, although I knew I should. When I didn't, Harold circled one arm around my waist and rested his free hand upon one of my breast, easily finding my nipple and gently caressing it between his thumb and index finger. When he finally released me, I caught my breath and placed one hand on my car door for balance. I could feel the wetness in my panties and hardness of my nipples. It took all of my energy to pull myself together.

"Harold, I do not want to give you the wrong impression, even though I fear I already have, but unlike my husband, I plan to stay faithful until after I am divorced." Even as the words left my lips, I felt like I had already committed adultery. A mixture of guilt and desire crowded my senses.

He placed an index finger on my lips, leaned over and whispered in my ear. "I respect and admire you enough to be willing to wait. My attraction for you developed a long time ago. I kept my distance because you are married. Now that you are getting a divorce, I thought I would take my chances and let you know I am interested in getting to know you much better." He straightened his posture and took a step back, never taking his eyes off mine.

"Thank you for understanding." Not knowing what else to say and unsure that I could remain standing any longer, I got into the car. Before I could close the door, he leaned inside.

"Shannon, whether you respond to my advances or not the job offer does not change. As long as everything clears with HR, it is yours if you want it." I smiled but did not respond. He stepped back and closed my door. As I drove away, I thought about what he said. The magnitude of what just happened sunk in. On some level, I probably just cheated on my husband and there was no way in hell I could take that job now. First, it would be an ethical dilemma. Second, based on the way my body responded to his touch and kiss, I did not think I could work around him and keep my legs closed.

Chapter Thirty-Eight

Daniel

The week Maddie stayed with her mother and grandparents gave me time to think. I had to figure out a way to talk to Shannon about her wanting a divorce. We walked by each other in the house like roommates who barely spoke. I came home early from work on Tuesday evening, thinking that we could talk before we got busy with the kids, but no one was home. I called her cell phone. She did not answer. I did not want to go back to work, so I decided I would break the ice between us by cooking dinner. Shannon loved Shrimp Alfredo, but does not eat it often, because of the fat content. Over the past few months, she had lost quite a few pounds, so I figured she could afford to eat a high fat meal once. I ran to the store, hoping to get back home and get dinner started before Shannon came in with the boys. I had just rinsed the pasta when they walked in through the garage. Jeran and Zach ran into the kitchen, dropping their coats on the floor along the way.

Zach made it to the kitchen first. "Daddy, whatcha doing?" Surprisingly, he did not go to the refrigerator like he usually did.

"Daddy is cooking dinner for you guys. How did your day go? Did you and Mommy have fun?" I poured three pounds of seasoned shrimp into a skillet coated with hot butter and olive oil.

"I had fun. I went over to Ms. Whitmore's house while Mommy went to a meeting for work." He stood on his tiptoes beside me at the counter. "What are you cooking?"

"I am cooking Mommy's favorite meal, Shrimp Alfredo. What did you and Ms. Whitmore do today?" I wondered what meeting Shannon had. I didn't think it had anything to do with any of her current assignments. I looked up to see her taking off her jacket. She had on a form fitting, navy blue, long-sleeved wrap dress, and leather three-inch peep toe high-heeled shoes I bought her for a birthday a couple of years back. She wouldn't look in my direction, but I saw she had on makeup. Her hair looked better than it had in a long time. Now that I think about it, she had taken her twists down, but I didn't think much of it. She usually wore it pinned on top of her head, but today she had it down, with curls framing her face.

"We went to the park and then we picked Jeran up from school. Then we went back to her house and had a snack. Ms. Whitmore helped Jeran with his homework, too." Zach went to the kitchen table and climbed into a chair.

"Oh did she now?" I stirred the shrimp a couple more times, poured it on top of the pasta and went to work on the sauce. I glanced at Shannon, but she still would not make eye contact with me. I began to wonder where she had gone.

Jeran jumped into the chair next to his brother. "Yeah, Dad, she did and she is smart, too!"

I laughed at the astonishment in Jeran's voice. "I bet she is very smart, son."

"Since I am all done with my homework, can Zach and I go and watch TV before dinner?

"If it is okay with your mom it is okay with me." I continued stirring the sauce, noticing Shannon still had not said anything or left the family room. She sat on the couch, seemingly distracted.

"Can we please watch TV, Mama?" Zach jumped down, ran over and hugged her.

She smiled and hugged him back. "You can watch TV if you pick up your jackets and hang them in the closet."

"Okay we will do that!" Jeran said, as he got out of his chair and ran to pick up his jacket. Zach ran and picked his up as well. I heard them laughing and talking down the hallway. I took advantage of us being alone.

Before I could say anything to Shannon, the boys were back in the kitchen. "Dad, is Maddie coming home tonight?" Jeran asked me.

"Yes, she is coming home. I am going to go and pick her up just as soon as I finish cooking dinner." Once they got the answer they wanted, they left again. I did not waste any time questioning Shannon about her day. "So, what meeting did you have today?" I turned the eye off under a now completed pasta dish and began preparations to make a salad.

Shannon remained silent a few moments longer. I continued cooking while waiting for her to answer. She finally turned on the sofa to face me, but she did not maintain eye contact.

"I went to a meeting today regarding another job."

"That dress does not look like something you would choose to wear to an interview."

"The actual interview occurred last Friday. Today's meeting was a follow up." She finally made eye contact.

"Oh…I didn't know that you had an interview lined up. Where did you interview?" I finished making the salad and walked over to the family room. "Do you mind telling me about it?" I sat on the sofa next to her.

"I interviewed last Friday with the English department at North Carolina Central University. Today was a follow up."

"Doesn't Richard's brother work for NCCU?"

"Yes, he does. He interviewed me for the position. He had a few more questions, so we met today to go over them." She brushed invisible lint from her dress. She looked as uncomfortable as I felt. I guess I had my answer to whether she really planned to move out with the kids and file for divorce.

"I guess congratulations are in order." I faked a laugh and smile.

Shannon dropped her eyes. "I am not sure that I am going to take it. Now that I have had a chance to think about it, I am not sure teaching is what I want to do." She was lying, I could tell. For as long as I have known her, Shannon has always expressed an interest in teaching at the college level. She taught at Waketech Community College before she got pregnant with Zach.

"When did you change your mind about teaching? You made getting back into the classroom your goal for when Zach started school."

"People can change their minds about things all of the time. I just don't think I want to be in the classroom again." She got up to walk out of the family room.

"Where are you going? I would like to finish talking." I went and stood behind her.

"What is it that you really want to talk about, Daniel? I know you are not all that interested in my job interview."

"Shannon, I am interested in your job interview. You up and decided to go back to work full time without discussing it with me. I am very interested in your plans to work." I found myself getting annoyed with her.

"Daniel, I do not need your permission to work full time." She turned to look at me with her hand on her hips.

"I never said you did, but I am still your husband and deserve to be consulted." I knew what her response would be as soon as I let those words out my mouth.

"You gave up your right to be consulted on anything I do when you found another woman to love."

I wished she would just let the past stay in the past. Every available opportunity, she threw Vaneetra up in my face. "Shannon, I don't love Vaneetra. I didn't love her then and I don't love her now. I made a mistake. When are you going to let it go?" I threw up my hands in frustration. "I have regretted getting involved with Vaneetra for months now. I wish you would just let us move past it."

She walked up to me, pointing her finger in my face. "As long as I am with you, I can't let it go. That is why I am filing for divorce, so that I can let it go and you with it."

"Shannon, I made a mistake and I know it is going to take a long time for you to forgive me, but I don't want to lose you." I reached out and touched her arm. She didn't pull away…progress. "Shannon, I love you…no one else but you. I regret ever even meeting Vaneetra and definitely becoming involved with her. I can't change the past and I love my daughter, but that does not take away from the love I have for you and our sons."

"I understand that you love your daughter, but how am I supposed to forgive you and get past what you did with her as a constant reminder? I know every single person in our family has accepted and fallen in love with Madison, except for me. How am I supposed to do that? How do I just ignore what you did and move on with business as usual?"

"Babe, I am not asking you to forget what I did, or ignore the fact that I have a daughter by another woman. What I am asking you to do is forgive me and accept Maddie. You don't have to do it as fast as everyone else, but please just try. I want you back. I want my wife back. I want to hold you and make love to you again, this time no one else but you." I moved my hand from her arm to her face, using my thumb to wipe tears from her cheek.

"I don't know if I can forgive you, or accept Madison. I just don't know if I can." Shannon's voice cracked and she turned her face away. I saw her hurt and felt like a complete monster. Never, in all my life, did I think that I would bring so much pain to her. I cupped her face, turning it toward mine, thankful that she did not pull away and kissed her forehead.

"Babe, what can I do to prove to you that I will never even think about being with another woman?" I brushed my lips against hers, grateful that she did not try to scratch my eyes out. I kissed her again, pressing harder this time. Wrapping my arms around her, I pulled her into me. My manhood rose and hardened against her thigh. At first her body stiffened, but quickly relaxed. "Shannon, I love you and miss being with you. I never want to be with anyone else again…only you." She released a low moan, as I kissed the nape of her neck. I positioned my arm to lift her up and move her onto the couch.

"Mommy, we're hungry!" Jeran's voice registered in my ears, stopping me dead in my tracks. I let Shannon go and looked over to find Jeran and Zach looking at us, trying to stifle their giggles with their hands over their mouths.

Shannon took a few steps back, cleared her throat and turned to the boys. "Okay, well let's go and eat the wonderful dinner Daddy made for us. It certainly smells delicious." She rushed into the kitchen, straightening her dress along the way. I excused myself to the bathroom so that I could situate my manhood inside my pants. After a couple of minutes, I relaxed enough for it not to be noticeable and went to join Shannon and the boys at the dinner table.

"Daddy, come and eat with us." Zach patted the space next to him at the table. "The food is good, thank you for making it." He shoved a spoonful of pasta in his mouth, using his hand to scoop up tendrils that hung from his bottom lip.

"Yeah, Dad, dinner is really good, thanks." Jeran ate a little more neatly than his brother did. "Dad, what time are you going to get Maddie?"

I looked at my watch, realizing that it was almost seven o'clock. "I should be going now, but let's all eat together and I will go after dinner." I spooned a heap of pasta on my plate and some salad.

"Can Zach and I go with you to pick her up?" Jeran put down his fork, waiting for me to answer.

"Well, buddy, we have to okay that with your mom. If it is okay with her then you can go." I looked over at Shannon who had her head bent down toward her plate.

She looked up and smiled at the boys. "Even though it is a school night, I think it will be fine as long as you come straight back."

Jeran and Zach chatted throughout the rest of dinner. Shannon and I ate in silence. I could not help but think something was bothering her. I wondered if she regretted letting me get so close, but thought better of asking her about it. I did not want to mess up the progress I thought I had made. I still had a very long way to go.

Chapter Thirty-Nine

Vaneetra

Four weeks into her second round of chemo, Vaneetra found herself once again sitting in Dr. Chen's office waiting to hear if she would get to live a little longer. The past few weeks had proven to be quite trying. So much had gone through her mind. Four weeks ago, sitting in the very same chair, she thought she would die. Today, her mind possessed no more hope than before. Even though her falls were less frequent, and she was not as nauseous, she no longer believed she would beat the cancer. She never thought she would come up against something that made her feel like she could not win, as if her life meant nothing; taken at a moment's notice.

Dr. Chen entered the exam room with what Vaneetra thought was a grim look on her face. She braced herself for the worst. "Hello, Ms. James. How are you today?" She sat on her chair with wheels, placed her laptop on the counter and opened it. "I have your latest blood work and test results." Dr. Chen turned and faced Vaneetra. Her expression flat, not giving away anything.

Vaneetra inhaled deeply, gripping the sides of her chair. "What are the results? Do I get to live another day or two?"

"Actually, with the progress you have made in the past four weeks, I feel comfortable telling you that you get to live longer than a day or two." She smiled at Vaneetra. "Your latest test results show a significant decline in the cancer cells present in your body. A few more weeks of chemo and I think we will have gotten it all."

Vaneetra sat for a few moments before she spoke in disbelief. "So, you are saying that the current treatment is working?"

"Yes, it appears to be working quite well. Tell me about your symptoms, are they better or worse?" Dr. Chen took out her stethoscope and listened to Vaneetra's lungs and heart. She allowed her to remain in the chair, instead of having her move to the exam table.

"My nausea and vomiting are a lot better. I can eat a little more, but everything still tastes like metal, except for chicken broth and crackers, those taste okay."

"That is good to hear. What about falling? Have you done any more of that lately?"

"No, I have not. After my last visit, I moved in with my parents. Between the two of them, my sister and her girlfriend, I have someone up under me around the clock. They have not given me any room to breathe out of fear that I may fall."

"Ms. James, you are very fortunate to have a family that wants to take care of you. A lot of patients have to go through this ordeal without the support of family."

Vaneetra pondered on that thought. "I guess I am fortunate. So what happens next?"

"You finish your treatment. We run more test. If we do not find any more cancer cells, you come back every three months for a checkup. The longer you go without any more cancer cell growth, the less frequent you come in for a checkup."

"What are my options to keep it from coming back?"

"Unfortunately, there is no guarantee that the cancer will not return. Some women have chosen to have a double mastectomy in order to reduce their chances of it returning."

"Is that an option for me?"

"It is something for you to consider." Dr. Chen typed something on her laptop.

"I will give it some thought." Vaneetra changed the subject. "When will I be able to go back to work?"

"That is entirely up to you, Ms. James. You appear to be somewhat stronger. I noticed that your parents are not with you today."

"My father is in the waiting area. I am still unable to drive and need help getting around."

"Try to increase your food intake a little more. That should help with your energy level. In the meantime, consider waiting until this last round of chemotherapy is over before returning to work. You may also want to start out working just a few hours a week and build up to full time again."

Back at her parents' house, Vaneetra lay down to rest for a while. So many thoughts clouded her head and she did not really know how to sort through them. Even though Dr. Chen told her the best news regarding her health than she had heard in a while, she would not allow herself to feel happiness or even relief. Sitting alone in her old bedroom, she felt like a child again, in the midst of a thunderstorm. When she was just about ten years old, a raging and violent thunderstorm tore through Raleigh, taking out the power on their block and several streets over. She remembered running into her parents' room and jumping into bed with her mother, seeking protection from the raging winds that banged the branches of the tall oak trees against the side of the house. Her father had gone out of town to visit relatives and her mother, not being the particularly nurturing type, made her go back to her room and brave the storm alone. Courtney had her own room, and loved thunderstorms. She lay in her bed under her covers reading a book with a flashlight. Feeling frightened, alone and powerless, Vaneetra forced herself to look out of her window and face the storm until it ended, promising that she would never be afraid of anything else in all of her life. She told herself that night that she could and would face the world alone and conquer all obstacles.

Lying in the same bed as she did as a small, frightened child, Vaneetra knew that a new fear had developed in the depths of her gut over the past weeks. The fear of dying clutched her heart and squeezed until she literally lost her breath. Being fully aware of the good news Dr. Chen delivered to her just hours ago, did little to assuage those fears. She knew she might never again live without fear, because she finally faced a monster so horrific that it took away her will to fight. Its strength and power overshadowed that of any thunderstorm, and even though she faced the attack head on and now seemed to be winning, she knew that it fought dirty and could one day return to battle once more. She knew breast cancer moved like a destroyer of all and did not play favorites. Her best bet would be to rid herself of its breeding ground. The things that she was told made a woman desirable, attractive and wanted—her breasts.

Vaneetra also thought about the other battle that she faced, getting her daughter back. She knew Daniel planned to pursue joint custody in the near future. Having spoken to her attorney, she also knew he had a chance at winning in court. She could not deny that Daniel and his family, at least his sons, loved Maddie. The day she met them, the interaction softened her heart. Their innocence to the entire situation and thinking of that lowdown worm of a father as super dad, gave Vaneetra a glimpse of what is good in life. In the back of her mind, it confirmed what she had always known. It confirmed that Daniel could have been everything to her if only he had allowed their love to flourish.

A knock at the door snapped Vaneetra back to reality. "Who is it?" Vaneetra shouted to the person behind the closed door.

Mrs. James opened the door and entered the room, carrying Madison in her arms. "Were you sleeping? I thought I you might want to spend time with Madison before her father came to pick her up." Mrs. James sat on the edge of Vaneetra's bed.

The thought of Daniel irritated Vaneetra. "What time is he coming tonight? I want to talk to him about her coming home." Vaneetra sat up in the bed and reached for Madison.

"He called and said he would be here by five-thirty. That gives you plenty of time." Mrs. James smiled as she handed Madison over to her mother.

"A few hours are not enough time, Mother. I am her mother and should not be reduced to spending whatever time that no good father of hers decides I should have with her." Vaneetra glared at her mother.

"First of all, Vaneetra James, remember who you're talking to! I am your mother and you need to lose that nasty tone. Secondly, her father does not dictate the time you spend with your daughter. It is dictated by your illness."

Vaneetra waved a dismissive hand at her mother. "This conversation is pointless. In a few weeks we will both be back in the comforts of our own home and can put this whole awful mess behind us." She stroked the top of Madison's head, enjoying her baby chatter.

"I take it Dr. Chen gave you good news today." Mrs. James leaned back and folded her arms.

"As a matter of fact she did. She told me that the current chemotherapy treatment is working and will be over in a few weeks, after which I can return to work." Vaneetra did not share her disbelief and fears with her mother.

"That's great, Vaneetra." Mrs. James hesitated before continuing. "Do you think you are ready to have Madison come and live with you full time?"

"Yes, as a matter of fact I do. Why do you doubt my abilities to parent my daughter?" Vaneetra's tone expressed irritation with her mother.

"Vaneetra, no one doubts your ability to take care of Madison! It's just that I think you should ease back into being a full-time parent. Madison is almost eight months old and is moving around a whole lot more. What I doubt is that you will be back to full strength and energy in just a few weeks." Mrs. James threw her arms open.

"I will be taking her home with me when my chemotherapy is over and that is really the end of the conversation." Vaneetra let Madison crawl around on the bed, being careful not to let her go too far.

Mrs. James stared at Vaneetra for a long moment with her arms crossed. "After all that you have gone through, you're still foolish enough to believe that you are in control. Well, let me put something on your mind. Madison has an entirely separate family that she has grown accustomed to. She knows them better than she does you at this point in time. Daniel and his wife have been loving and caring for her for the past four months and that makes a difference. You can't just up and snatch her away like they don't mean anything."

Mrs. James's words infuriated Vaneetra. "Just whose damn side are you on anyway? She is my daughter and I am taking her home with me. She will get used to not being around them, just like she got used to not being around me!"

"Well, since you have it all figured out, answer this one question for me!" Mrs. James glared at Vaneetra.

"It is not like I can stop you from asking it, so get it over with." Vaneetra's eyebrows furrowed. She reached out to grab hold of Madison, who now lay on her back trying to put her foot inside of her mouth.

"It's a simple question and statement combined. Daniel is an attorney, who obviously wants to be involved in his daughter's life. Hell, he is raising her while you fight for your life. What makes you think that he is going to just let you take her away and start calling all of the shots again? I don't think that he will and the minute you try he will have you in court, and let me tell you, baby girl, there is a huge chance you will lose."

Vaneetra bellowed out a bitter laugh. "My own mother is on the side of my sperm donor?" Mrs. James's attitude appalled Vaneetra.

"Vaneetra, please, I am on the side of right! Now you do what you want, but if I were you, I would work something out with that man. Like it or not, you need others and you especially need Daniel. One would think that you would have learned that by now. You ought to be thankful that you got knocked up by a man that, regardless of his circumstance, stood up and took on his responsibility. You just don't know how lucky you are." Mrs. James turned and walked out of the room, slamming the door behind her. The noise startled Madison and she began to cry. Vaneetra scooped her up into her arms and rocked her until she quieted down.

Her mother's words left her seething. Vaneetra wondered how in the hell her mother could think that she lucked out because he is doing what he is supposed to do. She would have preferred he stayed away. Even though her mother made her blood boil in anger, she knew one thing she said to be true. Daniel would not just hand Madison back over. She did not have to be a genius to know that.

Chapter Forty

Shannon

Girl, why didn't you tell me that you were going to interview at North Carolina Central?" LaVonda shrieked into the phone. "I would have put in a good word for you with Harold."

"I did not tell you, because I did not want you to put in a good word for me. I wanted to secure the interview and job on my own." I kept my voice level, not wanting my friend to pick up on my nervousness about having this conversation. Even though Harold obviously told her that he recommended me for a position, I am sure he did not tell her all that he offered.

"I guess I can understand that. So have you accepted the position yet and what does Daniel have to say about all of this?" She fired questions at me like she worked for a gossip column.

"LaVonda, I have not been offered the job yet." Even though I knew I would turn it down once offered, I chose not to share that news. She is not one to leave well enough alone and I did not want to have to explain my reasoning just yet.

"So what did Daniel say about your going back to work full time?"

"What could he say? He does not have a say in what I do! He gave up that right when he started another family."

"It may seem that way to you, but I bet he does not see it that way."

"It does not really matter how he sees it. It is what it is, and there is not anything he can do or say about it."

"Yeah, we all know where you stand, but you are still his wife, so you should discuss matters that affect all of you. And before you can go off on one of your tangents, I know what he did, but it does not give you cause to use it as a reason for everything you do."

"LaVonda, I do not use it as a reason for everything I do, but I can't just put it behind me and pretend like nothing happened."

"Yes you do, and no you can't. You have to find balance. Have you looked into counseling? I remember that topic coming up before."

"No, I have not looked into counseling. I have decided that I do not what to go."

"So what are you going to do? Do you plan to just sit around and be mad until you are no longer mad?"

I knew she was being sarcastic, but I answered her anyway. "No, that is not my plan. As a matter of fact, I have already told Daniel my plan."

"Which is?" She waited for my answer.

LaVonda is a strong advocate for working out difficulties in a marriage, even infidelity. Knowing that she would not like what I said next, I took a deep breath before I spoke. "I told Daniel that I want a divorce." Once I started telling her the story, I did not stop until she knew everything that had gone on over the last few weeks, except the kiss and romantic offer from her brother-in-law. I thought it best that I kept that bit of information to myself, at least for the time being.

"Shannon, it seems to me that you spoke out of frustration, but that does not mean that you have to follow through. I am not going to badger you, but I strongly urge you to slow down and really think about what you are doing. You still love Daniel and you know it. Running away is not going to make your life any easier. What you need to do is stop being stubborn and make love to him."

"For your information, I almost gave in the other night. He kissed me. I didn't pull back. If the boys had not interrupted when they did, I think I would have had sex with him right on the sofa." Thinking back on that day brought a fresh wave of guilt over me—for not being completely forthcoming with my friend about why I was so aroused, and for having been so turned on by another man that I was going to give in to my husband, just to have my own needs met.

"Girl, that is least somewhat of a good sign! Being turned on by your husband is a start in your healing process."

Her statement intrigued me. "How do you figure that to be so?"

"Honey, because I have been your friend through all of the ups and downs in your marriage and when you are angry with Daniel, making love to him is always the last thing on your mind. That man has gone months with not so much as a rub from you." She laughed and so did I.

"I guess you are right, but don't act like you don't do the same thing." I tried to shift the focus of the conversation.

"No, I give it up even if I am furious with Richard. Life is too short and the lovin' is too good to pass up. I get mine, he gets his and we either continue the fight, or work out our differences afterward." She laughed.

"But how can you just give yourself to Richard when you are angry? Why would you even want him to touch you?"

"I can do it, because I love my husband and I have a high sex drive."

"Well, I have a high sex drive, but I am not sure that I still love my husband." I sighed and shifted the phone to the other ear.

"Girl, you still love that man. You're just hurt and have not found a way to heal, but if you drop those drawers and let that man in, literally, you will begin to feel better. You will also be following the word of God."

I waited for the laugh I thought was coming, but it never came. "LaVonda, where in the world does it say in the Bible that by having sex with your husband, you are following the word of God?" I immediately regretted asking that question. LaVonda knew her Bible.

"Read 1 Corinthians, chapter seven, verses one through five; it addresses sex in the marriage. Anyway, that is only part of the point. Don't ignore the fact that you still love him. Also, even if you don't read the Bible, which you should, you should not withhold sex because you need it just as bad as he does."

"You may need it as bad as Richard, but I don't need it as bad as Daniel." I felt like a hypocrite.

"Girl, I need it more than Richard does! Sometimes, I think I ride him so hard, I don't know how he gets up and goes to work in the morning. It is a good thing our bedroom is on the main floor. Poor RJ would need therapy!" She laughed at her own joke.

"LaVonda, that just is not me. I do not see giving myself to a man who did not seem to want me in the first place."

"First of all, you need to change your mode of thinking. As long as you think that Daniel does not want you, you will continue to refuse to offer yourself to him, or be available when he tries to get something started with you in the bedroom. He wanted you then, just like he wants you now."

"I don't think, I know. He had an affair with another woman, didn't he?"

"Yes he did, but as hard as it is to believe, it does not mean he didn't want you. Men have a very difficult time expressing themselves and you know you are not easy to communicate with when you are upset, so that makes it even harder."

"So, you mean to tell me that the best he could come up with to show me how he felt was to start another family?" LaVonda's reasoning did not make sense to me.

"Okay, let's break this down. Daniel could have come up with a better way to demonstrate with you how he felt. However, you have to know that he did not intentionally go out and start another family. Secondly, it is time for you to allow some healing to begin, but first, you have to let go of the whole 'woe is me! My husband started another family' thing you have going on right now. Shannon, I am only telling you this for your own good and that of your sons, let it go!"

Listening to LaVonda made me want to smash the phone against the wall, but I maintained my composure. "Look LaVonda, I know you mean well, but how can you tell me what I need to let go of? Your husband did not cheat on you and make an outside baby. How do you expect me to just let that go?"

"You let it go by deciding that you are going to make your marriage work. You let it go by not basing all of who Daniel is off one indiscretion he had. You decide to love him and your marriage through this."

"Just how do I love through this?" I grew weary and did not want to argue.

"You go back and focus on the problems that caused the rift between the two of you in the first place. Understand that you made yourself unavailable to your husband and what's her name came along at a time of weakness in his life. Make yourself available to your husband both emotionally and physically. You have to forgive the man, not for him, but for you."

"LaVonda, that is going to be a very hard thing to do."

"Maybe so, but it is not impossible. Put yourself in his shoes for a minute. What if a man had come along, or comes along now, and made you feel desirable? Can you honestly say you would just walk away?" This last statement made me wonder just how much Harold had told her.

"I can honestly say that I would walk away. That's beside the point. He had options other than the one he chose, so please do not try and justify what he did."

"I am not offering justification. I am offering reasons, there is a difference."

"What is the difference?"

"Justification tries to demonstrate a person being right. A reason is just what it says. It tells you why a person makes a decision, it does not offer perspective on right or wrong." I could tell by her tone that she was impressed with her explanations.

"If you say so. I have to get off this phone and get some work done. I will talk to you later."

"Okay, but Richard and I are having a dinner party next Friday. You, Daniel and the boys are invited."

"Daniel won't be attending. What's the special occasion?"

"He is coming, because I already had Richard call and invite him. I knew you would not tell him. As far as why we are having it, you will find out next Friday night. I won't take no for an answer."

"I know you won't. See you next Friday night."

Chapter Forty-One

Shannon

The time between my conversation with LaVonda and her dinner party went by without incident. Daniel told me his partner and longtime friend, Josh, filed a motion of joint custody of Madison. He had a hearing coming up in a few weeks, and wanted me to attend with him, stating the judge may look upon my presence favorably given the circumstances. I knew it took a lot for him to ask me to go with him, but I could not readily agree. Ironically, hearing Daniel say that he had Josh file for joint custody of Madison did not bring about the pain it once had. I had been doing a lot of thinking and came to the realization that Daniel's character would not allow him to walk out on his child, regardless of the circumstances. Those same characteristics kept him at home with me and his sons. If only they had kept him from cheating, but LaVonda was right. I have to let that go. Even if we end up divorcing, I cannot continue to hold on to the pain. I need to find a way to forgive him. I just don't know where to begin.

I did not tell Daniel that I turned down the instructor position at NCCU and had begun to look elsewhere. I sent my resume out to other universities for online instructor positions. Having had a drama-free week, I really took the time to focus on how jumping back into the workforce would be a major disruption for Jeran and Zach. I loved my time with them and the flexibility of working from home. It allowed me the opportunity to volunteer in Jeran's kindergarten class often and to spend a lot more quality time with them both.

I know divorcing Daniel would only create more problems, but I convinced myself that those problems would be easier to deal with, but I cannot really be sure. I had stayed with Daniel this long; if I stayed a little longer, it would not kill me.

I also gave a lot of thought about making myself available sexually to Daniel. Since the day we almost had sex on the couch, he started making more subtle advances toward me again, most of which I somewhat responded to, but stopped short of putting myself in a position to have to decide to actually have sex with him. I would go to bed early, fall asleep in the boys' room on the floor, or sleep on the sofa. He'd try to wake me, but I would pretend not to awaken.

Harold called several times, I assumed to talk to me about why I turned down the position he offered, but I did not responded. I knew I could not work under him now that I knew what else he wanted from me. I was not as confident as I presented to LaVonda about staying faithful. My physical reaction to him was too strong for me to want to risk it. After our encounter, it took days and many long jogs to calm my libido. I knew it would be easy to satisfy myself other ways or by giving in to Daniel, but the first option just was not the same as actually being with a man and I did not want to be with Daniel because someone else turned me on. I actually wanted to desire him again.

The evening of LaVonda's dinner party, my nerves were raw from anxiety. I had spoken to her that morning and she had given me a rundown of the guest list. Much to my dismay, Harold would be in attendance. I did not know how I would react to having both him and Daniel in the same room. I feared my attraction to him would be obvious to everyone, especially Daniel. I decided my best course of action would be to avoid being in his presence, if possible, and to definitely not be alone with him.

LaVonda scheduled the dinner party to start at seven. Daniel had arranged with Mrs. James for Madison to stay the night with her. Vaneetra called during our ride to LaVonda's house, stating that she had Madison with her. I could not help but to overhear their conversation. She told him she had moved back home and proceeded to curse him out. He told her that he would be by Sunday night to pick up Madison and disconnected while she was in mid-sentence.

The start of the evening went surprisingly well. LaVonda and Richard hired caterers to prepare an extravagant three-course meal and an abundance of hors d'oeuvres. All guests, except for Harold, arrived by seven-fifteen, and we sat down to dinner promptly at eight. LaVonda's sister and her family were there along with a couple of Richard's colleagues and their families. Two of my and LaVonda's girlfriends that I had not spoken to in months were there with their families. I could tell by the looks that they gave me that they wanted to ask about Madison, but did not.

One friend, Wanda, pulled me to the side and told me if I ever needed to talk, she would be there to listen. Wanda shared that she and her husband, Michael, went through infidelity on both their parts, and survived. We shared a long hug and a few tears, before joining the rest of the dinner party. I made a mental note to schedule lunch with her. Maybe her experience could give me some insight into my own situation.

LaVonda's house accommodated all the families quite comfortably. Her open plan on the main floor made it easy to situate the children at the kitchen table and an additional one that she set up next to it and still be in the same vicinity as the adults, who would sit at two tables in the dining room. The natural flow of the ongoing conversations dictated the seating at each table. Daniel and I ended up across from LaVonda, Richard, Wanda and Michael with two empty seats next to me. That did not bother me until five after eight when the doorbell rang and Harold walked in. My heart fluttered at the sight of his physique and sunk once the guilt that I had managed to suppress erupted back to the surface of my consciousness.

After apologizing for being late, much to my chagrin, Harold opted to take the chair right next to mine. This move did not go unnoticed by Daniel, and neither did Harold's cool tone and overly firm handshake, but he did not say anything. My nerves stood at attention. I became keenly aware of their every move. I felt like my entire body began to tremble, but I could not see any outward signs and if anyone else did, they did not mention it. However, every time I looked away from LaVonda and Wanda, Daniel's eyes met mine. He seemed to be watching me closely. The expressions on Wanda and LaVonda's face told me they noticed.

Despite the tension I felt, the conversations between everyone else flowed easily. We all waited for LaVonda and Harold to make their big announcement. A few people attempted to guess at what it could be, without success. One person even suggested that LaVonda might be pregnant with twins. Another person guessed that they had won the lottery. Both garnered a hearty laugh from all.

Thankfully, for much of the dinner I did not have to interact with Harold. He spent most of his time, denying knowing anything about LaVonda and Richard's news and talking sports with one of Richard's colleagues. Just as I had begun to breathe easy, Harold caught me off guard.

"Shannon, will you please pass me the shrimp?" I almost dropped the platter when his hand lingered on mine a little too long. Daniel reached out and grabbed it from the other end, staring at me with what I thought was a look of suspicion in his eyes. "I am sorry to hear that you turned down the assistant professor position in my department. I feel like you were the best candidate for the job."

I sipped my wine before answering. Waves rippled across its surface, caused by my trembling hand. I quickly placed it back on the table, hoping Daniel did not notice…he did. "Thank you for having such confidence in me, but after careful consideration, I determined that the position would not be a good fit with my current needs."

Harold cleared his throat. "Well, the offer still stands for a couple more weeks, if you change your mind. I plan to travel for the next two weeks and will not have time before I leave to send the name of the next best candidate." I thought I noticed a change in his tone.

LaVonda, not to be left out of the conversation, chimed right in. "Girl, when were you going to share that news? Last week you said you had not even been offered the job yet."

"I had not told anyone yet, I only turned it down yesterday." I stared at her, hoping she would drop the subject.

She must have caught on, because she turned her focus to Harold. "Harold, where are you going, so close to the end of the semester? Aren't you teaching classes?"

"As a matter of fact I am, LaVonda, but I have two very capable graduate assistants who will grade all of the final term papers."

"So where are you going?" LaVonda paid no mind to the fact that Harold ignored the question the first time she asked it.

"I am going to Europe for ten days with some friends. We have been planning this trip for a couple of years. Now seems to be the best time for everyone to travel."

"Oh really! Would there happen to be a la—"

Richard cut her off before she could finish her sentence. "LaVonda, I am sure Harold does not want to discuss his personal business at our dinner party." She cut her eyes at him and sipped her wine.

Nearing the end of dessert, Richard and LaVonda stood up and tapped the sides of their wine glasses. The kids had gone to another part of the house to play. "Excuse me everyone, now comes the part of the evening you have been waiting for."

"It's about time!" LaVonda's sister shouted from her table. Laughter exploded around the room.

"So is it good news or bad news?" one of Richard's colleagues asked.

"Well, I wouldn't categorize it as good or bad." Richard hesitated, but continued. "It is good for our family, but it comes at a cost."

"So get on with it and stop making us wait." Harold stood next to his brother. I exhaled a little too loudly at his departure from my side.

"Come on, baby. Let's not keep them waiting any longer." LaVonda wrapped her arms around Richard's waist. Even at five-nine she seemed short standing next to Richard's six-foot-four-inch, broad, muscular frame.

"Okay then, I will get on with it. LaVonda, RJ and I are moving to Charlotte in July." My tears caught me off guard. I quickly used my napkin to wipe them away as Richard continued to talk. "I have been offered a senior director's position at a company based there and accepted."

Cheers of congratulations and claps echoed the room.

"It was not an easy decision to make, but it is best for us. We wanted to share the news with our closest friends and family before we announced it to everyone else."

Tears accumulated at the brims of LaVonda's eyes. She hid her face in Richard's chest, unable to stop them from falling. Wanda and I rushed to her side and hugged her. Her sister joined in. The four of us stood for what seemed like an eternity, crying, oblivious to the continued conversation around us. I finally managed to pull away and go to the bathroom to wash my face. Daniel offered to accompany me, but I declined.

I continued to cry in the bathroom for a while longer. Everything seemed to come down on me at once. In the midst of my life being in shambles, my best friend was picking up and moving over two hours away. While that was not a huge distance, to me it seemed like an entire world apart; too far to just pick up and visit anytime I wanted. I sat on the toilet for another twenty minutes, weeping about everything that had occurred over the past year and a half. A knock on the door prompted me to get myself together. "I will be out in a minute." When the person did not respond, I figured whoever it was decided to seek another bathroom. I washed my face, opened the door, walking right into Harold. He grabbed me by the waist to keep me from falling. I wiggled free and took two steps backward into the bathroom. He closed the distance between us, but stood right in the doorway, blocking my view behind him. "My apologies Harold, I did not know there was anyone standing outside of the door."

"No need to apologize. Actually, I had just walked up. I was not even aware that you were in here." He gazed at me from head to toe, once again resting his eyes on my breasts. This time I felt exposed. I crossed my arms over my chest.

"Oh, I thought maybe you had knocked a few minutes ago and waited until the bathroom became available."

"No, that must have been someone else. I'm glad they decided to leave. This gives me the opportunity to spend a few moments alone with you." He reached out for my hand, but I took another step back. He took a step forward, now standing completely inside the bathroom, but he did not try to touch me again. "I see some things have changed since our last encounter. Would those things have anything to do with why you declined the position in my department?"

I felt uncomfortable standing in the bathroom with him. My discomfort intensified knowing my husband could walk up at any moment. "Harold, nothing has changed since our last meeting. I just no longer feel like the instructor's position in your department is the best choice for me."

"Does it have anything to do with our interaction the last time we met? I meant it when I said that regardless of what happens between us, you could still have the job." His tone seemed genuine. I believed he would not have the Human Resource Department at NCCU withdraw the job offer. I did not believe he would not continue to pursue me. I also did not have enough confidence in myself not to give in to his pursuit.

"As a matter of fact it does. While I believe that you would not interfere with me getting the position, I do not believe it is a good idea for me to work under a man that I have been intimate with."

"What in the hell did you just say?" Daniel grabbed Harold by the shoulder, spun him around and violently slammed him against the bathroom door, breaking a whole in the plaster.

Neither one of us heard his approach. Both men stood above six feet tall, nose to nose, and in great shape. Not to be dominated, Harold grabbed Daniel's shirt and shoved back. They began to tussle inside the confined space of LaVonda and Richard's bathroom.

"Oh my Lord, please help me! Daniel, please stop. Harold, please stop!" Neither heard me over the punches and profanity. Daniel landed a right hook on Harold's left jaw, propelling him into me and knocking me off balance into the glass shower door. I felt it crack under the impact of my head slamming against it. Dazed, I had no idea what happened next. I seemed to float far away from the mayhem. I could hear myself begging Daniel to stop, but my weakened voice did no good. I slid to the floor. A strong hand reached out and pulled me up and away from the glass door. I later found out that Wanda's husband, Michael, pulled me into his arms in just enough time to prevent me from injury by the shattering shower door. Although I did not lose consciousness, the commotion made it hard to focus.

When things seemed to be under control, practically everyone in the house, including the children, had squeezed in the hallway outside the bathroom.

"What the hell is going on here?" Richard stood between Harold and Daniel, pushing them apart, while the other men held them back.

"Your brother has been fucking my wife!" Daniel lunged forward, taking along the two men that flanked him, almost knocking Richard down. Harold said nothing. Jeran and Zach were screaming for me somewhere in the crowd of people.

I pushed off Michael and stood up. "Daniel, I did not sleep with Harold!" I managed to get my words out through sobs.

"I know what I heard, Shannon. You said you two slept together." He sounded so convincing, I almost believed him.

"Daniel, I never said that. I said—"

"Don't tell me what I heard. I know what I heard." He shook himself free from the two men. I stepped toward him, but he pushed past me, knocking me back against Michael. I don't even think he realized that he had done it. "You want a divorce. I won't stop you, but you and the boys don't have to move. When you get home tonight I will be gone." I watched him exit through the gapping space the crowd created, getting out of his way.

"Why didn't you say anything? Why did you just stand there and let him believe that we slept together?" Harold stood several feet away, listening to me shout at him and breathing heavily, yet he said nothing. I could not read the expression on his face. I only knew that I had never seen it before. "Don't you have anything to say?"

Richard stepped in front of me and faced his brother, blocking my view. He obviously had seen the look before. "Harold, man, now is not the time for you to let your pride get in the way. Brother, I am going to need you to calm down and tell me what is going on." Harold didn't say anything for a long time. The other guests, children included, stood quietly awaiting his answer, except Jeran and Zach, who still called for me from somewhere in the crowd. Finally, Harold walked up to his bother and looked him in the eyes.

Never saying a word, he turned and departed from the same gaping hole in the crowd as Daniel. Richard turned to me, looking bewildered. I let my head fall on Michael's shoulder and sobbed. He wrapped his arm around me and stroked the top of my head. A sharp pain shot through my skull at the same time that Michael quickly snatched his hand away. It was not until that moment that I even noticed blood trickling down the back of my neck.

Chapter Forty-Two

Daniel

As soon as I left Richard and LaVonda's, I went home, grabbed some clothes and stuffed them in a duffel bag. I cleaned myself up in the bathroom. My knuckles stung under the running water from the faucet as I washed off Harold's blood. I drove around for hours after leaving my house, not knowing what to think, or how to feel. I could not believe what I had heard and that my wife actually slept with another man. I called Josh, who agreed to meet me at a local bar. By the time he arrived, I had polished off my fourth beer. Hearing Shannon say she screwed another man infuriated me. I didn't care that I did the same thing and have a daughter. The more I thought about it the more I wished that I had killed him. He had no right to violate my marriage. This brother knew that Shannon was married. He knew me! I wondered how long their affair had been going on. I wrecked my brain trying to figure out when this whole thing could have started and came up with nothing. I knew one thing for sure, the whole truth would come out, even if I had to beat it out the punk-ass motherfucker.

"Hey, dude, it is after midnight. This better be good. I ended a date early to come see about you. I could have gone another couple of rounds!" Josh slid into the booth across from me.

"You mean to tell me some woman was crazy enough to give you some?"

"Yes, some woman was smart enough to want to please me. You had two women wanting to please you at one time. I can have one."

"Had is the key word, now the one I thought I wanted is driving me insane and the one I know for sure I want, has someone else. Man, everything is crazy right now." I turned my fifth beer up to my lips and took a sip.

"What are you talking about?" The server came over and Josh ordered a beer.

"Man, you will not believe it if I told you, so I may as well not even tell you." I continued drinking.

"What I don't believe is that you are drunk and aren't making any sense. What in the hell is up with you, dude?"

"What's up with me? What's up with me? Nothing is up with me. You are supposed to be the best lawyer in town, besides me, and you aren't even asking the right questions. How did we ever become partners?" I sipped some more.

"We became partners because I am better than you, but I know you did not have me come all the way down here just so I could tell you that." The server returned with Josh's beer. He handed her cash and told her to keep the change.

"You are right! I did not call you down here to hear your deepest hopes and dreams. I called you down here to tell you about your scandalous-ass friend." I signaled for the server to come back over. Josh waved her off.

"Daniel, you are my only scandalous-ass friend, so what the hell did you do?" He turned up his beer.

"Me? What did I do? I didn't do shit. Shannon is the scandalous one, not me!" I grabbed for my beer, but Josh slid it away.

"Hey, buddy. Slow down on the drinking and explain to me just what in the hell you are talking about. What did Shannon do?"

"What did she do? What did she do? She slept with some punk-ass motherfucker, that's what she did. And you know what I did? I beat his punk ass…his motherfucking ass. That's what I did."

"Whoa, whoa…Shannon did what? You did what? Man, just how much have you been drinking?" Josh pulled my beer completely out of my reach.

"Man, give me my damn beer back. I haven't been drinking enough. That's how much I have been drinking…not a damn 'nough!" I reached across the table, grabbed my beer and took another sip.

"Okay, do you think you can put the beer down long enough to explain to me what the hell is going on? Can you do that?" Josh threw his hands in the air.

I sat my beer down and slammed my fist on the table, causing the few other patrons in the bar to look our way, but I didn't care. "I will start from the beginning. Shannon had a job interview with her friend LaVonda's brother-in-law, Harold, at NCCU in the English department. She told me about it after she had the interview, but said she did not know if she was going to take it."

"Yeah and what is the big deal about that? You don't want her to work outside of the home anyway."

"I'm not finished. The day she had what she said was her second interview she came home and was acting strange. I couldn't put my finger on it at the time, but now I know why. Man, she even almost let me make love to her."

"Daniel, she is your wife. What is so strange about her almost giving you some? Isn't that what you have wanted to happen for months now?" Josh finished off his beer, put the bottle down and stared at me.

"Yes, but I think she had been with old punk ass. Actually, she said that she was. I bet they were fucking then."

"Okay, dude, I don't need to tell you that you don't make any more sense now than you did a few minutes ago. Dan, man, where are you getting all of this crazy information from?" Josh ran his hands through his hair.

"We were at LaVonda's house for a dinner party. I caught Shannon in the bathroom with this motherfucker. She was talking about how she did not think she could work for someone she had been intimate with."

"Man, I don't believe that! You must have misunderstood her."

"I didn't misunderstand a damn thing! I know what I heard. She never even told me that she had actually turned down the job. I found that out tonight. And on top of that, this asshole had the nerve to sit next to her at dinner and rub her hand like I wouldn't notice. I should have knocked his ass out then."

Josh leaned over the table and whispered, "He did what? Dan, are you sure you are not misconstruing the situation? Who would be that stupid?"

"No, I am not misconstruing shit. He asked her to pass him a platter of shrimp and rubbed her hand when she handed it to him. She must have gotten nervous, because she almost dropped the whole platter. I had to grab the other side of it."

"Dude, that sounds like coincidence. You really need to think about this. Are you sure you heard what she said correctly?"

"Yes, I know what I heard! She said 'intimate'. What the hell else could she have meant?"

"Look, man, you will have to ask Shannon, but I just can't believe she would do that to you." Josh shook his head as if to signify his disbelief.

"Why wouldn't she? She could have been trying to get back at me."

"Shannon isn't the vengeful type. Why would she cheat after all this time? I think you are just trying to relieve your guilt for what you did. You need to talk to her and listen to what she has to say."

"I thought you were my boy? Why are you taking her side? When shit was messed up in your life, I supported you one hundred percent. It's fucked up that you can't do the same." I knew I was being unreasonable, but I was too pissed to care.

"I am going to ignore your rants, because you are drunk and just spouting off at the mouth, but if I wasn't your boy, I would let you completely ruin your marriage without trying to talk some sense into you."

"All I hear you doing is calling me drunk and defending my wife. You have not given me one solid reason why you think Shannon wouldn't cheat on me." I motioned for the server and Josh waved her off again. "Man, will you stop waving her off? I want another beer."

"She can come in a minute, but I want to finish our conversation first."

"Hurry the hell up. I want another beer."

"Look, when I cheated with my brother's girlfriend, you told me I should tell him what I had done and face the consequences. Now, I am telling you that you need to face the consequences of your actions. If Shannon did cheat on you, consider it a consequence to your actions. You brought that into your marriage."

"And how did that turn out for you?"

"We got into a fist fight. I ended up with two busted ribs, him with a black eye and didn't speak to each other until about two years ago."

"You told me you got into a bar fight when that happened."

"We were in a bar. I guess I didn't want to admit that I was wrong for what I did. I don't have a good reason for not telling you, so I won't make up one." Josh shrugged at me and waited for my response.

"So what happened to the girl?" I knew I was getting off topic.

"What happened to her is not important. We are discussing you and Shannon. You need to sober up and talk to your wife."

"I don't have anything to say to her. I know what I heard and I am done."

"You mean to say that after all you put her through, you are going to turn your back on her, because you think she did the same thing?"

I knew Josh was making sense, but I didn't think I could get past the idea of some other man making love to my wife. "Look, man, I need a place to crash for a few days until I can make other arrangements. I am not trying to go in behind some other man."

"Are you serious? Even if she did sleep with another man, you need to forgive her and call it even; just hope she is not pregnant."

"If she is, I am going to kill that motherfucker!"

Josh looked at me and shook his head. "There is no point in continuing to try and talk some sense into you. You are welcome to crash at my place tonight, but tomorrow you need to go straighten things out with your wife."

"Look, man, can we change the subject? I don't want to talk about this no more. You are killing my buzz." I waved for the server to come over and ordered another beer.

Josh shook his head and ordered one, too. "Dude, you are too messed up to drive, so this will be our last beer if you plan to crash at my place." Josh reached over the table and snatched the keys off the table. "I'll drive. We can pick up your car tomorrow, so you can go home to your wife and, if you're lucky, she will give you some."

"Man, get the fuck out of here! My so-called wife let another man run all up in her. How am I supposed to even think about being with her again? She disrespected me." The server brought our beers.

"So, now I guess you know how she feels. How many times did you run all up in your side piece? I still don't believe that Shannon cheated on you, but if she did, you deserved it."

Chapter Forty-Three

Shannon

I hid in Richard and LaVonda's bedroom with Jeran and Zach, until the commotion died down and their remaining guests left. LaVonda and Wanda came to my aid, not saying a word. Jeran and Zach clutched my shirt tightly with their tiny little fists and sobbed in my lap. I clung to LaVonda, wrapping my arms around her, begging for forgiveness between sobs. I am not quite sure if I wanted her to forgive me for ruining her party, or if those were words I wished I could say to Daniel. I should have never let Harold get that close to me. I spent months thinking my anger would block any desire to be caressed and stimulated by a man. I never once thought that another could awaken them.

I called LaVonda the next day, apologizing profusely and begging her to send me the bill for repairs they will need to have done. She refused to entertain the idea of my paying, stating that Harold held just as much responsibility, if not more, in the situation. Despite what she said, I felt solely responsible for the chaos Daniel, Harold and I created at their home. I was the one who let another man into the realm of my life meant only for my husband. Even though Daniel did it first, I should not have followed suit.

LaVonda may have ignored my requests to pay her for the damage we caused, but she did not ignore the reason for the damage. She pressed me so hard for that information that I agreed to have lunch with her the following Saturday, promising to explain everything.

I called Ms. Whitmore and asked if she would keep the boys for me. For some reason, I felt the need to explain to her what happened at LaVonda's party. She politely refused to keep the boys, inviting herself to join us for lunch instead, insisting that someone needed to pray for my marriage, and coach me on how to handle this situation. As much as I loved Ms. Whitmore, she really got on my nerves sometimes, always thinking she knew the right answers. Never mind she usually did.

Josh called me to let me know that Daniel was staying at his place. He listened while I explained everything, beginning with my telling Daniel I wanted a divorce up to his fight with Harold. When I finished, it felt like I had released a heavy burden from my soul. Ever since I have known Josh, he had always been a gentle listener and the voice of reason. He offered to pick up the boys a few nights during the week and take them to his house, if in fact Daniel chose not to come home. I accepted his offer and thanked him, not sure that I wanted Daniel to come home.

I needed time to think clearly. I felt guilty for getting so close to Harold, but not guilty enough to put aside why all this started in the first place. Despite the fact he cheated on me, impregnated a woman, and brought his child to live in our home, all with the expectation that I just accept it, he now chose to treat me like I did something wrong. Even If I had slept with Harold, how could he have the nerve to get so angry that he got into a fistfight, and storms out, leaving me and our children stranded.

I spent most of the week in a state of confusion and crying either out of anger, or out of despair. My stubbornness and pride refused to allow me to call Daniel. I kept telling myself him being gone would give the boys and me a chance to adjust to living on our own, but that did not help me deal with the situation any better. It did not turn out to be the easy transition I imagined it would, nor did I feel any better.

Most days I managed to get up, shower and take Jeran to school. During the day, Zach and I would lie on the couch and watch all his favorite television programs. He spent most of the time trying to cheer me up by rubbing my feet and telling me that Daddy and Maddie would be home just as soon as he finished helping Uncle Josh with his big case. Josh must have provided the cover story when he called to check on them. He ate a lot of cold cereal and peanut butter and jelly, which is not common. I pride myself on cooking hot meals for my sons daily. One day I did manage to warm up soup from a can.

The boys cried every night for their father and their sister, praying to God for them to come home. On Wednesday, Jeran's teacher called, suggesting I pick him up early from school, because he had spent the entire morning with his head down, sobbing. After that, I broke down and called Daniel, asking him to return my call…nothing. I could have driven to his office and choked the life out of him for ignoring our children. He had no right to be that angry. I may have wanted to have sex with someone else, but he actually did.

His stance on the situation pissed me off. I called Josh and asked him to pick up the boys Wednesday evening, sending them with enough clothes to last through the weekend and a note, explaining to Daniel that they wanted to stay with him for a few nights. I did not worry about how he would get Jeran to school, or who would care for Zach. I figured if our relationship was officially over, then he needed to learn how to figure these things out for himself. I loved my children with all my being, but believed wholeheartedly in joint custody.

I managed to pull myself together and spent Thursday and Friday planning my next move. Harold called several times during the week, but I refused to answer any of his calls. He finally texted me on Thursday afternoon, asking if I would meet him to discuss what happened. I responded, telling him that we did not need to discuss anything and I thought it best not to communicate with him. That did not stop him from continuing to text and call. I refused to acknowledge him, deciding to focus my attention on what to do about my marriage. Divorce seemed inevitable and I needed to prepare for the process.

On Saturday, I picked up Ms. Whitmore and we met LaVonda at Brio's in Crabtree Valley mall. I think they have the best appetizers and drinks. I needed both. LaVonda wasted no time firing questions at me like a gossip columnist. She did take the time to tell me that Richard refused to cash my check I sent to his job and tore it up in my face. "Shannon, you need to spill the beans and tell me what is going on between you and Harold. Sunday after church, he came back over to the house. He and Richard had the worst argument I have ever heard go on between the two of them."

"LaVonda, I am so sorry that I brought this mess to your house. I never meant for you and Richard to become involved in any of this." I used my napkin to wipe the corners of my eyes. I had gone two days without crying, but just thinking about what happened brought tears back full force.

Ms. Whitmore patted the top of my free hand. "Chil', don't worry about apologizing, just tell us what happened."

"That's just it! Nothing happened, absolutely nothing at all."

"So why does Daniel believe something did? Harold said Daniel came from behind, started making accusations and attacked him." The server brought over three glasses of iced water and a small bowl of lemons.

"That man of yours didn't just pull those thoughts out of the air. Something has him thinking that way. You have got to have some idea of what it is." Ms. Whitmore plopped a lemon in her water and swished it around with her spoon.

"I know where he got the idea from, but he is wrong." I sipped my water.

LaVonda grabbed and shook my hand. "So, get on with it. We are waiting to hear your side of this story."

"After I interviewed for the instructor position at NCCU, Harold called me for a second meeting. He said he had a few more questions for me."

LaVonda scanned her menu. "Did he call you personally?"

"Yes, he did"

"Uhm, Uhm, chil', that is a professional no-no, and a warning sign that something is not right. You should have known that." Ms. Whitmore added her two cents.

"Ms. Whitmore, I did not think anything of it, since we already knew each other. I simply brushed it off." Offense at Ms. Whitmore's declaration that I should have known better broke through in my tone. "Anyway, we met at the Bone Fish Grill for lunch one day. We chatted about random subjects, but after a while, his interest in me personally became apparent. When he walked me to my car, he leaned in and kissed me and told me he has always been interested in me."

"He did what?" LaVonda placed her menu down. "Did you say that Harold kissed you?" She stared at me with her mouth wide open.

"That is exactly what she said, chil'! What kind of fool do you have for a brother-in-law anyway? It is disgraceful for him to try to seduce a married woman. The Lord should have mercy on his soul, because he is truly lost."

"Now you just hold on, Ms. Whitmore. I do not approve of Harold's actions, but it is unnecessary for you to call him names and make such harsh judgments. You don't even know anything about him." LaVonda barely contained her annoyance at Ms. Whitmore.

"I know that he tried to take advantage of this poor girl, while she was weak in the flesh and in a state of confusion." Ms. Whitmore maintained her low opinion of Harold. "And I am not making judgments, I am making an observation. What would you call what he did? Tell the truth!"

LaVonda ignored Ms. Whitmore's suggestion that she may not be truthful about her feelings. "I am not sure what I would call it, but I know that Shannon is not a poor confused girl. She is a consenting adult, and if—"

Ms. Whitmore looked over her glasses at LaVonda, raising one eyebrow. "Are you implying that Shannon, a married woman, wanted to defile her marriage bed?"

"I am not saying anything, because you won't let me!" I detected defensiveness and irritation in LaVonda's voice and decided to interject.

"If both of you would just calm down and relax, I can tell you how it happened and my responsibility in it. I am sitting right here, neither of you have to make assumptions." Both women gave me there complete attention, not saying another word. It somewhat unnerved me. "Let me start by saying that Harold did not take advantage of me." Ms. Whitmore started to speak, but I held up my hand, signaling for her not to. "Almost from the very beginning of our lunch meeting, Harold made remarks and gestures that indicated his interest in me went beyond having me work for him, but I did nothing to stop it. At first, I ignored it, playing it off as nothing, but now that I have had time to think about it, I can honestly say that I enjoyed it. I liked his flirting, it aroused me."

"Shannon, what exactly did Harold say or do that aroused you?" LaVonda calmed her tone, but I saw unrest in her eyes.

"Do you mean what did he do other than calling and arranging a date disguised as a second interview and then kissing her?" Ms. Whitmore did not bother to calm her tone.

"Ms. Whitmore, I am not going to sit idly by while you continue to express your low opinion of my brother-in-law! This is getting out of hand." LaVonda clutched her cloth napkin in her fist so tightly I thought I heard threads tear.

I could not take their arguing any longer. "Ladies, I really need you both to stop with your bickering back and forth. Neither of you have a clue as to what really happened, nor will you let me tell you. If you are not going to be quiet and listen to what I have to say, I am going to leave. I came here because I need some help and sound advice. I thought I could get it from the two of you, but that does not seem to be the case."

For the first time since this entire debacle began, I admitted that I needed help navigating through this mess. I spent so long not knowing what I wanted to do, wanting to leave, but not being sure that I could. I spent over a year being furious with him, never once did I think of cheating or getting even until that day I met with Harold. I just wanted the entire situation to no longer exist. Now, a single moment of weakness has hand delivered to me the very thing I thought I wanted all along, to be free from Daniel and the mess he created. I thought I would feel a tremendous weight lifted from around my heart. Instead, I feel constant pressure like the air is being pushed out of my lungs and I cannot inhale to let any back in.

LaVonda let go of her napkin and rubbed my shoulder. "Shannon, you're right. We are not being very supportive. We apologize."

"Yes, honey. We're sorry. I, for one, will be quiet and listen. Whatever you need, but first let's start this conversation over the right way." Ms. Whitmore held out her hands for us to take. "Ladies, please join me in prayer, let's bow our heads.

"Lord God, I thank you for this opportunity for the three of us to come together and fellowship in Your holy name. Thank you for being our guide and protection. Lord God, Shannon is in great need of Your help. Her family is in peril and needs to be mended. Lord, You brought Shannon and Daniel together, but now this union is being torn apart. Lord, I ask that You remove malice and ill will from my and LaVonda's hearts and minds so that we can actually hear and be of support to our friend on this day. Lord, let Your will be done. In the name of the father, son and Holy Spirit, in Jesus name I pray, Amen."

"Ms. Whitmore, Harold did not try and take advantage of me or seduce me. He expressed his interest and let it be known that he found me attractive and desirable. I have not felt like that in a very long time. I let it go too far and accept responsibility for my part in the entire situation." Our meals arrived and I spent the next thirty minutes giving them details about what happened. When I finished, LaVonda spoke first.

"So tell me something, Shannon. Why didn't you just leave when Harold started coming on to you?"

I kept quiet for a moment, thinking about her question. "LaVonda, I guess the only answer I have for you is that Harold's actions and behavior turned me on." Just thinking about it created a tingling sensation between my thighs. I took a deep breath, willing myself to shift my focus to the present. "Had we been in a different setting, like his office for instance, I probably would have had sex with him right at that moment."

"Well thank God you were in a restaurant." Ms. Whitmore threw up her hands. "Lord knows both of you don't need to be steppin' outside of your marriage."

"Ms. Whitmore, I do not have a marriage. I have a shamble. Daniel and I have been dancing around each other since before Vaneetra showed up on my door step with her belly filled with his baby."

"So, are you saying that it is over between you and Daniel?" I detected pity in LaVonda's voice.

"I want to know what you plan to do about this Harold person. Are you planning on continuing a relationship with him?" Ms. Whitmore peered at me out of the corner of her eye.

"Harold and I do not have a relationship. We had an incident, a simple incident. I turned down the job offer and don't plan to see him again." I did not reveal that he had been calling and texting me. There was no need to add stress to the situation.

"And what about your husband, chil'? Just want do you plan to do about that situation."

"Daniel left and before he did, he told me he would give me a divorce. I am not going to beg him to come back. Over the past few days, I have thought about what to do next. I am still leaning toward just letting it all go. I hung in for a year after I found out he had an affair and a baby on the way. He bailed at the thought of my cheating."

"Shannon, what are you going to tell Jeran and Zach? How do you think they will handle it if you and Daniel divorced?" LaVonda's questions were valid. Questions I did not have good answers to.

"They will adjust. They will not be the first set of kids whose parents get divorced."

"Now, Shannon, that is just a bunch of foolishness. What do you mean they will adjust? They should not have to." Ms. Whitmore leaned forward and nearly spit her words at me. I knew her opinion on this matter favored Daniel and I staying together, but one would think that our divorcing affected her directly.

"Ms. Whitmore, it is not foolish for me to say that Jeran and Zach will adjust to Daniel being out of the home. He left me and, after all he put me through, I am not going to ask him to come back. If he can just walk out at the idea of my being with another man and he went off and created a new family, then he can stay gone." My words came out a little harsher than planned, but I did not apologize.

"Shannon, at the end of the day you have to do what you believe in your heart and mind is best for you and your entire family. If divorcing Daniel is what you think is best then so be it, but take some time and give it some real thought and consideration."

"LaVonda, I am tired of going through this. I am tired of talking about it. I am just tired. This mess has consumed every day of my life since I found out. That is why I want a divorce. I just don't want to deal with it any longer."

"Do you still love Daniel?" Ms. Whitmore asked the question.

"Yes…maybe. I don't know if I do or not. What does it matter? He moved out."

"You need to decide if you love him or not. If you don't then by all means divorce him and move on with your life. If you do, stop overthinking the situation and work on saving your marriage." Now it was clear why LaVonda made such a good therapist. She has a way of getting to the point and making the impossible seem easy.

"Daniel moved out. He obviously does not want to save our marriage."

"Has he moved completely out and have you tried to talk to him?" LaVonda asked.

"No, he only took a few things and yes I have called him several times. He has not responded once."

"You need to go and talk to him and explain what really happened. Open up about how you feel and why you let things go so far with Harold."

"Why should I do all of that? He has not done it. I still do not know what drove him to cheat on me."

"Chil', listen to an old woman. As women, we have to sometimes take the first step. Even when our men have not met our needs, or have hurt us, we have to stand tall and fight to save what is worth saving."

"That's just it. I am not sure what we have is worth saving. I cannot see any happiness in this for me."

"You have to create happiness, but first you need to go back to where the problems got out of hand for you and Daniel. You need to go back before this Vaneetra gal ever existed in your life and start there."

"Ms. Whitmore is right. Hon, I think you need to tear down the cracked foundation your marriage is standing on and build a new one. Think back to the biggest problem you and Daniel had pre Vaneetra and Madison and start there."

"We have had problems for a few years now. It is hard to pinpoint one specific issue."

LaVonda patted my hand. "The two of you need to figure it out together. Go and talk to him."

"If he wants to talk to me, he knows where I live. He pays the mortgage there."

"Shannon, go and talk to your husband. What can it hurt? He is already gone. Worst case scenario is that he stays gone." LaVonda shrugged and pushed her plate away.

"You need to talk to him, but I think you should go and talk to that Vaneetra person and give her a piece of your mind," Ms. Whitmore stated flatly.

"Ms. Whitmore, I do not have anything to talk to Vaneetra James about. I will not be doing that!"

"Actually, I think Ms. Whitmore may be on to something, Shannon." I nearly choked on my salad at LaVonda supporting such a crazy idea. "It may seem ludicrous, but I think it will help you heal. You have not really had an opportunity to get how you feel off your chest in a healthy and productive manner."

"So, you think confronting my husband's mistress will be healthy and productive? I know you are a therapist and I respect your opinion, but I can hardly see how that could be productive."

"You are helping to raise her child and will need to deal with her at some point, so you may as well clear the air and move on." LaVonda drove home her point and Ms. Whitmore nodded in agreement.

"Daniel and Madison have moved out. Besides, I wasn't really all that much help."

"Look, we can go back and forth all day and at the end you will do what you want, but I think you need to go and get your man and put that hussy in her place. Show her that you are queen and she was no better than a dumping ground…a toilet with legs!" Mrs. Whitmore tossed her napkin onto the table.

"Ms. Whitmore, need I remind you that the woman is battling cancer? No matter how trifling I think she is, I won't attack her verbally, or otherwise." I turned my attention to my salad, shaking my head at the very thought of confronting Vaneetra James.

"No one said anything about attacking her. Ms. Whitmore and I are merely suggesting you go and talk to her, tell her how you feel and move on. Whether she likes it or not, she needs to know how much damage she helped to cause. She obviously knew that Daniel had a family. After all, she knew exactly where to find you when she confronted you."

"Yeah, go on and give Ms. Thang a taste of her own medicine." Ms. Whitmore laughed at herself.

I had hoped discussing the situation with my friends would bring clarity and insight to my situation, but it did not. My husband cheated on me, walked out because he thought I cheated on him and my friends thought I should confront Vaneetra. I picked up the tab and went home, not having any clue as to what I would do next.

Chapter Forty-Four

Shannon

So many thoughts and emotions raced through my head at one time that I could not concentrate. I drove home, but felt restless and did not want to stay. I tried calling Daniel, but he sent me straight to voicemail. I texted him and told him I wanted to talk to our kids. Five minutes later, my phone rang. Jeran and Zach were on the other end, seemingly enjoying the time with their father and Uncle Josh. Jeran let me know that Daniel would be dropping him off at school on Monday and bringing Zach home. Zach told me that Jeran had not been to school since Wednesday and their dad took Thursday off to take them to the zoo, but they spent Friday with Madison and Mrs. James. He called her Grandma Evelyn. When I heard him call her that, I wanted to drive over to Josh's and rip into Daniel, but I knew that would not help the situation.

Restless and now furious, I paced around for a couple of hours doing chores, but frustration and restlessness clouded my concentration. The more I thought about my kids calling Mrs. James grandmother the angrier I became. I grabbed a duffel bag and a couple of suitcases out of Daniel's closet and started stuffing them with his clothes. I did not pay any attention to what I put in it. I just started dumping the contents of his drawers and snatching clothes off hangers. Thirty minutes later, I dragged and tossed each suitcase and the duffel bag down the stairs. Since he wanted to walk out on me after I put up with his crap all of this time, I would help his ass right out the door.

I drug everything to my SUV, loading it up, becoming more pissed with every second that passed. I stayed with him and let him bring his illegitimate child into our home. I at least tried to make it work. He thought I cheated and just walked out. By the time I reached Josh's block, my anger raged inside of me like a storm and I prepared to throw his bags at him and tell him to stay the hell out of my life. He at least should respect me enough to have a discussion with me, but since he didn't he could go straight to hell.

I saw Daniel standing in the driveway with the boys and slowed to a stop a few houses from where they were. Seeing our sons deadened the raging storm inside me. I could not let them see me lose my cool. Had he bothered to look in my direction, he would have seen me. Watching the three of them together for a few minutes, despair replaced my rage. Not seeing Madison, I was reminded of how my life used to be before she and Vaneetra came along. Reality set in and I knew that I could never return to yesterday. Today was all I had and it was filled with turmoil and destruction. I continued to observe, no longer feeling like I should approach them. They were playing tag; Daniel was the chaser. He would pretend to run after them as fast as he could when they were facing him, only to slow down when they turned and ran. For a moment, I thought he spotted me, but if he did, he did not acknowledge it in anyway.

I could hear their laughter loud and clear, but could not really make out what they were saying. They went on in this manner until the boys fell to the ground, doubled over in laughter with Daniel falling with them doing the same. Jeran and Zach's love for their father was obvious to anyone who saw them together and his for them. I realized their adjustment to not being with him every day would not be as easy as I had made it seem, instead they would be devastated.

After a while, Daniel loaded the boys in his car. I held my breath as the car rolled down the driveway, thinking he was going to drive in my direction. I wondered if he would drive past without even looking my way, or if the boys would see and call out for me, forcing him to stop. I exhaled when I saw him turn the tail end of his car toward me and drive off in the other direction.

I needed to go somewhere where I could clear my head and decide what to do next. I did not know exactly where. I just put the car in gear and drove, figuring I would drive until my full tank of gas ran low.

After three hours, I found myself at Carolina Beach. Something about it always made me feel better. It had a calming effect. I checked into a room at a beachfront hotel. Since it was off-season, the concierge gave me a room on the top floor with an oceanfront view. I went to the room, threw my purse on the bed and went down to the beach.

I picked a spot, took off my shoes and walked down to the edge of the water. The low tide washed out around my ankles, splashing the salty water onto the hem of my white peasant skirt. I remembered the first time Daniel and I came to this very beach during the late spring of our first year in North Carolina. We fell in love with the entire atmosphere, the quaint little boardwalk, the mesmerizing sound of the ocean at times slamming against it, other times enveloping the beach's edge; and the solitude it offered. Warmth engulfed my belly at the memory of our first time here. I had gone out into the water, daring myself to embrace its chill. I had closed my eyes, letting the peace overtake me, when suddenly I lost my footing at the same time a tide came in. The water overtook me, causing me to stumble and fall to my knees. I remember remaining calm and starting to push back and up on my feet using my hands. Before I could get one knee up, a set of strong arms wrapped around my waist, scooping me up out the water. Daniel walked me to shore, never releasing his hold. When he got me out of the water, he could not utter a single word. He only held me for what seemed like an eternity.

Later that night, after we had made love, he told me that for a moment he thought he had lost me forever, and promised never to let that happen. He promised always to protect and never leave me. That day seemed like it occurred in another lifetime, because here I was, back at the same beach, alone. So much had changed and happened. Somewhere along the line, Daniel fell out of love and used the first excuse he could to leave me.

Having walked for better than an hour, I found my shoes, went back to my room, grabbed my purse and went to the Shuckin Shack for dinner. Over two glasses of white wine, a serving of steamed shrimp and fried clams, I came to a decision about my next move. No matter what happened, I needed to forgive. I felt in order to do that I would have to face the people I blamed for my pain. I decided take Ms. Whitmore and LaVonda's advice and pay Vaneetra a visit. I had no idea what doing such a thing would accomplish, but I needed to do it. She came to my door and delivered mass destruction. I would deliver forgiveness to hers. Then I would face my husband. Even if he doesn't believe it, I will tell him the truth about Harold. I won't ask him to come home, and if he chooses to stay gone, he will make that decision knowing the truth. Back at the hotel, I stripped off my clothes and slipped under the covers naked, wondering if I still loved my husband. I drifted off to sleep knowing I did, but not more than I loved myself. It was time to decide to take care of me, no more tears.

Chapter Forty-Five

Shannon

I woke up the next morning feeling at peace for the first time in months. I showered, dressed, checked out of the hotel and drove the three hour distance home. LaVonda and Ms. Whitmore called to check on me. When I pulled over to fill up my gas tank, I sent them both text messages letting them know that I was fine and would call them later. Then I called to talk to the boys. Jeran answered on the first ring. "Hey, Mom, what are you doing?"

"Hey, sweetie, Mommy is on the way home from the beach. How are you and your brother?" I had no idea why I referred to myself in the third person when I was talking to them.

"Zach is taking a nap. Why'd you go to the beach, Mom? It is still a little cold outside." I could hear the concern in his voice.

"Mommy just wanted to take some time while you and your brother were with your father and get away. Do you miss me?"

"Yes, I am ready to come back home." His low, sad voice tugged at my heartstrings.

"If you would like, you can come home tonight. I will tell your dad to either bring you boys home, or I will pick you and Zach up after I run an errand."

His tone instantly lightened. "Great! I will tell Dad! I love you, Mom, bye."

Talking to my son reinforced what I needed to do. The time had come for me to put the mess Vaneetra and Daniel created behind me. No matter what happened, I would move forward free from anguish.

I entered Vaneetra's Brier Creek subdivision at about ten past two. Rain pellets hit my windshield with a soft steady thud. I briefly considered changing my mind, but did not turn my SUV around. Google maps on my phone took me straight to her front door. All the townhomes looked the same, with their neatly manicured lawns. She lived on a corner lot at the very back of the subdivision. Without hesitation, I got out of my truck, walked to her door and rang the bell…no answer. I waited a few moments and rang again…still no answer. I thought about leaving, but my feet would not move. I rang the bell a third time. "Who the hell is it?" The voice on the other side of the door sounded annoyed, yet tired. I did not answer. Instead, I rang the bell a fourth time. The door flung open. Vaneetra stood before me, a remnant of what she used to be, but not as frail as I had imagined. Her face registered irritation, then shock when she realized who I was. "What in the holy fuck do you want?"

Not bothering with niceties, I launched right in. "I want my life back, but since that is not going to happen, I thought we could talk woman to woman."

"We don't have a damn thing to talk about. Get the fuck off my door step."

"Not until you hear me out. You proudly walked into my life over a year and a half ago, with your belly stuffed with my husband's baby. I think you owe me five minutes."

"Bitch, you must be crazy, I don't owe you shit." She put her hands on her hips and leaned out the door toward me. Her use of profanity was getting old fast, but I knew to address it would do no good. Instead, I gave it right back to her.

"The hell you don't. You screwed my husband for months, knowing he had a family, got pregnant and had a baby. To top it off you get sick and I have been helping to take care of your child in my home. Yeah, you owe me and you are going to pay up." I took a step closer.

"Fuck you, I didn't ask you to take care of my child. But you don't have to worry, she will be coming home soon. Then I am going to sue for more child support and leave that trifling-ass husband of yours broke. Now get the fuck off my porch." Vaneetra took a step back and started to close the door in my face. I pressed my foot against it, and grabbed the knob. Her strength did not compare to mine.

"Look, I did not come here to fight and I am not leaving until I speak my peace, so you may as well listen." I pressed my hand against the door, but not enough to force it open.

"All I want to hear from you is the sound of your feet walking away from my damn house." She yanked the door out of my hand, breaking one of my nails.

As much as I was ready to slap the taste out of her mouth, I remained focused on my reason for being there. "I did not think you would make this easy, so I am going to just get on with it. I only came here to say that I forgive you." My finger with the broken nail throbbed and I could feel a trickle of blood run down it, but I did not let on.

"You what? Bitch, are you serious? Did I hear you just say you forgive me?" She stepped completely outside, stepping so close to me her nose almost touched mine.

"Yes, I said I forgive you. You and Daniel have dominated my entire existence since the day you rang my doorbell. Your hateful attitude has made the situation worse, but I have to let that go. I have to let you live with the fact that Daniel will always be your baby's daddy and never your husband. I have to let him live with the fact that he jeopardized the best woman he ever had for a few months of carefree nights of sex with you. I can no longer allow any of that to be my problem." My breath warmed the space between our faces, but I did not step back.

"Well don't you sound all high and mighty? You bring your raggedy ass to my house, talking all of this forgiveness shit, trying to be all noble and sophisticated, but I can see through you. I bet it burns you up to know that your man came to me to get satisfaction. How do you feel knowing that you were not enough for him?"

Her nasty and indignant attitude made it hard to maintain my forgiving demeanor. I abandoned that idea long enough to let her know where she really stood. "I feel about the same as you did when you realized that you were not woman enough to get him to leave home. You stand here and talk all of this trash, but you still go to bed alone at night. I know that you gave all of yourself to my husband, hoping that he would leave me, but instead he left you. Now you are over here by yourself, fighting for your life and my man is still at home, with the baby the two of you made. You think you can see through me, but I definitely can see through you."

She stepped back and started to wave her frail hand in my face. "Bitch, you don't know shit about me. I don't want your punk-ass husband. He just needs to run me my money when my daughter comes home."

"Is that why you are so damn bitter, because you don't want him? You can run that game on somebody else. I know better than to believe that. You are mad as hell, because he didn't leave me and you are stuck with a constant reminder that things didn't work out for you. I bet when you got sick, the idea of my taking care of your daughter almost killed you faster than the cancer. I kept my man and got your daughter," I said that with pride, knowing all I felt was anger in regards to that matter.

Vaneetra retreated into her house. I followed her to the edge of the door, stopping short of going in. "Fuck you, bitch. You better get the hell away from my door." She swung the door toward me. I raised my hands to keep it from hitting me, pushing it back toward her. Vaneetra stumbled backward, tripping over something. I had to reach out and grab her arm to prevent her from falling. She weighed nothing under my grip. "Bitch, are you fucking crazy?

I will have your ass killed!" She jerked one arm free, swinging it wildly, landing several blows to my face and head. Her hits felt like those of an angry toddler. I wanted to slam her to the floor, but something inside me that I cannot explain took over and kept me at peace. I grabbed her free arm, and pinned her against the door.

"You have to know that I did not come here to fight. No matter how angry you get, nothing will change. I am not leaving my husband." I had not planned to say that. I could not honestly say what would happen between Daniel and me.

She yanked her arms out of my grip. "Get your damn hands off me. I don't give a fuck if you leave him, or not." The look in her eyes told me she was lying. It was painfully clear that she loved my husband.

"You care and we both know it." I took a step back. I was sure she would not strike at me again. Her outburst left her breathless and visibly trembling. "I don't know how long Madison will be with me, but I can promise you that I will take care of her until she comes home to you. I won't let the sins of you and her father affect how I treat her. She, like me, is innocent in all of this."

Even though up until that very moment I resisted helping with Madison, I knew that I spoke the truth.

She laughed in my face. "Do you really think that you are innocent? I hate to burst your bubble, but if you had not been so damn frigid, Daniel may not have stepped out on you in the first place." Her statement caught me by surprise.

"Is that how Daniel described me, as frigid?" I could not help but to ask. It was the first insight I had on where we went wrong.

Vaneetra took advantage of the moment. "Oh, I see I have your attention now. Yes, your husband used to lay in my bed dickin' me down, all the while telling me that being with you was like screwing a corpse. He said you got so wrapped up in being a mother, that you forgot how to be a wife." She smiled at me as the last of her statement left her lips.

I struggled to maintain my composure. I could not let on that her words hurt deeply, but her eyes told me she already knew. "Even if he said all of that, he still did not leave. He is still with me. So, I guess I was not all that frigid." I knew lies rolled off my tongue, but she didn't and I used that to hold on to my pride.

"Whatever—you came over here all holier than though, thinking I needed your forgiveness. No, I am not the one who needs to be forgiven. You need to look in the mirror and talk that forgiveness shit to yourself. I don't regret what I did, but I bet you do. I bet you regret the day you first turned your man away from your bed. Now you know, he can and will be satisfied elsewhere." She smirked at me and crossed her arms in front of her.

I stared at her for a minute. Just long enough to detect a bit of hurt in her demeanor. I used it to my advantage. "Yeah, well, he is still my husband. He may have strayed, but he will not leave. I know because I asked him to and he refused. I can invite him back into my bed. I know for a fact if you get the chance, you will too, but I can promise you he won't ever come. He has tried you and you just weren't enough to keep him away from me." I returned her smirk and walked away without looking back, not letting on that Daniel had left me; that was none of her business. She did not say anything. I got into my truck and as I pulled away from the curb, her parents pulled up. I saw Madison's car seat in the back. I made eye contact with Mrs. James, but kept driving. Vaneetra could explain why her baby daddy's wife had been at her house.

Chapter Forty-Six

Shannon

It was no surprise that Daniel was waiting outside of Josh's when I drove up. He walked down the driveway and stood behind his car. I got out and walked toward him. Josh stood in the doorway. He started to come out, but I signaled him to remain inside. "I am here to pick up the boys. Are they ready?" I stopped about three feet away from him.

"Why in the hell did you go over to Vaneetra's house and what happened to your face?" He threw his arms out in exasperation. "She has cancer. What possible reason could you have for going to her home and upsetting her?"

The way he chose to defend her pissed me off. "Although I figured my presence would upset her that was not my intention when I decided to go. Are the boys ready? I want to take them home."

He stepped closer to me and kept his voice level, but I saw the anger dancing in his eyes. "Shannon, Vaneetra called me cursing, screaming and threatening to do harm to you. Tell me why you went over to her house and what happened. The left side of your face is red and welted."

"Daniel, I went over there to tell her I forgive her. I needed to come face to face with her and tell her how I felt, that I am moving past it, that I will take care of Madison until she is better. That is why I went over there. I needed to express myself to her."

"So what happened to your face? Did the two of you get into a fight?"

"You know her. She was your girlfriend, but to answer your question, we did not get into a fight. She did not like some of the things that I had to say, lost her temper and started hitting me, but I did not hit her back."

He threw up his arms and took another step forward. "Do you expect me to believe that you just stood by and let her hit you in your face?"

"No, because that would be inaccurate. I grabbed her arms and pinned her against her front door until she calmed down. Then I left."

"What exactly did you say to her?"

Frustrated by all his questioning, I threw up my hands. "Look, Daniel. It really does not matter what I said to Vaneetra. Just know that I let her know how I felt about what the two of you did and where I currently stand on the matter. I don't want to talk about it. Are the boys ready?"

He stood for a moment looking at me threw squinted eyes. I held his gaze, ready to take this argument to the end. Finally, he stepped back and let me pass. "Yes, they are ready."

I got about three feet away from him and turned back. "You know, I find it funny that you are more concerned about what I did and said to Vaneetra, but show no feelings in regards to leaving me and your sons stranded over something you think you heard. That is what we need to talk about, but I am not going to push the issue." I turned and walked to Josh's front door. He let me in to retrieve Jeran and Zach. After giving me a long hug, he called them downstairs and helped me get them and their belongings in my truck. Daniel had taken off without a word. I left and spent the rest of the afternoon enjoying my sons. I knew my marriage was over. Now it was time to prepare myself to move forward, and start again.

Chapter Forty-Seven

Shannon

As a treat for them, I took the boys to Jump Zone, a bounce house in our area and let them play for a couple of hours. Afterwards, we went to a Chinese buffet in Cary for dinner. I am not a fan of buffets, but they love it and this particular place serves good food. I placed all my attention and focus on them, ensuring they had a good time. I refused to think about Daniel's reaction to my altercation with Vaneetra. It made me wonder whether he still loved her.

By the time we arrived home, Jeran and Zach could barely keep their eyes open. I helped bathe and attempted to put them in their beds, but they found my bed to be more appealing. We piled in and I read bedtime stories from my favorite African American children's book until they fell asleep.

However, sleep evaded me. My mind kept wondering to what I would do with my life post Daniel and where to go from this point. I could feel an all too common ache growing from the center of my chest, but I refused to cry. I was tired of crying. What kind of fool was I to continue to cry over a man that put me through hell, only to walk out on me when he thought he would have to share in my experience? His recent actions today convinced me that he no longer loved me, that all those things he said about never letting me go and fighting to save our marriage were just lies. I needed to move on and begin my life without him.

The peace that had come over me last night, no longer existed. Turmoil filled my mind and I could not really understand why. Today confirmed that my marriage was really over and now it was time to move forward, but the thought of doing that just did not sit right in my spirit. Restless, I did something I had not done in months. I picked up my Bible off the nightstand and opened it. I did not know what I was hoping to accomplish. I stopped going to church months ago and had not prayed alone in only God knows how long. I didn't even know where to begin. So, I started from the most logical place…the beginning.

Reading about how God created Eve for Adam as a helpmate made me wonder if I had been created for Daniel. I always thought we were meant for each other, until Vaneetra introduced herself to me and I found out he had pulled her into our lives. Even when our relationship seemed not to exist and we could not speak to one another without arguing, I never questioned whether he was the man for me.

The chiming of the garage door jarred me out of my thoughts. "I really am not in the mood to argue with him. I hope he plans to just grab some more of his clothes and go." Tension gripped my neck, shoulders and upper back at the anticipation of an argument. I got out of bed, careful not to wake the boys, planning to head him off so that he would not disturb them. They would expect him to stay. I had gotten halfway down the stairs when he reached the base. I think I startled him, because he stopped dead in his tracks, one foot on the first step. "If you came to pick up more clothes, I did you the favor of packing you some things already. They are in the back of my truck."

For a moment, he stared at me not saying anything. "Actually, I did not come for more clothes. I came to talk to you and to see the boys before they went to bed." He climbed the steps.

"You are too late to see them. They've been in the bed for an hour." My stomach tightened into a knot, as he got closer. He needed to leave. I could not find the strength to argue. I didn't have any fight left in me. "You can go and check on them, but please don't wake them. We had a full afternoon and evening and they are exhausted." I moved aside so he could get past, but he stopped in front of me instead.

"I won't wake them. I'll just see them in the morning." He stood close, careful not to touch me, but my body heated in response to his proximity anyway. He just implied that he planned to spend the night. After walking out and leaving me stranded, then interrogating me about what I may have done to Vaneetra, I did not think I could handle his presence. I maintained my breathing level, mentally fighting what my subconscious was trying to push to the surface.

"I will have them call you when they get up in the morning. Maybe you can swing by and take Jeran to school like you originally planned." I moved past him down the stairs. "It's late and I am tired. I am going to get a glass of water and go to bed. You can let yourself out."

"Shannon, I want to talk to you. We need to finish the conversation we started earlier today." He turned and followed me downstairs.

The heat that had developed turned ice cold. No, he did not come to our home this late at night to finish a conversation about why I went to his baby mamma's house. "Daniel, it is late and I am not going to spend any more time talking to you about why I went to Vaneetra's house."

"Although I would like to understand why you went over there, I came to talk about you and Richard's brother. I need to understand why you slept with him. Did you do it to get back at me…to try and hurt me?"

I paused at the kitchen counter and contemplated my response. I wanted to yell, scream and ask him why in the hell did he have sex with and knock up some random chick that was now making our lives hell. However, now I really did not see how any of it mattered. If I were going to walk away and move on with my life, I had to let all of it go. "You heard part of a conversation and jumped to the conclusion that I had sex with Harold. Daniel, what have I ever done in all the years that we have been together to make you think that I would ever cheat on you?" I ravaged the cabinets in search of a wine glass. Water would no longer suffice. I was going to need some help relaxing.

"Shannon, I know what I heard. I heard you telling him that you could not have sex with him again!"

"Daniel, you did not hear me say that to him. I have not had sex with anyone but you since our first kiss." I went to the refrigerator to retrieve a bottle of wine, but he blocked the door.

"Shannon, you said you could not have sex with him again. Please don't try and deny that." He pressed his clenched fist against the freezer door.

"Daniel, this is going nowhere, so let me clarify for you what I said. You heard me tell Harold that I could not work under someone I had been intimate with."

"So are you going to play a word game with me? Shannon I don't feel like playing games." His attitude made me want to slap him, but I kept my cool. I kept telling myself that I needed to clear the air and move forward in my truth. "Are you really going to tell me that you are innocent of what I believe you did?"

"No, I am not telling you that." I tried to open the refrigerator, but he would not move. "Look, I never slept with Harold. I kissed him, but I did not have sex with him. I could not do that. I would not do that. I take my marriage vowels seriously." He shook his head and walked away, ignoring my dig about taking our marriage vowels seriously. "I know what you think you heard and I am not innocent, but I did not do what you accuse me of. That is not who I am. I am guilty of letting another man get too close to me, of kissing me, but not of having sex with him. What would make you think that I would cheat on you?"

"I could think of a couple of reasons. I thought maybe you did it to get back at me, or because you were horny as hell and couldn't bring yourself to be with me. It is not like we have had any kind of sex life. That vanished between us before any of this ever happened. The few times we were together, I felt like I was taking advantage of you. Your body was under me, but your mind was somewhere else. You stopped caring about us. It was like you used our sex life to punish me for not doing the things you wanted me to do."

His words stung like rain slapping across my face. "Is that why you told Vaneetra that I was frigid, that having sex with me was like having sex with a corpse? I didn't withhold sex from you as a ploy to get you to do what I wanted. I did not want to have sex, because I could not get aroused. You spent all of your time building your practice that you shoved me and the kids in the background. We never talked and every time I would try to strike up a conversation, you accused me of attacking you." The tears were stinging my eyes, but I refused to let him see me hurt.

Daniel placed his hands on my shoulders, trying to pull me closer, but I would not let him. Just yesterday, he treated me like a diseased animal. "Shannon, I never said those things to Vaneetra. I talked about being stressed out and unhappy, but never anything about our sex life. She never cared about what I was doing with you. All she ever cared about was making me happy. I assumed she knew we were not making love."

"What do you think I cared about? Do you think that your happiness was not important to me? As far as your assumptions about what she knew, let me tell you what I know. A woman that sleeps with a married man does not care if he is still sleeping with his wife or not. All she cares about is what she is getting from him."

"Shannon, I am sorry for what I did to you…to our family. I know and have known for a long time that I was wrong, but what can I do about it now?" He caught me by surprise. I never expected him to apologize. He had already done it once before.

"Why did you do it? You could have just left in the beginning of all of this. It would have been better for you to leave."

"I believed that you had forgotten how to be happy. We argued about every aspect of our lives, money, the kids, how much time I spent at work. I *felt* attacked all the time. It seemed like nothing I did satisfied you. I did not go out looking for someone else, it just happened. Even after it did, the idea of leaving you was not an option for me. I relieved stress with Vaneetra, but I never loved her."

"Yet, you did leave. The very minute you thought I had given myself to another man you turned and walked away."

"Shannon, I needed to blow off some steam. The idea of another man being with you and doing the things that I should have been doing…the things that I wanted to do sent me into a rage." I thought I saw his eyes moistened, but no tears fell.

"Daniel, how do you think I felt? To find out that you had been making love to another woman tore me to pieces! I have loved and been faithful to you from the moment I met you. Never did I ever think of giving what I had promised to you to another man. At least not until a couple of weeks ago, but even then, I still couldn't do it."

"Shannon, at the time it was all happening, I wouldn't allow myself to think about how all of this would hurt you. Even after you found out, I could not bring myself to face what I had done. I just tried to move past it and make the best of the situation."

"Daniel, it is not that easy for me. I can't just look past it. We had problems in our marriage, and instead of working them out, you went off and created another family without any regard for the one you already had. "

"Shannon, baby, I wanted to work out our problems, but you seemed so mad all of the time. I became resentful toward you."

I couldn't believe what he was saying. What had I ever done to him? "Why is that, Daniel? What have I ever done to make you resent me?"

"It seemed to me that you were ungrateful, that you didn't appreciate the fact that I was breaking my back all day, every day to provide for our family. I put in all of those hours building my practice so that you and the boys could be comfortable. So that you could have the option to live comfortably, but still be able to stay home and take care of our sons. I thought I was doing my job as a husband and a father, but it didn't seem like enough for you. You always found something wrong with anything I did."

"Daniel, I appreciated how hard you worked to provide for us, but I also needed you at home. I didn't think it was wrong for me to want more time from you. You put in long hours building your practice, not only for me and the boys, but for yourself, and that was fine. However, you forgot to put in hours to build up your family and every time I brought it up, you got defensive." I took a step back from him, because I could feel myself beginning to tremble. I could not understand why he did not see that his presence at home was as crucial as him being able to provide was. "What I don't understand is why you decided to cheat on me, which took even more time away from your family."

He went over to the kitchen table and sat down. Under the light, I saw that he was exhausted. He looked like he had not slept in days. "I did not *decide* to cheat on you. It just happened."

Now he had pissed me off. "How do you just happen to cheat on someone? Were you sitting down somewhere with your dick out and she fell on top of it, over and over again? I don't understand your statement."

"That is not what I meant. When I met Vaneetra, my frustration with our relationship was so high that I avoided coming home. She seemed very nice and to be honest, reminded me a lot of you." I had to bite my tongue to keep from cursing him out. What could he have possibly seen in her that reminded him of me? "Vaneetra made me feel like I was important and needed. She listened to me talk about my day at work, praised me for my accomplishments. She asked my advice about situations in her life and actually followed it. One thing led to another and before I knew it, things had gone too far."

"Daniel, things had gone too far when you got cozy enough to know that she was following your advice. You should have focused all of the time and attention you gave to her on me. I understand that I did not make it easy, but to just go and start another family seems a bit extreme. If you were really that unhappy, divorcing me would have been a better option."

"Shannon, I don't have an answer for why I did not put more effort into working things out with you." That did not surprise me. "I had already broken it off with Vaneetra by the time either of us found out she was pregnant. I did not intend to start a new family and I have not. Vaneetra is not my family. Madison is my daughter and I would like for her to be a part of this family."

"How do you expect me to except the child you made with another woman? I can't move forward from that. No one could!"

I walked up and faced him. "Please explain to me how you planned to move forward with your new baby, current wife and two sons?"

"I don't know. All I know is that I love you and want you back. I knew it would be hard for you to accept Madison, but I couldn't turn my back on her. I wanted to do what was right even though I knew it would only add to your hurt, but what else could I have done?"

"I did not think you could turn your back on your child. I don't know what you could have done short of not having an affair, but I can't get with your program. I can't be a mother to your child. Everyone, and I mean everyone, has accepted her and thinks that it is okay for her to be here, but, Daniel, it is not okay."

"Shannon, no one thinks that it is okay. I don't think that it is okay, but it's our reality. We have to figure out a way to move forward." He tried to put his hands on my hips, but I moved away.

"No, we don't have to figure anything out. I was planning to get a divorce, and when you thought I was cheating, you walked out. It seems like everything is figured out. All we have to do is tie up the loose ends." I walked into the family room and sat on the sofa. He followed.

"I am sorry for walking out on you like that. When I saw that guy in the bathroom with you and then I heard what you said, I just lost it. I couldn't handle the thought of you being with someone else." He sat down beside me, began to put his arm around me, but thought better of it. "Then I let myself think about how you must feel. Shannon, if you cheated, I deserved it."

"No one deserves to be cheated on and I did not cheat on you. When things get to the point where a couple feels like they can't communicate well enough to work out their issues, it is best to walk away. That is what I decided to do."

"Is that still your decision? Do you still want a divorce?"

"I want to be happy again. I think a divorce is my best chance at getting there."

"Do you still love me, Shannon?" He put his hand on my leg and the instant moisture in my panties told me I did. Here I was livid with him and his touch made me wet.

I thought about lying or saying I was not sure, but I told him the truth. "Yes, I do. I did not know that before you left, but your being gone helped me to recognize that I do."

His shoulders and face relaxed. He moved closer to me. "Then let's work it out. I don't expect you to immediately accept Maddie. I can only ask you to try. I won't ever turn my back on her and I don't want to lose you because of her. Shannon, I want it all—you, my sons and my daughter. I know I stormed out angry, but I am willing to do anything to prove to you that I am not going anywhere."

"Daniel, I am not sure that I can give you what you want. Even if I could accept Madison, I cannot deal with her mother. She is filled with spite and hate. I refuse to live with the type of stress she brings or in competition with her."

"Vaneetra is my problem and I will deal with her. There is no competition. I am done sleeping around on you. It has been so long since you have let me make love to you that I stopped counting at six months, but I have not even thought of being with another woman."

"I find that hard to believe. How do you go from having an affair to not even thinking about being with someone else, especially when you are not being satisfied at home?" I wanted to believe him, but I didn't trust him to be truthful about something like that.

"I will be honest with you. I became involved with Vaneetra, because I believed her to be a lot like you were before we began to have problems in our marriage. After it was too late, I realized that as much as she resembled you in motivation and sensuality, her general personality was very different, and nowhere near as beautiful."

"So you are telling me that our lack of a sex life had nothing to do with it?" I didn't believe that.

"If I told you that, I would be lying. What I am saying is that it was not the only reason." He pulled my hands onto his lap. I did not pull away this time.

I thought about what LaVonda said about not withholding sex. "So do you think that you would not have had an affair if I had not been so frigid?"

"Shannon, I never thought you were frigid. Vaneetra said that to get to you. I thought you stopped loving me, but I am not going to try to justify what I did. I was wrong and now all I can do is pick up the salvageable pieces to our relationship and try to build a better and stronger foundation."

I laughed a little too loudly. "I see you have been talking to my mother."

He positioned himself closer to me. "She is a wise woman."

My heart pounded against my rib cage. Keeping him out and moving on was not going to be easy and it wasn't because the boys needed him. I still wanted him. "Daniel, I still am not sure. I really have to think about it. I am still upset that you just walked out on me when you thought I slept with Harold. I don't understand how you could do such a thing if you love me like you say you do."

He cupped my face and stared at me so long, I thought he was not going to respond. "I walked out because no matter what I had done to you, I always considered you to be mine. The thought of another man being inside of you, making love to you, and fulfilling your desires enraged me. I know that is being hypocritical, but love is not always logical. This past week, I have realized that you are a strong woman to not walk away in the very beginning."

I focused on the bulge in his pants, afraid to look him in the eyes, as my tears streamed alongside his massive hands, down his wrist, disappearing into the cuff of his sleeve. Could he really still love me? Can a man love a woman that he cheated on? I thought back to my near mishap with Harold and knew the answer was yes. If you convince yourself that the person you love does not love you, it becomes easy to stray elsewhere. "I went to see a lawyer." He winced as if in pain, but did not pull away. "She suggested that we try counseling before I made any decisions."

"I am willing to try that." I glanced up in time to see the muscles in his face relax a little.

"I have been talking to LaVonda and Ms. Whitmore about this. They have helped keep me sane." I searched his face for disapproval, but could not find it.

"What did they say?"

"Ms. Whitmore said that I should pray."

"I can do that, too."

"LaVonda agrees with the attorney."

He chuckled. "She *is* a therapist."

A smile danced on the edges of my lips. "She also said that I should make love to you." I stared at him, hoping to relay the message of my pulsating pleasure spot. I was willing.

It did. "I am definitely willing to try that." Daniel pulled me to him, brushing his lips gently against mine. I opened my mouth slightly, allowing his tongue to enter. Each stroke of it drew my heart closer to him. After an eternal moment, he pulled away. "Are you sure you want to do this? I am willing to wait as long as it takes. I want you to be ready."

I rose to my feet, not answering him, just looking into his eyes, searching for a glimmer of the darkness of the past year and a half. I did not find it. Instead, I saw masked disappointment as he wrapped his arms around my hips, pressing his face against the lower part of my abdomen. His lips lingered at the tip of my pleasure spot. "I'll wait…as long as it takes. I will wait until you are ready."

Without saying a word, I placed my hands against his shoulders, pushing him back toward the sofa. They trembled as I pulled up my nightgown, looped my index fingers around the edges of my panties, pushing them down, and letting them fall to the floor. I saw excitement dance in Daniels eyes while his face maintained its composure. I kneeled down in front of him, unbuckling his belt and pants. His ripped abdomen quivered against the slightest touch of my fingertips. Gazing into his eyes, I pulled his pants and underwear down to his knees. Forcefully looking away, my gaze fell upon his erect manhood. Daniel pulled me toward him. I rose off my knees and straddled him, leaning in to receive his tongue once again. After a few moments, he withdrew from our entangled kiss, pressing his forehead against mine. Then he began to pray.

"Lord, please forgive me for all of the hurt and destruction I have caused in my home. Please forgive me for walking out emotionally and then physically, leaving my wife to bare the burdens of our marriage alone. Lord, thank you for giving me a second chance to be the husband and father that I am supposed to be. Please help us to be deeper in love and stronger than ever before. Never again will I stray from this gift you have given me. In Jesus's name, I pray…Amen."

The fear that clutched my heart released its death grip with each word of Daniel's prayer. He pulled me even closer. His manhood pressed against my pleasure opening. Without another thought, I raised and then lowered onto it like a queen receiving her thrown, slowly sliding up and down, allowing him to pulsate and throb inside me. Daniel rocked and moaned, each thrust becoming faster and more powerful than the next. I gripped the back of the sofa, squeezing my knees into his thighs, and throwing my head back so that I could take in every inch of him. He wrapped his arms around my waist, pulling me closer, going deeper, until I could feel myself explode all over his shaft. His body tightened and released soon after, as his love flowed inside me. Weak from the intensity of the moment, I tried to push away, but he held on tight. "I am never letting you go again."

For the first time since Vaneetra James delivered destruction to our door, we began mending our hearts and souls with passion and desire. For those few moments in time, no one existed but us. We made love well into the night, collapsing from exhaustion after what seemed like an endless amount of time. Afterwards, as I lay in his arms, my mind raged with conflicted emotions. Joy wrapped around me like a blanket, but doubt seeped in between the folds, forcing me to wonder if this revived commitment would last.

About the Author

Born in the South Suburbs of Chicago, Illinois, Nicole Hampton's love for reading developed at an early age. She often spent hours becoming lost in the worlds of characters of her favorite books. Reading offered an opportunity for Nicole to dream about life outside of her community and fed her desire to want to explore the world beyond her modest surroundings.

Wanting to find a way to help people see the struggles in their lives differently, Nicole wrote skits and plays for her church that addressed real life issues, and helped people to see God in their situations. The accolades given by those who saw her plays fueled her determination to write her first novel, *Glimmer in the Darkness*, and continue to address issues that occur in day-to-day life.

Nicole earned a Master's Degree in Social Work, and utilizes the skills and knowledge learned to address the issues presented in her debut novel in a manner that allows people to connect and understand the struggles of her characters.

Nicole lives in North Carolina, is a dedicated wife and mother of six, who spends any time she can snatch, developing characters and story lines to share with her readers.